A Deadly Legacy

A Lady Evelyn Mystery

by Malia Zaidi

For my parents

"What's past is prologue."
— William Shakespeare, *The Tempest*

"In each of us, two natures are at war – the good and the evil. All our lives the fight goes on between them, and one of them must conquer. But in our own hands lies the power to choose – what we want most to be, we are."
— Robert Louis Stevenson

Table of Contents

Prologue

She heard them coming through the fog that clouded her mind, made her eyes swim and head throb. The footsteps were heavy, pitiless in their approach. Pushing herself up, a rush of pain ran down her left side and she gasped and pressed her lips together. *I will not scream. I will not scream.* Tears shot to her eyes, but she swallowed down her agonized sob.

Steeling herself for the door to open, for it to begin anew, she sat as straight as she could, favoring her right side on the stiff straw mattress. Her brow was damp with perspiration. She could taste the salt on her lips. Her bare arms were covered in gooseflesh. Though she had hardened herself for this very occasion, the calm she hoped would descend upon her did not come. Her heart beat an angry rhythm in her chest. Counting in her mind, she waited, eyes shut. The steps grew closer. One, two, three... She opened her eyes. They were moving away. Her chest felt tight. Something was wrong. What was happening?

A door creaked somewhere down the hallway. The sound of movement, a scuffle. Raised voices and the unmistakable snap of leather against flesh. A cry. A howl. That voice...

No. *No!*

She flew at the closed door, but misjudging her strength and the ferocity of her injury, collapsed before crossing half the short distance. What had she done? She had known the moment the words slipped past her lips it would be her greatest regret. Yet the hope that her betrayal had been meaningless lived inside her until this moment, which proved the opposite to be true. Pressing her hands to her face, she could hold back her sobs no longer. The pain, the exhaustion and now this, this shattering confrontation with her own weakness, her moral failing was too much to bear. The ground was cold and welcoming as she lay down, and she could not imagine finding the strength ever to rise again.

Time became liquid, flowing around her until she lost her grip on it entirely. Hours passed, then days. Meals were brought, more questions asked, more bruises added to join the map of blue and green patterning her body, temporary tattoos of her permanent mistakes.

She did not beg. A tiny semblance of the dignified, clever woman she may once have been remained. Yet whatever clarity her mind possessed was focused on one fact alone, her guilt. Bruises could fade and sores heal, yet there was no balm to soothe away the damage she had caused. Every time her mind reached this conclusion anew, she sank into a heap of despair on the ground. The cold did not touch her anymore. The gnawing hunger in her belly felt like her just deserts, as did the shock of pain that ran along the length of her body with every movement. And yet…had there not been a sliver of hope, just the tiniest fragment, she might have dashed her head against the wall and been done with life, with suffering and pain.

One night – this much she could tell from the darkness beyond the tiny, filthy window set high into the wall - her door was opened. She was resting on her mattress. The sound of the key in the lock, the metal bolt scraping back made her open her eyes, crusty with sleep, and blink into the dim room.

"*Aufstehen!*" came the barked command. A torch beam sliced through the darkness, bringing tears to her eyes. The man in the doorway was tall, his voice young as he ordered her to get up. He shifted his weight from one foot to the other, as she made no move to obey. Let him command all he wanted, what could he do that had not already been done?

"*Los, aufstehen!*" he shouted once more, throwing a quick glance over his shoulder. Nervous. She did not recognize him. He was a new arrival.

"*Warum?*" she croaked, conjuring a smile to her cracked lips. It had its intended effect and, riled, he stepped forward.

"*Der Kommandant fordert es!*" So he had sent for her once more. She wondered what he could want. Hadn't she given them enough? Hadn't they wrung her dry like a limp cleaning rag? Curiosity got the better of her, curiosity and a vague hope that she might be able to alter what she had done.

Slowly, she peeled herself from the misshapen mattress she called a bed and, leaning towards her right side, pushed herself up to stand. Her whole body pulsed with pain, and she bit down so hard she could taste the metallic tang of blood on her tongue. The young man was impatient and though the lethargy of her movement was not by choice, she took some pleasure in making him squirm. By the time she reached the door, her legs trembled, and her hands were slick. She gripped for the doorframe, but the soldier, either impatient or taking pity on her, took hold of an arm and lent her support. He was younger even than her, she noticed. Just an overgrown boy like so many of them.

By the time they reached a bare room up two flights of stairs, the soldier was more or less carrying her. She was deposited on a hard, wooden chair in front of the window. It looked down onto a closed courtyard, illuminated by cold, electric light. The flagstones were slick with water. It must have rained. She knew nothing of the outside world, the whims and wiles of the weather. Her back was to the door, still she was aware of him before he made himself heard. The commander was a man with presence, whatever that meant. He was tall and lean, but filled a room to the point that she could hardly find the air to breathe.

"What do you want?" she asked, trying to steel her voice, to sound hard and bored, knowing the sorry sight she presented, emaciated and pale, told a different story.

"He stepped into the room, hat tucked under his arm. "You gave me something, so I thought it is only right I should return the favor."

He was standing behind her now, his powerful hand resting on her shoulder. She tried to shrug it off, but he only let out a low chuckle at her feeble attempts and squeezed painfully. Bending down, he whispered into her ear and pointed into the courtyard.

"Look."

Indeed, as he entered the room, her focus had shifted, and it was only now she noticed the commotion in the space below. Her breath caught in her throat.

A man was being dragged out between two soldiers. He was barefoot, his hands bound and face bloodied. She would have recognized him in a crowd of a million. She reached out, but glass and space separated her from him. *Look up,* she thought, then immediately shrank back. No, no he must not see her, must not know who brought him to this place.

"Now, now, so squeamish all of a sudden?" the voice in her ear whispered. Her chair was pushed forward so close she was trapped in front of the window.

One of the soldiers had produced a sack he pulled over his captive's head before marching him to the wall. She could not bear it, yet she could not tear her eyes away, willing fate to intervene, wishing the God she had forsaken herself would show his mercy after all.

The soldier walked back. The second drew a pistol.

A shot.

Her scream.

Silence.

Chapter 1

London, 1927

"Happy birthday!" These well wishes are not met with the intended enthusiasm. The birthday girl, startled and dazed from sleep, begins to howl and only her mother's soothing voice can calm her temper. Elsa turns one today and my cousin's house in Belgravia is filled with family, eager to bestow gifts and wishes of health and happiness upon the little one. Despite our good intents, Elsa only forgives our intrusion into her space when her mother places a slice of birthday cake in front of her, which she proceeds to convey almost everywhere but into her mouth. Nonetheless, it is a cream smeared face which smiles up at us moments later, benevolence restored.

"One year old," I muse, shaking my head as Briony and I watch the little girl and her siblings. "It seems only yesterday she was so small I might have held her in one hand." The room has been decorated with colorful streamers and small bunches of purple pansies. The half-demolished cake makes for a tempting centerpiece, just out of reach of sticky little hands. A mound of presents continues to grow in front of the fireplace as more guests join the celebration. I thought it wise to bring a little something for the other children, too. Areta and Timon are young enough to scoff in jealousy at their sister's gifts, though the eldest, Iona, would likely take little notice.

"I have grown acutely aware of the passage of time since becoming a mother," Briony observes with a smile, brushing a hand over Elsa's downy head of pale golden curls. "You will understand soon enough."

"Ah, yes," I say. How many times have I been told as much since Daniel and I announced our engagement earlier this year? As if *finally,* my life will have value, for I shall have a husband and before long a nursery full of children. I swallow my sigh. They mean well, of course, still it irks me. I am a traveled, educated woman with a business to my name, yet none of that seems to matter when placed on the scale beside a wedding ring. I must be careful not to take my frustrations regarding societal expectations out on my innocent cousin or fiancé. Daniel, for one, has never made me feel this way, and for that reason I am happy to finally have a date for our wedding set in stone. Only a little over a month remains and I will be Evelyn Harper, Carlisle no more.

"Briony! Darling, come say hello to Edith and Lloyd," Aunt Louise, Briony's mother, calls from the adjoining room.

"Mother has chosen today to invite all manner of people I hardly know," Briony whispers in my ear, rolling her eyes to great effect. I can tell she is not truly annoyed. Her mother wants to boast about her daughter's lovely family, and who can blame her? Obediently, my cousin trots off to greet her parents' friends. I am left in the pleasant company of my nieces and nephew. Areta and Timon already attend school, but at six and seven, they do not squirm in embarrassment when I kiss their cheeks or ruffle their hair. Iona at thirteen has always been older than her years and is even now playing second mother, wiping Elsa's face with a cloth before the little one escapes and toddles toward me with her slow, unpracticed gait. A wide grin reveals four tiny front teeth and chocolate smeared lips. I catch her in my arms as she topples forward and swing her into the air to squeals of delight. Cake crumbs remain lodged in her golden curls and the front of her dress is stained, but I have never seen a lovelier child. I suppose that opinion may change when Daniel and I have our own. For now, however, these four children are my very favorite in the world.

Speak of the devil! At that very moment, Daniel appears in the doorway. We exchange a smile. Before either of us can speak, Timon has spotted him and leaps from his chair, dark curls flopping onto his forehead.

"Uncle Daniel, I want to show you my new train set!" Timon announces and grabs Daniel's hand. He loves it when the children call him their uncle. He has so little family left and has yearned for it. We both suffered losses in our lives, but I was always fortunate to have Briony and her family, as well as Aunt Agnes and her late husband in my life. Of course, Agnes has a new husband now, the lovely Harold Finley, who must be around here somewhere. They married a few months ago, and I am happy to see her flourishing as Mrs. Finley, when she spent so many years mourning my late Uncle Brendan. In fact, I hardly see her these days, so busy is the new couple in making a circuit of London society. Were this not rather a relief, I might be offended!

When Areta and Iona lose interest in their food and disappear to read or play, I lift Elsa into my arms and we wander to the dining room. A large buffet has been set up for the adults, who did not wish to partake in the children's treats of sausages, roast potatoes and cake. Agnes and Harold are talking to Robert, Briony's father, in one corner. Briony is speaking animatedly with her husband, Jeffrey, in another. I haven't seen him all day, though Daniel and I arrived before everyone else. He is working on some all-consuming project for the British Museum, and it is driving Briony mad. They have weathered a few storms in their marriage thus far and always come out the other side of things, so I am not terribly concerned. Elsa mewls when she spies her mother, yet I decide to give the couple a wide berth to sort out whatever has etched that deep frown line into my cousin's face. Aunt Louise beckons me over.

"Evie, dear, come, meet Edith and Lloyd Ashbourne. We have known one another some twenty years."

"You age us, Louise," the woman introduced as Edith Ashbourne comments with a wry smile. Though Louise has indeed hinted at the lady's maturity, her demeanor is youthful, her bearing elegant, with the posture of a dancer and lively brown eyes, feathered by lines that tell of a cheerful nature. She wears a simple, impeccably tailored suit of emerald wool, the only indication of her wealth a thick string of pearls around her neck. Her husband wears his gray hair with dignity, and while his smile does not quite extend to his eyes, he reaches out to tickle Elsa's chin and she gurgles with glee. His military bearing and erect posture are explained when Louise announces he was a general in the Second Boer War.

"Evie is a detective, there is no hiding anything from her, age or otherwise, Edith," Louise observes with a wink in my direction. She has always supported my whims and fancies, even my foray into detection and the founding of The Carlisle Detective Agency earlier this year. I think her upbringing in France distanced her a little from the confines of the societal constraints which still influence Aunt Agnes, and we have always had an easy relationship.

"A detective! Yes, I read about you!" Edith exclaims, pressing her hands together in delight. "You solved the Devlin murder, didn't you? Clever girl, I remember saying as much to my husband. Women must learn to be enterprising nowadays. It is only a matter of time until all women have the vote, and then there is no stopping us!"

"Edith is quite a pioneer," Louise observes. "She marched with the suffragettes, didn't you?"

"I remember you in white, too, Louise. No need for modesty."

"Ah, but you and Emmeline were a pair. I was simply happy to march in your footsteps." I follow the exchange between the women, growing more and more intrigued by Edith. Elsa, in turn, grows more and more restless with our talk and squirms in my arms until I set her down. Before I can stop her, she promptly picks up a dropped piece of cheese from the carpet and pops it into her mouth. I will just have to hope Briony's maids made good work of cleaning the floor. Satisfied, the hunk of cheese making her left cheek bulge, she toddles toward Agnes and Harold, where I know she will be well looked after.

3

I turn my attention back to the Ashbournes and Louise, still engaged in conversation.

"Now that you are back from France, Louise, you should join us," Edith is saying. "Naturally, you are welcome, too." I have entirely missed the context of her invitation, but before I can ask, Lloyd Ashbourne is drawn into another conversation and his wife joins in. I have the impression the poor fellow must pounce on any moment his wife takes a breath to get a word in edgewise, still I have a pleasant impression of both.

"Where am I invited?" I ask Louise.

"Edith runs a chapter of the Women's Institute. She has asked me to help them organize a fundraiser next week."

"Oh," I reply. Fundraisers, though undeniably significant, tend to be events of interminable tedium given my past experience. Evidently, my lack of enthusiasm is badly disguised. Louise sighs and cocks her head in an all too familiar manner. I know a lecture is nigh.

"It is for a good cause, Evie. They help women become more independent, use their newfound right to vote, and even to leave abusive homes. After the Devlin case, I would have thought that must be a prime concern of yours."

"Yes, yes," I relent. "Perhaps we can persuade Briony to join us."

"I think she should bring Iona. The girl is another Edith and Emmeline in the making." Though I certainly think of my niece in the highest terms, I doubt she would relish the idea of spending an afternoon in the company of society ladies with a cause, when she could be holed away reading, her favorite pastime.

We chat a while longer, but Louise knows everyone at the party, and they all want a moment with her. I leave my aunt in the company of her former neighbors and find Daniel. This task, given my occupation as a bona fide detective, is no great challenge. All I need to do is follow Timon's excitable voice up the stairs to the nursery, where I am met with success. Daniel, sleeves rolled up to his elbows, is on the ground, laying tracks on the carpet, while Timon assembles a train to rival the Orient Express. Areta is busy with her doll house, and Iona is curled into a chair with a book. It is a picture I take in for a quiet moment, before stepping into it myself.

"What are you reading?" I ask Iona. Since I took her to Yorkshire as a birthday treat in the summer, she has obsessively consumed books by or about the three Brontë sisters. The tome cradled in her lap today appears to be no exception.

"*Jane Eyre*," she mumbles, not looking up. It must be her third time wading through the dense volume! I leave the girl in peace to ponder the dark corridors of Thornfield Hall and help Areta rearrange furniture in the doll house. They are such easy company, no false smiles, no inane chatter required to satisfy them. When Daniel and I finally leave, it is with a pleasant buoyancy in our steps. How much both of our worlds have changed in the few years we have known one another! I am an aunt four times over, have traveled to different countries, received my degree and founded The Carlisle Detective Agency, not to mention accepting Daniel's proposal of marriage. He has taken on a role in his family's company and though this continues to be a source of frustration at times, he is slowly growing closer to his cousin, the other president of the firm.

"Are you coming to Grosvenor?" he asks, as we climb into my motorcar, a midnight blue Bentley.

"I will pop into the flat and see if Hugh is there. He was meeting a client to wrap up a case this morning."

"The jewelry theft?"

"As it happens, the guilty party was not her maid, whom she had accused, but her own four-year-old daughter, who had taken a fancy to the sparkly bits and hidden them in her toy chest."

"Crafty," Daniel admires. "How did Hugh learn the truth?"

"The thief as much as confessed. Hugh saw her doll wearing a bracelet around her neck and, upon inspection, found it was quite the genuine article. He was worried this morning that the woman would refuse to pay, since the 'thief' was no real criminal but her innocent child."

"Surely not."

"I said the same. The woman signed a contract and her jewels were returned, but you know Hugh." I give Daniel a meaningful look, slowly edging onto the road. Hugh has always been quick to jump to conclusions, quick to expect the worst of people, a sad consequence of experience. Nonetheless, I could not have asked for a better partner in the detective agency. He has the instincts of a bloodhound with the grace of a ballerina.

"Are you still trying to make a match of him and Maeve?" Daniel asks as I turn onto Upper Belgrave Street. I do not see his face, still I can tell he is smiling. He has always viewed any and all matchmaking attempts on my part with sheer amusement. Perhaps, I grudgingly admit, because they all prove unsuccessful.

"No, I am not," I reply, not confessing that Hugh himself, in a rather embarrassing conversation for us both, asked me to cease my attempts. I had not realized my handiwork was quite so blatant. At least Maeve never remarked upon it.

"Good. He will find someone when he is ready to find someone. That is how it worked for us, isn't it?"

I sigh and nod. "I was only trying to help. He is so often alone. It can't be good for a man like Hugh who lives inside his head." The war left significant scars on Hugh's psyche and the trauma stole years of his life, turning him into a lonely, skittish man with an unpredictable streak in his behavior when we first met him. He is a perfect example of how the troubled veterans of the war can reintegrate into society, if they are offered a helping hand. Since our initial encounter, he has become Daniel's closest friend and one of mine as well. Unfortunately, we have very different thoughts on how to help him. Daniel wants Hugh to focus on his work and believes that he is happy enough as matters stand. I cannot imagine a truly happy man spends late nights writing up reports when it is not required, instead of going home, or that a happy man has nothing to fill his life outside of his occupation. I have watched him play with Briony's children and Maeve's little one, and I can tell he would flourish had he a family of his own. But then I suppose Daniel is right to say I cannot force it. Goodness knows how many times Agnes introduced me to eligible young men when I lived under her roof, and I scoffed at her presumptiveness. Then again, I want to help Hugh find a partner, not marry him off to ease my burden of care as I believed Agnes did with me.

"He has us. Sometimes family and friendship are one and the same."

"Things may change when we are married and have children. He will always be welcome and our friend, but we will have shifted course and I worry he will feel left behind."

"Did you feel that way when Briony's family grew?" Daniel asks when I come to a stop in front of his - our, as he keeps insisting – Grosvenor Square house.

"Sometimes, though of course I was happy for her."

"Well, we will see what happens." Daniel says with a shrug. "Perhaps I will be the one to find him a more suitable match." He chuckles.

"I thought you decided we should stay out of it?"

"I don't believe I said *we*." Daniel grins.

"You think you can find someone better for him than I can? You forget I spend almost all day with Hugh!"

"He is my best friend. Surely that qualifies me to better recognize what sort of lady would make a good companion for him, and he for her."

"We shall see about that!"

"A challenge?"

"Indeed."

"All right, though I suggest we keep it between ourselves." I can already tell Daniel is regretting his confidence. I hurry him out of the car before he changes his mind. Giving him a cheeky wave, I scoot down Brook Street in the direction of St. James, my mind already busy sorting through the list of eligible women in my acquaintance. It is surely quite impossible that a man such as Daniel is better suited to the task of matchmaking than I am!

Chapter 2

When I arrive at the flat, I run into Mr. Singh, the butler and friend of my neighbor, Dulcie Hazlett. He doesn't seem to notice me. His brow is creased, and circles rim his dark eyes. Dulcie's dog tugs on the lead, and before I can ask Mr. Singh whether something is troubling him – which is quite evidently the case – he is out of the door. I consider popping up to see Dulcie myself. Over the course of the past few months we have become good friends, not merely neighbors. I decide to leave it until later. If she is unwell and Mr. Singh out, I do not want to rouse her from her bed. Lost in thoughts of Dulcie, I wander up to my flat.

My neighbor is perhaps ten years Agnes' senior, but she has aged considerably faster than my straight-backed aunt. No doubt her self-imposed confinement in her flat plays a significant role in her pale skin and low energy. I learned months ago that the death of her son at the end of the war caused a shift in the demeanor of the previously adventurous woman. She does not trust the world outside her own four walls and will not leave them no matter the coaxing, no matter the sunshine, or the eager yapping of her dog.

Upon entering my flat, I am welcomed by the delightful aroma of gingerbread. Maeve has always been an excellent baker and since her son, Aidan, and the boy's grandmother, Kathleen, moved into a spare room, she has been honing her skill ever more. If I was worried Aidan's presence would distract my maid from her tasks, I was entirely mistaken. She is far cheerier and less preoccupied than she was when kept apart from the little lad, and for his part, he has been a quiet and friendly presence, never disrupting a meeting, nor leaving mayhem in his wake the way Briony's children often do. In fact, I rarely see him. During the day, Kathleen usually takes him out; in the evenings, he is in bed early. Today, however, I spy a flash of copper hair peeking out from behind the door to the kitchen.

"Well, hello," I greet him and tousle his hair. He is a sweet, quiet lad, pale complexioned, with a halo of flame-colored curls. A beautiful child. I feel a stab of sadness that his father will never have the chance to meet him. He died before he knew that Maeve was with child and though Kathleen, his mother, told me that Aidan is the image of his father, I see only Maeve in both his appearance and his manner.

Malia Zaidi

"Say hello, Aidan," Maeve instructs, wiping her hands on her checkered apron. Aidan's eyes grow wide and he tucks his thumb unto his mouth, hiding behind his mother. A boy only months older than Elsa, Aidan is easily forgiven this slight.

"It smells delicious," I say, though my stomach is still full of cake from Elsa's party. "Is Mr. Lawrence in?"

"Yes, miss, in the study. Kathleen meant to go out with Aiden so he wouldn't be in your hair, but it's perishing cold out today."

"Yes, winter has certainly arrived early this year. Best to stay in where it's nice and warm. Isn't that so, Aidan?" When I tickle his chin, he gives me a shy smile. I leave the mother and son to themselves. Maeve is very conscious of being any trouble, and I know she is afraid her son and his grandmother could be sent away again. The little lad is as uncomplicated as his mother and Kathleen, once she warmed to the idea of living here, has been as easy a housemate as I could wish for. Not that I spend many nights here. Grosvenor Square is my home now, though I intend to keep this flat both for the purpose of owning my own property as well as providing an office for the business Hugh and I operate, The Carlisle Detective Agency. We had a stroke of luck – though I ought never think of murder in such terms – when a wealthy and prominent (if despicable) man was killed. He happened to be the father of my old friend, Percy. The case became ours and we solved it to the accolades of various publications, who seemed fascinated with the notion of a titled lady detective and her war veteran partner. I will not lie, the publicity of that first case is undoubtedly responsible for our continued growth and success. No such shocking case has come our way since the Devlin murder was solved, however, though we have been occupied with various smaller mysteries. The notable families of London are never keen to involve the police when confronted with a dilemma of a somewhat dubious nature, where discretion is required and a quiet resolution the desired result. Blackmail, household theft, and infidelity are only a few of the cases with which Hugh and I have kept busy these past few months. That being said, I did experience a twinge of envy when I met my friend, police inspector Lucas Stanton, for tea last week, and he told me about a spate of robberies he was tasked with solving. But there are advantages and disadvantages in being a copper. He may have the more intriguing, adventurous caseload, but I have easier access to many places he does not. This fact was particularly evident in the Devlin murder, where the upper echelons of society would hardly stoop to answer Stanton's queries, while he tried to find the murderer. Through my connection to Percy and the dead man's acquaintances, people were more willing to speak to me. Or, though I do not like this theory as much, they thought I was a silly girl with whom they might

9

share easy gossip. In any case, the mystery was solved, and the name of The Carlisle Detective Agency was on many a lip in the following weeks.

Pushing open the door to the study, I spy Hugh hunched over his writing pad, the lamp on his desk throwing tall shadows across the wall as the day beyond the window grows dark. It is only a quarter to four and the sun is already shifting its focus to other lands, turning away from us in our cold, gray London. This year has slipped by like water through a closed fist. The months have run, but moments such as these, when we are without a specific task, without a case to occupy our time and our minds, seem interminable in their length. I look at Hugh hoping this tedium can be avoided, that he will tell me of an urgent call, a new mystery to be solved.

Hugh glances up and sets down his pen, resting his arms over the pad of paper, a vague attempt at nonchalance, though I recognize it as an attempt to hide what he has been writing. "Oh, hello. I didn't expect to see you here today." Do I detect a hint of discomfiture in his manner? Perhaps he did not wish for me to know that he is spending another long day at the office with no urgent work calling his name. Or, I feel a tingle of excitement at the thought, is he possibly interested in my maid after all and simply wished me to cease my meddling? I have been told to curb the latter impulse on previous occasions...

"I wanted to come in after the party, see if there is a new case now that the jewelry theft at the Wilkinson house is resolved," I explain hopefully.

"Nothing so far." He shrugs. "How was the party?"

"Lovely, you really should have come, you know you were quite welcome," I say, setting my bag and hat on the table and draping my coat over the chair at my desk.

"It was a family affair, I didn't want to intrude."

"Nonsense," I dash aside the notion. In truth, I suspect he was overwhelmed by the prospect of the many well-heeled strangers in one place, too much idle chatter, inquisitions into his connection to the family and his past. I can hardly blame him for opting to send a small, carefully wrapped parcel for the birthday girl instead. Elsa unwrapped it with glee and proceeded to bash the small wooden dog against the floor with surprising ferocity for one so young. Yet she did so with a wide smile, suggesting the gift was met with her approval. Hugh would have enjoyed himself, I think, but decide to let the matter rest. "What are you working on?" I ask instead, perching on the edge of my desk, my gaze on the paper in front of him.

"Oh, nothing really." He makes a dismissive gesture like swatting a fly. He is quite obviously lying, though I cannot imagine why. Has he accepted a case he does not wish to discuss with me? No, he is loyalty personified and would not go behind my back, of that I am convinced. I will have to trust him to tell me in his own good time. I settle down, rearrange some papers, sign a few invoices. When I started the agency, I thought it would be a challenge to make a name for ourselves, thought our peers would scoff at the nature of the business. Fortunately, the success of our first case prevented this initial hurdle. All the same, the wait for an intriguing mystery to trickle in has proven a tedious counterpart to the thrill of actual detecting.

"You should go home," I tell Hugh, a few minutes later. "Hopefully tomorrow we will have something new to work on. I will telephone Mr. Napier from the paper to learn whether he has a little scoop for us. He owes me a favor, after all." I met the determined newsman in the wake of our first case, and for the promise of a future favor, gave him exclusive insight into the crime, with the permission of my old friend and employer. Percy agreed that it was best to tell the truth in his own words, before other papers threw mounds of speculation at the broken family. I have not yet called in the favor, but if tomorrow is as quiet as today, I may have to. Stanton certainly won't invite our agency to help him solve any crimes, nor will the victims in his cases be likely to hire us.

Though Hugh is reluctant to leave before five in the evening, he finally gets to his feet and picks up his hat and coat. Not long after the door has fallen shut, I decide to follow suit, reminding myself that it is a good sign our telephone is not ringing with the frequency of London rain. It must mean the world is more at peace than I anticipated. I have somewhat convinced myself of this fact, when the apparatus in question lets out a shrill cry. I am not entirely proud of the speed with which I leap at it and wrench the mouthpiece from its cradle.

"Carlisle Detec-"

"Evie, dear!" My shoulders slump at the sound of my aunt Louise's voice ringing down the line.

"Yes, Aunt Louise," I say, trying not to let my disappointment be known. Why would she call me here? But then she probably assumes, as does almost everyone else, that I live at this address, as is proper for an unmarried lady.

"I didn't have a chance to ask before you left, but Edith wanted to show me around the Women's Institute tomorrow and said to invite you along. Since you do not have a case at the moment, you might as well join us."

"Oh, all right, though a case could come in at any minute."

"Hugh will cope without you for a few hours. Besides, I want to show off my clever niece. Edith was rather impressed, and it takes a lot to impress a woman like her."

"I think you are making this up. We hardly exchanged more than a greeting." If it makes my aunt happy, I suppose it can't hurt. Besides, I cannot deny the Women's Institute is a worthy cause.

"Excellent. Briony cannot tear herself away from her little ones, sadly. I should have liked to take Iona were it not for school. Yet somehow I do not think Edith endorses compromising even a day of a girl's education for an extracurricular excursion."

"Is she so formidable, this Edith Ashbourne?" I cannot help but tease. Aunt Louise herself is hardly a tame little lady. Her friend must truly have left an impression.

"I remember her at the end of the war, Evie. She and Emmeline were so brash and brave, we all wanted to be like them, even as they intimidated us a little. From what I gather, her current second-in-command is a rather respectable lady, too. Worked in the War Office or something like that."

"Well, you have roused my curiosity," I concede, and it is true. I remember the women in white, with their proud sashes gracing the covers of newspapers when I was a girl. Agnes never participated in the movement, but I could detect a flash of pride in her when she read their stories. When women over thirty were finally granted the vote in 1918, I know she went to the polls the next election with her head held aloft. It was the end of the war, and the country needed a burst of hope, a flash of progress, even if some disagreed with the notion. I am still ineligible to vote and so can hardly shirk involvement in furthering the cause, even if it is up to my aunt to give me the necessary push.

Chapter 3

I am halfway down the stairs, when I remember Dulcie and the weary Mr. Singh. Turning on my heel, I retrace my steps and climb the extra flight to her floor. Hesitating a moment before knocking, I hear no sound beyond. Maybe I should let them be? Suddenly, the door is pulled open to reveal Mr. Singh's bearded face. He musters a smile, but there is little vigor behind it. Leaning on his cane, he steps back and beckons me inside.

"Is everything all right?" I ask, lowering my voice to a whisper, though I am not certain why. A heavy, spicy aroma hangs in the air and the lights are low, throwing long shadows down the hall. If I did not know Mr. Singh and Dulcie, I might be a little spooked by the atmosphere.

Mr. Singh runs a hand over his face. "Come, let me make you a cup of chai."

I follow him into the kitchen. A pot of fragrant lentil stew is bubbling on the hob, and various jars of colorful spices line the counter. I sit at the long wooden table and wait for Mr. Singh to pour the tea. Since meeting my neighbors some months ago, I have become fond of the warm, spicy Indian chai. On a bracing day like today, it is particularly comforting.

"Is Dulcie unwell?" I ask, when he sits opposite me, steam from our cups rising into the air between us.

"The tenth anniversary of her son's death has come and gone, and she has not dealt with it well." Mr. Singh takes a sip of tea and closes his eyes for a moment. Dulcie told me her son died at his own hand at the end of the war. She has never recovered, as I suspect no parent ever really could. I wrap my hands around the cup and remain silent for a moment, allowing my friend to gather himself. His relationship with Dulcie far exceeds that of an ordinary butler. He has been her companion for many years and as such must have seen her at her very lowest. Perhaps he is lonely, too. Though there is a certain fascination with his native land amongst the English, he will always be an outsider here; his turban and dark features see to that. I myself have noticed the stares when we take a turn around the park together. When Dulcie is well, she is his dearest friend, but when she is not, when she is lost to the past, crippled by grief, to whom does he turn?

"She was better for a short while. When we met you, and you brought a bit of vibrancy into our lives, I even let myself hope she might recover, might come back into the world again." He shrugs.

"Is there anything I can do to help? Would she speak to me?"

"Her doctor came by earlier and gave her laudanum. I do not approve, but even in her ill health she maintains her obstinacy." A weak smile touches his lips before falling away again.

"I saw you with the dog and thought something was wrong."

"She sent me away while the doctor visited. I don't trust him. He seems willing to do anything for the right fee. I have said as much to Dulcie. She will not listen."

"What is his name, perhaps I can inquire after his reputation?" I dislike the thought of anyone taking advantage of Dulcie's weakened state and seeing Mr. Singh so distressed. "I am a detective, after all," I remind him with a little nudge.

"Ah, yes, it can do no harm, can it? His name is Calvert. Dr. Roger Calvert. His practice is in Soho." He lets out a mirthless chuckle. "Leave it to Dulcie to choose a physician based on the fact that his practice is located in a bohemian neighborhood."

"I will look him up. If you have a bad impression of the man, I trust your intuition."

"More than can be said of Dulcie," Mr. Singh mutters sadly, staring into his half-empty cup.

"She is not well," I offer reassuringly, though I suppose there is little comfort to be found in my words. I determine to put my metaphorical magnifying glass to this Dr. Calvert and his practice.

It is with a heavy heart that I leave to drive the short distance to Daniel's – *our* – house in Grosvenor Square. The wind nips at my face when I step onto the street, and I wrap my scarf tightly around my neck. The square is empty, as it often is on a late afternoon. Children are indoors, nannies avoiding the chill of the park and runny noses that are part and parcel of the onset of the season. Warm electric light radiates from behind gauzy curtains and a pale moon glows faintly above the rooftops, a peaceful oasis in the madness that is London. When Kathleen first arrived with Aidan to join Maeve in the flat, she could hardly believe how quiet it was after her life in an East End tenement. As I walk to my car, footsteps echoing through the square, I feel a twinge of sadness that the flat will never truly be my home. After I left Oxford, I was determined to live on my own for the first time. Then I accepted Daniel's proposal of marriage. I certainly do not regret my decision, yet it meant I never quite settled into regarding the flat as my home. Rather, Daniel insisted I should think of the Grosvenor Square house as ours. And it is a lovely house, just lovely, and Daniel is the only man for me. Why then, do I feel so restless whenever I consider the future?

I climb into my car and shiver, sitting on the icy leather seat. It isn't uncertainty about Daniel being the right one for me, of that I am sure. Perhaps it is more of a worry that my role as his wife will change something in me, something I do not wish to alter? That it will force me to adapt, to bend in a way I wish to avoid. Yet Daniel has never tried to curb my impulses. He knows I have my own mind. Perhaps it is more the constant and unsolicited advice I am receiving from every married woman of my acquaintance that is setting my teeth on edge. I wonder whether the married men in Daniel's circle do the same, or whether they simply assume everything will remain the same for them, for it is often so. Women have children, women manage the home, the family, and still it is the husband who is the head of the household, the one with the final say. The thought irks me and while I do not suspect Daniel of a tyrannical disposition as a husband, I am suddenly energized for tomorrow's visit to the Women's Institute. Perhaps the ladies will offer me better advice for the future than to remember that my husband's shirts ought to be starched just so.

Chapter 4

I meet Aunt Louise at her house. No one is meant to know I essentially reside in Grosvenor Square already. While my aunt is far from prudish, I prefer not to test her liberal views.

"Goodness, it's cold, isn't it!" she says, bundling into the passenger seat of my car and bringing a gust of chilly air with her. We are traveling to Bloomsbury, where Edith's chapter of the WI – the Women's Institute – is located. I slept badly and can muster only moderate excitement for today's outing, even though I generally enjoy Louise's cheerful company.

"What are we going to do there?" I ask, trying to inject enthusiasm into my voice as we drive past St. James Park and towards The Strand. Traffic this morning is busy and for a good while we slowly roll along behind a bus which stops every few moments, testing my patience.

"Edith said they focus on voluntary services and helping women become more independent."

"A significant cause."

"It is," Louise says, hesitating before she continues. "I hope it can be for me, too. Briony is so busy with her family and you are with your business, I feel I must do something of value as well. Something satisfying. Robert is happy at Chesterton," their country estate, "but I need something more stimulating than bracing walks and hosting the hunt every year. Even Agnes has moved on with her life!"

"I hardly see her and Harold. They are so busy!" I agree.

"Yes, well, I want to be busy, too." Louise sounds a little lost, and I reach over and give her hand a gentle squeeze.

"Then I am happy to join you. Goodness knows I have the time once a case is resolved. They come in fairly frequently and pay Hugh's wage, but there has not been a real mystery to sink my teeth into for months."

"Evie, you should not moan about that! Surely, you do not yearn for murder and mayhem in your life again?"

"No, of course not, but maybe something a little more stimulating than a child stealing her mama's jewelry. Stanton is always going on about robberies and fraud and the like, I wouldn't mind poking my nose into one of those cases."

"You must not make such wishes, dear girl, it will get you into trouble. We all know you have been there before."

"Yes, yes," I grumble, half agreeing and half wishing all the same.

"Ladies, welcome, how good of you to come. You are not the only newcomers today. May I introduce Miss Juliet Nelson." Edith nods at the woman standing beside her. She is pale and almost painfully thin with high cheekbones and watery blue eyes. We are standing in the wide hall that houses the WI. Women's voices echo around us, and the general atmosphere is one of joviality

"Evelyn Carlisle. Lovely to meet you," I introduce myself, and Louise echoes the sentiment. Miss Nelson's clothing is plain, though well made, and she wears not a scrap of jewelry, which lets her appear younger than she may be, nearer my age than that of her host.

"And you," she answers in a low voice, deeper than I had expected.

"My daughter, Adeline, will be around somewhere," Edith continues, turning her head this way and that, seeking out her daughter in the crowd of women. I must say, I am surprised by the energy in the room. I always assumed these institutes were all about cooking jam and teaching ladies how to knit. My ignorance does me no credit, I realize. One wall of the large room is adorned with posters advocating women's liberty and ladies of all ages are milling about, chatting and breaking into groups. I am not certain what role I am meant to play. Edith and Louise have turned away, talking to another woman in a bright orange dress and I feel ill at ease, too conspicuous in my ambiguity.

"Are you new to the WI, Miss Carlisle?" Juliet Nelson asks softly. I hardly noticed she was still standing beside me and startle at her voice.

"Oh, yes. Yes, I am. My aunt and Edith are old friends, and she invited us along. I confess, I am not sure what to do."

"I feel much the same. I received an invitation in the post." She gives me a little smile, merely a twitch at the corner of her mouth really, as if the muscles are ill-used to the exercise.

"I think my aunt didn't want to arrive alone."

"As someone who did, I cannot blame her."

"Do you live in the area?" I ask, trying to keep the conversation alive, but sensing she will not contribute much without my inquiry.

"Not far, yes. And you?"

"I live in St. James and have my business there, too." She raises an inquisitive brow, which I take as encouragement to elaborate on the nature of said business. The way parents are always keen to expound on their children, I need little prompting to discuss The Carlisle Detective Agency. The flicker of a smile reappears, and this time it seems to reach her pale blue eyes.

"A detective agency, that sounds like a fascinating endeavor. Too exciting for me, though."

"Oh, I do not know about that." I explain the rather tame nature of our current caseload.

"All the same," she insists. Moments later, we are interrupted and drawn into a group which now includes Edith's daughter, Adeline Markby, a cheerful woman a few years my senior with a head of chestnut curls and a heart-shaped face. Two rosy spots tint the apples of her cheeks, matching the color of her suit, a bright magenta with overlarge buttons. She is the picture of a frivolous society lady, and yet she is here and well-liked and respected. I wonder what the regulars of the WI think of me? Perhaps they view me with the same skepticism with which I view Adeline? I give myself an inward kick to set judgement aside. My uncharitable attitude stems from the fact that I do not feel at ease. I am itching to return to the office and feel guilty for hoping an intriguing case has presented itself in my absence.

We congregate around a large table, and cups of tea are pressed into our hands as Edith commences with the meeting. Plans for an upcoming fundraiser are discussed, and I vaguely register Louise volunteering our services to host a luncheon in the near future, as well as organizing a trip to Covent Garden to distribute food on Armistice Day.

"Your aunt is taking to our group rather well, isn't she?" Adeline whispers, nudging me gently.

"Indeed, she is always very capable when she has a cause."

"You seem as though you do not quite believe in the WI's work?"

"Do I? I must apologize," I stammer quickly, embarrassed she has discerned the skepticism in my manner. "I suppose, well…"

"You think it all rather dull?" There is a twinkle in Adeline's eyes telling me she does not mean to chastise.

"Not dull, so much as limited, perhaps. My work took me to the East end earlier this year. I saw true squalor, people struggling. Women struggling. I wonder whether the business of teaching how to knit and run a home is the best we can do for women."

"Then you do not know very much about the WI, Lady Carlisle." Again Adeline's tone is not critical, so much as eager.

"Probably not, but all this talk of fundraising and holding workshops strikes me as a step removed from more critical work to be done for women in this city. Many are still illiterate, others work in factories only to have their men drink away their earnings."

"Teaching women independence can begin with simple tasks such as how to run a home."

"Certainly, it can," I acknowledge, already regretting my moment of assertiveness. It is not my intent to disparage the work of this institute, for good evidently comes out of it. Yet my mind often returns to what I saw in Whitechapel earlier this year. Although I have since contributed to charities aiding the desperately poor, I still wonder how to help beyond simply supplying funds.

"I have been to the soup kitchens in Seven Dials, Lady Carlisle. Something must be done, I agree. Yet we must start somewhere, and for me the WI is that place."

"You speak more wisely than I might, Adeline," I concede and offer her a smile. Despite the fact that I am still uncertain how to be of use here, I understand the meaning of her words perfectly. We must begin somewhere. I hoped taking in Maeve and her family and finding a position for the widow I met in Whitechapel last year were solid beginnings, but there are countless more women who live a life weighed down by the burden of perpetual destitution and drudgery. When I glance around the room, I see clean faces, none drawn taut by worry and hunger, but even here, I cannot see beyond the surface. My last case taught me that anyone, even women of the highest social standing, can carry the weight of the world on their shoulders. I should not dismiss the work of the Women's Institute so easily, Adeline is right. For the first time this morning, I am glad Louise asked me to come along.

Chapter 5

By the time we leave, I find myself signed up to participate in all manner of events, and my head is veritably spinning. Juliet Nelson appears to be in much the same state, though she remained silent much of the time. She projects a certain fragility that speaks of loneliness. Maybe that is why she came here today. She does not wear a ring, so is likely single.

"Can I offer you a lift home?" I ask, as we leave the building amid a crowd of enthusiastic WI ladies.

"If it's not an inconvenience." She agrees with a faint smile.

"Evie, dear!" Aunt Louise breaks away from a group and walks toward us. "Edith has asked me to tea, to chat about the old days and all that. You don't mind, do you? Naturally, you are welcome to join us."

"No, no, you go on. I will take Miss Nelson home and go to the office. Perhaps Hugh has news of a case."

"Shall I cross my fingers, my dear?"

"Do, please!" I laugh and wave her off. "The car is this way."

"You can call me Juliet," she says so quietly I almost miss it. "Miss Nelson makes me sound like a spinster." She chuckles. "Which I am, make no mistake, yet I do not entirely bear the banner with pride."

"Oh, you are so young!" I exclaim, judging her to be a few years older than I am.

"I will be thirty-four next month," she says with a shrug.

"That is hardly an age to qualify you for spinsterhood," I observe with a raised brow. Her slight figure lends her youth, but there is a weariness in the set of her shoulders, a near translucence of her skin I observe as we walk side by side down the road.

It has grown busy, and street vendors line the pavement. A boy selling matchsticks trails us until I buy a box. The WI premises are located in a lively area, not far from the main stretch of theatres and down the road from Bloomsbury Square with its beautiful garden. A few streets on is the magnificent building housing the British Museum, Jeffrey's place of work. We turn onto Bury Place, where the Bentley waits patiently for my return. I notice a slight limp in Juliet's gait that robs her of some of her willowy grace. It also makes me remember Dulcie's doctor – the potential quack – whose premises are not far from here.

"Where can I take you?" I ask when we are settled in the car. Juliet names an address. "Have you lived there long?"

"Several years."

"What a lively area," I comment, sensing Juliet is one of those people who will not, on her own, move a conversation forward.

"One can live more unobtrusively the louder the neighborhood," she observes. "It came as a surprise that the WI even found me to send an invite."

"Perhaps a neighbor or colleague recommended you."

"Unlikely," she replies, not elaborating on her reasoning. I am at once fascinated by this enigma at my side, and frustrated by her opacity. Never one to abide drawn out quiet, it is my task – or so I view it – to fill the silence. I ramble on about Daniel and the upcoming wedding, only realizing once the words are out of my mouth, she may interpret them as insensitive, given her earlier bemoaning of her spinster status. If so, she makes no show of it, simply nodding and responding with short answers. It is a relief when we finally arrive at her block of flats on Guilford Street down the road from Russel Square. It is a nice address, and I wonder how she maintains it. By her own account, she is single, and no mention was made of a profession. Her plain clothing suggested that her means are modest, yet her home indicates a different status. My observation is not judgement in either case, but it is in my nature to be curious, as my profession demands.

"Thank you, Miss Carlisle," she says, opening the passenger side door.

"Evelyn, please, and you are quite welcome. I hope to see you at the next event. I would welcome a familiar face in the sea of strangers. My aunt will doubtless desert me as soon as a noble task calls her name, and there seem to be plenty of those in the WI."

"I will see you there," she says and closes the door. *Odd fish.* The thought may be uncharitable, but not unwarranted. I shrug to myself and adjust the gear before rejoining the London traffic.

Chapter 6

Three uneventful days pass. No new case rolls in, and Hugh and I twiddle our thumbs before half-heartedly agreeing that patience is the key. I telephoned my journalist contact, Hollis Napier, but he was out of the office and has yet to return the courtesy. Even Stanton is too busy to meet, or perhaps too wary to let me in on any mystery he is currently trying to solve. I looked up Dulcie's doctor, but could find little information regarding his practices, beyond the fact that he is an advocate of antiquated healing methods, or, as he put it, "heart and mind means of healing". I worry about my neighbor. When I ventured to see her once more yesterday, Mr. Singh told me she was resting again. If only I could think of a way to lure her out of doors, to invigorate her closed world, perhaps she would find some desire to experience life again. Sinking further and further into herself, drugged and sedated, I worry she will never emerge from her sinkhole of grief.

Beyond my anxiety for Dulcie's well-being, I have little to do. Hugh is moving into new lodgings and has taken the day off, and Maeve is quietly pottering away as she always does, while Kathleen and Aiden have gone to church. It is thus when Adeline contacts me to help with an event at the WI that I jump at the invitation. Idleness does not suit my temper.

"It is a cause that should appeal to you, Evelyn. We are petitioning the Metropolitan Police once again to increase the number of female patrols."

This is indeed an intriguing cause, one that has been championed since the end of the war. During the war, with the men away, it was up to women to maintain order, and many effectively worked for the police. When the men came home, employment was returned to them and taken from the women who ably held their positions. The campaign to reinstate women into the police force has been ongoing since the early 1920s. Sadly little progress has been made. Women are not considered as efficient, as strong, as intimidating as men, and thus incapable of fulfilling the role for which they appeal - or so men in power claim time and time again. In my experience, however, women find ways beyond brute force to get the job done and would do so again, if given the chance. This is indeed a cause I can get excited about, and I agree to meet Adeline and the other women at the Bloomsbury chapter house the following morning.

The day is gray and damp just like the previous one when I set out to the WI. My windshield is spattered with a soft drizzle and the pavement is slick. I see a number of women closing their umbrellas as I park my motorcar across from the WI. Not looking where I am going, my hand clamped onto my hat, I nearly collide with Juliet. "Oh, pardon me!" I exclaim as we shuffle inside. The air carries the scent of damp, mingling perfumes and strong tea. At a table near the end of the hall, I see Adeline and Louise busily dispensing cups and saucers. My aunt, it seems, is in her element. I am happy for her to find purpose in this new endeavor, I only hope to be met with a similar sense of fulfillment. Adeline seems cheerful, too. Although her dress of vibrant fuchsia would make her appear so even in the deepest doldrums.

"I must admit, I was not certain I would see you here again," Juliet observes with a smile.

"Perhaps I was not terribly enthusiastic at our last meeting," I acknowledge taking off my hat and smoothing my hair, while Juliet tucks her gloves into her pocket. I notice a number of small, circular scars in the palm of one hand, but she moves quickly, and I cannot get a better look.

"Neither was I, initially. Then I thought, why not? I am doing little else of use. I may as well try my hand here, even if the only result is that I learn how to make a decent jam."

"I think we underestimate the WI," I observe in a low voice, telling her of my exchange with Adeline Markby at our last meeting. "I deserved her chastisement, when I consider the reason for today's discussion."

"You approve of women in the police force?"

"Naturally!"

"Ah, yes, you are a detective. Quite close in professional terms. I do not suppose your family would have approved of any attempts to join the Met?" Juliet smiles, and it enlivens her wan face, revealing straight white teeth and bringing a brightness to her near translucent blue eyes.

"I cannot imagine the notion would have been met with excitement. May I ask, what do you do?" Though her smile remains in place, the brightness leaves her eyes, and I hope I have not caused offense. Before I can retread my steps, however, she replies.

"I am a lady of leisure, more or less. I do some secretarial work at the British Museum a few days a week. The position was not so much merited as gifted. A friend owed me a favor." I am surprised she admits this so easily.

"My cousin's husband works at the museum," I say. Before I can elaborate on Jeffrey, a woman who hurriedly introduces herself as Priscilla Lewis, Adeline's secretary, interrupts us. She carries a pad of paper and insists we sign our names to the petition. Tiny in stature, she reminds me vaguely of a terrier, nipping at our heels until her attention is diverted elsewhere. Our duty done, we shuffle through the groups of women to the table. Adeline spies us first, for Louise is busy chatting with Edith and another woman with a regal bearing and a ruby the size of a grape sparkling at her neck.

"Have you signed the petition?" Adeline asks, filling my cup. I have lost sight of Juliet and glance around.

"Yes, I did." I focus my attention on Adeline. Juliet will be fine, though I feel strangely protective of her. She seems so fragile and reserved amid this crowd of animated women. "I did not get a chance to read it. My uncle would be appalled that I put my signature to a document without proper inspection."

"And you, a detective at that!" Adeline laughs.

"Indeed."

"Well, it will be our secret. I was not sure you would return, that is why I called you myself."

"So I could not weasel out of the engagement?" I ask, warming to her. For all her frills and penchant for eye wateringly colorful attire, she is not to be underestimated. I admire her directness and tell her as much.

"Ah, well, with a mother like mine nothing less is acceptable," she says, smiling though I detect a hint of irritation in her tone. A bold suffragette for a mother could be a source of inspiration, yet undoubtedly her expectations for her child – a daughter in particular – must be substantial. Perhaps that is why Adeline dresses in so overtly feminine a manner, a tiny rebellion against her mother's no-nonsense attitude to attire and behavior. She wears a wedding band. I would like to meet the man who has married into this family. He must be either as meek as a lamb or formidable as a lion. Adeline's father, Lloyd Ashbourne, seemed a combination of the two when I met him. I do not doubt his wife is the head of that household, and I feel a twinge of pleasure at the thought. It makes me think of Agnes and Harold, where the situation is much the same.

"I am having a little luncheon at my house this weekend. Only a few women are coming," Adeline says, lowering her voice. "I would be thrilled for you to be one of the party. You will see, we are a fun bunch."

"You are determined to win me over?"

"You are independent, educated, have made a name for yourself -"

"Please, do continue!" I laugh.

"What I mean to say is that the WI could use someone like you in our ranks. You strike me as a woman who can knuckle down to a task." Adeline's passion is catching, and I find myself agreeing to her invitation, asking her whether she might invite Juliet as well.

"She seems a little lonely to me," I say quietly, hoping the woman in question is not within earshot.

"I had the same impression." Adeline nods thoughtfully, tapping her bottom lip with a finger. "Don't you worry, we will make her part of the group in no time at all."

"Adeline, look." Priscilla Lewis squeezes into our conversation, holding the petition under Adeline's nose. "Everyone has signed it."

"Brilliant, now we will send it on to other chapters and the Met will not know what hit them!" Adeline's praise conjures two spots of color to Priscilla's cheeks. I can understand her eagerness to please. There is a catching intensity, a vivacity about Adeline Markby, and I find myself considering the tasks ahead with some enthusiasm. She spoke of the pressure of having a mother like Edith Ashbourne, but quite evidently some of the older woman's hunger for change has rubbed off on her daughter, and she has made it her own.

"Ladies, ladies!" Edith claps her hands. The room falls silent. "Thank you all for coming today. Many of you have been working on this campaign for years, and we have seen some progress, but simply not enough. The WI may at times be regarded as a quaint organization for housewives to keep busy. However, we all know, if we were given the power to effect change, it would be done ten times faster than our male peers could hope to achieve it, and to the greater benefit of society as a whole!" Her rousing speech is met with cheers. I find myself clapping along with shared excitement. A politician was lost on Edith Ashbourne, but her daughter or granddaughter may find a seat in Parliament yet!

"Shall I give you a lift to Belgravia?" I ask my aunt, when she appears at my side at the end of the meeting. She is pink-faced and smiling, tucking stray strands of hair back into her bun. Like me, she appears enlivened by Edith's encouragement, and I am glad to note the sense of purpose she sought in coming here may have been found already. Or if not purpose, at least a sort of sisterhood.

"If you don't mind, dear."

"I will offer to take Juliet home. It looks like more rain," I say, gesturing to the high windows beyond which the sky is an ominous shade of gray, clouds dense, no valiant ray of sunlight breaking through. I have taken on a strangely protective position towards Juliet, despite her being several years my senior and likely well able to make her way home, rain or shine.

"I think I saw her slip out just a moment ago," Louise says, slipping on her coat. I cannot spy the other woman anywhere in the slowly emptying hall. When Louise and I step outside, nearly swept off our feet by a frigid gale, I see Juliet's white blond hair at the end of the street. She is bent forward against the wind. I call out to her, yet she does not seem to hear, for she walks on and quickly disappears around the corner.

"Adeline invited me to a luncheon this weekend," I tell my aunt in the car, the motor rumbling as I maneuver onto the road.

"Yes, Edith insisted I come, too. I was meant to visit Agnes on Saturday afternoon, but there is no saying no to Edith Ashbourne."

"Ha! I noticed much the same about her daughter, though I daresay Adeline possesses a gentle nature beneath her fervor."

"She seems a lovely woman. Ill-advised when it comes to her dress, though. I suppose I ought to be above noticing such things, if I want to be a part of the sisterhood that is the WI," Louise says with a little chuckle.

"She wears a wedding ring. Who is her husband? He must be a man of some fortitude in a family of enterprising women."

"I met him once, but his name escapes me." Louise furrows her brow. "Oh, yes, I have it! Graham, Graham Markby," she announces with a pointed finger punctuating every word.

"The name is not familiar," I note. "Do they have children?"

"No, to Edith's disappointment. They have been married for a good while, but then some never have children. I can't for the life of me remember what he does." Louise shrugs, dismissing the topic.

We roll past the pillared beauty that is the British Museum. It reminds me of Briony's husband, and I ask, "Have you seen much of Jeffrey lately? I hardly caught a glimpse of him at Elsa's birthday party." Louise sighs, which confirms my impression that something is not quite right.

"Briony is frustrated with him these days. You know how it goes with those two. Up and down, up and down. I tell her, 'You have children now, a family. You cannot be arguing about all manner of things.' Then again, I see Edith and remember Emmeline and how we used to march, and I think, all right, let him have it if Briony is upset." Louise shrugs.

"I think he is afraid to seem to be taking advantage of Briony's fortune. He is proud of his work, and could not bear it if others thought he was idling simply because he can."

"I know you are right, but Briony is my daughter. There will be no argument he can win against her, as far as I am concerned," Louise says, smiling to soften her words.

"I feel exactly the same. She is a sister to me."

"Jeffrey is restless in London," Louise observes, and I hear a note of sadness in her voice. "I could not bear it if they left England again."

"Has there been any indication they might?" I ask, concern creeping into my own voice. Surely, Briony would have told me? "Not yet. It is likely I am making myself worry for nothing. Then again, if Jeffrey decided there was valuable work at some site far from here, I wonder whether my daughter would defy him and remain in London."

"Separate from Jeffrey?" I ask, aghast at the thought. Whatever troubles have plagued them in the past, they have four children now.

"Unofficially, maybe? Oh, what am I saying, Evie!" Louise presses a hand to her mouth, an expression of guilt on her face. I stop at the side of the road and pull my aunt into a half embrace.

"Briony will not leave and neither will Jeffrey. They are simply in the middle of one of their spats. It will be over in no time, you shall see," I soothe, uncertain what has brought about the shift in mood in my aunt. Her jubilant mood after the WI meeting has evaporated. I have only ever known Louise as an unwaveringly stable influence from my childhood into adulthood. I suppose I never considered her to be merely human like the rest of us.

Chapter 7

Instead of driving straight to my flat in St. James after dropping Louise off at her house, I go to Briony's, a convenient five minutes from her parents' home. When the maid opens the door to admit me, I find myself standing in a surprisingly silent hall. The older children are in school and Elsa may be asleep, for not a wail, nor a giggle can be heard. It is almost eerily peaceful. The maid leads me to the sitting room used for informal occasions, recognizing me as a frequent guest, and goes off in search of her employer. The room is large and airy, with a window looking out at the garden, now the dull green of early winter. A cherry tree at the end of the small expanse is nearly bare of leaves and a lone squirrel, cheeks puffed out, makes a hurried dash across the lawn.

"Admiring the garden?" Briony's voice rings out from the doorway, and I turn. My cousin wears a smile, but her eyes are rimmed red, her expression pinched.

"The garden is the least of my concerns," I say, giving her a meaningful look. Her smile melts away like ice cream in the sun, and she slumps onto a sofa.

"Did mother send you?" she asks, a note of petulance mingling with weariness in her tone.

"No, but she is worried, and now I can see why." Sitting down beside her, I press a handkerchief into her palm. "It is Jeffrey, I presume?"

"I think he is having an affair, Evie!" Briony closes her eyes and drops her face into her hands.

"No! Surely, not!" I exclaim, incredulous. Jeffrey may be many things, but I never believed him charismatic enough to charm another woman into bestowing her affections upon him, though even in my shocked state, I realize this is not the right approach to take with my cousin.

"When...how?" I stammer.

"He is always away at work, sneaking out even on the weekend! It is ludicrous!" She lets out a weary sigh and thumps the sofa cushion with a closed fist. "And before you say that proves nothing, we were at an event for the museum two weeks ago, and there was a woman, a pretty, young one, whom he quite overtly tried to avoid. When I asked him who she was, he mumbled something about him not knowing everyone, and I should stop fretting." Her eyes grow wide. "It was such an unsuitable reaction to an innocent question, Evie. There must be more to it. He has been distant ever since."

"There could very well be a simple explanation," I muse, my mind tripping over possibilities to calm my cousin's fears.

"Did you know he was walking out with another woman when we met?" she asks in a quiet tone, avoiding my eyes.

"What? You never said!"

"It is hardly a fact with which to endear my dearest friend to a new beau, is it?" Briony shrugs, her fingers fidgeting with the cushion's trim. "He assured me it was nothing serious. Now I wonder."

"Jeffrey loves you and the children. We are both aware how possessed he can become when given a task at work. Maybe his new project is simply his latest obsession. There need not be a third party involved."

"I hope you are right. What would I do if my suspicions were confirmed?" She pulls the cushion to her chest and raises her eyes to meet mine. "Mother has been telling me of the WI and the way they are advocating for female independence. If Jeffrey were betraying me - his family - would you all view me as a coward if I stayed with him?"

"You know we would not," I say, privately wondering whether her concern holds a grain of truth. I would judge Jeffrey, and harshly at that, yet would a part of me be critical of my cousin, too? No, I think, not critical so much as sad for her.

"Yes, you would, and I could hardly blame you. I would hate myself for it, too."

"Don't speak like this, Briony!"

"It is easier for you. If you want to walk away, leave the country, do whatever you wish, you have that freedom. I have four lives for whom I bear the responsibility, and I cannot act rashly. Not that I wish it to be any other way, of course. Without our children, goodness knows where I would be." It is true that I am not bound by the responsibility of motherhood, but whatever she thinks of my carefree ways, I am rooted by other means. There is Daniel, my aunts and uncles, my business, and significantly, Briony herself and the children. They may not be mine to watch over, but I hate to imagine a time in which I cannot see them all as often as I do now.

"Let us not be hasty," I encourage her. Now is not the time for elaborate explanations regarding my own duties. Briony is in turmoil, and I happen to be in a position to ease her burden. "You may have forgotten, but you have the great advantage of a cousin who is also a celebrated detective! I will discover the truth behind Jeffrey's behavior. Once we know more, you can make a decision. You and the children will never be alone, whatever you decide."

"You mean to spy on my husband?" Briony gives me a curious look, her frown slowly shifts into a bemused smile.

"With your permission, naturally."

"Jeffrey would be furious if he found out I had set you and your bloodhound's nose upon him." A giggle bursts from her lips. She presses a hand to her mouth, as if caught belching.

"He will not find out, unless I find *him* out," I declare with confidence I have little right to feel. It doesn't sit quite right with me to spy on Jeffrey, whom I have always considered a friend. Nonetheless, he is causing Briony worry, and for that he deserves my clandestine intrusion, at least as far as I am concerned. Besides, even making the proposal was worthwhile, for it conjured a smile to my cousin's lips.

Chapter 8

The following day our office telephone rings with a frantic woman on the other end, crying about how her darling Freddy has gone missing. The police are not interested, and we absolutely must help her. Naturally, her words and manner capture my attention, and Hugh, who sits opposite me, leans forward, eyes wide with curiosity.

"How old is Freddy?" I ask, trying to sound calm and reassuring, to soothe the poor woman's nerves.

"Six! Oh, he will be so frightened!"

"Six years old, and the police are not interested?" I ask, appalled. Hugh narrows his eyes.

"So dismissive," the woman sniffles. "He has never been out alone."

"Yes, yes, I understand why you would worry. Do not be afraid, Mrs. -"

"Baker," she supplies.

"Mrs. Baker. We will set out to find young Freddy right away. Can you give us a description? When did you last see him? Are you certain he is not at school, or at a friend's house?"

"School? Whyever would he be there? No, no. He is lost, the poor lovey. He has a short brown coat and goes up to my knee."

"Your knee?" Suddenly comprehension dawns and my shoulders slump. "Mrs. Baker, is Freddy a dog?"

"Yes, of course he is! Such a sweet little pup! A darling spaniel!"

I try my best to swallow a sigh, and Hugh sits back, rolling his eyes. Nonetheless, I take down the information Mrs. Baker supplies and promise that one of us will be at her Mayfair home within the hour.

"I can do it," Hugh says, rubbing his eyes as he gets to his feet.

"Do you mind?"

"No, I will get a bit of exercise combing the gardens for errant Freddy. At least he chose a sunny day to make his escape."

"Thank you," I reply. Hugh just nods, doffing his hat and sliding his arms into the sleeves of his coat.

The day is fine indeed, a contrast to the interminable gray of the past week. The sky beyond the window is a cool, cloudless blue that tells of a nip in the air. The sun shines into the office, making dust motes dance in its bright rays. It is not a day meant to sit in a quiet office. Even Kathleen and Aidan left for a walk a while ago, the little lad tottering along beside his grandmother, as I watched them from my perch at the window.

My promise to Briony comes to mind, and I decide now is as good a time as any to begin my surveillance of her husband. I hope, in this case, to be entirely unsuccessful in confirming her suspicions.

Putting on my coat and grabbing my bag and hat, I call out a quick goodbye to Maeve, who sits at the kitchen table, bent over a pad of paper. Like Hugh did a few days ago, she covers it up on my approach, her cheeks coloring. I do not stop. She is entitled to her privacy. Goodness knows what she is doing, perhaps writing a romantic poem, or perhaps a love letter? Maybe she is merely doing household accounting and slightly overspent this month?

Outside I realize the brilliant blue sky and sunshine have conjured a false sense of a mild day, for the air is frigid and a wind bites at my cheeks and makes the bare tree branches shiver.

I seem to be driving the route to Bloomsbury constantly these days, though today's visit is for less congenial reasons than on other occasions. The closer I get to the British Museum, the more I wish I were simply dropping in on another WI assembly, where tea and cake and pleasant conversation would await me. I have come without much of a plan. My promise to Briony was easily made, but how to go about it? Jeffrey will recognize me a mile away, and I will have to leave the Bentley somewhere well out of sight. It is not the most inconspicuous of motorcars, after all. Further, the British Museum is a colossus of a building. At least I know the department where Jeffrey works. Should I wait until he comes out? The notion strikes me as a remarkably tedious way to spend a day. Besides, he may not emerge until evening, and then he will probably not be joined by his supposed paramour. Clearly, I did not think my plan through. Perhaps I ought to have gone to whistle for Freddy, while Hugh with his wily ways undertook this more challenging enterprise. But then he is there, and I am here, and I may as well try my best. Should Jeffrey happen upon me, he will not be suspicious. He is well aware how much I enjoy the vast collection of the museum, and that I frequently wander these halls and marvel at the Rosetta Stone and Elgin Marbles. Jeffrey feels quite the same, and the thought that he has charmed some lady who shares this passion is, perhaps, not quite so far from the truth as I insisted it was to Briony yesterday.

While I saw much in the way of classical architecture when I lived in Greece, the British Museum, with its towering Ionic columns and elaborate pediment high above the main entryway still has the power to awe me every time I visit. It is nearing noon, and a group of schoolchildren standing in a crooked queue complain of their rumbling bellies, only to be hushed by harried teachers. I move past them, giving a little boy a sympathetic smile. Undoubtedly, a great number of visitors come to see the vast offerings of the collection every day, yet the size and scope of the museum means there are rarely crowds. I wander inside, admiring, as I always do, the soaring ceiling, the light, airy atmosphere so at odds with the dust-borne artefacts on display.

Once inside, I wonder how to begin the actual process of detection. I dismiss asking after Jeffrey. I am not a good enough actress to avoid unwanted attention, and if he becomes suspicious, he may take better care to cover his tracks...If there are tracks to cover, that is. I remain skeptical.

To my left is a Roman gallery, displaying marble busts of emperors and orators, their expressions stern, as they peer down at me from their plinths, the weight of history resting on their shoulders. Apart from some goddesses and muses, I notice not for the first time, that they are all men.

I move along the gallery halls, towards the area where the staff's offices for the Department of Greek Antiquities are housed. It is where Jeffery will, or at the very least should, be spending his days. I glance at my watch. Nearly lunch time. I will take the chance that Jeffrey plans to eat out. Thus I dawdle about a small gallery from where I see the door to the departmental offices. Sometime last year, Jeffrey gave me a personal tour to show off some new acquisition and in doing so, revealed the location of his office. Hopefully, it remains the same. The museum itself is gargantuan. Jeffrey hinted that one department is, in fact, little connected to another. The Egyptologists, for example, shun the scholars of Greek antiquity and so on. Perhaps it will not be a challenge to spot Briony's husband after all. He is a man of habit and would never miss lunch. Unless, perhaps, he has more tempting plans. I grimace and purge the thought from my mind.

Before Hugh and I took on the mantle of detectives, no one told us how much time is spent waiting. A detective's greatest challenge lies not in solving a crime, rather in honing her patience. Hours are eaten up by observation, or the inane task of waiting near a telephone. I mentally prepare myself that patience may be required today, when the door opens, and my breath catches in my throat. Yet it is not my cousin's husband I spy, but Juliet Nelson.

I recall she told me of her secretarial work at the museum, but my mind was consumed with other things, I nearly forgot. Instantly, I wonder whether she may be Jeffrey's illicit paramour. She is pretty and enigmatic, which some men find appealing. Furthermore, she is unattached.

Today she wears another of her plain suits of navy serge. Her hair is pulled into a tight bun at the nape of her neck. She walks rigidly, straight as an arrow, yet from this distance, her limp is more pronounced. Juliet carries a small bag and her coat is draped over her arm. I cannot explain what compels me to abandon my post staking out Jeffrey and follow her instead, but so I do.

Quickly, we pass through one gallery after another. As unobtrusively as I can, I try to blend in with other visitors, all the while keeping an eye on her. Juliet moves with purpose, eyes ahead, never caught on the marble curves of Aphrodite's hip or the rippling contours of Apollo's muscles. Half-way to the door, I wonder what I am thinking! I came here to watch Jeffrey, and now find myself so easily distracted by an enigmatic woman I barely know. I pause for a moment, ready to turn on my heel when the true object of my interest steps into my line of sight. He walks quickly, a bundle of papers in his hand. I just about manage to duck behind a pillar and out of sight. Perhaps he is distracted, perhaps he truly does not notice, but in a movement that makes me wince, he collides with Juliet. She drops her bag, and he scatters his papers. They bend and fumble about, gathering up their things. Jeffrey's lips move, doubtless in apology. Juliet smiles and says something in return. Their hands brush as she helps him collect his papers. I narrow my eyes, watching for any sign of clandestine affection, but find none. They nod at one another and move apart, Jeffrey sweeping past me, unseeing, while Juliet disappears from view.

I wait a few moments behind the pillar, feeling silly, yet unwilling to compromise my position should Jeffrey turn back. If Juliet is his secret lover, both are remarkably good actors. No, in truth, I suspect her of nothing apart from the misfortune of having been in Jeffrey's way when his mind was elsewhere. The more I think on it, the less convinced I am of Briony's suspicions. I step out from my hiding place and sink onto a bench in front of a display of tall Minoan urns. Jeffrey's lover, I believe, is not of flesh and bone, but rather dust and clay.

"Evelyn?" a familiar voice draws my attention and I turn. Juliet stands behind me, a curious expression on her face.

"Juliet, what a coincidence!" I exclaim, with more cheer than I feel. Today has been both disappointing, yielding no proper case, nor information, as well as satisfying in that I did not catch Jeffrey out doing anything untoward, well, not yet at least.

"I was on my way to lunch, when I noticed I was missing a glove and came back." Juliet smiles and holds up the errant article. She must have dropped it when Jeffrey collided with her. I wonder whether I could turn this meeting to my advantage.

"Do you know a good café in the area? I spent the morning exploring the museum and am famished. Won't you join me? Unless," I add quickly, "you have other plans."

If my proposal is met with displeasure, I would never know it judging by Juliet's expression. "All right," she agrees.

"This is my favorite part of the museum," I tell her, as we walk towards the doors. "I lived in Greece for a time with my cousin and her husband. I told you of him, Jeffrey Farnham. Have you met?"

"Farnham?" Juliet seems to consider the name, her forehead creasing as she frowns in thought. "Yes, I think I have heard the name."

"He is an archaeologist in the department of Greek Antiquity."

"Yes, I remember. In fact, I believe it was him I ran into just a few moments ago, now that you mention his name. That is why I dropped my glove. His mind seemed rather somewhere else." She offers me a small smile. Nothing to learn from it. At least she did not deny meeting him as she might have if their acquaintance was deeper than one ought to suppose.

"Do many women work in the department?" I ask, trying to sound merely curious, not inquisitive.

"I have only been there a few months myself, but there are two other female secretaries and one archivist."

"Jeffrey never mentions anyone, I think he is completely absorbed by his work." My comment earns no response from Juliet. I almost regret having asked her to lunch. How are we to make conversation, if I am the only one willing to open my mouth?

Juliet leads the way around the corner to a small eatery with fogged windows and a blue door. We are welcomed by a wave of pleasant warmth that takes the chill of the short walk right out of my bones. We sit at the small window table looking out at the street, both ordering the beef stew.

"Do you enjoy your work?" I ask. The café is not terribly busy, despite the time of day, and the silence between us would stretch if not filled with conversation.

"It is neither the most challenging nor compelling task, but I do not mind. Do you enjoy yours?"

"Most of the time, yes," I say, shrugging. "I have not had the agency for long, so should still be quite passionate about it, and for the most part, I truly am. I want to do something useful and feel I am helping, only sometimes the cases seem so inconsequential. Missing dogs or mislaid jewels."

"Clearly, they are of consequence to someone, or else they would not pay you to solve them," Juliet reasons.

"Yes, I suppose you are right. Very sensible, too," I concede, slightly rattled by her cool manner, her unwillingness to slip into banter. Her responses are direct, unwavering. At least I have learned there are more potential lovers for Jeffrey in the department. If I continue to ask, will Juliet, in her forthright way, continue to answer? I decide to test this theory. "Are you a Londoner? I cannot distinguish an accent, though I have tried." Do I detect a flicker of something like irritation dance across her seemingly immovable features?

"Yes. I am. I moved around a bit in my time, though. Some people, when they travel, are quick to pick up foreign accents and dialects, but I am much the opposite."

"I have a cousin, Teddy, who is brilliant at it. He just needs to spend a few hours in one place and can emulate the dialect with fluency. Do you have a brother or sister? I have no siblings, but am close to many of my cousins."

"No, none."

"Is your family in London now? Mine has more or less congregated here, just as I returned to live in the city."

"Where were you before?" she asks. I do not miss the fact that she has gracefully swerved around my own question. Is she intentionally slippery, or am I painting a picture on the blank canvas she offers, because I have a tendency to do so? I tell her of my time in Greece with Briony and Jeffrey, watching her carefully for a reaction at the mention of her colleague's wife, but find none. I speak of my time in France, then my studies in Oxford and before I know it, our meals have come and gone.

"Well this was very nice," says Juliet with a placid smile. "I really must be getting back to work. Thank you for the pleasant company." Somewhat bemused I nod, shake away her offer of payment, and watch her slender figure slip out onto the street. I order a cup of tea. Usually, I am the one to compel others to speak, confident that most people, if you give them the chance, prefer talking about themselves, or at the very least their concerns, far more than listening. Somehow Juliet turned the tables on me. She now knows half my life's story, while all I know of her is that she moved around and possesses no talent for accents. What sort of a detective am I?

Dejected, I order a slice of Battenberg cake.

The day is not a complete failure, for I manage to obtain the names of the other women working in Jeffrey's department with remarkable ease. I telephoned the museum, claiming to require the information for a governmental survey. I was very vague, yet the man on the other end was willing to believe my subterfuge, which I put to him in a wholly unnecessary false voice. He thus provided their names and positions. Miss Lara Bennet, Mrs. Joan McMullin and Mrs. Frances Bell, the latter of whom is the archivist, the former being the only unmarried of the three. Of course, there is the possibility that Jeffrey is entirely innocent, or that he met his lover elsewhere. He may have avoided some woman at the party, as Briony observed, because she is a colleague whose company he simply does not enjoy. Little to go on, still I will persevere. If truth is to be had, it shall be mine.

Chapter 9

Over the course of the next few days, Hugh locates Freddy and returns the pup to a tearful and terribly grateful mistress, and I am able to eliminate two of the women from my list of Jeffrey's potential mistresses. I play spy again, this time with greater success and discover Joan McMullin to be quite certainly and robustly with child. Although it is perhaps presumptuous and unfair towards my sex to think so, I strike Frances Bell from my list as well. She appears to be nearing her sixtieth birthday and when I looked her up in the newspaper archives, I learned she is recently widowed. Her late husband's obituary, if written by her, is tender and sorrowful. I cannot imagine her to be much inclined to throw herself into a love affair given this recent loss.

Lara Bennet remains. From a distance, I estimate her age to be near my own. She is small and slightly plump, with a sharply cut blond bob. Of course, I cannot entirely discount Juliet. Yet from her manner, which is so entirely different from that of my cousin, I struggle to imagine Jeffrey's attraction. Then again, I struggle to imagine him with anyone else altogether.

I plan to keep a close eye on Juliet, when I see her at Adeline's luncheon today. Louise will be there, too, for she and Edith have rekindled their old friendship. Further, I have finagled an invitation for Briony. I want her to tell me whether Juliet is the one she noticed at the party. From the way she described the woman, blond and pretty, it could be Lara or Juliet or any number of women. Surely, she would recognize her, if faced with her again.

Briony is all nerves when I come to pick her up. She has dressed in a perfectly cut suit and a new hat, clearly meaning to impress. I give her hand a squeeze before we ascend the stairs to the Markby house, not far from my cousin's in Belgravia. It is a tall, slim building with decorative wrought iron balconies and a lion's head as the doorknob. We can hear the sound of lively voices even outside, amplified when a maid opens the door and bids us enter the warm, tea-scented hall.

"Evelyn, you came!" Adeline, this time in a grass green dress, takes both my hands in hers, before moving on to my cousin. "And you must be Louise's daughter, I can see the resemblance." When she turns to greet another arrival, I offer Briony a little shrug.

"Is she here?" she whispers, as we enter the salon. A few of the WI ladies are seated on sofas and chairs, while others mill about in small groups, teacups in their hands. It seems an informal setting, well in keeping with Adeline's easy manner. A pair of young maids move around with trays of small cakes and sandwiches. The atmosphere is one of warmth and good cheer. I feel Briony relax slightly at my side. Perhaps she expected a den of anarchists, plotting how to overthrow the government, not a group of women set on formulating petitions and ironing out peaceful campaigns over tea and pastries.

"Over there." I gesture in the direction of a pale blue sofa occupied by three women chatting away. Juliet nods along, but her lips do not move.

"It isn't her," Briony whispers, and I catch the relief in her voice. I share the sentiment, though perhaps it is mixed with a twinge of disappointment, too. How easy it would have been, if Juliet was the woman in question. I would have come much closer to learning the truth. And yet...I cannot imagine the quiet, closed-off woman from the WI as anyone's illicit lover. She strikes me as a solitary creature, and though I know little about her – she has ensured that much – I am inclined to trust my intuition.

Juliet becomes aware of us, raising her gaze and breaking away from the conversation. Her companions hardly seem to notice, as she gets to her feet.

"Juliet Nelson, may I introduce my cousin, Briony Farnham."

"Very nice to meet you." Briony smiles.

"And you. Evelyn said your husband works in the British Museum, as do I."

"Indeed. Do you enjoy your work?" Briony chats easily, now that she feels less threatened by the willowy blond. I let my attention wander.

A man, tall and slim with dark hair enters the room, clearly in search of someone, eyes roving about, touching upon stranger's faces, until they alight upon the one he seeks. I take him to be Graham Markby, Adeline's husband. He appears to be near his wife's age, in his mid-thirties. He nods at a few of the women, who greet him with an ease that speaks of a prior acquaintance, and touches his wife's arm, drawing her away from the conversation and bending down to speak in quiet tones. I watch them, trying not to stare. They seem at ease, a small island in the middle of this crowd of ladies. Adeline wears a private smile and when they move apart, she notices our little group.

"Graham, darling, come, meet some newcomers," she says loudly and pulls him towards us. To his credit, he does not appear ill-at-ease in this milieu. His wife probably turns their home into a women's clubhouse rather frequently. Introductions are made, polite chit-chat exchanged.

"Very nice to make your acquaintance. I think we may have met before?" he observes, nodding at Briony.

"Oh, it is entirely possible, do forgive me for forgetting. My memory is a sieve nowadays," my cousin notes with a smile.

"And I have met your father, Robert Carlisle," he adds. His gaze is direct and not unfriendly as he regards us, waiting for a reply.

"Yes, in what small circles we travel!"

"I am afraid I do not recognize your name. Nelson, you said it was?" Graham asks Juliet, who has remained silent.

"Juliet has been away from the city for some time," his wife explains, as though the fact that her husband cannot place a woman in this bustling city requires explanation. Then again, he seems to be a man who prides himself on remembering a face.

Before the conversation can take flight, we see Lloyd Ashbourne, Adeline's father, lingering in the doorway, his hand raised in a wave. He seems unwilling to cross the threshold into the sea of women. I would have thought it is many a man's dream!

"Graham and Papa are going to the club," Adeline says. "Go on then, my love." She kisses Graham's cheek, and we bid our goodbyes. "They are both used to being shunted out, when Mama or I invite some of our WI friends over. I hope you are enjoying yourselves. Perhaps I forgot to mention it at our last meeting, but a group of us plan to volunteer at the Salvation Army on Armistice Day, next Friday. We did it last year and felt it was worth repeating. Louise has already agreed to join, but we all lead busy lives, so I would understand if you are otherwise engaged."

"As long as my agency remains without a new case, I am quite happy to join you," I say.

"I do not work on Fridays, so it suits me as well," Juliet agrees. Briony promises to try her best, but with four children, her time cannot always be scheduled.

"Wonderful! Priscilla, my secretary, has arranged the event. I would be lost without her, and so would Mama! Speaking of whom, where has she disappeared to?" Adeline's attention drifts once more.

"If you like, I can come and pick you up on Friday," I offer Juliet. A part of me regrets the offer as soon as the words slip past my tongue. Will the drive be filled with silence or my nervous chatter?

"That is kind of you, but I can make my own way." I accept this without argument. We talk a while longer, yet Briony, too, has little more success at luring Juliet out of her reserve. In fact, she is so good at deflecting each question, I almost wonder whether she is Jeffrey's mystery woman after all. What other reason would she have to remain so opaque on the simplest of matters. My cousin makes much the same observation when we leave the Markby house and walk the few blocks to her own.

"She does have a certain allure," Briony notes, a worry line creasing her brow.

"Perhaps you should simply confront Jeffrey," I suggest. Having told my cousin of the other women in the department, I think it may be best to challenge Jeffrey. He is a terrible liar. If asked outright, I do not think he could tell a falsehood. Or if he attempted to, I know my cousin would recognize it as such.

"What if I did and he confirms my suspicions?" she asks, sidestepping a puddle, and casting me an anxious look.

"Then at least you would know, at least you would not have to go through every day with uncertainty."

We walk a little while in silence, the click-clack of our heels on the pavement and the rustle of the wind through leafless branches the only sounds accompanying our thoughts. I understand Briony's dilemma, but if it were me, I think I would go mad from the weight of the suspicion. I would grab Daniel by the shoulders, give him a good shake and force him to confess, if indeed there was anything to confess. As yet, I have no reason to believe Jeffrey has taken the path of infidelity except for Briony's fears, which, I must acknowledge, if only in my mind, have been wrong before.

"I do not know whether I am ready to confront him, but I am going to pay a surprise visit to him at work to find out if this Lara Bennet is the woman he wanted to avoid. If she is, and Jeffrey remains as distant as he has been lately, I will ask him directly, come what may." Briony sounds resolute, though the words must stick in her throat. She hates confrontation even more than I do, and I wish I could take the task out of her hands. Well, I suppose I could...

"Do you want me to ask him?"

Briony hesitates. To her credit she shakes her head, pulling back her shoulders a little. "No. I am not a child anymore." She sounds regretful. Sometimes we all yearn for the simpler days of youth.

When we arrive at her house, she convinces me – no great challenge – to say hello to the children, and so the rest of the afternoon is spent listening to eager voices recounting the day, to Iona's eloquent argument against Mr. Rochester – "He kept a woman in his attic!" – and Elsa's cheerful, if less eloquent, attempts at conversation. All the time, I wonder how Jeffrey could risk all this, the happiness of his family, his children. I come to the conclusion that the Jeffrey I have known for many years now, simply would not, and I am going to prove it.

Chapter 10

Good intentions aside, proving someone's innocence can be even more of a challenge than proving someone's guilt, or so I have found in the past few days. I have been on Jeffrey's and Lara's tail, and even once followed Juliet all the way from the museum to her house. Nothing suspicious occurred, yet neither do we have proof that Briony's fears are unfounded. She has not yet confronted him, or ambushed him at work. I say as much to Daniel, while we ready ourselves for a dinner at Agnes and Harold's house, or rather my aunt's home, which she now shares with her husband. There was no way she would have moved into his bachelor's abode.

"I am not encouraging your involvement," Daniel says, buttoning his shirt in front of the mirror. "But what if she had a peek at his weekly diary? If there is a suspicious appointment, maybe it will make it easier to discover the truth." He grimaces at my excited expression, already regretting setting this idea into the wild.

"You are a detective, Daniel Harper! Why did I not think of it?" I drape my arms around his neck. He smells of soap and laundered cotton, so familiar I think I could sniff him out like a bloodhound, though I somehow doubt he would deem the metaphor particularly romantic.

"Perhaps I ought to join you?"

"Perhaps you should. We could make a family business of it."

"I would have to change my name to Carlisle," Daniel observes with a smile.

"And what of it?"

"Nothing at all, a lovely name."

"And yet I shall sacrifice it for you. What greater gesture of devotion can there be?" I give him a kiss. "My aunt is waiting." I grin, and he sighs.

"Did I tell you," he says, as we climb into the car, "Wilkins believes he is being followed?"

"You certainly did not! Since when?"

Daniel raises his hands in a placatory gesture, and I cross my arms over my chest. Really, keeping such a mystery from me, when he knows it is my passion!

"He only told me yesterday. Mentioned he had the feeling someone was watching him when he went to the bank and later again, when he came back to the house."

"Does he think it has something to do with his past?" I ask carefully. We recently discovered Wilkins, Daniel's butler, has a rather checkered history and potentially earned the ire of one of the more unpleasant villains I have ever come across, Reg Hogan.

"Why now, though?" Daniel wonders aloud. "He seemed rattled, but since the lies about his past and his theft became known to me, he has been desperate to prove himself trustworthy." Months ago, Wilkins was arrested for the murder of his brother-in-law. He was innocent and proven thus, I am happy to say, by the efforts of the Carlisle Detective Agency. Yet he had not been honest, and though his indiscretion was understandable, it formed a slight chasm between him and Daniel, who previously thought of his butler, a former soldier like himself, as a friend.

"Maybe I can ask Hugh to look into it? He has the skill of a phantom when he sets his mind to it."

"Is that meant to be reassuring?" Daniel asks, but I detect humor in his tone.

"At the very least, it will give him a task. I feel guilty that he has been forced to search for errant pups and stolen jewels."

"It is good for him. He doesn't need more tragedy in his life, whether it is his own or another's."

"He is doing well," I say gently, placing a hand on Daniel's arm. Hugh was a broken, erratic man when we met him a few years ago, and Daniel sometimes fears his friend will relapse into such a state again. I am not too worried. Hugh was alone before, but he has friends now. We are here to see him right, and he knows it.

I lean my head against Daniel's shoulder as the driver winds his way through evening traffic. Droplets of rain glisten on the windshield, tinted golden from the light of the streetlamps. The pavement shimmers and dark figures under umbrellas hurry to cross the road, rush for a bus, or duck into their homes. So many lives that drift by us on a daily basis, yet so few leave even the faintest impression. The thought saddens me, even if little can be done about it. We can join in with our community, take care of our family and our friends, still we must accept that many stories - most stories - will forever elude us. For a curious soul such as myself, the notion is a rather tragic one. It has to do with my reason for becoming a detective, both a need to learn what hides behind the façade, as well as an insistent desire to right wrongs in the world. Children of the war, or orphans such as myself, may feel this urgency more acutely.

Sometimes the results of my detecting may right one wrong, but throw another life into disarray. There are always innocent victims, no matter how satisfying the result of an investigation. There is never a perfect balance. Sometimes the truth reveals such unsavory facts, I wonder whether they would have best remained hidden. But then, the resolution of a mystery generally brings about at least some form of justice, which must be worth it in the end.

"What are you thinking?" Daniel asks, giving my hand a gentle squeeze.

"Contemplating the state of justice in our world, and you?"

"Wondering what's for dinner?"

"Our thoughts are aligned then. If the meal is disappointing, with us dragging ourselves out of the house on such a cold and wet night, there surely is little justice left in the world," I observe with a dramatic sigh.

"Do you think Harold has succeeded in incorporating his love for spices into mealtimes?"

"Wonders do exist, and Agnes is in love. We may find ourselves knee deep in curry tonight."

Mr. Harris, Agnes long-time butler, opens the door to her Eaton Square home and we bundle inside. The night is cold and a sharp wind whistles around the corners. The house radiates comforting warmth, and we gratefully shrug off our coats and hand over our hats.

"Mr. and Mrs. Finley are in the lounge," Mr. Harris says in his deep, polished voice. I wonder whether he struggles calling Agnes by a new name after so long and with having a man in the house once more? Even if Mr. Harris was Agnes' employee, she depended on him tremendously when Brendan died, and while she may not say so, he is a part of the family.

"Thank you, and how are you?" I ask, as he leads us down the hall. Of course, I know the way to the lounge blindfolded, for I lived here much of my life.

"Quite well, quite well. Bit of a creak in the bones, but that is the way of life," he says with a chuckle. "Here we are, enjoy your evening." Mr. Harris steps back to allow us entry. Agnes and Harold are seated on a sofa in the lavender lounge, their heads bent together, though they move apart upon our entry. Harold stands and reaches for Daniel's hand, while I kiss my aunt's brow.

"Sit, sit. A drink?" Harold asks, already at the trolley, a decanter in hand. We agree, and he busies himself with his task. Agnes looks well, bright-eyed, if slightly restless, shifting about on the sofa, settling only once Harold has distributed the glasses and perched beside her again.

Malia Zaidi

"How is business?" Harold asks. I am gratified he has directed the question not only at Daniel, but at us both. I suppose any man who marries into this family, in particular making Agnes his wife, will learn to understand that women are as formidable – if not more so, given my aunt's temper – as men.

"Quite well, nothing new, really," Daniel offers, taking a sip.

"Our cases are coming in slowly. Nothing terribly exciting, though," I admit.

"The world is at peace? Hallelujah!" Harold laughs.

"If only," Agnes says and raises her eyebrows. "All we read about in the papers is one tragedy after another."

"Do not be so grim, my love!"

"Let us speak of other matters," I say, taking a sip.

"Yes, let us discuss the wedding. I have spoken to the cooks and the menu is set, the dress is nearly ready and almost all the guests have agreed to attend. Isn't it marvelous?"

"Excellent," Daniel nods, giving me a wide-eyed look. Both of us would have preferred to elope, but my relationship with Agnes, which has only recently warmed, would be struck back to the Ice Age should I displease her so. She has taken it upon herself to plan everything, and I generally do not mind, though I am beginning to wonder what I agreed to. My sole demand was that she should whittle down the guest list of over a hundred to something nearer fifty. She was appalled, but I get my willpower from her and she grudgingly accepted my wish.

"The dress fitting is next week, don't forget," Agnes reminds me. I take another fortifying gulp.

"I wouldn't dare," I reply.

"Well, that brings us to a matter we wanted to discuss with you." Harold and Agnes exchange a fleeting, almost conspiratorial look, which leads me to believe they rehearsed this before. I glance at Daniel, who shrugs.

"Is everything all right?" I ask, worried they are about to confide some personal calamity. "You are not ill, are you?" A sudden tension squeezes my chest and I grip my glass more tightly, as though it might provide support.

"No, no," Harold reassures us, and my muscles relax.

"Nothing like that," Agnes agrees, though she does not appear entirely at ease.

"Well, out with it!" I demand.

"Just like her aunt," Harold observes with a glint of pride in his eyes. "Well, what we wanted to tell you -"

"Harold is going into politics!" Agnes interrupts her husband.

"Oh," I say, relieved, though surprised.

45

"Politics? In what capacity?" Daniel asks with greater eloquence than I seem capable of mustering.

"I want to be an MP. Retirement does not suit me. Agnes agrees we are too young to sit around while the world is spinning, and we could be involved in a meaningful way."

"Very admirable," I say. "Naturally, we are happy to support you." Given a moment to let the proposal sink in, I believe Harold would make a brilliant politician. He is a genial fellow, who has seen the world and gets along with most everyone, and his military bearing gives him a powerful sense of authority when he intends it to.

"The Shoreditch constituency is open, and I intend to become the candidate for the election." Harold smiles. "Naturally, I have to better acquaint myself with the area, be active in the community."

"There is much to be done for that part of the city," I observe, remembering its East End neighbor, Whitechapel, where I witnessed some of the greatest squalor I have ever come across. I wonder what people will think of a moneyed man like Harold, with his Belgravia home and plummy accent? He spent much of his adult life in India, and told me of the strife and scarcity he saw at times. Perhaps his existing connections with the political elite, as well as his grounded attitudes and kindly nature will prove a perfect combination. In any case, I wish him luck.

"If it is anything like Whitechapel, poverty, unemployment and crime will be high on your list of priorities," Daniel muses, doubtless recalling the hollow-eyed children we saw on the street, the line of men standing in tattered jackets outside the Salvation Army, toes poking through the thin leather of their shoes, cheekbones sharp against sallow skin. I try to envisage Harold and Agnes in those streets and my imagination struggles to conjure the image, but then few of my own acquaintance would have been able to picture me there either. I have only been back a handful of times to help Maisie, Wilkins' sister, move and bring her things to Grosvenor Square, where she is now employed as Daniel's housekeeper.

"Despite all I have experienced, it still strikes me as shocking that some have so very little, while we sit here with so much we hardly know what to do with it," Harold says somberly, surprising me with his observation, but also with the shadow of genuine melancholy in his eyes.

We are silent for a few moments, lost in our thoughts. The crystal glass in my hand suddenly feels too heavy and I set it aside, amber liquid sloshing at the bottom. It is Agnes who draws us back to the present, giving a sharp little clap, making me jump.

"Yes, yes, and it will be very good for those poor souls to have a man like Harold as their champion."

"Indeed," I agree, though not with quite the same fervor my aunt has invoked. Harold has a steep mountain to climb. With Agnes at his back, though, he is unlikely to fall.

Chapter 11

Daniel is full of ideas on how to help Harold when we go home after dinner. So much so, I wonder whether he might be suited to politics as well. He is certainly not finding great satisfaction in his family business, but his guilt over having abandoned it for years will not make it easy to acknowledge this reality.

When I wake the next morning to a brilliant blue sky and the insistent caw of a raven perched on a tree beyond the window, Daniel has already left. The room is cold, the fire in the grate has died down to ashes. I have to battle with myself to get out of the cozy bed. Today I am meeting with the WI for our Armistice Day volunteering in Covent Garden.

Nine years have passed since the armistice to end wartime hostilities was signed. Yet the pain of those terrible years has not simply dissolved, faded from the earth as though signatures on paper could erase the grief of millions. I know few families who have not, in one way or the other, been touched by the war, by the voids it left behind. Daniel's family was shattered to pieces, both of his brothers gone too soon, his parents broken by their loss. Hugh became a shell of himself, skittish and afraid. I shiver to think what this day represents, the memory of a dark time in our history and of those who were lost. Those who went away because they wanted to be brave and good, or because they had no other choice, and who never came home.

The official two minutes of silence seem too little, the food we distribute to the poor, the maimed, the veterans, inadequate. I feel helpless and inconsequential in face of it all. Maybe Harold has it right, though, and action is the only way forward to improve matters. In that spirit, I resolve to try my best today, and hopefully on many more days after that.

When Briony, Louise and I arrive in Covent Garden, a bustle of volunteers is already busy setting up large pots and organizing people in the hall to queue. There are men and women and even a few children, weary and shivering every time the large doors open and a gust of November wind rushes in on the heels of a new arrival. We are handed aprons and assigned positions. Adeline and Edith are talking to a man with a cane, wearing a medal on his jacket, while a child with the same color hair fidgets at his side. The atmosphere is somber, but also vaguely celebratory. Food is passed around and I hear snippets of stories, names mentioned with a hint of melancholy, a soft smile of memory. Priscilla Lewis flits about, making certain everything is as it should be. She need not worry. People have come for food and company and both are in good supply. I glance over at Briony, unfamiliar in an apron, face flushed from the steam rising up from the stew she serves. She is smiling, talking softly with a man whose front teeth are missing, not much older than us. At eleven, though the queue is not at an end, Edith calls out over the din of voices and the clanking of spoons.

"It is eleven. A moment of silence, please."

One cannot but be moved by the solemn and immediate hush that descends upon the crowd. Men and women lower their eyes, and even the children, sensing something important is happening, cease their eager chatter. The customary two minutes pass, yet I suddenly feel closer to these strangers. We have shared something, regardless of our differences. It is by sheer circumstance that I stand here serving food, while they stand in line, hunger in their eyes and weariness in their bones. How easily could the situation be reversed? I resolve in that moment to do more. My monthly donations may bolster the supplies, but I recognize now the value of presence. A kind smile, a gentle touch, an open ear may provide a balm for tired souls, and I hope to offer just that, even if it is fleeting.

"I am glad we came," Briony whispers to me, when the last of the bowls has been filled, the final pot emptied. She smiles, eyes bright, cheeks rosy, her apron spattered with gravy.

"So am I."

"It is easy to forget, you know. I had no brothers who went to fight. Father and Jeffrey did not go to the front. The shadows of the war touch me so little in the day to day, I could almost put it out of my mind." She gives a sorry shrug. "I have done the same when it comes to the poor of this city. They must look at me and think I am a silly woman."

"They look at you and see a kind woman," I soothe, placing a hand on hers. "But you are right in other ways. We can do more, do better in the future."

"Next time I will bring Iona."

"Ladies, thank you very much for your help today. And how wonderful to have you as part of the group, Briony," Adeline interrupts our musings, moving between us and draping an arm around both of our shoulders.

"We were happy to help."

"I lost two cousins in Belgium, it nearly sent my uncle and aunt mad with grief," Adeline observes quietly, looking at the groups of people huddled together in the hall. "The WI isn't only about furthering the women's cause, it is about community. We want to bring people together, not focus on our differences. I sometimes think that is where many politicians go wrong. They get so caught up in their own self-worth, they cannot see the problems right in front of them anymore."

"Perhaps more women ought to be in politics," Briony muses, and though there is a trace of humor in her voice, Adeline nods enthusiastically.

"That's the way of the future, my dear." She smiles and looks around. "Say, did you see Juliet Nelson today? I spoke to her on Wednesday, and she said she was going to come."

"I haven't seen her, actually," I admit, vaguely embarrassed to have yammered on about fellow feeling, all the while neglecting to notice the absence of a woman I hope to make my friend.

"Hm...I will go and ask Priscilla. Where has she gone?" Adeline looks around before raising a hand to wave Priscilla Lewis over.

"No, I haven't seen her. Her brother telephoned this morning to say she was ill. She suffers from migraines, apparently."

"Poor dear," Adeline says with a frown.

"Yes," Priscilla agrees, though a line has creased her brow.

"I don't want her to slip out of the fold again without notice. She is a quiet woman, but I believe she is lonely. At least she has some family nearby, it seems."

Something in Adeline's words strikes me as not quite right, and then it comes to me.

"Priscilla, did you say Juliet's brother telephoned?"

"Yes, I could barely hear him, the connection was terrible!" She frowns and shakes her head.

"That is odd," I observe. "Juliet told me she has no siblings."

"Maybe you misunderstood?" Adeline shrugs.

"I do not believe I did, though she was very reserved when it came to telling me about her family, or herself, to be honest. I found myself going on and on, simply to fill the silence."

"Maybe she didn't want to come. It's a cold day, and she is off from work. Maybe she wanted an excuse to stay inside," Adeline suggests.

"The man could have been a lover," Briony whispers with a smile.

"Or maybe it was her putting on a voice," Priscilla notes with a shrug. "I really couldn't say. I did have a sense about her, the first time we met, that she was not particularly devoted to the cause.

Struck me as a flighty creature, and proud, too, if you pardon my saying so."

"Pris, really!" Adeline replies, raising her brows, as she stares at her secretary. The women are almost of a height, both small in stature and yet Adeline seems to tower over Priscilla at this moment of admonishment. The other woman lowers her gaze. There is something formidable about Adeline, which belies her penchant for magenta dresses with lace cuffs, and her quick and easy smile.

"I am sorry, that was unfair," Priscilla acquiesces.

"Well, I will give her a ring later to hear how she is. If she does not wish to participate in the WI, I cannot force her to, but I do not share your cynical view of the woman, Priscilla. What do you think, ladies?" She turns her attention to Briony and me, who have followed the exchange between the two women with rapt attention.

"That sounds like a plan. I wouldn't be surprised if she felt under the weather from this sudden nip in the air."

"Right, that settles it. Now let us set about cleaning up. A few of the women are coming round to Mother's house afterwards. You are very welcome to join us."

"I really ought to go to the office. My colleague may have news of a case," I say, though my expectations are not high. Briony, too, makes an excuse, and we set about tidying up. After another hour, hands red from washing pots and bowls, Briony and I bundle up and say our goodbyes. The air feels biting cold after the hazy warmth of the crowded hall, and we hurry as we walk the short distance to the car.

Briony is silent as we climb inside, and I rub my hands before taking hold of the frigid wheel. When, after a few moments, she still has not said a word, I can tell something is weighing on her.

"Briony? Is everything all right?"

"What?" She asks, raising her head, eyes wide as if roused from sleep, having been caught snoring. I repeat my question. "Oh, I...I don't want to say."

"Well, now you must! You know I am a curious creature, you cannot tease me so, it is cruel." I am only half-joking. It is surely one of life's great irritations to be handed a morsel when we want the whole cake.

"I am embarrassed even to think it, Evie."

"Out with it!"

"When Priscilla said Juliet was not coming and that a man, allegedly her brother, had telephoned with an excuse, I wondered whether Jeffrey is with her right now?" The final word comes out as a squeak. Briony shakes her head and presses a hand to her mouth. Muffled, she mutters, "Tell me I am mad."

"You are not mad, my dear. Mistaken, I do hope, but surely not mad. I thought we had eliminated Juliet from our list of suspects?"

"We could easily be wrong. Jeffrey works around the corner from where she lives. He could be there and back in the lunch hour, and no one would suspect a thing was amiss."

"What do you want to do?"

"Maybe we could pop round to the museum, see if he is there?"

"If he had gone to her in his lunch hour, he would be back by now. It is nearly two already." I hesitate, then pull to the side of the road.

"What are you doing?" Briony asks when I open the door.

"See that telephone kiosk? I am going to call the museum and ask for him. If he is there…Well, then he is there."

"Which proves nothing, as you pointed out," she notes.

"If he isn't, I will drive to Juliet's flat, and we will wait to see if he emerges." I seriously doubt this endeavor will prove fruitful, still it may provide Briony with a sense of relief or at least a better understanding of where she stands. She nods, looking entirely unconvinced. I step outside. The kiosk offers shelter from the sharp bite of the wind, but it is a dingy, frozen space. I dial and ask to be connected to the museum, then to Jeffrey's department. The secretary's voice on the other end is definitely not Juliet's. We can assume she is truly at home. The question whether she is alone, however, remains.

"May I speak to Jeffrey Farnham, please?" I ask.

"I am afraid he has stepped out. Can I take your name?"

"Oh, no need. I will try again another time. Thank you," I say quickly, and hang up the receiver. Hesitating a moment longer in the kiosk, I contemplate how to put this news to Briony. It hardly means anything. He stepped out. That could merely imply he was relieving himself. Then again, a more dubious option has been planted in my mind. I do not expect to catch Jeffrey at Juliet's flat, but I cannot go back on my word now. I think it would be easier, as I have told my cousin, to confront her husband than to stake out his potential lover's flat on the off chance he will be spotted there.

Briony already knows the outcome of my call before I have said a word. She is my best friend and can read my expression like a cartographer a map.

"It doesn't have to mean anything," I say quickly.

"He is obsessed with his work. He never even comes home for lunch. He would not take a long break without good reason."

"It could be a business lunch. Something related to his work. Daniel has certainly complained of those on more than one occasion."

"Jeffrey is not a businessman. He is an archaeologist and curator. The only place he wants to be is among dusty old scrap."

I swallow further protestations. Briony has a hard set to her jaw, and there is no going back. Silently, I set the car in motion and we roll on towards Bloomsbury.

Chapter 12

"Is it that one?" Briony points at Juliet's building.

"Do you really want to do this?" I ask.

"Unless you have a better plan?"

I do, but I am not sure she will like it. The thought of sitting here in the cold car for hours on end seems entirely a waste of time. "What if we go up? We can buy some bread or flowers and claim to have brought them upon hearing of her illness. If she is truly unwell, we will simply hand over our little offering and be gone."

"Do you think she would let us in, if Jeffrey was there?"

"We will have to see," I admit, seeing the flaw in my plan.

"What if she is at home with her brother, or a lover who isn't Jeffrey?"

"Then it hardly concerns us, does it? As long as she is not up there with your husband, she can host orgies for all I care." This, at least, provokes a tiny smile on my cousin's strained face.

"All right, then." She sighs.

"Let's go."

We turn around the corner to a grocer and buy a loaf of crusty bread and a bottle of apple cider. Clutching the parcel, we enter Juliet's building. There is no one at the front desk. Though a sign saying, "Mr. Button" indicates it is typically manned by a fellow with that delightful moniker. For our purposes, his absence is ideal. We slip by, noting Juliet Nelson's name on the mailbox for Flat 9.

"I feel a bit sick, Evie," Briony mumbles when we climb the stairs. Her face is pale, and her lips pressed into a thin line.

"We can still turn back."

She hesitates, taking a steadying breath before climbing on. I share some of her anxiety, for I in no way desire to catch her husband with a lover. I do not want proof. I only want to be able to see Jeffrey the way I always have.

We reach Flat 9 too soon, and I feel my heartbeat quicken.

"Ready?" I ask, feeling a little silly. We have orchestrated all of this purely on a vague suspicion. We could be spectacularly wrong. Oh, how I hope it will be so! I raise my hand to knock. We wait, ears pricked to the slightest sound. Nothing.

"Maybe she is truly ill and sleeping?"

"Are you looking for Juliet?" a voice calls out from the stairwell. I jump, startled by this new presence. A man, perhaps seventy, clinging to the bannister peers at us with watery blue eyes. "Yes." I try to collect myself. "We heard she was unwell and wanted to bring her something to cheer her up." I hold up our parcel. "Ill, is she?" The man slowly descends the remaining stairs, stooping as he moves. "I am Mr. Button. I work the desk downstairs, and I water the plants for a lady who is out of town on the fourth floor. Quite a climb, I tell you. Takes me a good while to get up and just as long to get back down." Mr. Button smiles and it transforms his face, brightening his eyes and bringing to life the brackets of lines around his mouth, the feathered creases at the corners of his eyes.

"I wonder whether her brother has left," I muse, an idea coming to my mind. "He is tall, blonde with blue eyes," I describe Jeffrey as best I can, hoping the man who called Priscilla – if there was a man - does not match the description.

"I haven't seen anyone I didn't recognize come or go today," Mr. Button says, scratching his chin. I give Briony a quick look. "Well, Juliet does not seem to be in." She shrugs. "She knew we were coming."

"Did she now? I can take the parcel and give it to her later. Maybe I missed her leaving when I was upstairs." Mr. Button holds out his hands. As he does so, he loses his balance, tumbling forward. I try to catch him, but he falls against the door, reaching out to steady himself on the door handle. The handle, however, provides no support, for it twists in his grasp and the door swings open. We scramble to help the poor man to his feet, when I notice my cousin's attention has shifted to the dim hall now open to us.

Briony peers inside and I follow her gaze, my breath caught in my throat. The hallway is in utter disarray. A vase lies smashed on the ground, violets scattered, trampled into the carpet. A mirror hangs crooked while a small table has been upended, resting on its side.

"Goodness!" exclaims Mr. Button in a whisper, as if he has come across Ali Baba's cave, his eyes wide in disbelief.

"Juliet!" Hesitating, I step across the threshold. "Call the police, Mr. Button," I say as calmly as I can.

"Evie -" Briony appears torn between holding the shaken man upright and following me. I do not believe either of us expects to catch her husband here anymore. I take care not to step onto the shards of pottery, the crushed flowers, though I bend down to touch the patch of carpet, finding it dry. This rampage happened hours ago. Briony has followed me into the hallway, and I sense her presence behind me. It is dim, no electric light switched on. I feel a draft from somewhere, an icy chill at the back of my neck.

Cautiously, I poke my head into the sitting room. It is in a state of similar disarray, yet empty of an occupant. I exhale a shallow breath, turning and shaking my head. The next door reveals a kitchen. Pots scattered on the floor. A reddish liquid, I quickly realize is soup, spattered across the wall. My chest feels tight. Mr. Button has disappeared, hopefully to call the police. Clearly, Juliet's flat has been burgled. I step to the next door, turn the doorknob.

A gasp is stuck in my throat and I hurtle inside, towards the pale figure lying on her back, her limbs at awkward angles. Bruises form a chain around her neck. My shaking hands feel for a pulse. I find nothing.

"Evie?" Briony calls out from the hall.

"Don't come in!" I shriek, hardly recognizing my voice in my desperation to keep her from this sight, this horror that will otherwise be etched into her mind forever. Of course, she does not listen. Responding to the tone of my voice, not the meaning of my words, she hears alarm and comes running. I move to block her view of the body – Juliet's body! – but she will instantly understand what has happened.

"My God! Evie, is she…is she dead?" Briony stammers, eyes wide with horror in the dim of the room.

"Yes," I whisper. "She has been strangled, Briony."

Chapter 13

In hindsight, everything happened very quickly. The police arrived and a coroner covered Juliet's body with a white sheet. Briony and I sat shivering in Mr. Button's tiny kitchen while they took our statements, cups of sweet tea in front of us. Yet in the moments after finding Juliet, it felt as though the clock had slowed. I remember the realization registering on my cousin's face, her stepping back, colliding with a chair, nearly falling. I remember the touch of Juliet's pale skin, cold and waxen. The window was wide open, the curtains dancing in the breeze, but it was not the chill of the wind that pricked my skin with gooseflesh. I was frozen to the spot, while Briony ran to tell Mr. Button what we discovered.

While I sat, waiting, unwilling to leave Juliet alone, I felt a sting of guilt. Had I not complained of boring cases, of a lack of excitement? But I never, never wished for this, for murder.

I still haven't managed to dislodge the pang of conscience, even at home in Grosvenor Square, waiting for Daniel to return from work, unaware of what has happened. I tried to contact him, but he was in a meeting, so I called Hugh, who came to Bloomsbury and drove us home. When we dropped Briony off in Belgravia, I promised to telephone that evening. I hope I was able to shield the body from her view, but even being in the proximity of murder is a terrible experience.

Hugh is still with me, and we sit in the lounge sipping whisky. Wilkins presses the drinks into our hands, saying, "Good for the shock," while Maisie goes to fetch a blanket to drape across my shoulders. I almost begin to cry then, faced with their gentle care, but swallow my tears to spare them the embarrassment.

"Feeling better?" Hugh asks, eyeing me with an assessing gaze.

"Yes and no." I give a little shrug. "I had a strange feeling when I saw the disarray in the hallway, a sort of premonition, though I did not want to believe it until I saw the body."

"She was strangled?" Hugh asks and I grimace, the memory of the bruises around her neck flooding my mind. No murder weapon.

"It looked that way." Taking another sip, I hesitate before saying, "I have been complaining of our dull caseload, Hugh. I feel as if I wished something terrible to happen and now it has."

"Don't be silly, Evie! Of course, you had nothing to do with this. The person who ransacked Juliet's flat and then proceeded to strangle her is wholly responsible." There is vehemence in his tone, his gaze locked on my own, willing the meaning of his words to sink in. I know he is right, still I cannot quite shake my feeling of accountability.

"She lived on the third floor. It seems odd that a burglar would go upstairs, ignore the other flats on the way. It was a workday, after all, they may well have been empty and made for easier spoils. Instead, they broke into Juliet's flat, looted about and, coming across her, murdered her. Mr. Button did not see anyone unknown to him enter or leave. Quite honestly, though, someone could still have slipped by. He was not at his desk when Briony and I arrived either." I take a steadying deep breath, shaking my head.

"If a burglar comes across the owner of the flat, the natural instinct should be to retreat and run, not to attack."

"My thoughts exactly. But then, if he chose her flat for a reason -"

"He may have intended to do her harm," Hugh finishes my sentence.

"It's possible, isn't it?"

"Quite," he agrees. "Were there signs of a forced entry?"

"None, come to think of it. Had there been, we would have been alarmed even before poor Mr. Button fell against the door and it swung open."

"Maybe she made a habit of leaving the door unlocked, so an intrusion was easy," Hugh suggests.

"Or she knew her killer and willingly let him or her inside"

"Possibly. I wonder whether anything was taken."

"The place was in such disarray. How would anyone be able to tell? She lived alone, so who else would recognize if it had been a successful robbery?"

"Likely it wasn't. Assuming the killer intended to burgle the flat and was surprised by Juliet, one might suppose he would flee the scene quickly after the murder, not wait around to collect the most valuable bits and pieces."

"I wonder whether the neighbors heard a commotion of some kind?"

"You said the carpet where the vase had been toppled over was dry, and Juliet's skin waxy to the touch. The murder must have occurred several hours before you came upon the scene. Maybe the burglar planned for most people in the building to be at work?"

"So many questions!" I say in exasperation. "I wonder who the investigating officer will be."

"Do you think Stanton will get the case?" Hugh asks, echoing the question bouncing around my own mind. I know it is unlikely, but what if I telephoned my friend, the police detective, and made him aware of the case and my connection to it? Perhaps he can find a way to take it on, if he gets there early enough. It is bound to be messy, and from my experience, a lot of coppers prefer to avoid those cases.

"I will call him now."

Hugh waits in the lounge as I go to the study. It takes a while, but when I am finally connected to Stanton, the story of today's events bursts out of me without much prompting.

"Another murder? Evelyn, this is serious. How did you get involved *again*?" I ignore his emphasis on the last word, which sounds a little too much like an accusation...

"Do you think you can find out who has the case? Or," I hesitate, choosing my words with care, "do you think you might -"

"You want me to make a play for it? Evelyn, the police is not a schoolyard. There are rules and regulations, a system of order."

"Yes, yes, but can you?"

I hear Stanton sighing at the other end of the line. "I will try. I have just cleared up a bank robbery and am owed some goodwill. Do not get your hopes up. And if I do get it, do not imagine I am working *with* you. This is a murder investigation. You would do well, for once, to keep out of it. The only reason I am entertaining your suggestion is so that you know someone trustworthy is investigating, and you do not have to poke your nose in any further."

I consider his judgement of my nose a little harsh, given the circumstances, but I refrain from saying so, simply relieved he has agreed to look into the case. I thank him and return to the lounge.

"No guarantee, but he is competent and whatever he says now, he will be more willing to share information than a stranger."

"Exactly. We have to ask who had reason to wish Juliet harm, why and when. We know the where and the how already." Absently, I drum my fingers on the surface of the table.

"Evie?" Hugh raises his eyebrows.

"Yes?"

"We are investigating, aren't we?"

"Oh, I would say that much is certain, Hugh," I reply, draining the last of my whisky, the burn sliding down my throat. "Yes, I would say we have a new case."

Chapter 14

The question of who might hire us to solve the murder – for we would naturally prefer to have a paying client – is answered the following day, when Edith Ashbourne calls on us at the office. I slept badly, tossing and turning, then came in early, despite Daniel's insistence that I should stay home and rest. Ants seemed to crawl beneath my skin. Whenever I closed my eyes, I retraced the steps into Juliet's flat, each time with the same result of me sitting up, roused from the nightmare, then realizing the nightmare was reality. I did not know Juliet well, and though I sensed she preferred it that way, I now wonder why.

Hugh slips out while I offer Edith a seat, and Maeve arrives bearing a tray of tea and biscuits. She casts me a curious glance, but I merely nod, and she leaves again, closing the door behind her.

"Evelyn, I heard what happened to Juliet. Goodness, what a tragedy!" Edith shakes her head, pressing her lips together.

"It's terrible," I reply, unable to think of another word to summarize the brutal murder of a young woman in her own home. Nonetheless, my choice seems insufficient.

"I feel awful that you and your cousin found her. How thoughtful of you to bring Juliet some food when she was ill." Edith shakes her head. "I keep wishing she had come to Covent Garden yesterday, unwell or not. She could still be alive."

"I have thought the same," I confess.

"It seems improper to ask it, still I must. Do you think the killer or burglar, or whatever one might call him, interfered with Juliet before he committed that final cruel deed?"

The meaning of Edith's words is obvious, and I am shocked not to have thought of it already. In my mind's eye, I revisit the scene of the murder. Juliet was sprawled on the ground. Apart from her bruised neck, I noticed no other signs of violence against her. She wore a pair of trousers, and while they bore marks of a stain, likely a loss of bladder control, it did not appear as though they had been forced on or off. But I cannot be certain. The coroner would have an accurate answer. It is infuriating to think of Juliet being subjected to such further indignity and suffering before she was killed. I feel a sob rising in my throat, but swallow it down, trying to control myself. Edith is the picture of composure, and I aim to mirror her.

"I do not think so," I say carefully. Edith nods.

"You are quite upset, unsurprisingly, but I detected a spine of steel in you even when we first met. Your reputation has only strengthened my initial observation. I have little faith in the police, when it comes to matters of delicacy, and I would like to employ your detective agency to look into the crime. It is a lot to ask, and Louise would probably disapprove. However, I feel a sense of responsibility for the women of the WI. Juliet, if only for a short time, was one of them. Lloyd, my husband, said I was being insensitive in coming here, asking this of you, but I told him he ought to have learned by now not to underestimate a woman's resilience. What do you say, Evelyn? Naturally, I will pay whatever is the going rate."

"My partner, Mr. Lawrence and I discussed the situation prior to your arrival and are in agreement. We intend to take on the case, and I am grateful to you for your trust in our capabilities, but truthfully, I could not have let it rest, even without your support."

"I respect you all the more for your honesty, my dear!" Edith smiles and gives a sharp clap. "Now, I will let you get on with your work, as I must with mine. I have been trying to locate Juliet's brother, an unsuccessful endeavor thus far. I telephoned her place of work, but they, too, know next to nothing of her family. I suppose someone will make arrangements, but it seems she lived a rather solitary life. Perhaps you could -"

"I will look into it," I finish her thought.

"Very good, then." Edith gets to her feet, her posture ramrod straight. She possesses such natural authority, many a man would surely envy her for it. "I am holding a meeting of the WI tonight to explain what happened. Thus far I have only told my husband, Priscilla and Adeline, and I suppose she told Graham. It is only right the other women are made aware of the state of affairs. You are quite welcome to attend, but I will say nothing you do not already know."

"I hope we will soon have a better understanding of the situation."

"Good luck, Evelyn." Edith holds my gaze for another moment before turning away. I detected sorrow in her eyes and do not think it would be far from the truth to say Edith feels a certain degree of obligation for every woman at her chapter of the WI. Now one of her flock has been murdered.

When she leaves and Hugh returns to the office, I share the news of Edith's proposal.

"So, it's official," he says, a glint in his eyes.

"It is. I plan on going to the museum today, to see if I can learn anything about Juliet there."

"One of us should try to find out whether the press has got hold of the story. It is bound to be a bit of a scandal, a fairly well-to-do, single woman robbed and killed in her flat."

"Will you look into it?" I ask.

"Of course."

Hugh is already putting on his jacket, grabbing the notebook on his desk, when I add, "Edith made me wonder...Well, she made me think whether Juliet was assaulted before her murder."

"What was your impression?" he asks, a frown creasing his brow.

"I cannot be sure, but I don't remember a sign of violence against her, apart from the horrible bruising around her throat. If Stanton becomes the investigating officer, I am sure we can learn the results of the coroner's report."

"Fingers crossed," Hugh says. "Give him a call later, see what he says. They must have made a decision by now, and after the Devlin case, he is surely in favor with his commissioner."

"The question is, does he want to take the case. It is bound to be fraught with complications. Juliet led a very lonely life, it would appear."

"We will soon know more about her. Have you noted down everything you remember about the scene of the crime?" I nod. "Good. Let us meet here again in the afternoon. Hopefully, we will have more to discuss."

After Hugh has gone, I glance at my watch and decide it is a reasonable time to call on my cousin to find out how she is faring after yesterday's shocking turn of events. I could drop by her house before going to the museum. Will Jeffrey even notice Juliet's absence at work today? We can be reasonably certain he did not go to see her yesterday. It all seems so silly now, our reason for going to her flat. I don't suppose Briony and I will tell anyone – except for Daniel, whom I am afraid I told immediately.

The telephone rings once, twice, three times, before it is wrenched from its cradle. "Farnham residence," a harried voice announces. I recognize the butler and ask for Briony. "Just a moment, please."

It takes a good few minutes for Briony to arrive. "Evie?"

"How are you?"

She sighs. "It was a difficult night. I couldn't sleep and I didn't want to alarm the children this morning, so I tried to act normally. Now I am exhausted, and it is only a quarter to ten. I am still in my nightgown," she whispers.

"Good, you should rest. Don't worry about the children. They will be taken care of. Does your mother know? And Jeffrey?"

"I called Mother last night. She and Father came over immediately."

"You didn't tell them why we were at the flat, did you?"

"No. I said it was to bring poor Juliet some food. Oh, Evie, I am so ashamed! There we were, about to accuse her of adultery with my husband, when she had been murdered!"

"We couldn't have known. I only wish we had come earlier, to help somehow." I shrug. "What was Jeffrey's reaction when you told him?"

"He was shocked, but no more than my parents. He didn't seem heartbroken or personally affected. I feel such a fool having suspected the two of them."

"Put that out of your mind, nothing is gained by making yourself feel worse than you already do. Go to bed and get some rest, or shall I come to keep you company?"

"No, no, I think I will take your advice. I am not alone in the house, and the children will be back soon. My parents have taken them to their home for a bit."

"Is Jeffrey around?" I ask, wondering whether he abandoned his shaken wife to go to work on a Saturday.

"Yes, although he has been ensconced in his study since breakfast. For once, I don't really mind. It is best we give each other a little space, even if he doesn't realize he is doing it."

"I am going to stop by the museum, see if I can learn something new," I say. "I keep wondering who the man claiming to be her brother was. If she told the truth and has none, was he her killer? It would make sense."

"How eerie! You think he killed her, then telephoned Priscilla to say Juliet was ill and not coming? That suggests a high degree of premeditation, don't you think? How would he even have known she was meant to be in Covent Garden?"

"Exactly," I agree. "The more I consider it, the more I believe whoever killed Juliet was not an ordinary burglar."

"What do you mean?"

"It means Juliet had an enemy."

Chapter 15

Before I set off to the museum, I try to call Stanton's office, to no avail. He does not answer. I hope this means he is out investigating Juliet's murder. I am itching to know the results of the coroner's report. Modern medicine is a marvel, and though it is too late for Juliet, we should be able to learn around what time she was killed. In my estimation, it must have been hours before we found her. That being so, the window was open and the room cold, it could have even happened the day before, which in turn would call into question my theory that the person who telephoned Priscilla to explain Juliet's absence was in fact her killer. Why excuse her from the Armistice Day event, if the killer was long gone and in no danger of being found at the flat, should anyone from the WI come to investigate? Unless they simply wanted to delay the time when her body was discovered? It having been Friday, she would not have been expected back at work for a few days at least.

The day is cold, but the streets are busy with people enjoying their Saturday. I get caught behind a bus, stopping and starting, stopping and starting until I finally turn onto Shaftesbury Avenue. It is satisfying to be in control of the wheel, to move forward and not sit anxiously behind my desk. Motion has always had a way of setting me at ease. When I leave the car behind on Great Russell Street, I take the short walk to the museum. Weaving around a family with four wide-eyed children and a harried mother, I enter the building.

It is strange to recall that the last time I was here, I ran into Juliet. How I wish I had pushed for more answers at our lunch, not spoken so much of myself to fill the silence. Maybe then I would know more about her. I wonder whom she took into her confidence? She seemed to make a practice of going unnoticed, slipping by, slender, pale and silent. If my theory about her death being a calculated murder is correct, she must not have done as well in being overlooked as I thought. Someone with dark motives did notice her, and took against her for a reason I do not yet understand.

At the reception to the Department of Greek Antiquity I notice Lara Bennet sitting behind the desk. Today she wears a tight red dress with a matching cardigan and lipstick. Though she may appear the office temptress, the thought of awkward, disorganized Jeffrey making a play for her seems almost laughable.

"Can I help you?" she asks.

"I was hoping you could, yes." I initially contemplated whether to wait until news of Juliet's death became more public knowledge, but I want to observe the reactions of her colleagues. If the police are dawdling that is hardly my fault, after all! "I have some rather troubling news."

"What news?" she asks, eyes narrowing.

"You know Juliet Nelson, do you not?"

"She has been working here a little longer than I have. Why do you ask?"

I look around. The offices are empty, and I see no one else about. "Juliet was a friend of mine," I explain, well aware this is a fib.

"Was?" Lara asks. She is a sharp one, I must acknowledge.

"Juliet died yesterday." Lara's hand flies to her mouth, and her eyes grow wide. I give her a moment to collect herself, gauging her reaction as genuine. She may well be a talented actress, but my guess is this sad truth is entirely new to her.

"Died? How? I-I don't understand. I saw her a few days ago. She looked perfectly well."

"When did you last see her?" I ask.

"Let me think." Lara taps her forefinger against her bottom lip. "It was Thursday morning. She had Friday off, but I saw her on Thursday, yes," Lara nods. "I remember it well, because I asked what her plans were for Friday and she told me something about the WI, some Armistice Day event. To be honest, I only half listened." She shrugs sheepishly. "We were colleagues, not friends. Not that I had anything against her," Lara adds quickly, lest I consider her heartless.

"She liked to keep herself to herself," I observe sympathetically.

"Very much so. In fact, I hardly know anything about her. I don't think she had any family and didn't wear a ring." Lara frowns and shakes her head. "Tragic, really, that she died, and I know next to nothing about her, even though we saw one another almost every day for months. Poor Juliet. How did it happen, an accident?"

"It isn't quite clear yet, I am afraid." Hesitating a moment, I ask, "She didn't seem different, worried in some way?"

"Not that I noticed, but as I said, we were not friends. I wouldn't have confided in her, just as she didn't confide in me. She always seemed a little subdued, but maybe that was just her manner. She had that limp. Maybe her leg was giving her trouble. My nan has a gammy leg, and this weather makes it so painful she can hardly leave home sometimes!"

"Hm…yes, I wonder what happened to her," I muse.

"How did you know her?" Lara asks, narrowing her eyes.

"We met at the WI," I say quickly.

"Really?" Lara gives me an up and down look, probably taking in the cut of my coat, the Chanel scarf and fur edged cuffs. "I always thought of it as an organization of frumpy homemakers." She giggles, and my conviction that Jeffrey could not possibly be involved with her solidifies.

"You would be surprised," I reply, swallowing a sharper remark, for did my own thoughts not echo Lara's not long ago?

"I will come to the funeral, if I am not working," she says generously. "There probably won't be many attendees."

The thought weighs me down, as I leave the department and make my way along a colonnade of busts and vases. Lara is right. It is terribly sad that Juliet died alone and might not have been found for days, and now she may well be buried with only a smattering of people come to remember her. If Edith's power is anything to go by, though, at the very least the women from the WI will attend. Homemakers, as Lara called them, many may be, but likely that occupation has expanded their hearts, honed their patience and strengthened their sense of community, all great virtues in my book. Women in the workforce may not be uncommon, but it does not flatter one to look down on the work of another, be it paid or unpaid.

"Excuse me!" I turn at the sudden shout, and so do a few other people. From my earlier efforts at spy work, I recognize Jeffrey's colleague Frances Bell hurrying after me. She is a tall woman, broad shouldered and dressed in a boxy suit, that Lara would undoubtedly scoff at behind the woman's back. The expression on her face is one of concern. I can guess what she is about to say.

"Is Juliet truly dead?" Her brown eyes are wide as they focus on me.

"I am afraid so."

"Oh, God!" She shakes her head, suddenly pale. For a moment, I worry she may faint and offer my arm, but she steadies herself and shakes her head once more. "Lara just told me. I can't believe it! I saw her a few days ago. She seemed well."

"Were you friends?" I ask hopefully.

"We were more like old acquaintances. I knew her many years ago. Then she came back to London looking for work, so I helped her find a job here. I have been an archivist for some time and am friendly with the director of the department. He was acquainted with my husband, too, before he died."

"I am very sorry," I say, feeling false, as I already knew this. Juliet said she had lived at the flat for years, yet only worked at the museum a few months. Something doesn't quite add up.

"Yes, well, that is life, it ends at some point. Howard was no young man. But Juliet, she was young and had been through so much."

Frances sighs deeply. My ears prick, caught on her last words. What had she been through? I realize I must tread carefully now. If Frances was a mentor to Juliet, she will be protective of her memory and she does not know me or my intentions. I decide to be honest. Beckoning her to an empty bench across from a marble statue of Daphne trying to flee Apollo, I begin to explain.

"Mrs. Bell, my name is Evelyn Carlisle. I met Juliet at the WI, and I am also a detective."

"Carlisle?" A crease lines her brow. "I have heard the name."

"A case my agency solved some months ago received considerable attention."

"Right," she nods, a hint of wariness creeping into her features.

"Though I had hoped Juliet and I would become friends, I will be honest with you, we did not know one another well nor long enough for a friendship to have developed. However, I have been hired to look into the circumstances surrounding her death. As you might know, she did not have a wide circle of friends, and it is a challenge to learn much about her that could move the investigation forward. If you have anything that could help, I would be very grateful, and it might go some way to find justice for your friend." Falling silent, I hope my little speech has softened her towards me.

"Juliet was murdered?" she asks.

"I found the body." To her credit, she does not gasp. "That is why I feel particularly invested in learning the truth." I watch her carefully. Her features are even, but there is a twitch in her right eye and her hands are clasped tightly in her lap.

"I see."

"Can you help me? I promise, I am trying to do right by Juliet."

"Who hired you?" She asks, ignoring my own question.

"A woman from the WI. I cannot say more. You will understand some need for discretion is involved."

"Why does she want your help?"

"She does not hold the police in particularly high regard and hopes I will treat the matter with caution and delicacy." I reach out and touch her arm, just for a moment. "Mrs. Bell, I truly only wish to help. It was horrible to find Juliet, and whoever took her life must be brought to justice. I will work with the police as much as I can, for I am not a reckless person and the murderer is undoubtedly dangerous. That being so, I must learn more about Juliet's life, her past and present to understand what would motivate someone to kill her."

"Please, call me Frances. Yes, I understand. Juliet was a private, quiet person. I fear I do not have much to tell that would aid you in your efforts."

"You said she had a difficult life. What did you mean?" I ask gently, sensing she is still reluctant to speak, though her distance may simply be a manifestation of her disbelief. If she was close enough to Juliet to know of her past, to have been allowed entry into that realm of her life, their relationship must have been deeper than what I am being led to believe. She glances down, a strand of her gray hair slipping from behind her ear, before she meets my gaze again.

"She lost her parents when she was a young woman. They had been very close. Some people lean more on others when such tragedy befalls them, while others pull back and grow ever more reserved. Juliet belonged to the latter category."

"How terrible," I say, feeling the prick of gooseflesh on my arms. Juliet and I share this past, both of us orphans. As Frances says, some of us have others on whom to depend, as I was fortunate to do. Maybe Juliet did not choose to pull back, but was forced to. Not everyone is lucky to have people who care enough to break one's fall. I had aunts and uncles who were willing to take responsibility for me when, aged four, I lost my parents to a terrible fire in our home. I imagine Juliet must have felt quite untethered. By all accounts she was a reserved woman, and losing two people she loved, with whom she had felt at ease must have cut her to the core. Again, I am saddened that we could not have known one another better.

"You understand why I felt for her? I wanted to help. Keeping her close seemed a good idea to me."

"How did you two meet, if you do not mind me asking?"

"My husband and I already knew her family. Not well, but we were acquainted. We never had children of our own, and Juliet was at an age that she might have been our daughter when her parents died. I felt a strange sort of responsibility for her when she came to London."

"Juliet mentioned that she moved around a bit in the past. What did she do?"

"She didn't like to settle in one place, took odd jobs here and there. There was some money from her parents, and she was able to make it stretch. The flat where she lives – lived – was theirs as well, as far as I know." That answers one question.

"She never married?"

"No," replies Frances shortly, glancing around. I can tell she is itching to leave, to return to the privacy of her office, to be alone with her grief. Before she does, I press one of my cards into her hand and make her promise to contact me if she remembers anything to help the investigation. She agrees, yet her demeanor is closed off, as though she already regrets any word that slipped past her lips. As though by speaking, she has betrayed the dead woman. I wonder why…

"The police will likely wish to speak to you," I say as we part.

"I suppose they will," Frances mutters, a frown lining her brow. Turning, she walks briskly away from me, her height and straight posture making her stand out among the groups of museum visitors in the gallery. I shake my head and get to my feet. At least I learned more about Juliet from her than I did from Lara, and yet I am convinced she was not entirely forthright in her answers. I am afraid Frances Bell has not heard the last of me, whether she likes it or not.

Chapter 16

As I walk into my building in St. James, I hear a familiar yap and turn to see Mr. Singh with Dulcie's little dog on my heels. I raise a hand in greeting and wait for them to catch up. He is slow moving, leaning on his cane. Mr. Flynn at the front desk gives me a nod, then returns to reading his Saturday paper.

"Mr. Singh, how are you?" I ask, offering my arm and leading him towards the lift, a contraption I usually avoid, for it rattles and clangs alarmingly on ascent and descent alike.

"I am well enough," he replies, though his voice is hoarse, and his general demeanor suggests otherwise. He leans against the wall of the lift. Rudy, the dog, looks up at us with curious brown eyes.

"Why don't you leave Rudy with me for a few days. Or I can come and take him for his walks. It is so cold, you shouldn't go out if you are unwell."

"You see through me, my dear, but the fresh air does me good."

"Has Dulcie improved at all? I made some inquiries about this physician, but there seems nothing much to learn apart from his penchant for outdated, though not illegal, treatment practices."

"I suppose I was simply trying to blame someone. Maybe he is doing his best. I hardly know anymore," he says, as we are jolted to the side. I steady myself on the brass handrail.

"I wish there was something I could do to help. Would she see me, do you think?"

"Perhaps. She was feeling brighter yesterday, had some mad idea of holding a séance, if you can believe it! My clever Dulcie turning to such claptrap." Mr. Singh sighs and gives a little shrug as we arrive at his floor.

"Desperate people are willing to believe many strange things. I confess I once toyed with the idea myself in an effort to contact my parents. In the end, I never went ahead. Even if Dulcie does hold a séance, it is harmless and might give her some small measure of peace. Why not allow it to happen?"

"I cannot stop her in any case," he says with a sad smile. "Even in this state, Dulcie has a mind of her own and a will of steel. Nonetheless, I worry that once this measure is taken, it will only be the beginning. Will she be tricked into more and more outlandish practices simply because someone made her believe she is reaching her son? I could not bear to stand by and watch such a descent."

"Let me talk to her," I say. "Perhaps I can help somehow."

"You are welcome to try, my dear."

The flat is warm, almost unpleasantly so. A fire burns with temper in the grate of the sitting room where Mr. Singh leaves me. The first time I came here, I marveled at the trinkets and decorations Dulcie brought to London after her many years in India. The walls are peacock blue and a small collection of porcelain elephants sit on the mantelpiece. Piles of cushions in jewel colored silk plump the sofa and chaise lounge, a few lie in piles on the plush rugs. There are framed photos of Indian men and women in elaborate dresses and robes on one wall, and a large framed painting of a green valley, depicting the scenery of Dulcie's beloved Simla. It must be difficult, at times, to be surrounded by all she loved of that country while knowing she is unlikely ever to return. She has created a time capsule of all that matters to her in this flat, and has not left in a long time. This room is a shrine to India, while a few doors down is her son's room as she keeps it, untouched. Likely, she hoped to pretend he was still here, but in the end, the truth tends to catch us up.

"Evelyn, how good to see you." I hear Dulcie's voice from the doorway and turn away from the painting. Swallowing a gasp, I take in my neighbor's appearance. Her small body seems to have shrunk even more. When only a few weeks ago she looked slender, she now appears frail, her hands, holding the doorframe, are bony and the skin near translucent, revealing a network of blue veins beneath. I have not seen her in a few weeks, but her transformation is startling.

"Dulcie." I plaster a smile to my lips, as I give her a gentle embrace, almost frightened I will cause her pain. Taking her hand, I lead her to the sofa, an action she would have balked at when first we met, not long ago. She now accepts my assistance without a word.

"You are not well. I am so sorry not to have visited earlier, I did not know-"

"As I wished it to be," Dulcie interrupts, and I am relieved she still possesses the strength to make a point, as Mr. Singh suggested. "I did not want to burden you, my dear. There is nothing you or anyone can do for me."

"I might have brought food or books or offered my company, at the very least," I protest.

"I have a physician who comes to the flat, and you know I am well looked after. What ails me cannot be healed." She swallows, and I pour her a glass of water from the jug on the table. After taking a sip, she continues. "Sunil likely told you, the tenth anniversary of my

71

son's death came and went. Rupert would be almost forty by now. What a life might he have lived? I could have grandchildren tottering about my knees, breaking my porcelain figurines." She smiles a melancholy smile that does not touch her glistening eyes. "When you lose a child, the what-ifs never end. Never. Not a day goes by without the thought of all that might have been. The pain of knowing it never will be is endless."

"Oh, Dulcie," I say softly, taking her hand in mine.

"Sunil worries for me, and I worry for him. He is too young to be trapped here with me, a woman lost to the past and unable to step into the present. I have tried to let him go, but he would never leave me. In truth I am grateful, very grateful."

"You are not alone, Dulcie. I have been a bad friend, but I will be better," I promise earnestly, still clutching her hand. She gives mine a squeeze.

"I am happy to have met you, my dear, but you are young. Do not worry yourself about me."

"Mr. Singh mentioned you want to hold a séance?" I ask, ignoring her request.

"If Sunil says so, it must be true. He never lies," Dulcie observes, rolling her eyes. "Will you try to dissuade me?"

"Any such attempt would be entirely futile," I say with a wink.

"You know me well, Evelyn. What harm can it do? I once balked at the very notion of making contact with the dead, but there are many things we cannot begin to understand or explain in this world or even the one beyond, if such a place exists. Why then not allow for the possibility of the supernatural? If aeroplanes can fly across the sky, why cannot spirits of our lost loves reach out to us?"

"I cannot answer that," I concede.

"Exactly!"

"Yet I cannot pretend to believe in it either. If I did, I would be drawing black curtains and lighting candles all the time. I miss my parents, too, yet I cannot imagine they would choose to contact me – if we allow for this possibility – through the medium of a séance. If they could, I must believe they would speak to me or send signs whenever they pleased and whenever I wished them to."

"Maybe not all of us possess the power to call upon those who have passed," Dulcie suggests.

"Maybe."

She sighs and leans against her pile of cushions. "I won't be dissuaded, Evelyn. Not by Sunil and not by you."

"Then you must do what you think best," I say with sincerity. I hope Mr. Singh will help her find someone who is not a complete charlatan to orchestrate the event. Dulcie has set her mind to it, and it will be done one way or another.

"Won't you join us? You could see if you might contact your parents after all. Or Daniel his brothers?" I want to decline, want to say, no, I absolutely do not wish to join her. Then I see the eagerness in her eyes, recognize her desperation and find myself nodding against my will or better judgement. Could I persuade Daniel or Hugh to attend as well, I wonder?

When I leave Dulcie's flat, I feel heavy with her troubles and my own, or rather those concerning Juliet Nelson. It is only two o'clock, but I feel this day has twice the number of hours as ordinary ones. The prospect of having to summon dead people with my upstairs neighbor leaves me with little appetite. Nonetheless, I wander into the kitchen.

"Oh, hello, miss. Can I make you something to eat?" Maeve asks, sitting up at the table as though caught idling.

"Maybe some soup, if there's any left?"

"Of course." She gets to her feet. "And there was a call for you. Mr. Lawrence wasn't in, so I answered it. Mr. Stanton, the policeman called. He said he would be out of his office until the evening, but wanted to let you know that he got it?" She looks a little confused, doubtless questioning what the enigmatic *it* may be. I feel a rush of excitement. If Stanton is on the case, he will, if grudgingly, be willing to listen and perhaps share the odd morsel of information with me. The first good news today!

"Perfect. I understand his meaning. I will take the food in the study. Thank you, Maeve."

Once in the office, I begin to write down the scant amount of information I have acquired today. Lara and Frances echoed my suspicion that Juliet was a rather solitary figure. At least I learned a little about her family and background. Who wished someone living as unobtrusively as Juliet Nelson dead? Who was willing to take the risk and kill her in her home, where the caretaker could see everyone who entered and left the building? Then again, Mr. Button proved yesterday that he is not the most vigilant of fellows. Nonetheless, a neighbor might have taken notice of a stranger, too. Unless it wasn't a stranger. Unless the killer had visited Juliet before, was maybe even a regular fixture?

I must speak with Mr. Button again, and hopefully Stanton will get some answers from the neighbors. He will have greater authority to question them than I do as a private investigator. However, once he has done so and shared his knowledge, I can go back with a more targeted approach. Really, I think Hugh, Stanton and I would make for a rather formidable enterprise!

Once I have finished my soup and set about continuing to write my notes, the telephone rings. I pick up the receiver.

"Evie?"

"Daniel!"

"Is everything all right? How are you feeling?" I hear some shuffling of paper. "I wanted to call earlier but constantly got held up."

"No need to apologize. Why are you at work at all, it's Saturday!"

"Dominic wanted to discuss something with a few of the managers. What have you been up to? You were out of the house so early today."

"I couldn't sleep and wanted to see Hugh to discuss what happened. I've been out much of the day." I tell him of Edith's call, her intention to hire us to look into the murder and my subsequent visit to the museum.

"The police are surely on the case. Why would Edith hire you? Not that I don't have confidence in your abilities!" he hastens to add. "But this is a murder, after all."

"Edith feels a sense of responsibility for Juliet. She didn't have many people in her life."

"I can understand that. Though, futile as my misgivings may be, I am none too thrilled to have you looking into a murder again."

"You mustn't worry so much. Hugh and I will be cautious, and Stanton has been assigned the case -"

"Surely, that is too coincidental?" Daniel interjects. I detect a hint of irritation in his voice at the mention of the detective's name. When Stanton and I met a few years ago, Daniel had the notion that the detective set his sights on me. Both men have since developed a sort of cordiality, yet I doubt they are destined to become bosom pals.

"I told him about the murder and suggested it was an interesting case. It seems his superior is willing to give him a chance after the success of the Devlin investigation," I explain very matter-of-factly.

"You want him on the case?"

"It is helpful to have a connection in the Met, Daniel. Stop being silly. Lucas and I are friends, and you and I are going to be married in a month's time. I will hear no more of this."

"Yes, yes, all right," he concedes. "What is Hugh up to? I imagine he is chomping at the bit just as you are to have a new case."

"We are both keen to solve it, if that is what you mean."

"I am sorry to sound tactless, but you have been in harm's way before and you will forgive me if the thought of just that happening again is not a happy one."

"Is everything all right at work?" I ask, sensing his tense manner is not so much a result of Stanton's involvement in the case or even

74

mine, as something else entirely. He hesitates before confessing that my suspicions are true.

"Dominic wants to close one of the shipyards on the Tyne. It's not profitable anymore, and he thinks we should cut our losses." I hear him sigh and can picture his expression, pained, rubbing his eyes with one hand. "During the war years there was demand for constant production, but now trade is our main concern and we use the vessels we have. Closing this yard will put hundreds out of work."

"Is there no way to save it?" I ask. Daniel has made it his mission to keep workers engaged, having witnessed the devastating effects of unemployment since returning to the city. It will hurt him to be the cause of it, but not as much as it will hurt the shipyard workers and their families when food runs out. I often think Daniel is not made for the world of business. He grows defensive when I suggest this, guilt binding him to the company his grandfather founded, a company he abandoned for many years in the wake of the war.

"Dominic and I are friendly now, yet when it comes to business, he can be ruthless. I have to trust him, because he has run the organization for so long in my absence. It is still frustrating, though. He wants to make the announcement on Monday."

"I am sorry."

"Yes, well," he sighs heavily, "I am not quite giving up yet."

"Will you be home for dinner?" I ask, eager to see him, to exchange ideas face-to-face. Daniel may worry when I begin a new investigation, particularly one concerning such a grim crime, yet he quickly gets drawn in, putting his mind to the puzzle, considering this angle and that. We are well matched, and I wish, not for the first time, that the wedding was already behind us.

"I will try to get away soon. Shall I pick you up at the flat later?"

"No, I will come to Grosvenor. I am waiting for Hugh to arrive. He wanted to find out whether the newspapers are aware of the murder already."

"Good luck! I am sure you will have more to report tonight."

"Good luck to you, too." I replace the telephone on its cradle and just as I do, hear the front door open. It can't be Kathleen with Aiden, there is no squeak of the pram, no childish chatter to be heard. Moments later, the office door opens, and Hugh walks in.

"Any luck?" we ask as one, and both grin, our thoughts are so evidently aligned.

"You go first," he offers gallantly, shrugging off his coat and sitting in the chair opposite me. His expression tells me little of the success or lack thereof he had today. I tell him what I learned from Lara and Frances and end with the news that Stanton is on the case.

"At least we will have a contact in the police, though we should branch out beyond Stanton. It was lucky he was owed a favor and was willing to take this case, still we should try to befriend a few other coppers."

"That should be your project. I do not think it very likely they will share a pint with me and gossip about a hard day's work"

"Point taken. Well, it seems we still don't know much about Juliet, but I think we must focus on her past. If she moved around, as we were so ambiguously informed, perhaps she made an enemy somewhere who only recently found her again?"

"Where to begin? No one can tell us much about her, it seems. While I believe Frances was being a little secretive, I am not certain even she knows where Juliet lived in the years following the death of her parents."

"That would have been during or right after the war, a chaotic time," Hugh agrees, scratching his chin. "Perhaps I have an answer to the problem. I met with Hollis, and he was all ears." Hollis Napier is a slippery fellow whom I don't trust beyond the ties of mutual advantage, but he is wily, too, and good at what he does.

"What did he say? Had he heard of the murder?"

"No, not yet. He was thrilled to be the first, though. I think the police were a bit slow, and so it didn't leak to the press yet. Hollis was quite excited, a bit unfeeling given the circumstance. He proposed to look into Juliet's background and share the information with us, if we are willing to work with him as we have in the past."

"I marvel at his resourcefulness, all the while hoping he never turns his probing eye on me," I observe with raised brows.

"Quite. I also heard that there have been a few robberies in her neighborhood recently. Nothing violent. Some trinkets taken when the residents were out. I doubt they are connected, but Hollis wasn't sure. He is salivating at the prospect of a scandal or a big story to expose." Hugh wrinkles his nose with distaste, though I cannot fail to observe, if only in my mind, that we are not much better, even if our motives are.

"I have been wondering how to come by more information about Juliet's parents. She was unmarried, so their last name would have been Nelson, too. The flat used to be theirs, apparently, so perhaps one could find out who they were and where they came from. That might help us to better understand Juliet as well. I will drop by her flat later and see how Mr. Button fares. He is elderly and alone, as far as I could see, and I want to make certain he is well."

"And while you pour him a nice cuppa, you can slip in the odd question about previous tenants," Hugh muses with a sly smile, tapping his head. "I understand how you think, Lady Evelyn."

"So you do," I concede. "But I am genuinely concerned about the man. He seemed frail and shaky on his feet yesterday. In fact, had he not stumbled, we may have failed to discover Juliet at all."

"I take your point. I don't suppose you will be allowed entry into the flat."

"Doubtful. With any luck, Stanton will tell us what - if anything - they found."

"Shall I join you?"

"Maybe best not to. I don't want to overwhelm him." Hugh nods and pulls out his notebook, beginning the task of transcribing the information he gathered onto a separate sheet of paper for our files. We work so easily together one might think we have known one another all our lives, not merely met a few years ago and under rather difficult circumstances at that. When we met, Hugh was lonely and lost after the war, and I cannot help but think of Juliet in a similar way. From what I gather, hardly anyone even knew she existed. Will mourners attend her funeral? If Daniel and I had not found Hugh, might the same have been said of him? I shudder at the thought and banish it from my mind, taking comfort in the scratch of his pen on paper and knowing he is my friend.

Chapter 17

"Oh, hello, it's you," Mr. Button says when he looks up.

"Mr. Button, you are back at work already?" I ask, nodding at his desk. "Are you well enough? After everything that happened yesterday, I did not have a chance to ask whether you were all right, given the circumstances."

"You are a kind young lady. Miss Nelson was the same. Everyone walks by, some touch their hat, others give me a nod, but for most I am invisible." He gives a little chuckle, but there is not mirth in it. "I am not complaining. It is what it is, my father always said, and it is true. Miss Nelson, on the other hand, she would stop, ask after my day, notice if I was limping more when I fetched the mail. She had a limp, too, though I never said anything. She wasn't the sort who wanted to speak of herself, but she could listen, yes, she could listen." Mr. Button sighs and shakes his head, his arms crossed over his chest, shoulders rounded as he sits hunched on the chair. I feel an urgency to reach out and embrace this small, fragile man who has no one to ask after his day, no one to take notice. How much loneliness is right before our eyes, and we simply remain blind to it? I refrain from embarrassing Mr. Button with any displays of affection, offering a simple smile instead.

"I know so little about her," I admit. "We had only been acquainted a week or so. Had she lived here very long?"

"For some years, six or seven maybe. Before that the flat was empty much of the time." Juliet told me it had been some years, but not quite that long. I remember what Frances said of Juliet having only recently returned to the city. Maybe she just contacted Frances a few months ago instead of when she actually arrived?

"She lived here all this time?"

"She was away frequently, but yes, it was her home."

"Did the flat belong to her parents?" I ask, thinking back to Frances' words and questioning them now, given Mr. Button's new testimony.

"Not that I know of. The previous owners were not called Nelson." Mr. Button's forehead creases with concentration. "I have been here nearly all my adult life, so I have met just about everyone who lived in this building in the past half century. Miss Nelson was the first with that name."

"I see. You cannot remember the name of the previous owner?"
I ask lightly, hoping he is not concerned about my inquisitive tone.
"It's in the register. I could look, if you like?" He offers eagerly.
"I don't want to put you to any trouble, but if you don't mind?"
"Come along, then." He gets to his feet, glancing around the
empty entry hall. "I don't suppose anyone will notice my absence."
Though the observation is made with a vague smile, I cannot help but
feel a stab of pity, for there is likely truth in his words.

Following him down the hall, we arrive at his own flat, a small
space allotted to the caretaker of the building. The corridor is dim,
even when he tugs the cord for the electric light and leads me into a
small sitting room. It is sparsely furnished and for a man who has lived
here for decades, little evidence of individuality emerges. The walls
are bare, save for a few faded drawings of an anonymous landscape
and a clock which ticks loudly with every passing second. Mr. Button
ambles over to a cabinet and draws out a thick ledger, paging through
it with a furrowed brow.

"My eyesight is still good enough to read without specs," he
says, looking up for a moment with a proud smile. "Do make yourself
comfortable," he adds, nodding at the faded sofa, the hue of sun-
bleached moss. Everything is slightly drained of color. The walls, the
furnishings, the carpet. I want to do something for Mr. Button, inject
a flash of brightness into his life, but I cannot think how.

"Ah, here we are. The name was Bell. Howard Bell. He owned
it. The reason I could not recall the name was that he never spent any
time in the flat. I have no image of the man in my mind and, if you do
pardon the boast, I never forget a face."

"Bell?" I repeat. It cannot be a coincidence that Juliet's
colleague, the woman who procured the job for her is called Frances
Bell. Then why did she tell me the flat belonged to Juliet's parents if it
may have been hers or her husband's? Then again, I cannot discount
the fact that it is a common name. There must be a great number of
Bells in this city alone.

"Yes, in fact..." Mr. Button frowns at his ledger, turns a page,
then turns back again before looking up. "I cannot find a record of the
ownership changing hands. It seems even when Miss Nelson lived
here, it still belonged – or rather belongs – to Mr. Bell. I suppose
he rented it out to her. I am not sure why this surprises me, but I
assumed it was her property." He shrugs, though his words carry
more weight than he realizes. If Juliet rented the flat from Frances
and her late husband, then there is a deeper connection to the museum
archivist than the woman wished to let on. I did have the impression
Frances was not being completely forthcoming, but why mislead me?
Why keep the fact that the flat was her husband's a secret unless she

was hiding something? Could it be possible that Frances is unaware of the flat? Was Juliet, perhaps, her husband's mistress? So many possibilities flood my mind, I barely hear Mr. Button and have to ask him to repeat himself.

"Now that I think on it, I did meet Mr. Bell!" He announces, triumph in his voice. "It must have been at least ten years ago. I remember it now because it was the day the Battle of Cambrai had begun, and I read it in the paper. It was the winter of '17." He nods. "He came with two others, all wearing long dark coats and dark hats. Nothing unusual about that, I suppose, but it meant I could barely see their faces. You remember I never forget a face. Well, I only saw his in shadow. He did greet me, told me the number of his flat and went up. After that I do not think I saw him again. Occasionally, people would come to the flat, but they never stayed longer than one or two nights. They never gave me their names. It was his property, so I could hardly object. The times were so muddled already, with the war and young men leaving all the time, terrible news in the papers. Whatever was happening here seemed irrelevant in the grand scheme of things."

"Do you think you would recognize Mr. Bell if you saw him again now?" I ask, wondering whether a photograph of the late Howard Bell could be procured. It would be far easier if I could ask Frances outright whether it was her husband or someone related to them who owned Juliet's flat. Being friends of Juliet's parents, the Bells could have rented the place to them, but Mr. Button insists that no Nelson has ever lived here. I decide to trust his powers of recollection

"I might. He was tall, slim built with broad shoulders and he had a nose that looked like it had been broken before and badly reset. I would guess by now he might be past sixty or even close to seventy. He was not a young man even then, though I ought not be talking," he chuckles. "I will be seventy-four next month."

"Your memory puts people half your age to shame, Mr. Button. Thank you for telling me all of this. I am trying to get a better picture of Juliet. It is strange, we hardly knew one another, yet finding her as we did connects me to her. It won't bring her back, but it might make the memory of her a little more substantial."

We return to the entry hall together and Mr. Button slides behind his desk with a gentle sigh. I feel sorry to leave him, but I ought to be going. I pull a card from my bag and hand it to him.

"Thank you for your assistance, Mr. Button. Please take my card and do contact me if you remember anything else or if I can be of assistance in any way."

He squints as he reads the card, and when he looks up there is surprise mingling with something like admiration in his blue eyes.

"A lady detective? Who would have thought I'd live long enough to see that?" He chuckles and rummages around beneath his desk, pulling out a book and waving it in the air. Arthur Conan Doyle. "Am I one of your sources? How exciting! Always happy to help." He gives a little salute and I mirror it, before slipping out of the door and back into the chilly December afternoon.

Chapter 18

That evening, Daniel and I sit in near silence as we pick at our food, dragging pieces of chicken through gravy, which don't find their way to our mouths. Daniel's mind is undoubtedly occupied with the closing of the shipyard, while I cannot shake the image of small and kindly Mr. Button all alone in that anonymous flat from my mind. It makes me almost as sad as Juliet's death, which is absurd, of course.

"What will you do tomorrow?" Daniel asks, interrupting my thoughts. I told him about our recent discoveries, and though he struggles knowing I am back in the middle of a murder case, he has accepted it with weary resignation. Besides, he may complain at times, yet once the case gets underway, he is as keen to hear of developments as anyone.

"I will speak to Jeffrey. At the very least, he must be able to tell me a little more about Frances Bell."

"That sounds logical, though I would not rely too heavily upon Jeffery's powers of observation. He can stare at a clay urn for days on end, but his interest in people is not quite so profound."

"You may be right. I wonder whether the shock of Juliet's murder has pushed Briony's suspicions about him aside. I forgot to ask her today, my mind was so full of other things."

"What of the man who called the WI to excuse Juliet's absence. Do you have any notion of who he might be?"

"I haven't a clue. I want to speak to Priscilla. Perhaps she was not entirely truthful, though I cannot think why? It was obvious she did not like Juliet much. I assumed it was mild envy, because she was diverting Adeline's attention. Priscilla dotes on the Ashbourne ladies."

"Have you heard anything from Stanton?" Daniel asks, taking a sip of wine, his eyes not leaving my face.

"No, I have not. You remember, you can call him Lucas now."

Daniel grins. "You don't."

"I suppose I don't. I know you are not a great enthusiast of the fellow, but it is so very useful to have a contact in the police. There are places he can go that I am sure you prefer I did not."

"Well, when you put it like that…" he concedes with a smile.

"I went to Dulcie's today. She is quite unwell." I explain the state I found her in, and the reason for her decline.

"The poor woman. I feel for her. My father took his own life, and you never quite stop asking yourself if and how it could have been prevented." Daniel pushes away his plate and leans back, shaking his head.

"She wants to hold a séance." I watch for Daniel's reaction. He only raises his brows. "I think Mr. Singh had hoped I could dissuade her, but whatever strength has been sapped from her body, her mind is sharp, and she remains stubborn."

"Desperate for her son."

"I wonder how trying to contact the dead is regarded in Mr. Singh's religion. He is a Sikh, I believe."

"Maybe you should ask him, he has always been forthcoming. Whatever his beliefs, I cannot blame him for being put off by the notion."

"Yes, well, she wrangled me into agreeing to participate," I say with a helpless shrug. Daniel sits up, a bemused expression on his face.

"Do you believe in it?" he asks, and I cannot tell whether he is teasing or serious.

"No...well, maybe a little?" I reply, vaguely exasperated with myself. "Logically, no. I cannot believe spirits of the dead choose to contact us only through a paid medium at a table with blacked out windows and flickering candles. If it were possible, why not speak to us whenever they please or whenever we have need of them?"

"And illogically?" Daniel asks.

"Illogically I think, what if it could happen? The world is a strange place. There is so much we cannot understand. Why not this?"

"And yet you do not go to church, do not believe in the power of prayer."

"I have never discounted the idea of a greater power," I note. "It is simply a difficult notion to allow, considering the lack of benevolence the world has experienced in this century alone."

"Maybe he is not a benevolent being?"

"Or maybe *she* cannot be blamed for the greed and folly of men?"

"Had I known tonight's conversation would advance into the realm of philosophy, I might have asked for whisky instead of wine," Daniel says with a smile.

"Do not tease me, I am quite serious!" I throw my balled-up serviette at him. He deftly avoids my rather weak attack.

"I know you are. I am, too."

"Daniel!"

"All right, all right," he says, holding out his palms to appease me. "I am sorry. It is a rather unexpected turn of events, you must admit. I did not imagine you would ever attend a séance, let alone entertain its validity."

"I don't want Dulcie to go through it alone in case Mr. Singh cannot be convinced to join her. You are not, by any chance, interested?" I ask, focusing my eyes on his.

"Evie…"

"It is only one evening, and it may be interesting!"

"Must I?"

"I cannot force you."

"But I wouldn't hear the end of it, if I didn't go?"

"Denying me may not be the best way to start our marriage," I suggest with an exaggerated wink.

"And blackmail is? Speaking of marriage, do you have any hand in the planning of ours, or is it all in your aunt's control?"

"Since she does not listen to me one way or the other, I have decided to yield all wedding related decisions to her. I am curious to see what sort of dress she plans to put me in."

"I am, too."

"Don't distract me. Will you come or not? Maybe Hugh can join, too."

"Making it sound like a party won't make it more appealing."

"You hate parties."

"Exactly. But I have been well and truly roped in, and you tie a firm knot, my dear."

"If I did not, I might frighten you off." I smile, pleased to have convinced him. Well, maybe *convinced* is the wrong word…

"Never," he replies, smiling, too, and I know he is not truly upset about the prospect of attending the séance. I will ask Hugh tomorrow, or maybe Aunt Louise? The thought of my aunt makes me think of another. Oh, dear, I have completely forgotten to tell Agnes about the latest murder I stumbled upon. A few years ago, I would have actively tried to keep parts of my life secret from her, yet our relationship has since warmed considerably, and she will be quite put out to be the last to hear. After dinner, Daniel settles down with a stack of papers, while I give my aunt a ring.

"Another murder!" she repeats quite shrilly once I have presented her with a summary of recent events. "I thought it was a brilliant idea of Louise to join the WI with you. I thought, surely it is a safe, peaceful environment for that girl. But, no, of course not! You somehow manage to turn even that haven of jam making and local chatter into a den of iniquity." I let her rant on for a while longer, realizing her sharp words are not a sign of anger directed at me, rather her strange way of expressing concern. It has taken me a good quarter of a century to decode my aunt's manner, but from a safe distance, it is quite bearable.

"The WI is far more than I first anticipated, and Edith Ashbourne and her daughter are formidable. They remind me of you, actually," I say, happy she cannot see my smile.

"Edith was always a troublemaker, but of a good sort, I suppose," Agnes says, the fire draining from her voice. "You will be careful, won't you? Mr. Lawrence is making himself useful?"

"Yes and yes," I reply dutifully.

"Well, there is little else to say on the matter. I won't change your mind, I know that much."

"Some might observe I acquired my obstinacy from you."

"Obstinacy?" she repeats, as if the word is foreign to her ears. "I have never been obstinate in my life!"

"All right, then. Tell me, how do Harold's political ambitions progress?" I ask, trying to turn the conversation to a less controversial subject. Agnes is easily diverted, which surprises me on account of her *very* obstinate nature, but she is in the flush of love and her new husband is on the forefront of her mind. She tells me a little about Harold's plans, and it is almost soothing to listen to something wholly unrelated to murder and mayhem. However, when the subject turns to Harold's concerns regarding unemployment in his constituency, my ears prick up.

"He wants to impose a penalty on the companies who let go droves of their employees, while the owners continue to drown in their wealth," she says. I can tell it is a direct quote from Harold, for such words would never have passed my aunt's lips in the past. In her grand home on Eaton Square, she is far removed from any socialist leanings.

"Quite a noble cause," I observe, thinking of Daniel and his worries about closing down the shipyard.

"Indeed. He met with a number of community leaders in Shoreditch yesterday. They complained about the lack of responsibility companies and factories feel towards their workers. Harold came back aflame with plans!"

"I wish him well. Do let us know if we can help in some way. Perhaps you ought to join the WI as well. There must be a Shoreditch chapter."

"Oh, I am not sure if I am suited to something like that," she says, suddenly reserved.

"Of course, you are! Ask Louise to put you in touch with Edith. I am convinced she can help. If you are interested in being better acquainted with the troubles women face in this country, it is a good place to begin. I myself was surprised by the advocacy the organization proposed."

"Perhaps," is all she offers. We end the conversation with her warning to me and greetings for Daniel, as well as a reminder – rather too stern, in my view – that my fitting for the wedding dress is in a few days and I best not be late, or else! I lean against the wall for a moment, pondering Harold's proposed initiative. It is a worthy cause. But can it be done, or will my aunt's well-meaning husband soon be disappointed by the hurdles placed into the path of anyone who tries to do good?

As I am lying in bed, it strikes me that, given the good will displayed by Mr. Button when I visited, I might have gained access to Juliet's flat. Perhaps my conscience prevented me? Then again, if the police do not have a guard there, they would be very careless indeed. I will ask Stanton for permission tomorrow, and if he does not agree…well, then I will be forced to make the most of my new friendship with the genial Mr. Button. This business of detecting is bringing out a cunning side in me. I cannot say I am unhappy about it!

Chapter 19

"She's elusive, that Miss Nelson," I hear a familiar voice behind me when I walk to my car the next morning. Swinging around, I spy Hollis Napier, leaning against the neighbors' iron fence, a grin on his face.

"Mr. Napier," I say, crossing my arms. I do not comment on the fact that he has found me outside Daniel's house at eight in the morning, rather than my flat in St. James where a well-behaved, as yet unmarried Evelyn Carlisle ought to be spending her nights.

"For a detective, you do not cover your own tracks very well," Napier observes, stepping towards me. He is a nondescript man in his mid-thirties. Ash-brown hair, blue eyes, a long face and wide mouth prone to crooked grins. "Your motorcar is hardly inconspicuous, though I daresay," he glances around, "it may be in this neighborhood. Well done!" He lets out a wolfish whistle, and I roll my eyes.

"What do you want, Mr. Napier, I hardly have time for games."

"No games, Lady Evelyn, I am all seriousness." To illustrate his point he frowns, which only serves to lend him a more comical appearance. Some faces are meant to laugh and his is one of them, even if the laughter is frequently fueled by mischievous glee.

"Have you learned anything new?" I ask, narrowing my eyes.

"What will you give me for it?" he asks, stepping closer.

"Nothing at all, since I already tipped you off about the murder in the first place," I remind him.

"Hm...yes, true." He shrugs. "Thought you might be forgetful."

"I am sorry to disappoint. Now tell me what you know."

"It is mighty cold," he says with an exaggerated shiver, eyes veering to the house from which I just emerged.

"Oh, all right," I huff. "Only for a few minutes, just so that is clear."

"As the waters of the Thames," he replies and follows me to the house. Daniel left earlier than I did, but Wilkins gives us a strange look when we enter. He remains professionally silent after his offer of tea is rejected. In the sitting room, facing the square outside, Hollis slides onto one of the brocade sofas as if he owns it, leaning back and taking in the room.

"Rather plainer than I imagined," he observes with a disappointed dip in his features.

"My sincerest apologies," I retort, sitting down opposite him. For one reason or another, he brings out a rather prickly side in me. I am not at all sure I like it.

"I assume you already know your pretty policeman is on the case?"

"Inspector Stanton is not *my* anything, but yes, I know."

"Thought as much. Did you also hear he has not been able to locate a single friend or relative to formally identify the victim? Naturally, we all know she is Juliet Nelson, but official channels and all that should be able to provide for more." Hollis makes a dismissive gesture.

"No one at all?"

"Added to that, I have not been able to find any public record of her until the year 1919. Well, that isn't quite true, I did find her birth registered in Reading, but her adult life has been spent as a phantom."

"No records of employment?"

"None until she started working at the museum."

"I was told she moved around, but the caretaker in her building says she has lived there quite a few years."

"No family money, I would guess. Father was a clerk and mother a homemaker. No siblings."

"How did you find this information?"

Hollis taps the side of his nose. "A good journalist never reveals his sources, but you can trust their accuracy. Her parents were called John and Margot Nelson."

"So, they really are dead?"

"Yes, an accident in a bus fourteen years ago. It was run off the road and toppled down a cliff." He winces.

"Good heavens!"

"She was nineteen."

"I wonder where she went, what she did? What of the house where they lived? Did she sell it?"

"Must have. How else would an unmarried nineteen-year-old make her way in the world?"

"Maybe." My thoughts wander to a younger Juliet, alone then and still, more than a decade later. "And during the war?"

"Nothing. That does not tell us much. Those years were a muddle and record-keeping not the highest priority for many employers. She might have worked on the land, a factory girl, anything. Maybe she found herself a lover who kept her? Was she pretty?"

"Hollis!"

"It's relevant!" he counters with a sheepish smile.

"Yes, I suppose. She had a delicate look about her."

"Can be appealing," Hollis muses, waggling his brows. Agnes would be appalled by the man's behavior. However, the notion of Juliet having a lover is not far removed from what I have been considering as well. The fact that Howard Bell owned the flat does not discount the possibility that Juliet lived there as his mistress. Especially since Frances, his wife, seems unaware he was the owner. The more I recall Frances' expression when she told me the flat belonged to Juliet's parents, the more I doubt she realized she was lying. Why volunteer the information at all? Unless she is far more cunning than I believe her to be, which is possible.

"What are you thinking? You have someone in mind, don't you?" Hollis regards me with a bemused expression, head cocked slightly to one side. I am not entirely confident of his discretion, yet he has proven useful thus far and I decide to trust him with my suspicions.

"Howard Bell? You want me to find out whether he was Frances Bell's husband?"

"I assume he is, but can you?"

"Can I? What a question! If he is dead and his late wife is in her sixties, he must have been a bit of a rogue when he picked Juliet for a mistress," Hollis observes. I choose to ignore his licentious grin.

"If he did, *if*."

"He would hardly be the first to do so."

"It still seems a little too crude for him to have had an affair with a woman he and his wife met through her parents. She must have been a child at the time!" I grimace, and Hollis' grin widens.

"You are easily shocked, Lady Evelyn!"

"Not shocked, disturbed."

"Then you have much to learn of men."

"Perhaps I need not know everything."

"What happened to your curious heart?" Hollis places a hand over his.

"I really ought to go soon." I get to my feet. He sighs but follows suit. "Contact me at the office next time, please."

"Afraid your fella won't like your male company?"

"Afraid for you, perhaps," I say, meaningfully. Hollis only smiles, doffs his hat and slips through the open door. He has the ability to rile me, though beneath all his teasing and bravado, he is a decent chap.

Reaching for my own hat, I am about to step outside when the sharp trill of the telephone stops me in my tracks.

"Lady Evelyn!" Maisie West, the housekeeper and Wilkins' sister rushes into the hallway.

"What is the matter, Maisie?"

"It's your cousin, Mrs. Farnham, on the telephone. She says it is urgent!" Maisie's eyes are wide, and I am gripped by a sudden terror that something has happened to one of the children. Hurrying past her, I rush into the study.

"Briony? What is it? Has something happened?"

"Evie, the police were here. They have taken Jeffrey in!"

"In for questioning?" I stammer, my mind racing.

"I don't know! I was upstairs with Elsa, and I heard the door. Someone answered it, so I didn't bother looking. Next thing I know, one of the maids is running into the nursery calling for me to come quickly, Mr. Farnham is being taken away by the police!"

"Why? Did they explain anything?"

"Oh, Evie, it's Juliet. He was seen with her on Thursday." And on Friday she was dead.

Chapter 20

"How could you arrest Jeffrey and not tell me?" I practically shout at Stanton, when I stand in his office hours later. He sits behind the desk, his expression impenetrable.

"First of all, lower your voice, I don't need more attention than your not infrequent visits have already garnered," he says in a low, controlled voice. I frown and cross my arms, scowling down at him, refusing to take the proffered seat. "Fine. Secondly, I did not arrest anyone, just so it's clear."

"You brought him in for questioning?"

"As was my right, Evelyn. Juliet Nelson was seen climbing into Jeffrey's motorcar with him on Thursday, the day before you found her dead. How could I ignore that?"

"Who saw him?"

"A person whose name I cannot disclose."

"Was it Lara Bennet? Frances Bell? I have reason to believe Mrs. Bell is not being quite honest."

"What makes you say that?" he asks, frowning.

"It was her?"

"No, it was not."

"She lied to me about her connection to Juliet," I say.

"Sit down and talk to me. I cannot concentrate with you glaring down at me like a menace." Hesitating, I sigh and give in to his demand, explaining all I have learned thus far and my suspicion towards the archivist.

"That does not prove much. She might not have known Juliet rented the flat, or, as you say, Juliet may have been her late husband's mistress."

"Which would give her a motive, don't you think?"

"If she knew, and if it is true," Stanton notes. "Her husband's name was Howard Bell. She mentioned him when we questioned her, just by the by."

"Which should push her higher up on your list of suspects."

"If we are going by that, Jeffrey Farnham and your cousin, for that matter, might be on the list as well." He raises a hand to silence my objections. "You visited Juliet on Friday because you suspected Mr. Farnham of having an affair with her. Now it transpires he was seen with the murder victim the day before her body was found. It looks somewhat suspicious, doesn't it?"

"Jeffrey is not a killer, and I won't countenance what you suggested about Briony."

"The coroner claims Juliet could have died Thursday night. Mr. Farnham's alibi is that he was in his study at home alone."

"Surely a maid saw him?"

"A maid he pays, who will be frightened to deny anything her employer suggests?"

"Do not paint him a villain. What is happening now?" I left Briony and her father with the solicitor they brought for Jeffrey, while I made a fuss to speak to Stanton.

"He will be released again, which does not mean his innocence is proven. Whatever you say, you clearly think him capable of devious behavior, otherwise you would not have suspected him of infidelity with Miss Nelson."

"Infidelity and murder and two very different things, Lucas," I remind him.

"And yet, in my experience, one can sometimes lead to the other. When powerful emotions are at play, people can be unpredictable. Maybe Juliet wanted him to leave his family, made demands, blackmailed him. When pushed far enough, even the meekest of men are capable of villainy."

"Not Jeffrey," I remain firm.

"Strangulation is a crime more often associated with men than women. It requires physical strength and Mr. Farnham, though slim, is quite tall."

"Juliet was a slip of a thing! I don't think it would have taken a sturdily built man to overpower her."

"I realize you are trying to link Mrs. Bell to the case, but as of yet, I have no reason to suspect her. So, she didn't know Juliet rented the flat from her husband." He shrugs. "Many women are not informed of certain business arrangements their spouses make."

"The flat is still in the Bell name and Howard is dead."

"Then she may simply see a bit of extra money coming into her account, hardly something to be alarmed about."

"Why are you so willing to view Jeffrey as a suspect, but not this woman who may have overtly lied. What reason does Jeffrey give for being seen with Juliet on Thursday?"

"He claims he offered to drive her home, because it was raining."

"Well, that sounds utterly plausible. I saw the two of them bump into one another at the museum some time ago. I could swear they hardly knew each other. Jeffrey was just being friendly."

"Maybe," Stanton acknowledges. "So far we have few leads, and he happens to be one. Now, Evelyn, I really must get back to work."

Getting to my feet, I say, "As do I, Lucas, as do I," and turn on my heel. Stomping down the corridor to meet Briony and the others, I realize I am not being fair. Stanton is doing his job as he sees fit, and it does appear less than ideal that Jeffrey was seen with Juliet on the day before we found her dead, possibly the very day she was killed. However, Stanton did not mention anyone seeing Jeffrey actually entering Juliet's building, which is something, I suppose.

"We were told they will release him in a few hours," Uncle Robert says when he sees me. Briony is leaning against him, and her skin looks almost green in the dim light of the station.

"I spoke to Stanton. It doesn't seem that he has a strong case against Jeffrey, still it isn't ideal that he was the last person seen with Juliet as far as we know." I could have minced my words, but my cousin and uncle will appreciate honesty more than tact at the moment. All the same, Briony lets out a sigh of distress and Robert tucks her arm into the crook of his elbow, patting her hand.

"He was trying to do her a favor, driving her home in the rain," he soothes, yet when he meets my eye, I read in his expression he is not wholly convinced. While I cannot be certain of Jeffrey's innocence when it comes to adultery, I am utterly certain he could not have harmed a hair on Juliet's head. I have seen this man with his children, have known him for years, lived with him and Briony. He is not a murderer, and I say as much with the full force of my conviction.

"Can you take Briony home, Evie? I should wait for Jeffrey."

"Of course."

Briony does not put up an argument, and I gently lead her outside. We garner a few curious stares from policemen, and the fettered criminals in their care, as we leave. The cold air feels pleasant after the stale warmth inside the building. I take a deep breath. My car is just across the road, but when I look at my cousin, I worry she may not be able to cover the short distance. Only when I have safely deposited her in the passenger's seat do the muscles in my shoulders relax slightly. I do not start the car just yet.

"What should I tell the children?" she whispers, not looking at me.

"Nothing. There is nothing to tell, is there?"

"Iona saw her father being led away. There is no school today, remember?" She sighs and rubs her eyes before turning to face me. Her expression makes for a sorry sight and I curse Jeffrey for being the cause of it, innocent of a crime or not.

"Iona is a bright girl, but you should tell her it was a misunderstanding. As far as we know, that is precisely what it was. Jeffrey was driving a colleague home. That says nothing about his character apart from the fact that he is considerate."

"Maybe," she says in a weak whisper. "Can you take me home now?"

We roll down the streets in silence. Everyone we pass walks with their shoulders forward, coats drawn tight against the cold. I pull into the square opposite Briony's house, where the tree branches are bare and reach like frail limbs into the white sky. A hardy sparrow pecks at the ground. The front door opens before we have climbed the stairs leading up to it. Iona flanked by Aunt Louise stand in the doorway, worry tugging at the corners of their mouths. Briony pulls the girl into a tight embrace, and I whisper to my aunt, "Jeffrey will come home today." I sense her sagging with relief, and do not have the heart to tell her I suspect the ordeal is not quite over yet. Stanton made his suspicions clear.

"Come inside, come inside. The neighbors will be itching for more gossip." Louise ushers us into the entryway. To me she mutters, "I cannot believe the police came and picked him up for everyone to see."

"I suppose they thought if he is a criminal, he doesn't deserve better."

"But his family, his children? Don't they?" Louise is vibrating with anger. Areta and Timon are upstairs. I hear their excitable chatter through the ceiling. For once, I am relieved they are out of sight. Poor Iona is as pale as her mother. She has had enough upset in her short life, an orphan until a few years ago, when Jeffrey and Briony adopted her along with the other two children.

Louise and I leave mother and daughter alone for a moment, and go into the library where Louise closes the door behind us. The space is dim, though it is only eleven in the morning. I turn on the electric light and the room is suffused in a warm, artificial glow.

"He did not kill her," I repeat.

"Of course not. I know it isn't fair, he is a victim in this, too, but I am so angry with him." Louise slumps into a chair and presses a cushion to her chest. "When Robert was initially opposed to the match, I supported Briony. I insisted Jeffrey was a fine fellow."

"He is a good man. He has his flaws, but we all do," I argue in Jeffrey's defense. He has upset Briony, and the question of his fidelity remains unanswered, but he has just been hauled in by the police in front of his wife and eldest child, been questioned and made to wait, alone and likely afraid. I cannot but feel compassion for him at this moment.

Another two hours pass before we hear the front door open and voices, low and male, breaking the silence. Iona has been reading quietly, while we three women sat together waiting. I called Daniel and Hugh earlier and told them not to come, though both offered. It would be too overwhelming to have more people here. We all spring to our feet and rush into the hallway. Jeffrey is ashen, dark circles rim his eyes, as if he has been sitting in a cold police cell for the past week. Uncle Robert reaches out a hand to his wife, who takes it gratefully. Iona, usually so reserved, is the first to launch herself at her father with a fierce embrace. Jeffrey looks startled, then a smile and an expression of relief soften his weary features.

"It's all right, Iona, it's all right," he soothes, and when the girl steps back, I see tears in her eyes. Jeffrey looks at Briony, who has hung back. "Briony?" She hesitates, then allows him to pull her close. His lips move, but I cannot hear what he whispers into her ear.

"There are no charges, of course. Jeffrey has done nothing wrong," Robert announces to our teary gathering.

"I was only trying to be helpful." Jeffrey shrugs weakly. "She had a limp, and it was raining. I thought it silly not to offer her a lift. I stopped in front of her building, she got out and went inside. That was the last I saw of her." He shakes his head in disbelief.

"We should all have something to eat, and then Jeffrey needs to rest," Louise decides. "Evie, are you staying?"

"No, I think I should go, let you have some peace. Call me if there is something I can do. I spoke to Stanton, Jeffrey, and it seems they do not have anything on you apart from the fact that she was seen climbing into your car."

"And that is all there is. I wish I could be more helpful, but I hardly knew the woman! She was quiet, kept to herself, got the work done. Nothing more, nothing less." There is an apology in Jeffrey's voice. I think, had he not been taken in by the police, Juliet's death would hardly have touched him. She was almost anonymous to him, just as she was to nearly everyone else. At the very least I am certain Jeffrey, if he is going behind Briony's back, did not do so with Juliet Nelson. He is a terrible liar, and I would have seen guilt and discomfort in his eyes, had he been lying just now. I give Briony's hand a squeeze and kiss Iona's cheek before slipping away. Making my way through Belgravia towards St. James, I am exhausted, and it is merely afternoon. Hugh must be waiting for me, and Daniel will want to hear the news.

Stanton may still suspect Jeffrey, but as far as I am concerned, he is innocent. I made pronouncements about Frances Bell to him, yet when I reflect upon my words, was I simply trying to divert attention from my family? Perhaps I was. Nonetheless, the question remains.

Did Frances intentionally lie about the flat, or is she truly ignorant of the fact that her husband rented it to Juliet? And if she lied, was she aware of something between Howard and Juliet that would provide a motive for murder even after her husband's death? The thought makes me startle. How did Howard die? A rush of energy floods my body as a new direction of inquiry comes to mind. What if Frances knew of an affair and first killed Howard, then his mistress? It sounds like the plot ripped straight from a sensationalist novel, and yet…

I decide to put the question to Hugh as soon as I have assured him that Jeffrey is home and well and, in my view, innocent. Perching on the corner of his desk, I watch for his reaction. Hugh rubs his chin in concentration.

"Definitely possible. In any case, more likely than Jeffrey harming a fly. I do not know the man well, but on the last occasion we met, he wouldn't even discuss rugby on account of it being too violent." I cannot help but smile, which was Hugh's intention. He must have read the strain in my features the moment I entered the room. "As for Mrs. Bell," he continues, "We need to look into her more thoroughly. She has met you and is aware of the investigation, but she does not know me yet. I will dig deeper. In the meantime, we should not discount the WI. Before you protest, listen for a moment." Hugh leans forward. "I have been thinking about it, and it strikes me that the one new aspect of Juliet's life was her participation in the WI. Everything else was going according to a well-honed routine. Nothing out of the ordinary."

"I suppose that is true. I would be curious to find out whether other women in her building were invited to join when she was. If only Juliet received an invitation, it seems likely someone at the WI tried to lure her in."

"I agree. You said Priscilla showed some dislike towards Juliet for one reason or another. It may be useful to learn more about her."

"Then there are Edith and Adeline, both act as leaders of the group."

"Mrs. Ashbourne is the one who hired us," Hugh observes.

"Perhaps she underestimates our abilities and wishes to divert attention from herself?" I suggest, far from convinced. Edith's reaction to learning I was a detective was one – I believe – of genuine admiration. Could she be so good an actress, so underhanded to have meant none of what she said?

"It seems unlikely. What of the daughter?"

"I have no reason to suspect Adeline, but I also have no reason to discount anyone at the WI. The women are practically strangers to me. I admire their spirit, yet there is no telling what anyone is capable of, as we have learned from past experience."

"Are you becoming a cynic?" Hugh asks with a smile.

"Like you?" I counter.

"Goodness, I hope not!"

Getting to my feet I say, "If either of us were truly cynical, we would not believe in the possibility of justice, and our work would be pointless."

"Maybe I do not truly believe in justice."

"Hm...sometimes I wonder if I do. Juliet won't come back to life, even if we find her killer."

"When we find her killer."

I smile. "See, you are an optimist after all."

Chapter 21

After exchanging ideas with Hugh over bread and lamb stew that Maeve prepared, I decide to call on Edith. She is owed an appraisal of our progress, minimal though it may be, and I want the chance to observe her more carefully and to question her myself.

The Ashbournes live in Lowndes Square in Belgravia, not far from Aunt Louise and Uncle Robert, in an elegant Georgian house with a view of the currently bare gardens in the square. It is a quiet afternoon, the distant sounds of busy Sloane Street and Brompton Road barely register in this enclave of wealth and privilege. I climb the steps to the front door and sound the knocker. A small, rotund man in a butler's uniform opens the door and, upon hearing my name and the purpose of my visit, places me in a sitting room to wait. It is a large room with high ceilings and a paining that looks very much like a Turner above the mantelpiece. On the wall opposite hangs a framed newspaper front page. I step closer and see a photograph. It is grainy and faded, depicting Edith beside Emmeline Pankhurst and three other women in white, wearing sashes. The headline announces, "Women Win the Vote". I cannot but smile, wishing desperately that any suspicions Hugh and I foster against Edith are speedily dispelled.

"Evelyn, what a surprise. Don't tell me you have solved the crime already?" Edith's voice interrupts my thoughts, and I turn to see her striding into the room hands outstretched. Following her is Adeline, dressed, for once, in a subdued navy blue suit.

"No, I am afraid we are not quite as swift as we would like to be. Hello, Adeline. I hope I am not interrupting?"

"Not at all," says Adeline, gesturing for me to take a seat while tea and a tray of biscuits are laid out for us. "Have you any news? I still can't believe Juliet is gone." She shakes her head, her expression one of bewilderment. "And you and your poor cousin were the ones to find her. How very dreadful!"

"It was. I wonder how long it may have taken for anyone to miss her, if we had not been the ones to do so," I say, before explaining that Hugh and I have found next to nobody who knew much of anything about the deceased.

"I suspected she had few friends. That is why I was keen to engage her when she joined the WI," Adeline says, stirring sugar lump after sugar lump into her tea.

"It is in Adeline's nature to include everyone," Edith says with more than a trace of pride. As her only child, Adeline must have been the recipient of a great measure of motherly attention, even if the mother in question was rather busy with other matters as well.

"Could you tell me a little more about her? You said you were barely acquainted, but perhaps there is something you forgot to mention earlier?" My gaze moves from one woman to the other. "Then there is Priscilla. I would like to ask her about the call she received, excusing Juliet's absence."

"Oh, yes, the caller!" Adeline's eyes grow wide. "Do you think he was the murderer?"

"I cannot discount it, though if it is so, they must have been well acquainted, for no stranger would know of Juliet's plans to join us on Armistice Day."

"Imagine that, a confidante doing her harm. It is awful." Adeline grimaces.

"We can give you Priscilla's details. As for myself, I cannot think of anything I forgot to tell you. We occasionally send out letters to local households inviting women to join us. I never met Juliet before, nor do I handle the invitations. In fact, you can ask Priscilla about that. She is a very organized secretary. You were probably better acquainted with Juliet than the two of us. You both joined on the same day. Didn't you spend some time talking to her?"

"I did. We even had lunch together one day," I admit.

"That is what I like so much about the WI. Friendships can blossom from shared causes," Adeline says with a smile.

"Well, we weren't friends exactly, but I hoped we would be. She was very reserved. I fear I dominated much of our conversation. But as I said earlier, I remember her telling me she had no siblings, which has been confirmed. Further, she had lived in London for some time, and was born in Reading. Her parents are deceased. No family has come forth to identify her body or to organize a funeral when the police release it."

"I cannot decide whether it is worse to be forgotten, or to leave behind loved ones who would be shattered by grief," Adeline muses, her perpetual smile slipping slightly. I wonder the same. Can one even speak of one being better than the other? Both options are entirely hideous for the dead and the living.

"We must hold a memorial service for her at the WI," Edith decides. "We may not have known Juliet well, but for a short time she was one of us."

"Well said, Mother," Adeline agrees. "Speaking of being one of us, I meant to invite you and your fiancé to dinner this weekend, if you have the time, Evelyn. I want you to properly meet Graham, and I will also ask your cousin if she would like to join us."

"Oh, that is kind," I reply, though I doubt Daniel will muster much excitement for a dinner party with strangers, and Briony and Jeffrey will likely beg off. "I am sure we do not have a prior engagement."

"We look forward to it. Perhaps by then you will have learned something new. If there is anything else we can do to help, or the WI, of course? When we told the women yesterday, they were quite upset, though I daresay many would not have recognized poor Juliet," Adeline observes with an apologetic shrug.

"All the same, it is deeply disturbing for them and all of us that a woman in our ranks has been killed," her mother adds. "Yes, a small memorial event for Juliet would be quite appropriate. It is a shame we will have so little to say about her."

"If no one comes forward to arrange the funeral, the WI must step in," Adeline announces. I smile at the mother and daughter sitting opposite me, both eager to help, to lend time, money, a hand or an ear. Juliet would have found friendship with both of them, had she lived. Feeling a little disappointed not to have learned anything new, I take my leave. At least I have Priscilla Lewis' details. Adeline told me she would likely be found at home this time of day. She has a ten-year-old son and a barrister for a husband.

I glance at my watch. It is only a quarter to four, so the husband will not be at home yet and I, hopefully, won't disturb the family by arriving unannounced. I decide to chance it and climb into the Bentley to drive around Hyde Park to Marylebone.

Chapter 22

The Lewis house is a modest, well kept, three story brick with a small wrought iron fence. Priscilla herself answers the door wearing a harried expression, a few curls of her ash brown hair having escaped her chignon, two rosy spots coloring the apples of her cheeks.

"Lady Evelyn, what -"

"Priscilla, please excuse the interruption. Have I caught you at a bad time?" I ask, hoping my use of her given name will evoke an aura of friendship that has not, as yet, developed.

"No, I suppose..." she hesitates then pulls the door open. "Please, come in." It is pleasantly warm after the chill outdoors, and I feel heat rising to my cheeks as Priscilla leads us to a small lounge overlooking the street. I accept an offer of tea, and she calls for a maid. The room, I cannot fail to notice, is surprisingly untidy. A stack of children's books lies in a tumble slightly too close to the fire crackling in the hearth. A few of the sofa cushions rest on the ground and there is a stain on the carpet. It seems Priscilla's ship doesn't run quite as tightly outside the WI, though I can hardly be one to judge. If I had a child, I suspect it would soon have the run of the house as well. Perhaps she relishes her organizational work at the WI, where she can use her skills without small sticky hands interfering?

"You must excuse the mess," she says, and I feel a flush of guilt for having taken notice of it, for Priscilla is evidently a mind reader.

"Adeline told me you have a son?" I ask, trying to turn the conversation to lighter matters before asking about potential killers and murder victims. Balance is the best friend of harmony, after all, and that is precisely the state I wish to achieve between the two of us.

"Yes, Bertie," she replies with a tight smile.

"How old is he?" I ask, knowing the answer already.

"Ten. Just turned ten." Her expression softens a little, though I cannot ignore the tension remaining in her eyes and the set of her shoulders. I am inclined to interpret it as guilt. But to be fair, I must acknowledge it is more likely annoyance at having been called upon unannounced.

"A lively age," I comment inanely, adding, "And he likes to read," with a nod to the books.

"Yes, although I have told him endlessly not to leave his books near the fire." Priscilla gets to her feet and stacks them up on a side table. The maid enters and sets down a tray of tea and biscuits before disappearing again.

"Priscilla, I am sure you are wondering why I am here. We do not know one another very well yet, though I hope that will change in due course." I smile and accept a cup of tea, my stomach turning at the sight of yet another one.

"I assume this is about Juliet Nelson." Priscilla does not meet my eye, pouring her own cup and selecting a biscuit from the plate.

"It is. Perhaps Edith or Adeline told you, my detective agency has been hired to look into the case."

"Edith made a reference to that extent. I thought I misheard," Priscilla observes evenly. I cannot quite judge whether she disapproves or is merely uncertain what to think of the whole matter. She cannot be blamed for feeling dumbfounded by the recent turn of events.

"My partner and I have started investigating, trying to learn more about Juliet. We barely got acquainted with one another before she was killed."

"It is a tragedy, truly, but I do not see how I can help. I hardly exchanged more than a few sentences with her, and when we spoke, I had the impression she was not wholly present." She shrugs and takes a sip. "One ought not speak badly of the dead, and that is not my intention. However, I cannot speak well or ill of someone I hardly knew, someone I felt intentionally kept me at a distance."

"You are not the first to make such a claim," I admit.

"To be honest," she says, her posture relaxing, "I am relieved to hear you say so. I wondered whether she had taken against me specifically, which might have made me a little prickly towards her. I feel ashamed of it now, but I was a bit short with her the last time we spoke. And when her brother called to say she wasn't coming to help us on Armistice Day, I thought she was being lazy. I lost a brother in the war, and remembrance is important to me. I think I felt worse, because she still had hers. I may have taken it personally. Now, of course, I know she is not to blame." Priscilla falls silent, watching me. The urge to express her thoughts has been sated. The words have tumbled out of her, a monologue fueled by guilt. Not, however, guilt of a murderous kind, I suspect.

"I am sorry for the loss of your brother, but I have strong reason to believe Juliet was an only child."

"Yes, the police said as much."

"You spoke to the police?"

"Briefly. I could offer them as little as I can offer you. I told them about the telephone call. He called at our meeting hall, where I was gathering a few things with some of the other ladies, about an hour before we left."

"Very late notice."

"Do you know whether it was truly coming from Juliet's flat?"

"No," she says slowly. "I suppose I hadn't considered an alternative."

"I do not wish to alarm you, but I suspect you have come to the same conclusion I have. The person who called -"

"Could be Juliet's murderer," Priscilla finishes my sentence and presses a hand to her mouth. I reach out and take the teacup from her other hand before she can drop it.

"I know it is appalling to consider, yet I must ask, can you recall anything in particular about the caller's voice? An accent, perhaps? Anything distinctive?"

Priscilla bites her bottom lip, her brows knitting together in concentration. "No, no, I cannot recall anything exceptional. I was frazzled, gathering things together, irritated she was backing out so late. I hardly paid the caller much attention. As I said earlier, it was a bad line, almost muffled. If I heard the voice again, I doubt I would be able to recognize it."

"The caller might have tried to disguise their manner of speech. If this person was aware of Juliet's intention to join the WI ladies on Armistice Day, then I have to believe it was one of her few confidantes."

"How dreadful!"

"Quite." We sit in silence for a few moments, each pondering the horror of poor Juliet dying at the hands of someone she not only knew but possibly even trusted.

"What will you do now?" Priscilla finally asks.

"I will continue to ask questions. Juliet lived on this earth for over thirty years. She must have left a trace of that life, and I intend to find the trail of breadcrumbs."

Chapter 23

Though Priscilla was unable to shed much light on Juliet or the caller, I do not regret my visit. I misunderstood her as an irritable, short-tempered woman, impressions based purely on the few minutes we spent in each other's company. Having spoken to her now, sensing her guilt when she confessed to disliking Juliet, I feel closer to my fellow WI member. When her son barged into the room, hair wild, demanding his tea, I saw another, more nurturing side of her still. That all being very well, it does not bring me much – if any – closer to unmasking the killer. I suspected someone from the WI, but who, apart from Edith, Adeline and Priscilla did Juliet interact with? She attended no more events than I did and was usually in my company, yet I know as little of her as seemingly all the others do. There must have been someone else in her life, surely, and that someone, the caller maybe, could be the villain I seek.

Sitting in my car by the side of the road, I close my eyes, letting the events of the day wash over me. It seems impossible that Briony's frantic call only came this morning. What a relief that Hollis left just before. I certainly do not trust him enough to let him in on my family secrets. He can be useful to me, if I am useful to him, beyond that, I am not so sure. Then there is Stanton, who brought Jeffery in for questioning, causing the family such distress, and for what? I ought not blame him for doing the work I asked him to take on, but I cannot help feeling a twinge of betrayal tugging unpleasantly at my heart. Daniel has told me not to forget that Stanton is a policeman, not my partner like Hugh, yet I always put his misgivings down to jealousy. I have little right to be disappointed in Stanton's actions, but I am all the same.

Perhaps it is this sense of frustration or maybe my innate inquisitiveness that has me driving back to Bloomsbury, to Juliet's flat. From a telephone kiosk, I ring our office and am put through to Hugh.

"Hugh, can you come to Bloomsbury?" I ask.

"To Juliet's?"

"I want to have a look around, and I trust Mr. Button will allow it. You should be there, too, with your hawk eyes."

"My eyes and I are on our way!" he says, and I hear a click at the end of the line. True to his word, Hugh arrives just when the sky begins to turn a soft orange, presaging sunset. I see him from a distance, unobtrusive in a long gray coat and dark hat, blending in with the evening crowd. Climbing out of the car, my muscles are stiff from waiting, eager to move. I hope Mr. Button is around and not put off by my return or my companion's presence. I considered going in alone with Hugh following secretly when I give a sign, but I cannot countenance deceiving the kindly older man and thus hope he will be amenable to our request. I might say I lost something in the flat – I've used this method with success in the past – yet I do not think it will be necessary today. In any case, I suspect he will feel more warmly towards me than the police. The advantage of a private detective is that she appears, to most, a human being, not an imposing figure of the law, watching to catch every minor wrongdoing. Maybe I am a tiny bit sensitive when it comes to coppers today...

Mr. Button is sitting at his desk, a newspaper spread out in front of him, the space illuminated by the bright glow of a lamp. He looks up when the door opens, bringing in a gust of icy air that makes me wish the poor fellow did not have to sit here all hours. However, he strikes me as the sort who would not wish to shirk a duty for which he is compensated. I suspect the fact that he did not see anyone on the day of Juliet's murder rests heavy on his conscience. Perhaps he nodded off and the killer snuck in without his notice?

"Mr. Button," I greet him with a bright smile. "Good evening. I hope I am not making a nuisance of myself. May I introduce my colleague, Mr. Lawrence. Hugh, this is Mr. Button." The men shake hands and I can tell the elder is slightly ruffled by our arrival, though he smiles his usual kindly smile.

"Very good to meet you, and to see you again, Miss Carlisle."

"May I be very bold, Mr. Button?" I ask, leaning forward in a conspiratorial manner.

"Please," he says, a bemused smile on his lips.

"I wonder whether I might have a quick look at Miss. Nelson's flat? I suspect the police have already nosed about and abandoned it again?"

"Well, I suppose...The police was round earlier, two chaps. They left a few hours ago. Not the chatty sort," he observes, raising his bushy white brows.

"Could we have a peek? We won't be long, but I want to do right by Juliet and for that, it would help to know how she lived. It seems strange, wrong even, to be in her flat, yet I have to believe, for the sake of justice, she would not mind the intrusion."

"I think you are probably right," Mr. Button agrees. "Can I give you the keys? I am afraid my knees are giving me trouble today. The chill gets right into my bones in winter."

"Of course." I gratefully accept. While sorry for his pain, it seems simpler this way. Sitting in the drafty entry is no way for a man of his years to live, though. It is only a matter of time before he catches a cold or something worse. It is not my business to make such observations, however. I know Mr. Button is a proud man. I accept the key he presses into my hand and promise to return it as quickly as we can, before Hugh and I climb the stairs to Juliet's flat.

"You discount Mr. Button from the list of suspects?" Hugh whispers, when we have reached Juliet's door. I turn to him with wide eyes.

"You saw the man, Hugh! He is fragile and not in good health. I cannot imagine he could have anything to do with the murder."

"He may be acting. How difficult is it to complain of a bad joint, slow movement and thus avert suspicion?"

"Hugh, sometimes people simply are who they seem to be," I say. He lets it pass without further comment, and I turn the key in the lock. Our entry this time is so different from the last, though the scene in the hallway is not much more encouraging. The police have rooted about, and it looks even more chaotic than before.

"It could have been a distraction, the killer going on a rampage, but what if he – or she, I suppose – was searching for something specific?"

"And in which order did events take place?" Hugh muses as we step into the eerily silent space, closing the door in our wake. "Did Juliet let him in willingly, he killed her and then rooted about? Or did he enter without her invitation, start his search, notice she was home and killed her?"

"I want to speak to the neighbors. Likely no one was home or heard anything, since Stanton seems to have come no further in the investigation than we have, and he must have questioned them. All the same, I want to hear their answers for myself."

"Talk me through the scene as you came upon it," Hugh says. I oblige, gooseflesh rising to my skin as I remember. We begin at the door and progress along the hall, looking into every room as I did with Briony, finally reaching the space where we came upon Juliet's body. Everything looks much as it did then. The furniture has not been righted, but the window is closed, leaving the air stale. It is nearly dark outside, and we pull out our torches, unwilling to turn on the light, in case it should arouse suspicion. I do not want Mr. Button to be penalized for allowing us entry, nor for us to be caught out.

"No photographs, hardly much of anything on the walls. Strange, given the fact that she lived here for years," Hugh observes.

"Books, though." I gesture at the shelf, in front of which lies a pile of scattered volumes, clearly pushed aside by a violent hand.

I glance at the titles, surprised to discover that our reading tastes aligned. *Might we have become friends?* I wonder not for the first time.

"I will search the kitchen and sitting room. Why don't you take the bedroom and bath?" Hugh suggests. I know he would not feel right intruding into this most private space. I am not eager to do so myself, still I nod and accept the task. The flat feels hollow, so lifeless, it is difficult to believe it was a home to someone not long ago. I want to complete our search quickly and leave. It is not a place to linger. I wonder whether Juliet was happy here. It certainly seems as though she did not put much effort into making it a comfortable home.

An open door at the end of the hallway leads to the bedroom where Juliet was killed. The bed is unmade, not gently rumpled, rather angrily torn apart, sheets pulled away, mattress not quite resting on its frame. Juliet cannot be offended anymore, but I am angry to find her small sanctum so cruelly invaded. I suppose the police conducted their own search and did not think to restore any sense of peace to the room, but I intend to go about my investigation with care. I find nothing under the bed, the mattress, behind the cold metal frame or the nightstand. There is nothing of interest in the drawers, which hold a few handkerchiefs and a balm for headaches. I open her wardrobe, revealing a few good suits in drab tones of green and gray, a few hats and nylons rolled up in a box at the bottom. I pull out the box to feel around the back wall of the wardrobe, when it topples over, spilling out serpentine coils of stockings and something else…I narrow my eyes and reach for the small black box, a jewelry box. Opening it, I see a glint of metal, a slim gold band. Is it a wedding ring? Was Juliet married? A widow? Or did it belong to her mother? It is small, doubtless a woman's ring. The gold carries the dull patina of age. I return it to the box and, and, without much thought, tuck it into my coat pocket.

I find nothing else of note in the bedroom. No wedding dress reverently folded into a long box, no dried bouquet of faded flowers. Perhaps the ring is an heirloom, a memory of the family she lost, and she thus kept it out of sight, her fingertips brushing against the small box every morning when she got dressed.

"Any luck?" asks Hugh, when I join him in the kitchen after having carefully combed through the bath. I tell him about the ring. "Interesting that she kept it hidden."

"Have you found anything?" I ask, glancing around the kitchen. A few plates were smashed on the ground and remain as shattered shards, a mosaic of destruction.

"Nothing. Some canned food, hardly anything fresh. A stale half loaf of bread. Only four plates, counting the broken ones. I don't suppose she was one for hosting dinner parties."

"Nothing in the cabinets or drawers, or attached underneath them or hidden behind them somehow?"

"I felt around, there wasn't anything. I must say, my rooms in Lambeth are not a testament to individuality, but Juliet lived like a monk, or a phantom in comparison."

"I wonder whether she did not care for material comforts, or whether she preferred to slip by unnoticed?" I muse, taking in the small room.

"If it is the latter, there has to be a deeper reason," Hugh observes. "She may have liked her privacy, but no one likes to be invisible, not for years on end, a lifetime even." He speaks from experience, so I do not add further comment.

"Ready to leave?" I ask instead, slightly dejected, though I hardly know what I hoped to find. Ideally a diary noting down the time she expected a visitor on the day of her death and who this person was. Alas, our search yielded no such vital clue. I suspect the one conducted by the police was similarly unsuccessful, or else they would not be grasping at straws and questioning Jeffrey.

"Ready?" Hugh asks and turns. As he does, the floorboards creak and he pauses.

"Hugh?"

"Just a minute," he says absently and kneels down, pushing aside a thin rug and running his hands over the wood. I join him on the floor, shining my torch downward, watching him as he pulls out a small pocketknife and levers it into a slit between the boards. To my surprise, it lifts easily. I let out a little gasp and shine the light into the small space now exposed.

"I felt an unevenness as I stepped on the board, and remembered I used the same trick when I lived in France. My landlord liked to poke about, and I did not want him to discover the little money I had."

"Consider me impressed," I say. "Do the honors." Hugh nods and reaches into the blackness. His hand emerges with a box, decidedly larger than the ring box in my pocket. This one is wooden with a delicate inlay of lighter wood patterning the lid, about the size of a dense book. Holding my breath, I wait for Hugh to open it.

"Look." He holds it up so I can see the contents. Resting in the box are two medals and a thick wad of pound notes.

Though only my friend can hear, I whisper, "Quick, hide it in your coat and let's go. I can't see properly in this light, and I want a good look." Not hesitating for a moment, Hugh obeys my hushed command, tucking the box into his coat and replacing the wooden plank and carpet as we found them. Fortunately, the mess disguises any trace we may have left behind, and we slip into the hallway and down the stairs undetected. Mr. Button is dozing once more. He bids us a bleary-eyed goodbye, when I press the key into his hand and thank him for his help. Together, Hugh and I step into the night, precious cargo between us, minds flush with sudden possibilities.

Chapter 24

"Oh, hello -" Daniel breaks off, giving us curious looks as we bundle into the house on Grosvenor Square, almost missing him in our haste to get to the library to examine our loot.

"Daniel," I say, stopping for a quick kiss. "We may have found something important. Come with us." He does not hesitate, and we are soon ensconced in the library, both boxes on the table, us hovering above. Hugh opens the lid and carefully takes out two shiny medals and the wad of money. Daniel raises his eyebrows, and I explain how we came by them. My explanation is interrupted when Hugh makes a startled sound, pulling another object from the wooden case. A photograph.

It depicts a young man, smiling timidly at the camera. The picture is creased and the corners are bent, but it was clearly cherished by Juliet.

"A lover?" Daniel suggests.

"Possibly, since she had no siblings."

"Different coloring, too. You said Juliet was pale with nearly white blond hair," Hugh observes. Indeed, the man in the photo seems to have dark hair, and his features, too, in no way resemble Juliet's. He is handsome, with a strong jaw, large eyes, and a dimple in his chin.

"Maybe he was the one who gave her the ring," I wonder aloud, reaching for the small case containing the golden band and showing it to the men. "She may have been in love, may have had someone who cared for her. That would mean she wasn't always this secluded person, whom no one really knows."

"Tragic, though, if it didn't last," Daniel muses.

"Maybe that is what made her withdraw?" Hugh suggests, squinting at the photograph. I suspect he may require specs, but then he points at something in the picture. "This was taken in France." Daniel and I almost knock heads, leaning in to see. "Here in the corner you can make out a sign for a *boulangerie*," Hugh explains, referring to the French name for a bakery.

"He could have been a soldier. Might have gone to war and sent her the photo," Daniel says, and I can tell from his expression that he is thinking exactly what I am. Did this man ever make it home?

"It's possible," Hugh says. I know they are remembering Henry and William, Daniel's brothers, the former of whom was a dear friend to Hugh. Neither returned from the war.

"What a terrible story, if it is true."

"Not uncommon, though," Hugh notes.

"What about the medals and the money? Could they have belonged to this man? Maybe they married and she received them after his death. They are clearly military. Look," I hold one up.

"A British War Medal," Hugh says approvingly. "But the real stunner is this one." He lifts the other with reverence. "A Victoria Cross."

"Remarkably few were awarded after the war," Daniel explains, taking in my blank gaze. "It signifies great valor in the face of the enemy."

"Juliet's man must have been a remarkable chap."

"Another one gone too soon, if our suspicions are true." Hugh carefully returns the medals to the box.

"What of the money?" Daniel picks up the wad. "This is a substantial sum."

"Perhaps she didn't trust banks. Lots of people don't," Hugh says, and I suspect he is one such person.

"The flat is small, but well situated. I don't suppose the rent – if she paid any – would be cheap," I say. "Maybe she needed the money for that. The question remains where she got it from."

"She could have saved up. As you said earlier, you don't know anything about her past until she arrived in London. Perhaps she earned a great deal of money somewhere," Daniel suggests, sounding unconvinced.

"Or she robbed a bank?" I counter. "We have to find out whether she had to pay rent to Howard Bell, or now to Frances, who still owns the place. I wonder how Bell died and whether our suspicion that Juliet was his mistress is true. If she was and he died suddenly, there may not have been time to make arrangements for her to be left the flat without his wife learning of its existence."

"That is assuming she truly was unaware. For all we know, Bell had a number of flats he rented out. Perhaps it was an ordinary business arrangement, and he was simply doing Juliet a favor because he had been friends with her parents." While I ponder Hugh's words, I cannot quite accept that it is all coincidental. There has to be more to the Bell connection than a rental agreement. I begin to write down all of our theories, including the possibility that the killer went on his rampage through the flat with the aim of finding the box, until we can think of nothing more and Daniel suggests we eat. Hugh agrees to stay for dinner, and we share a pleasant evening, even if we cannot help ourselves from occasionally lapsing to the subject of the murder, hardly the sort of conversation to stoke one's appetite.

"Has Evie told you of the séance?" Daniel asks, when Hugh and I start wondering about the meaning of Juliet's cash hoard once again. If Daniel prefers to speak of Dulcie's séance, we must be tiring him with our talk!

"A séance?" Hugh wrinkles his nose and puts down the fork that just speared a chunk of roasted parsnip. "You mean one of those productions to summon the spirits of the dead?"

"That's the one! And production is a very apt word for it," Daniel says approvingly, giving me a meaningful look.

"It was hardly my idea!" I say, holding up my hands.

"What are you both talking about?" Hugh looks from Daniel to me and back again. Daniel takes pity on his friend and explains.

"Dulcie wants to commune with her dead son?"

"She is very low at the moment," I explain. "It is a desperate move, but I agreed to join her and so will Daniel. Won't you my love?" I say pointedly in my fiancé's direction. His nod is punctuated by a sigh.

"Will you try to contact Henry and William?" Hugh asks with a surprisingly grave expression. Daniel drops his fork.

"You must be joking?"

"Why discount the possibility?" Hugh asks with a shrug.

"Because, well…because it's absurd, it's a farce!"

"How do you know?"

Daniel looks startled that Hugh could even entertain the endeavor as potentially effective. I decide to help him, interjecting, "Will you join us? I am sure Dulcie would be comforted to have someone in our group who shares her belief that it might not be a charade."

Hugh hesitates a moment, then nods.

Daniel rolls his eyes, and I jab him with my elbow. I haven't forgotten our bet to find a special lady for Hugh either. Perhaps I will be met with success in that department as well!

Chapter 25

After Hugh has left, I call Briony. It is almost impossible to believe it was only this morning when I received her frantic message that Jeffrey was taken in by the police. I want to hear how she, Jeffrey and the children are coping with today's upheaval. To my surprise, she sounds rather bright when I get her on the line.

"It was not really so bad, Evie," she whispers.

"What makes you say that? This morning you were distraught."

"It forced me to confront him. After seeing Iona so upset, I couldn't ignore it anymore. I asked him outright whether he is having an affair, who the woman I saw at the museum was - the one he seemed keen to avoid - and whether he truly did not know Juliet better than he claimed."

"Goodness, you are bold!" I exclaim proudly. "What did he say?"

"Oh, Evie, I am so relieved," she sighs into the telephone. "He promised he did not know Juliet personally, he was not having an affair – the very suggestion seemed to confound him! – and the woman was a colleague with whom Jeffrey had a bad argument about the origin of some silly pot or other. They were simply trying to avoid one another out of a mutual dislike, not shared duplicity."

"You believe him?" I ask, relieved to feel that I do. I never did think Jeffrey capable of adulterous behavior, let alone the scheming such actions would have demanded.

"I do. He is a terrible liar, and the ordeal with the police truly upset him. I feel so foolish having concocted this tale, when there was nothing to be found. It doesn't repair all the cracks, but at least Jeffrey is aware of them now, too."

"That is certainly something," I observe.

"I suggested a holiday after your wedding. Mother and Father will see to the children. He said he thought it was a good idea. Maybe Crete? He misses it, and it would be good to visit the villa." I let her chatter on, relieved some troubles can be mended, and that she seems to have recovered from the shock of finding Juliet's body, though she does ask about the funeral.

"The police have not released the body, and as far as I know, no one has come to claim her as their kin. The WI is going to organize the funeral, if no one else comes forward."

"Adeline called before dinner and said her mother has an obituary written already. She invited Jeffrey and me to dinner this weekend and said you and Daniel are coming, too. I am afraid I begged off. I want us to spend time as a family this weekend."

"Understandable. Not to worry, Daniel and I will be quite all right on our own. Besides, I like Adeline and am curious to get to know her husband better." We talk a while longer of this and that, easy gossip after a wearisome day. I am truly happy for my cousin to learn that her fears were unfounded. However, this is not the first time in their fairly short marriage that the two of them have been in crisis, and I doubt it will be the last. Perhaps a holiday in Greece would do them both good. I miss it, too, sometimes, the view from the villa, the rustle of olive trees beneath my balcony, the clear sky, balmy breeze and stretch of endless blue sea. I would not mind returning someday. Daniel has decided to arrange our honeymoon and is very secretive about it. Has Crete wound its alluring way into his mind? Or someplace exotic where we have never been? It will be a relief to have the wedding behind us, and for it just to be the two of us on an adventure.

Tomorrow Agnes has commanded me to a fitting for the wedding dress. The last time I saw it, it was plain muslin underlay. I wonder what Agnes has concocted with the seamstress, given full control. A mass of flounces and frills? A high collar of strangling lace? It is uncharitable, yet I hardly know what to imagine. Agnes and I have had our problems, but I am the daughter she never had, she has told me as much in her rare confessional moods. This is the only wedding she may ever plan for someone else, and I want her to be happy. The wedding itself matters not so much to me as the life which follows. It took me a long time to accept Daniel's proposal – repeated proposals, I should say, the poor fellow! Now I am eager for our relationship to be formalized, for me to have a rightful place in this house, not to feel I have to sneak about, using my flat in St. James as a pretense when I am here. Will Daniel and I weather storms as Briony and Jeffrey do? Thus far, the trials we faced have not been in our relationship but outside of it, and thus served to bond us closer together. What does the future hold for us? It will be strange not to be Evelyn Carlisle anymore, but Evelyn Harper. I will keep the agency under my maiden name, however, if for no other reason than as an homage to my parents who are gone. I was a Carlisle for more than a quarter of a century and part of me will remain so until the day I die. At the same time, I feel a tingle of excitement at the thought of sharing Daniel's name, of our children sharing it as well. We will be the Harper family. Although I have a family in Briony and Agnes and many more wonderful people already, I am excited to create one with my soon-to-be husband. The thought of motherhood frightens me, but not as much as a short while ago. The closer the wedding day nears, the more I feel ready to take a step further into the realm of adulthood. It has taken me long enough, but better wait for the right one and the right time than settle for something that is neither of the two.

The next morning, I drag myself halfway across town to West Kensington and to the exquisitely appointed bridal salon for the wedding dress fitting. Agnes wanted a local designer to make the gown, nothing French, nothing *continental*. The day is cold and gray and a fine mist dusts my windshield. Although I am early, Agnes is already here and gives me a vaguely reproving look. The studio is small, but the few furnishings and décor are of high quality. A delicate chandelier sparkles above our heads and the walls are covered in a rose colored paper, while the carpet is thick, and the sofas upholstered in the finest mauve brocade. The seamstress, Mrs. Hollyfield, greets us warmly and sends her assistant, a bright-eyed girl with corkscrew curls, to fetch Agnes tea, while she ushers me into a dressing room at the back. The seamstress is perhaps my aunt's age, though her plain dress and tight chignon make it difficult to judge. Her face is long and unlined, her eyes the color of toffee, her movements elegant, like those of a ballerina. Reluctantly, I peel out of my cozy layers, shivering a little when I stand in front of Mrs. Hollyfield in my undergarments. She does not seem to take notice, and calls in her assistant to help dress me as though I am a doll. I step into the pile of cream colored lace and let them button me in, Mrs. Hollyfield expertly stepping back every once in a while, plucking pins from a cushion on her wrist and making whatever adjustments she deems necessary. There is no mirror in the room, perhaps to add an element of surprise? I let them work, wincing when an errant pin pricks my skin. Finally, the seamstress appears satisfied, a smile touching her lips as she nods at Kate.

"That'll do. Come, let us show your aunt." She opens the dressing room door and I step onto a platform. Around me are three large mirrors. I hardly register Agnes' words of approval, for while I claimed little interest in the details of the wedding planning, my eyes have caught on my reflection.

To my surprise, the dress Agnes thought up with the seamstress is beautiful. Soft cream lace, light as a spider's web, cascades down my body, tiny pearl buttons crawl up the curve of my back and the long sleeves emphasize my arms and wrists in a most flattering way. It is modest, but elegant, with a high neck and flowing lines. I have never been a girl to fantasize about my wedding, yet if I were, I imagine I would be wearing a gown such as this one.

"What do you think?" Agnes asks, gazing up at me, expectation in her voice.

"It's perfect," I breathe, carefully running my hands over the soft lace, feeling the swish of silk underneath.

"You like it? Oh, I am glad," she says, allowing herself a smile.

Cautiously, I step down from the platform and take her hands in mine. "It is exactly what I wished for without even realizing it."

"I hoped you would think so. Your mother's dress was destroyed in the fire, and mine is outdated. I did not think you would want to wear it for the sake of tradition," Agnes explains, looking at me with an unfamiliar vulnerability in her eyes. "But I thought you might like to wear this?" She holds out a rectangular velvet case. I open it to see a slim gold necklace, a sapphire at its center flanked by two small diamonds. It matches the ring Daniel proposed with, which I wear always.

"Oh, Agnes!"

"Do you like it? Brendan gave it to me as a wedding gift all those years ago. I think he would have been very glad to see you wear it on your own wedding day."

"I am honored," I say, genuinely moved and surprised by the prick of tears in my eyes. "Will you help me put it on?" My fingers run across the delicate jewels, and I look at my reflection. I am a bride. What a strange notion!

"You look beautiful, my girl," says Agnes. The wet glimmer in my eyes is reflected in her own. We cannot help but laugh, wiping away the tears. "Brendan would have loved to have seen you on your wedding day, and James and Vera," Agnes adds, the tears flowing more freely now. "We must not be sad. It is a happy occasion." I reach out and squeeze her hand.

"We will always remember them, but I am happy to have you here, and I am grateful for all the planning you have done."

"Of course. Who else would do it?" she asks, and I smile. Who else indeed? My parents may be gone, but I am not alone. Whatever past struggles Agnes and I faced, she is as close to a mother as I have known. I realize in that moment, there is no one alive with whom I would wish to share this moment more than her.

Chapter 26

I am floating on a cloud when I reach the flat in St. James. Agnes and I had a lovely lunch after the fitting, filled with reminiscences. It served as a happy and necessary distraction from the darker matters that have occupied my mind of late.

Hugh is at his desk, but he is not alone. Hollis Napier sits across from him, legs crossed, leaning back in his chair as if he owns it. He tilts his chin and gives me one of his crooked smiles, while Hugh crosses his arms. He has never been terribly impressed with the journalist and has made no secret of the fact that he dislikes my arrangement with him.

"This is how it works when you are the boss, is it? Swanning in at two in the afternoon." He makes a tutting sound. Hugh pulls a chair up to his desk for me and I sit down, ready to listen. Hollis will not have come simply to tease me. Then again...

"Mr. Lawrence told me you already discovered Howard Bell was Frances Bell's husband. I decided to look into him a little more. Hopefully, what I gathered is news to you and I am proving my worth," Hollis says with a wink. He must have arrived mere moments before I did.

"Go on, then, tell us what you know."

"Well, he died eight months ago. A sudden death, heart attack at sixty-two. He is survived by his wife, fifty-nine, no children. They own a house in Fitzrovia, near Regent's Park, not far from Miss Nelson's, or rather Mr. Bell's flat. Frances Bell brought a considerable amount of wealth into the marriage, but both lived quite modestly. The house is nothing to boast about, I went to see it."

"Goodness, you work fast!" I cannot help but marvel.

"How do you know all of this?" Hugh asks, less willing to heap praise upon the man who evidently requires little encouragement.

"That isn't all. I have my connections. I asked around, and would you know it? The obituary for Bell ran in my paper. Frances Bell was the one who sent it in. Howard Bell was quite an enigmatic figure. His wife is an open book in comparison. Grew up in Reading – like Juliet and her family if you recall – and studied at Girton College. Apparently extremely bright, but she was relegated to secretarial work for fifteen years. During the war, she was granted a higher position and even when the men returned, it was not taken from her." Hollis glances at a notebook balanced on his lap. "She has been an archivist for the museum's Department of Antiquity for the past seven years."

"Quite an admirable rise. I must remember to ask Jeffery his opinion of her when I next meet him," I observe, unreasonably proud of Frances for having proven her capability and attained this position. My time in Oxford taught me much of what is possible for women, but also that our sex still has a far way to go, and the climb is often over much rougher terrain than for men.

"Have you found out how they knew Juliet's parents?" Hugh asks, his expression beginning to thaw a little.

"I think Frances Bell and Juliet's mother grew up together," Hollis shrugs. "Maybe Frances knew Juliet as a child before her parents died and wanted to keep an eye on the young woman."

"Certainly possible. If it was so, the theory of Howard making her his mistress sounds a little unlikely, one would hope," I observe.

"And what a titillating theory it was," Hollis says with a not altogether savory grin. I forgive him his lack of tact, for he has proven useful. Frances must have known Juliet quite a bit better than she let on. I need to talk to her again and get answers. I could ask Jeffrey about them both, since he must have seen them together, but he is so unobservant when it comes to most things except antiquities, I would not like to depend on him as a witness.

"Have you learned anything else about Miss Nelson?"

"Goodness, you are never satisfied, are you? Like a pair of bloodhounds." Hollis shakes his head. "I am afraid the twenty-four hours since you put me on the case were not sufficient time to delve into her character as well. Many pardons, Lady Evelyn." He makes a mock bow while remaining in his seat.

"Thank you for your help," I acknowledge. "Hopefully, it moves us further along. Juliet herself is an enigma. Hardly anyone knew her. So, if Frances Bell was lying and was better acquainted with her than she led me to believe, I may be able to drag some information out of her."

"However, if she wasn't lying and truly remained in the dark about her husband's connection to Juliet, we have to wonder why that could be."

"As I said, Howard Bell was a mystery as well." Hollis raises his brows. "While an affair may not be the most likely answer, could they not have worked together in some other capacity?"

Hugh and I throw each other a quick glance. The money in the box. Is it the result of some illicit deal between Bell and Juliet? Hollis, shrewd and quick as a cat, does not miss our unspoken interaction.

"What are you keeping from me? I gave you what I had, you ought to repay the service."

"You have my promise that the story will be yours as soon as we solve the case, Hollis. For now -"

"For now, you are keeping your aces close to your chest? I thought better of you, Lady Evelyn," Hollis says with mock reproof. He understood our bargain from the start and cannot argue the merit of its details now.

"My apologies, but you can trust us. If we solve the crime, the story is yours. I assume you will handle it with tact?"

Hollis gets to his feet and tucks his notebook into an inner jacket pocket. "You assume correctly. Whatever you two think of me, I am a serious reporter." He gives me a hurt frown.

"We think of you as such, you can be sure," I reply, though Hugh remains silent.

"Then I shall be on my way. I have other work, besides running my poor little feet ragged on your account. Ta-ta!" With that, he turns on his heel and before long, we hear the front door close.

Hugh sighs, and I chuckle. "Oh, come now, he is not so bad. And he has been helpful!"

"I don't like working with someone who thinks tragedy is a story."

"Better a story than forgotten entirely, do you not agree?"

"Grudgingly, take note of that." He stretches out his arms, his fingers cracking. "How was your wedding dress fitting?"

"Lovely. Agnes chose well. Sorry for coming in so late."

Hugh makes a dismissive gesture. "Daniel asked me to be his best man, did you know that?"

"I knew he planned to. Have you accepted?"

"How could I not? I was surprised, though," Hugh says, a smile tugging at the corners of his mouth.

"You are his best friend, I expected nothing less."

"This case has made me think a lot," Hugh says slowly, not quite meeting my eye. "Juliet lived almost as a ghost, just like I did for so long before you two met me. If I had died or been killed, no one would remember me. No one would have noticed. The world would spin on as it always does."

"You shouldn't think such things, Hugh. You are not alone, that is what matters."

"Yes, well, I was lucky."

"We were lucky, too. Now, stop being morose and tell me, could the money have come from some business Juliet was running with Howard, something illicit?"

"Definitely a possibility. We must learn more about them. If we know more about Juliet's past, we have a far greater chance of discovering why anyone would have wished her dead."

"I am going to visit Frances again. Do I confront her with our knowledge or go about it in a more subtle manner?" I frown, contemplating the advantages of either approach. If I barge in and throw my questions at her, I risk alienating the woman. But it would also give me the chance to gauge her reaction. If she shows surprise, shock even, might I believe she truly knew so little of Juliet? Or will she simply refuse to speak about it? I have no authority to make her talk, and even the police have no reason to suspect her.

"There is more to be gained by confronting her. You don't suspect she killed Juliet, do you?"

"I cannot be certain. It would not take a very strong person, given Juliet's slight build, and Frances is a tall woman."

"Be careful. Maybe I should come along."

"I will ask her to meet me in a café. We will be in public, and I am not afraid of her." The latter statement is, perhaps, not entirely true. Though so far, I have no reason to consider her a danger. Frances seemed genuinely shocked to hear of Juliet's death. Why would she draw attention to herself, if she had something to hide? But then, people are strange...

Hugh has made it his mission to get his hands on the coroner's report, and I am all too glad to leave this morbid task to him. I suppose we could call Stanton and see what he is willing to share, yet we parted badly yesterday. I am not quite willing to make the first move. Perhaps Hugh can do so in my stead?

He goes off on his quest, and I decide to have a quick cup of tea before venturing into the cold once more. My hope to find Maeve in the kitchen is met with success. Aidan is sitting on a chair, propped up by a stack of cushions, stuffing small cubes of cheese into his mouth. Maeve has her back to me and is humming quietly, falling silent when she notices my presence.

"Could you make me a cup of tea, Maeve? I am going out again in a bit and need something hot before I venture into the cold. Is Kathleen out?" I step into the kitchen and brush a hand over Aidan's soft hair. He gives me a shy smile, holding out a piece of cheese, which I decline. The offering hand glistens with saliva and fond though I am of the little boy, that would be taking it a step too far.

"She went to Aidan's grave," Maeve says in a low voice, though I doubt her son, named after his late father, could understand.

"Does she go often?"

"At least once a week."

"And you?"

Maeve sighs and shrugs. "I go occasionally, but sometimes it feels like I only knew him in a dream. It was such a short time and so long ago. I...I don't know. He was Aidan's father, even if they can never meet. I will think of him fondly always. All the same, it doesn't help to look back too much, wondering what might have been." *Like Kathleen does,* are her unspoken words. Maeve is usually quiet like her son, yet once in a while, when drawn out of her reserve, she shares the odd morsel of profundity that belies her youth.

"It's good to look to the future. You are so young, after all. But he was Kathleen's son. The past will never release her, I suspect."

"She says Aidan looks like his pa. I think he looks like me," Maeve says with a smile, pouring hot water into a cup, glancing over her shoulder at her son, who is staring with some concentration at his diminishing plate of cheese. He really does look like his mother. The milky white skin, the flame-colored hair. Their eyes are different, though, and I suspect Kathleen sees her lost boy every time she looks into them.

"Perhaps it is none of my concern, but do you know people your own age? I don't want you to think you must stay in every day." The flat is always spotless, despite the tiny child residing here. Maeve never shirks her duties. She has a day off, but she spends it exclusively with Kathleen and Aidan. Maybe she would like to go out, explore a little, or be on her own for a few hours.

"I have met a few other maids," she says dismissively, as if vague acquaintances are enough for a young woman who ought to be giggling and gossiping with her friends.

"I have joined the WI with my aunt and cousin. You are welcome to come along some day, if you like."

"That is kind, but I doubt I would fit in very well, a single mother, and a maid at that."

"It is nothing like that, don't worry. I had my prejudices, too, but they have proven unfounded."

"Didn't the woman you met there get killed?" she asks, lowering her voice on the final word, her eyes wide as she sets my tea in front of me – a drop of milk, a lump of sugar, just as I like it.

"Well, yes, that is true," I admit. "Though I do not have reason to believe her membership in the WI is connected to her death."

"Maybe she met someone there who wished her ill. If she had been living peacefully until she joined, I would suspect the WI first."

"Possibly," I muse, taking a sip. I do not mention that I, too, entertained the notion of Edith, Adeline or Priscilla bearing blame, yet I discounted them after our conversations. Now, though, Maeve has reawakened a sense of doubt in me. I am curious to see Adeline again, and hopefully create a better picture of her. Maybe Daniel will notice something I do not. Perhaps she will behave differently in the presence of her husband.

I finish my tea, chatting about the miserable weather, answering Maeve's questions about my wedding dress. I am surprised that Aidan follows me to the door when I leave, waving shyly with a small, pink hand before toddling back into the flat. I have grown fond of him and of Maeve, and even Kathleen is pleasant to have around. As I descend the stairs, reminded of Dulcie and Mr. Singh in the flat above, I think of how much my life has changed in the past few years. I may have fallen out of touch with some of my society friends, ladies with whom I drank tea, discussed the latest fashions and marital prospects, but I have gained so much in their stead. Stepping into the haze and mist of the November afternoon, I cannot but smile.

Chapter 27

I wait until five, sitting in my car across the main entrance of the British Museum. Hopefully Frances does not use a side door, or put in late hours. My plan is to catch her when she is leaving and convince her to have a cup of tea with me. An imperfect plan, yes, but I do not want to ambush her in her place of work. While I know her home address, it is far too intrusive to arrive at her door. It is nearly dark by now. Fortunately, the street in front of the museum is well lit with a number of streetlamps and Frances Bell is a tall woman with a broad-shouldered build. I feel certain I would recognize her easily. I admire her, achieving what she has, attending Girton and working and waiting patiently until she had her chance. It must be difficult to go on alone after one has been married for so long. Is she as lonely as Juliet was? Or am I misjudging them both? Clearly, Juliet had a life before we met, if only I could learn more about it. What did she do in those years between the death of her parents and her return to London? Were the Bells in touch with her? Did she seek them out? Did they have something to do with the money in her hidden box? Then there is the question of the young man in the photograph and the medals. I wonder whether they could be traced, whether they bear a number that signifies to whom they were given? A catalogue number with the recipient's name in some office of records? Harold has connections to the War Office from his time in the military. I will ask him what he thinks.

My thought is interrupted when I spy the tall figure of Frances Bell descending the stairs of the museum. I step out of the car and hurry across the street towards her. I can tell she has noticed me even from a distance. She stiffens, her features tense. Evidently, my visit is not particularly welcome.

"Mrs. Bell," I say, offering a smile. "Do forgive me for disturbing you. I hoped to find you here."

"I told you to call me Frances. How may I help you? It has something to do with Juliet, no doubt?" If she does not sound excited, she at least sounds resigned to talk.

"Indeed. Do you have a few minutes for a cup of tea?"

She hesitates, then nods, no doubt finding it is preferable to standing in the damp cold. Perhaps she has an empty house to return to and does not truly mind a delay in getting there.

We find a small tearoom, almost empty, save for two men arguing quietly at a table in the corner. One wears a deep frown, while the other scowls, his face rivaling the color of a ripe tomato.

"When is the funeral?" asks Frances, her hands cupping a steaming mug.

"I don't know. Soon, I expect. Will you attend?"

"Of course." Frances meets my gaze. "Forgive me for being frank, but what do you want from me?"

"I welcome your candor and hope you do not mind if I speak openly as well." A nod. I continue. "I think there is more you can tell me about Juliet to shed light on who she was and, maybe, who could have wished her harm."

"What gives you that idea? Do you suspect me?" Her tone has sharpened, her eyes remain fixed on mine. It takes some discipline not to squirm under her stern look.

"I suspect everyone unless they give me reason not to," I say, mirroring her manner. "But I would rather eliminate your name."

"How very good of you!" she exclaims, voice thick with unambiguous sarcasm.

"Please, we have started on the wrong foot. Let me explain myself," I say.

"I wish you would." And so I do.

"Did you know the flat Juliet lived in belongs to you?" Her expression tells me she was not expecting this.

"What do you mean, it belongs to me? Juliet's flat?"

"Or rather it belonged to your husband, Howard Bell."

"You are mistaken."

"I am afraid not." I watch her carefully. Unless she is a brilliant actress, she truly is unaware of her husband's holdings, let alone Juliet's connection to them.

"But why was she living there? Why did Howard...I don't understand." Suddenly, I feel very sorry for her, for forcing her to confront this news about her husband when she is still mourning him. I don't want to paint him a liar in her eyes when he can no longer defend himself. Nonetheless, fact is fact, and Howard Bell owned that flat.

"You said you knew Juliet's family, did you grow up together?"

"You have been reading up on me," she notes, though the sharpness has faded from her voice.

"I am doing what I have been hired to do."

"Yes," she says slowly, "I knew them both, but mostly Juliet's mother, Margot. We went to the same school. I was older. We weren't friends then. She was beautiful, born in France, everyone loved her. I was tall and quiet, clumsy, never touched by her light, though she was kind enough, not one of those beauties who thinks cruelty will make her even more desirable. She spoke fluent French because her mother came from Lille and Juliet learned, too. It always made Margot seem a little exotic. I think she only traveled to the continent once in all the time I knew her. It was only when we were older, when she was married, and I came home from university during the holidays that we became friendly. I liked Margot well enough and her husband, John, too. I held Juliet when she was born, and I went to their funeral. By then I was married to Howard. He came with me." Frances sighs. "Juliet was shattered by their loss. They had been very close. I hardly knew her as she grew up. I lived in London, so we drifted apart. This was before everyone had a telephone in their house, and we only wrote the occasional letters."

"What happened to Juliet? Did Howard meet her?"

"Well, yes, but we weren't close enough that he would rent out a secret flat to her. I cannot believe it. She always told me it had belonged to her parents. This surprised me, I admit. Margot and John were comfortable, but not wealthy by any means. Keeping a flat in London would not have been cheap, even then."

"You must be getting rental income from it."

"Truth be told, after Howard died, I couldn't be bothered with all the legalities surrounding his estate. I tried to keep going as I had before, which was difficult enough. Maybe there is a rental income. If so, it does not go into our shared account and the solicitor made no special mention of it. Then again, I may not have been paying much attention, to tell you the truth."

"Do you know where Juliet went after her parents died? You said she moved around, but do you have any details? Did you keep in touch? Was it she who sought you out in London?"

"You have a lot of questions," Frances observes, but I detect a hint of a smile.

"I may have been accused of being too curious before, though I daresay it was called something less flattering."

"There is nothing wrong with curiosity. I am the same. I think my parents thought sending me to university – not at all the done thing at the time – would calm my mind, instead it served to do just the opposite. I wanted to learn everything I could, and I still do."

"Then you understand my motivation," I observe, wishing once more for this dignified, interesting woman to be innocent. What a waste it would be of her intellect and hard work to make a murderer of herself!

"I admit I do. You might have to soften your means for satisfying that curiosity, though," she says, yet the chastisement is tempered by a gentle tone. "To answer your question, we sporadically exchanged letters. When the war started, the letters stopped coming and I was busy with my new role as archivist. I did not take notice."

"You never saw her?"

"She came to London a few times and had dinner with Howard and me. Juliet didn't like the city much."

"And your husband? Did he keep in touch with her?"

"He had no reason to. They hardly knew one another…or so I thought."

"Perhaps he wanted to help her find a footing when she came to the city, and she did not wish to trouble you. Was she a proud woman?" An image of the quiet person I met those few times materializes in my mind. She seemed reserved, but Priscilla may not have been wrong in considering her proud, too. Secretive seems the most apt word to describe her.

"Maybe he did. I can think of no other reason I would wish to contemplate." So her mind has leapt to the possibility that Juliet was Howard's mistress as well. I grimace, sorry to have conjured these thoughts in her mind. Yet I believe Frances is not the sort to run from her troubles, the sort who prefers not to know.

"I spoke to the caretaker of the building, a Mr. Button, and he says he only saw your husband a few times and not while Juliet lived there. It appears unlikely that she was anything more to him than a young woman in need of help."

"I will take your word for it. Howard was a complicated man, but I always trusted in his devotion to me and to our marriage."

"Then I am certain he was. I did not know him, you did. Do not let this spoil your memory." We sit in silence for a few moments, the tea before us growing cold. The two other men have left, and we are alone, save for a bored looking server hunched over a paper in the corner.

"I didn't kill Juliet, you know," Frances whispers. I sit up straight, taken aback by her directness. Is she telling the truth? There is a weariness in her features I had not noticed before. Tired eyes, pale skin used to days spend indoors, bent over ancient texts and catalogues. She appeared so surprised when I told her of her husband's connection to Juliet. If she truly did not suspect an affair or another duplicitous plot, what reason would she have for harming Juliet? I suspected she could have even gone as far as killing her own husband in a rage, discovering he had taken a lover, but now I know he died naturally, if suddenly.

"Do you have any notion who could have wished her dead?" I ask, not quite acknowledging her claim of innocence.

"None. I would gladly tell you or the police if I did. I also want to know who killed her, and frankly, now that you told me about it, how she and Howard were connected. If he wanted to help her, he knew I would not oppose him. Why the secrecy?" She shakes her head.

"You must miss him," I say.

"Every day."

"What did he do?"

"He worked in the government. The War Office. Nothing high up, by any means, though. He often complained about dull administrative tasks, but he liked it, really. He did not have to stay in employment he loathed. The house was bought with my money. I do not know how he came by the flat unless he was lying to me about his income." She shrugs, takes a sip of the cold tea, grimaces and sets the cup down again. "I think I would like to go home now." Not waiting for my reply, she scrapes back her chair and gets to her feet. I drop some coins on the table and join her. Outside, I offer her my hand. She hesitates, but takes it before turning away. I watch her, clad in a long dark coat, posture straight and proud, as she walks along the street and disappears around a corner. Taking a deep breath of the frosty evening air, I cast one last look at the illuminated museum across the street and turn away, myself to go home after a long day.

Chapter 28

The streets are busy with people climbing into and out of buses, and it takes me an unusually long time to arrive at home. Time to think of everything Frances told me. I believe her. I am convinced that she did not kill Juliet, that she did not know her husband kept the flat and his connection to the young woman a secret. I wonder how she is feeling now. Does she think he betrayed her? Depending on the marriage they shared, she likely does. Lies are a betrayal, even if they do not conceal infidelity. If I learned that Daniel had done the same, I would be terribly disappointed.

When I finally arrive in Grosvenor Square, I am exhausted and hungry, happy to allow Wilkins to take my hat and coat and glad for the scent of cooking lingering in the air. He offers to fetch me a hot toddy to warm me up, which I decline. I have had altogether too many hot beverages for my liking today.

"Is Daniel home?" I ask

"In his study." Wilkins offers me a strained smile. There is something in his manner to give me pause, a crease between his brows, a new hollowness to his cheeks.

"Is everything all right?" I ask, for we have gone far beyond the usual relationship between butler and employer. Only a few months ago Daniel, Hugh and I had to save Wilkins from prison, when he was wrongfully accused of nothing less than murder! The investigation brought us closer, even if it also illuminated things about him that gave us pause. Daniel was more disappointed than he likes to admit.

"Yes..." he replies slowly, emotions clearly warring within him. "No."

"No?" I ask, wishing he would just come out with it.

"I think I am being followed." I remember Daniel said me as much a while ago and then I forgot, distracted by the murder.

"Do you suspect anyone?"

"At first, I believed it was someone from my past, but why now?"

"Would it be wise to contact the police?"

Wilkins instantly shakes his head. "No, no. I have had quite enough of the police in recent times." He manages a smile. "Maybe I am overly suspicious."

"Be careful," I say, reaching out to touch his arm. He nods and leaves me to find out when dinner will be served. I wander down the hallway to Daniel's study. It is a small room, which he chose because it faces the garden and a tall French window opens onto the terrace. Not that this is particularly useful on blustery November evenings, but he likes the sense of openness it affords. After the war, after his years of travel, of trying to escape, he still fears feeling closed in by his surroundings, though he does not like to speak of it. Still, he hardly ever ventures to his grand old family estate in the country. Too many memories can be a cage as well.

Knocking lightly, I do not wait for an answer, a habit he should probably get used to earlier rather than later, since we are soon to be wed. I find him seated behind his desk amid a scattering of papers and two cups of half-drunk tea, milk curdling on the surface. Daniel's sleeves are rolled up to his elbows, and he has a spot of ink on his cheek.

"What are you doing?" I am slightly bemused to find him so.

"Trying to understand whether we can save the shipyard. Long and short, we cannot." His shoulders sag. I move around the desk and wrap my arms around him.

"It isn't your fault, Daniel."

"It is, because it's my company. Well, mine and Dom's. The responsibility rests on our shoulders. He wants to make the announcement in the next few weeks. I am trying to convince him to hold out until after Christmas. Or is that crueler?"

"No. Let the workers have a few more weeks of peace and a celebration with their families."

"Before we pull the rug from under their feet."

"Will closing the yard help the company?"

"Undoubtedly. Dominic wants to go into commercial liners, branch out from transport vessels. Sometimes I think I should never have gone back to the business, rather started something new, or gone into politics like Harold. I admire him, I really do."

"You still can. You are a young man, Daniel. Harold might be the source of even more frustration for you, if he is elected. He plans on proposing some sort of penalty on companies who close mills and yards and let workers go without compensation."

"He is right to do it," Daniel observes. "I feel terrible, but the way I see it, we either close the yard and save a greater number of jobs by keeping the company afloat or we keep it and risk losing everything." He rubs his eyes and leans back in the chair.

"Our wedding is fast approaching," I say, smiling as I crouch on the corner of his desk. "That should create some diversion."

A DEADLY LEGACY

"Is it cowardly that I can hardly wait for us to go on our honeymoon afterwards, to get away for a while?"

"I thought much the same earlier."

"You tried on your dress today, didn't you?" he asks, smiling. I am glad to provide some distraction when I tell him of the day, not offering the slightest detail of the dress, however. I must draw the line somewhere, and now that I know what Agnes has chosen, I am strangely excited to see the rest of her arrangements.

Throughout dinner, we try to distract each other from the respective hurdles in our professional lives and instead discuss the wedding, Briony and Jeffrey, Harold's ambitions and finally, Wilkins' strange suspicion that he is being followed. Spooning the last of the pear crumble into my mouth, I lean back in. "He must be quite apprehensive to talk to me about it," I note in a low tone, though the door is closed and no one else about. At times, even living with trusted servants, one feels observed.

"I think he is trying to be transparent after everything that happened. Maybe we should ask Hugh to look into it? He has always been good at trailing people."

"A slightly dubious talent, but I cannot argue."

"Have you given any thought to our little bet?" Daniel grins.

"I have been rather occupied recently, what with murder and mayhem and the like. Still, I had a little think on the matter."

"Any conclusions?"

"Not quite. I am choosing carefully. I intend to win our bet!"

"Poor Hugh, with us as matchmakers plotting behind his back."

"I suspect he is a little lonely. He said he is grateful to have us, comparing himself to Juliet. Maybe he would rather like a family of his own? He hasn't had one since he was a boy. And from what he has told us, his father never cared for him." We fall silent, and I swirl the last of the port in the bottom of my glass. It is a strange world we live in, where fathers abandon sons, where mothers like Dulcie and Kathleen lose theirs too soon, where children grieve parents they never knew, and where war and murder and all manner of cruelty crack the fragile peace we strive to maintain. Yet there is good, too, so much good which never finds mention in the pages of newspapers, the gossip of the parlor rooms. Kindness, honesty and love may not quite restore the balance completely, but remain the greatest foe of misery and regret. I think it is the best we can hope for, in this flawed and fascinating world of ours.

Chapter 29

Near two in the morning, after tossing about in tangled sheets for the past three hours, I give up and quietly slip out of bed. The house is dark and feels hollow somehow, as I make my way down the stairs, past silent room after silent room to the library. Once arrived, I close the door and turn on the electric light. The object I seek rests where I left it, on a table beside my favorite armchair. Juliet's box.

Carefully, I lift the lid and take out the medals. Daniel put the wad of money into a locked drawer, but these he left where they were. I sink into the chair and turn them in my hands. The cross is less tarnished than the other, attached to a crimson ribbon. I run my finger over the front, the crown and lion. It is made of bronze, cold and heavy in my hand. When I squint, I can read the inscription, "For Valour". The other, the more common British War Medal is round, the ribbon slightly frayed along one side, with the dates of the war 1914-1918 and an image of St. George on horseback on one side, and King George V on the front. The bronze is a dull disc, but as I turn it front to back, running a finger along the edges, I feel an unevenness and, holding it up to the light, see something imprinted upon the bottom edge. There are tiny letters that have been scratched, almost as if intentionally rubbed away on a rock, but I can tell they were there. Taking out a magnifying glass, and feeling a proper sleuth, I can make out an S followed by an O or a D and an N or M at the end. I do not need to write the letters down to conclude the name Nelson was once imprinted upon this medal. Nelson. There follow a series of numbers, but they, too, are marred and mostly illegible. No letters telling of a rank remain visible, if they were ever present. Who scraped away the name? Was it Juliet? Was this her medal, or did it belong to her father? Or perhaps another relation we know nothing about? It could not be a husband, for he would not have shared Juliet's maiden name.

What does it all mean? I want to wake Daniel and ask him what he thinks, but decide to be reasonable. The questions will keep. Nonetheless, I take out a sheet of paper and write them down. I realize, in the back of my mind, that I will have to turn the box and its contents over to Stanton at some point in the very near future, but the police had their chance to conduct a thorough search. It is not my fault I have a clever chap such as Hugh for a partner. Then again, I think, tapping the pencil against my bottom lip, I do not wish to alienate the police,

Stanton in particular, by being seen to obstruct their investigation. I want us to work together, even if, at the moment, I feel frustrated with the detective. Yet Briony has come through the ordeal the better for it, and so I suppose I have no reason for irritation towards Stanton. Tomorrow I will contact him, tell him I have something the police might find interesting. If I show myself willing to cooperate, maybe he will be, too. We would certainly have an easier task of learning of the coroner's findings if we ask Stanton outright, rather than Hugh sneaking about. Sometimes I have to remind myself that I wanted to be a detective to bring about resolution, to help the survivors find some small measure of peace, not to compete in a battle of wits and efficacy with the police.

I turn the medals over again, discovering nothing else and gently replace them in the box. There is something at the back of my mind as I tip-toe up the stairs and slip into bed, but it is out of reach. Even as I try to grasp it, I drift away into the realm of sleep.

In the morning, Daniel can distinguish no more of use on the medals than I could, though he agrees that the name must be Nelson. While we cannot be certain who that Nelson is just yet, I am convinced this small discovery has brought us closer to knowing more about Juliet.

Daniel trudges off to the office, while I finish my tea and read the morning paper. Hollis has written an article chronicling the death by freezing of more and more homeless people in the streets this winter. I push away the remains of my breakfast, my appetite dissolving, as I picture those poor souls huddled into doorways. I must mention it at the next meeting of the WI, though I would not be surprised if the women are already well aware of the problem. This thought leads me to Edith and Adeline. They said a memorial was being planned for Juliet, even suggested the WI would organize her funeral, if no one else stepped forward. I don't suppose Frances wishes to take responsibility.

I should telephone Edith and ask her whether any arrangements have been made. The police will likely release the body soon. Though I am reluctant to do so, I must also contact Stanton about our findings. However, I want Hugh to have a chance to inspect the medals before we are forced to hand them over. Despite my reluctance, I drag myself into the study and call the police station. It takes several minutes until I am finally connected to Stanton, and I almost decide to give up, when his voice rings down the line.

"Lucas, it's me, Evelyn. There is something I need to discuss with you. Do you have an hour or so this afternoon?"

"Does it concern Miss Nelson?" he asks, his wariness patently evident.

"I may have discovered something," is all I say.

"Can't you tell me now?" His words are impatient, even if his tone is not.

"Not exactly. There is something you need to see."

"Must you be quite so cryptic?"

"I am afraid I must. Bring some good news for me. What I am offering is worth something significant in return."

"Are you trying to barter facts about a murder investigation with me?"

"You know me so well!" Quickly, before he has a chance to argue, I add, "Around three? Perfect. See you then!" I end the call, even as I hear him trying to speak. Oh, well, so he is a little riled. He will come. Stanton may be many things, but immune to curiosity he is not.

Hugh and I arrive at the flat in St. James at the same time. I send him ahead, hurrying upstairs to ask after Dulcie. I mustn't let time slip by again without keeping a closer eye on her. Mr. Singh looks tired, yet he tells me that Dulcie, though resting, is better. She is buoyed, he continues with disapproval, by the prospect of the séance which shall take place Monday of next week on account of a full moon, whatever that means. Perhaps the medium is a werewolf? I promise to be there. Mr. Singh insists with a firm shake of the head that he will not participate. I wonder whether his disdain comes from a belief like Daniel's that it is an utterly farcical undertaking, or whether his religion forbids any involvement in contacting the dead. I have never asked him much about Sikhism, perhaps I should. Religion always strikes me as a complicated subject of conversation, particularly between a believer and a non-believer. Yet if ever there was a patient soul, it is Mr. Singh, so I do not doubt he would be willing, even happy, to humor my curious mind.

Hugh's eagerness to set off again is plain when I enter the office. He is still wearing his coat, hat tucked under his arm and with a plan to get his hands on the coroner's report. Having made the acquaintance of one of the coroner's assistants, an ale enthusiast, apparently, Hugh believes the man would easily let the details slip if he knows any. He is not altogether pleased when I tell him Stanton may be persuaded to trade the information in exchange for the medals.

"I don't entirely like handing the box to the police," Hugh says, finally shrugging off his coat.

"Nor do I, but we must work together. In the end, we want justice for Juliet, or whatever comes close to it, not the glory of beating the police to the chase."

"Well…"

"Oh, all right, it would be a triumph to solve the case first, and we may still do so. Forget about that for a moment. I made a discovery." I beckon him to my desk and pull the box from my satchel, placing it gently on the table. Taking out the medals I show Hugh the tiny etching on the bottom edge.

He touches his forehead. "How could we have missed this!"

"It is almost illegible," I soothe.

"Still, I should have looked more closely, not that I've held any war medals in my hands before. I wasn't that sort of soldier." He does not sound remotely perturbed by this.

"It spells Nelson, doesn't it?"

"Hard to say with complete certainty. It would be the only logical name, though, wouldn't it?" Hugh holds the medal up again, examining it with one eye closed. "Nothing on the other medal?"

"No, though I gather it is very rare."

"Awarded for acts of great valor."

"The question remains, was Juliet herself the recipient, or someone she knew? The man in the picture? A relative?"

"All are possibilities. I wish the service number were not so damaged, then we might have a chance of looking it up in the records."

"Maybe Stanton has another way to trace it?"

"I want to make an imprint of the medals. I am going to get some clay, so we can have a copy and show it to Harold. He might know more."

"An excellent idea," I say, pleased with my partner's quick thinking. "When is Stanton coming?"

"Not for hours." Sinking into my chair, I wonder what to do in the interim, when I remember my conversation with Daniel. "Hugh, do you think you could keep an eye on Wilkins? He suspects he is being followed, sounded rather spooked in fact. He is worried someone from his past is after him."

"I don't know." Hugh looks down.

"What do you mean?"

"He is probably fearful for no reason."

"I think he is genuinely troubled. He would hardly have told me of his concerns were he not. And now Maisie is living with us. I believe he fears for her as well."

"No one would hurt Maisie," Hugh asserts, still not meeting my gaze and a very strange thought comes to me.

"Hugh?"

"Yes?"

"Have you been following Wilkins?" A moment of hesitation gives me the answer. "Goodness, whatever possessed you?" I ask, mystified by his actions.

"I want to make certain he is not lying again, not sneaking about behind Daniel's back! It was mad of him to take that man back into his employ, into his home! I mean, Maisie is lovely, she deserves all the help you give her, but Wilkins is a proven liar!" It all erupts from Hugh in a torrent of words. I sense he has been holding on to his frustration for months. Hugh is very protective of Daniel. He was a close friend of Henry, Daniel's eldest brother who died in the war, and I suspect he has, intentionally or not, taken on the role of a guardian. All the same, stalking Wilkins simply will not do and I say as much.

"Daniel is too loyal for his own good," Hugh announces, though without the righteous force of his previous outburst. "It will get him into trouble one day. I understand Wilkins' treachery was not ill-intentioned, but he lied and betrayed Daniel nonetheless."

"And yet Daniel forgave him. If he can do that, you must accept it. I agree, it is not easy to forget what happened, but Wilkins was desperate when he stole from us and lied about his past. He never intended to cause any harm. Then there is Maisie to consider."

"Yes, well, I haven't done anything, only kept an eye on him occasionally."

"And now you must stop. You cannot go frightening people." The words that remain unspoken have a greater impact than those I say. When we met Hugh, he was in a bad state, bent on vengeance, stalking and threatening a man he deemed a killer – a suspicion which was, to his credit, proven true. But he is beyond that now, or so I hope. I am careful not to call his actions mad, a word that, even if spoken half in jest, would cut him deeply. It is not so much for Wilkins' sake as Hugh's that I am so insistent that he must cease his pursuit. He is too good a man to fall into such a trap once more, even if I initially shared some of his suspicions towards Wilkins.

"I'll stop."

"Then we need never speak of it again." Hugh nods. He leaves soon after. I feel for him and appreciate his loyalty, but over the past few months, I have come to sympathize with Wilkins, too, and thus Hugh's behavior cannot be tolerated.

While Hugh is out to find clay so we can make imprints of the medals, I busy myself with another case, concerning a missing Pomeranian in Green Park. It is a tedious task, trudging through the park, calling out "Fluffy" every few minutes, my pockets full of treats for the naughty fellow. He is located just as my fingers go numb, and I return him to his grateful "Mama", as she calls herself. It was tempting to reject the case when it came in this morning, but I have to remember this and the like are the agency's bread and butter at the moment. We are still establishing ourselves, even if Juliet's murder is constantly at the forefront of my mind.

By the time I return to the flat I am half-frozen, and welcome the steaming toddy Maeve presses upon me after she helps me peel off my winter layers.

"You'll catch your death out there today," Kathleen observes, wiping Aidan's nose. "We're staying well indoors, isn't that right, Aidan?" The boy's big eyes move between the three of us, and he clings to his grandmother's leg. It must be a comfort, at least a small one, to have a part of her lost son nearby. If only Dulcie had the same, if only she had someone who knew and loved her son as she did, with whom to share memories, who could remind her of the happy times, not only of her loss. Mr. Singh tries his best, yet it is not the same. Perhaps Kathleen and Dulcie could be friends. I do not think they have ever met. Kathleen is only in her mid-forties, though grief, loss and many years of hard life have aged her prematurely. She is a widow, a childless mother. Still, the bright light that is her grandson enlivens her expression with frequent smiles nowadays. A thought comes to me, but I dismiss it as silly. Kathleen is a devoted Catholic, surely, she would not be interested in joining Dulcie's séance? Remembering what Maeve told me of the older woman spending much of her time visiting her son's grave, I nonetheless decide to put the idea to her when I catch her on her own. In Maeve's company, Kathleen may be unable to agree to something generally viewed through a lens of suspicion.

"Is Mr. Lawrence back?" I ask, slowly feeling warmth returning to my fingers and toes.

"He was in shortly after you left, but then he went out again. He said he would be back by the time Mr. Stanton arrives. Would you like a square of gingerbread? I made it fresh."

"You spoil me. Thank you, Maeve."

"Best you have some now. This young man has been eating it and will be spoiling his appetite before dinner," Kathleen says, giving Aidan's hair a playful ruffle, though her words seem a reprimand directed at the young lad's mother. I hope there is no discord brewing between the women on the subject of raising Aidan. He seems unaffected, sticking a thumb in his mouth and watching me with big blue-green eyes. I smile at him and he smiles back, before hiding again behind his grandmother's skirt. I might pity him, for he will never know his father, but he is loved fiercely by these two women, and that is more than many can say.

Having finished my gingerbread and written down the bare details of the case of the errant Pomeranian, I wander to the window, peering out at the white sky above the rooftops of St. James. Cold emanates from the window, and as I lean closer my breath leaves a cloud of condensation on the glass. I trail my finger through the haze before it fades away. I used to hate winter as a child, being trapped indoors, more rain than snow, no pony rides or running about with the dogs. When we stayed in town, my nanny and Agnes rarely had the desire or patience to trek out of doors with me. I would keep a close watch on the gardens, eyes keen for the delicate heads of the crocuses and snowdrops breaking through the earth, for the bright blossom of magnolia, beckoning the arrival of spring. Even now winter is not my favorite season, but for different reasons; slippery pavements and slick roads, a chill caught every time I leave the house. All the same, I cannot deny the change in seasons has something of a cleansing effect, a preparation for something fresh as the old year draws to a close and the new year with all its possibilities is on the horizon. Next year I will be a married woman, a wife, Evelyn Carlisle no more. What awaits me and us in the months to come? Unbidden, a vision of Juliet enters my mind, not of her as a corpse, but of the quiet woman I first met. 1927 was her final year on this earth. Whatever comes next in the world will be as nothing to her and to so many others. I shiver and pull my shawl closer. Endings and new beginnings. It is as it always was, even if this truth is rather bittersweet.

The sound of the front door opening draws me from my musings. It must be Hugh, for were it Stanton, I would have heard a knock and Maeve's hurried steps. Indeed, a moment later Hugh steps into the office. He shivers and rubs his hands together, setting his hat on his desk, but keeping on his coat.

"Biting, isn't it? I spent the past few hours hunting down a missing pup, but at least it ended well. The dog, sweet Fluffy, has been returned to his Mama."

"You should have waited for me, I would have helped," he says, frowning, not meeting my gaze. He thinks I am angry with him. He is always shifty when he believes others are judging him.

"It worked out well enough. Feeling is finally returning to my extremities. You made the impressions of the medals?" I gesture at the clay drying on his desk. "We ought to put that out of sight when Stanton comes."

"If I had known there was a new case -"

"Do not waste a thought on it. I got some fresh air, and on my return was fussed over with freshly baked gingerbread."

"So, your suffering was tempered." Hugh allows himself a smile.

"Quite. I am sure Maeve will make you up a plate."

"In a bit, maybe." Hugh takes a breath as though he wishes to say more, but stops himself.

"Come now, Hugh, are we not beyond that? Tell me what you are thinking. Out with it!"

"You know me too well, Evelyn."

"I am a detective. For me there is no such thing as knowing someone too well."

"I went to Grosvenor Square."

"Hugh -"

"Do not worry. I spoke to Wilkins, didn't stalk his shadows this time."

"Oh?"

"I told him it was me." He raises his gaze to meet mine. I wait for him to continue. "I can't say he was pleased, but there might have been some relief, realizing it wasn't one of his old friends – or rather foes."

"It was decent of you to go, brave." I smile, pushing aside any doubts I fostered since this morning's revelation. "You are a good man, Hugh Lawrence."

"Maybe not good, but I don't want to be bad." He swallows, glances at his shoes. "I'll go see about that piece of cake, then."

Chapter 30

Whether to illustrate his authority or purely by chance, Stanton makes us wait. He only arrives when Hugh and I have almost given up on him, well over an hour after I had asked him here.

"Finally!" I announce, when Maeve leads him into the office. She has taken his hat and coat. The suit beneath is creased, as is his forehead, for that matter.

"I am working on other cases, I'll have you know," he says, sinking into the chair opposite me, while Hugh pulls his closer. "Some are deemed far more pressing than Miss Nelson's murder, it pains me to admit."

"Anything interesting?"

"None of your concern, Evelyn," he says sternly. "Now why did you order me here in the middle of a workday? I gather you have something important to share?"

"That depends on what you have to offer us."

"How many times? That is not how this relationship works!"

"What Evelyn is trying to say," Hugh interjects, as if handling two squabbling children, "is that we have found something rather interesting the police evidently overlooked. While we are honor-bound to inform you of our findings, we hope for some degree of reciprocity."

"Thank you, Mr. Lawrence." Stanton grins and raises his brows at me. "At least one of you has some manners, *Lady* Evelyn."

"Fine." I pull open a drawer and set the box on the desk. "This belonged to Juliet Nelson."

Stanton sighs, carefully opening the lid, as though expecting a rattle snake hiding inside. "Where did you find this?" he asks, taking out the medals, then the money, the photograph and finally the jewelry case with the ring inside. His eyes meet mine.

"In Juliet's flat."

"When?"

"A few days ago, after the police had searched the place," I admit, feeling like a chastised child. "We didn't do anything wrong. It is hardly our fault your people overlooked it."

"Where was it?"

"Er...under the floorboards in the kitchen."

"Right," he says, nodding. "Not exactly hidden in plain sight."

"Not exactly," Hugh agrees.

"You had no business poking about a murder scene, though I know you have no self-control when it comes to such things. So I can't say I am surprised."

"And you must admit, it is quite a find, is it not?" I push him a little more than is perhaps wise. He simply nods.

"Notice the imprint on the bottom of the British War Medal," Hugh says, leaning closer to show Stanton. The policeman squints, then runs his finger along the edge.

"Nelson?"

"Seems likely," I say.

"Indeed, it does, given what I have just learned of Miss Nelson."

"I suppose you won't tell us what that is until we give you everything we have?" I observe. He is not making it easy for me to forgive his behavior towards Jeffrey.

"We suspect the man in the photograph was a lover, whereas the wedding band suggests Juliet could have been married. Maybe she was a widow. As for the money, well, it could have been a fund for a rainy day or savings with which she did not trust the banks. I doubt her salary as a secretary at the museum allowed her to save much. The question of her rent remains unanswered." Reluctantly, I explain what we have learned of Howard Bell and his wife and their connection to Juliet. I repeat what I already told Hugh, of my belief that Frances truly did not know that Howard and Juliet had been in contact, let alone that he was allowing her to live in his flat. It would be very interesting to learn about Juliet's financial affairs, to peek into her bank account, if she had one, which seems likely, despite her hidden trove of money. If Stanton has any notion of granting Hugh and me this insight, his expression does not show it. He listens without much of a reaction to anything we say, and I worry he may already know it all. But then Frances did not let on that she had an enlightening conversation with the police, and she could not have told them of the flat, since by my estimations, she was unaware of it.

"I interviewed her colleagues, but nobody had much to offer. Mrs. Bell mentioned that she had been friendly with Juliet's parents, which was neither here nor there."

"And you have struck Jeffrey from your list of suspects?" I ask, raising an eyebrow.

"For now," he replies.

"What have you learned? And when is the funeral to be held?"

"Edith Ashbourne has volunteered to organize the funeral. Quite admirable, given her rather trifling acquaintance with Miss Nelson. What do you think of her?" Stanton asks, ignoring my other question like a seasoned interrogator.

"She hired us, so I am inclined to believe she is innocent. Why draw more eyes to the case, if she has something to hide?"

"It could be a ploy. Perhaps - and try not to take offense - perhaps she underestimates your abilities?"

"She marched for women's suffrage, was arrested more than once and leads a WI chapter. If you are implying she does not believe in the competence of women to complete a task typically assigned to men, you are mistaken, Lucas," I reply with conviction.

"And I am here, too," Hugh adds with a shrug.

"Right. For the moment, I have nothing against her. It seems no one who knew Juliet has much to say and no one from her past, who might have greater insight, can be located. My superior is keen for me to hand the case over to someone else and concentrate on the armed robbery of an MP."

"You won't, will you?" I ask, knowing his answer already. He shakes his head, running a hand over his eyes.

"All right. I should not be ungrateful, you have done good work before and doubtless will do so again. I very much hope you can, for once, avoid placing yourself in harm's way in the process. The coroner came back with his report, which is why we are able to release the body for burial." I slide forward in my seat, eager to hear what he has to say. "The cause of death was asphyxiation by strangulation, as we suspected. Juliet seems to have put up a bit of a struggle, though. Blood under two of her nails, suggesting she tried to fight off her assailant. Unfortunately, this doesn't mean much, for we haven't come across anyone with a scratched face. Other body parts are easy to cover up in winter. There was no sign of rape, which is something at least, though it would have proven her killer was male. As matters stand, we do not even know that much with certainty." Stanton shakes his head before continuing. "That being said, Roger, the coroner, was surprised by something he found. Juliet Nelson had a network of scars across her back and arms and circular ones on her arms. Different sizes. Some long, as if from lashings, some small and round like burns from a cigarette." I gasp, and Hugh narrows his eyes. Stanton goes on, "She must have had a limp, for Roger said it was evident her ankle had once been broken and healed badly. Looked like an old injury."

"Juliet did limp, I remember noticing it," I say quietly, his words sinking in. "What happened to her?"

"I am trying to find out. There are no records of a marriage to be found, which does not exempt a lover or even a parent as the source of this abuse."

"Poor Juliet. Frances said she was very close to her parents, but then she did not even know her own husband had a secret flat and let

Juliet live there. So there may be much more of which Frances was wholly unaware."

"I intend to question her again. These medals, the photograph…" Stanton scratches his chin. "They point firmly in the direction of the war, so I have to suspect Juliet was either connected to the person to whom they belonged, or they were her own. I will try to trace them, but with the service number scratched away and the name hardly legible, it will be a challenge."

"Hollis Napier is looking into Juliet's history and that of her family as well. He may find a cousin or an uncle who was close to Juliet."

"Maybe this person was her abuser, and she got hold of his medals and kept them secret as a strange memento of sorts?" Hugh suggests, crossing his arms, brow furrowed.

"Possibly," Stanton concedes. "I don't think very highly of Hollis Napier, but I suppose I can't stop you working with him."

"No, you can't." I dismiss the notion, though Hugh sits up at Stanton's suggestion, which echoes his own feelings towards the journalist.

"Other than the scars and the ankle fracture, Miss Nelson seemed a healthy woman. She should have lived to a ripe old age. I see far too many cases of people dying too young in my profession. Just the other day, a boy was stabbed to death, not three years older than Thom." Thom is Stanton's thirteen-year-old son. The thought of another child not much his senior being dragged far too early from this earth sends a shiver down my spine. We are quiet for a moment, each of us remembering, I think, a person in our lives who left too soon, who never reached middle age, let alone old age. It is Hugh who breaks the silence, and I am grateful. His words force the memory of the baby brother I never knew from my mind.

"Have you spoken to any of Juliet's neighbors? Mr. Button claims not to have heard or seen anyone suspicious. Kind though he is, he does not strike me as a paragon of attentiveness."

"Most neighbors were at work on Friday morning. We now believe the murder likely happened Thursday night. To answer your question, no, nobody has come forward with any useful information. One woman, a Mrs. Grant, says she heard some movement of furniture below her, in Juliet's flat, around eleven. She was in her kitchen getting a glass of milk for her son who couldn't sleep. It doesn't have to mean anything. The carpet might have dulled the sounds of the rampage."

"Unless it wasn't a rampage," I suggest.

"What do you mean?"

"What if the killer wanted to make it look like that, a burglary gone wrong? What if it was orchestrated, the destruction a careful part of the plan? If the killer wished to avoid anyone knocking, he could have created the disarray without the noise of wanton destruction drawing attention to what was happening. I believe the chaos in the flat was planned, not a random burglary. For if she was killed in the evening, most other residents would have been home and might have heard something."

"Unless this was a reckless burglar, it still leaves us with the question of the door and its lock. They were not tampered with. Either Juliet made a habit of leaving it unlocked in the evening, which strikes me as very unlikely, or she let her killer in." Stanton shrugs.

"We agree," says Hugh. "It must have been someone she knew."

"He also had to be aware of her plans for the following day. Yet why telephone Priscilla to say Juliet could not attend the Armistice Day event?"

"My guess is, doing so would buy the murderer time before the body was found." Stanton replies. "And whoever it was opened the windows, keeping the flat cold to better preserve the corpse." I try not to wince at his choice of words.

"Back to the neighbors." Hugh sounds unaffected by Stanton's clinical terms. "Were any other women in her building invited to join the Women's Institute, or only Juliet? Priscilla Lewis, the secretary, told Evelyn many invitations were sent out, but she did not produce a list."

"I wondered the same. Indeed, four women living in the same building received invitations. None but Juliet had the time to attend, though. One was quite appalled I even suggested it. She said the WI was for self-indulgent women with nothing better to do than harp at men."

"Right," I say with a deep sigh. My own opinion of the WI was admittedly faulty, but I quickly changed my mind. With experience comes wisdom, does it not? Stanton glances at his watch and raises his brows.

"I have to be going. I am working on two other cases at the moment."

"Then you can be glad we are helping with Juliet's," I observe.

"I'll be glad if you don't get yourselves in trouble in the process. I trust you will keep her tethered to the ground, Hugh?" Stanton gives Hugh a half smile.

"That is a task beyond the ability of any mortal man, inspector." Hugh winks at me, and I feel a stab of pride for my partner in crime - so to speak.

"I best go, my words are wasted here," Stanton replies, rolling his eyes and putting on his coat and hat. "Stay safe and keep me informed."

"The same goes for you, Lucas," I say and wave him off. When the front door is closed, I turn to Hugh.

"Well..."

"Indeed."

"Do you think it was the young man in the photograph who treated Juliet so cruelly?"

"Would she have kept it, then? I believe the contents of the box were treasures to her, the medals, the money, the photograph. Of course, I could be wrong." Hugh leans back and takes a deep breath. "I wonder whether Stanton's revelation really brings us any closer to the truth. To me it seems every clue we gather compounds the image of the enigma Juliet was. She hasn't become more of a real person in my mind, so much as a figure in the shadows."

"I can't say I disagree," I admit reluctantly. "Let us hope Stanton has luck on his side in tracing the medals, and that he will share his findings with us."

"Of course, he will, Evelyn." Hugh gives me a meaningful look. "He likes to act unenthusiastic, but you are the only one who cannot see that he is – how do I put it? – overly fond of your company."

"Hugh -"

"Evelyn, he is enamored with you! I swing between contempt for him, Daniel being my closest friend, and pity when you call on him, and he cannot deny you." I am surprised by the turn our conversation has taken. Hugh's accusation of my inattention is not quite accurate. I realize Stanton may view our friendship differently than I do, but I have done my best not to give him false hope. I never realized that Hugh was aware of any of this.

"What would you have me do?"

"When you asked him to take on the case, I wondered whether it was fair, but then I reasoned, selfishly perhaps, it would be good for our work. I expected he wouldn't want to disappoint you, and more so, he wanted the chance to keep watch over you in case you were in trouble."

"He always acts as if I am making a nuisance of myself!"

"Acts, yes, but not very convincingly for anyone other than you."

"Again I ask, what shall I do? I will not cut him out of my life. I am marrying Daniel in a matter of weeks. It is quite clear where I stand."

"It should be, but you are being more rational than the human heart, Evelyn." Hugh smiles and rests his elbows on the table, meeting my eye. "I am only telling you to be aware and to be gentle."

"I would never hurt him intentionally," I say with a helpless shrug. Hugh nods, moving back to his own desk. The words he spoke remain lingering in the air. Have I been careless with Stanton? Doubt wars with my desire to solve this case for the rest of the day, and does not release me until I drift off to sleep that night.

Chapter 31

Although detectives keep notoriously unpredictable hours, I have decided to spend much of Saturday with Briony and her family. After our conversation with Stanton, I need a few hours of distance from the case, even if it constantly threatens to encroach upon happier thoughts in my mind.

The day is fine, cold with a bright blue sky, not a cloud in sight. The last of the dying leaves tumble from their branches, leaving colorful heaps along the pavement. Briony and I have taken the three older children to a tearoom. On the way back, energized by buttery scones and abundant squares of gingerbread, Timon and Areta jump into every mound of leaves, throwing them at one another and shrieking with pleasure, while Iona gives them a benevolent look and rolls her eyes to the heavens. When I arrived in Belgravia this morning, Jeffrey was noticeably present, happy to chat, asking questions, answering mine. What he had to say, however, did not add anything to further the investigation. He is not observant, but at least he is trying. Briony seems livelier than I have seen her in some time. Her eyes are still rimmed with circles, but her manner is cheerful. How long will it last? It is only a matter of time before another crisis assails her marriage, and I wonder whether these constant ups and downs are normal. Will it be so for Daniel and me? Will he drive me mad with frustration? Will we forget how to speak to one another, or grow suspicious and resentful? I want to believe the answer is no, but there is much in life – nearly everything, I suppose – we simply cannot predict. I push aside these qualms, at least for the moment, and enjoy the easy company of the children.

"This one looks like a fish!" Timon holds up an oval leaf.

"This one looks like a star." Areta presents her own red hued offering. By the time we arrive back at the Farnham home, both of them have collected a bouquet of brilliantly colored leaves. Briony humors them and allows them to bring the collection inside, while Iona looks on with disapproval.

"Elsa might put them in her mouth."

"It will be all right, Iona," Briony reassures her. "Go on and wash your hands," she commands, and they trudge off, giving us a moment to talk.

"You look well," I observe as we wander into the sitting room. I sink into one of the velvet armchairs, while Briony stands by the fireplace, stretching her hands towards the flickering fire.

My cousin glances at the door, making certain it is closed. "Jeffrey is making an effort, coming home at a reasonable hour so we can have dinner together, asking after my day. I think he was genuinely shaken when I told him I suspected him of adultery."

"He wasn't angry?"

"You know Jeffrey, he does not really get angry." Briony leans against the mantel, a thoughtful look on her face. "But then nothing quite stirs his passion beyond the finds of an archaeological dig." She tempers her words with a smile, but there is truth to them, at least the way she sees it. I cannot decide what to say and Briony, sensing this, moves the conversation along to my wedding.

"Areta is giddy over her dress, I hope you like yours at least half as much as she does hers."

"Agnes chose well. I am getting rather excited, imagining what else she has planned. Well, excited and apprehensive."

"Not about Daniel, though."

"Of course not."

"Isn't it funny to think, if you had never come to Greece and Jeffrey had not invited Daniel at the same time, you two would never have met? You might have given in to Agnes and married some tiresome aristocrat with a wobbly chin and fondness for fox hunts and cigars by now!"

"It doesn't bear considering!" I laugh. Hugh's words come to mind again, and I decide to put them to my cousin. No one knows me better than she does, after all.

"How very forward of Hugh!" Briony cries, not without a hint of admiration. "But what are you to do? Stanton will be hurt all the more if you sever your ties, poor chap. Better to play match-maker and find him someone else."

"I am tasked with that already in Hugh's case, though he is to know nothing about it. Have you any ideas? I boasted to Daniel I would find someone perfectly suited. Thus far, I am afraid I have come up blank."

"Hugh needs someone with both feet on the ground, someone who is kind and patient and makes him laugh."

"Isn't that exactly the person we all want?"

Briony shrugs. "I read Areta fairy-tales at night, and the princesses always want to be rescued, or need to be rather. Their savior is forever a handsome man, strong, usually royal. When I listen to myself telling my daughter these stories, I am tempted to change them. When you are grown, you realize fairy-tale princes are hard to come by, and in the end, kindness, compassion and humor are worth more than golden locks and chivalry."

"Iona is rubbing off on you," I tease. "The other day she held forth, denouncing Mr. Rochester and was vastly disappointed that Jane Eyre forgave him."

"That girl is the future. Our mother's generation had the suffragettes, but for which cause will Iona be a pioneer?"

"Maybe she should accompany us to the next meeting of the WI. Well, maybe not the next one," I add, remembering Stanton's words. "I suspect there will be plenty of talk about Juliet's funeral. Edith and the ladies of the WI have taken on the task of planning it for Tuesday. Edith telephoned this morning. I agreed to meet with her for breakfast tomorrow. I can't imagine having much of an appetite when that subject is on the table."

"You don't suspect her? After all, the WI was the one novel feature in Juliet's life before she died."

"I can't deny the thought crossed my mind. The trouble is, I can simply find no motive for anyone to wish her harm. She seemed to live in an intentionally modest, almost secluded, manner." Now that we are on the subject, I cannot prevent myself from telling Briony of the box we found, and of its contents.

"The man in the photograph must have been a lover," she decides, and I can see romantic stories being constructed in her mind. Despite her earlier words, she still shares Areta's love for a fairy-tale. Even if this one did not have a happy ending.

"Maybe. There are still too many unanswered questions in this case." I hesitate, then tell her of the coroner's findings, my cousin blanching at my words.

"How horrible! Poor Juliet, goodness! Who did this to her? Do you think her killer was a prior abuser, returned to take some final revenge?"

"It is possible. Perhaps she lived so quietly to avoid notice, sensing someone was on her trail?"

"You think it was a man?"

"I honestly do not know. The only suspects so far seem to be women of the WI and work colleagues, no one specific. Daniel and I are having dinner with Adeline and her husband tonight."

"Now I wish I had agreed to join, but it is important for us to spend time together as a family after what happened."

"I understand, of course. Nonetheless, I am hopeful something will come out of the evening besides friendly chit-chat. Adeline says she did not know Juliet better than I did, but maybe there is something she remembers that could help. I am clutching at straws, but the more time that passes, the easier it will be for the killer to slip away, if he or she has not done so already. London is a large city, how are we to find this person?"

"You must give the police some credit. They will do their best. Even if Stanton is busy with other work, he will likely expend a fair amount of energy on Juliet's case, because it connects him to you."

"Don't be silly, Briony! He is a good policeman, that is why he is working on the case."

"If you say so." Briony grins and waggles her brows. I give her a stern look, and it isn't long before we are both giggling like fools. The door is pushed open, and Areta with the other children, Elsa in Iona's arms, stand in the doorway. Areta wrinkles her nose, big brown eyes moving from her mother to me.

"Why are you laughing? What's so funny?" she demands.

"Come here." Briony stretches out her arms. The little girl throws herself at her mother, so unaffected at the age of six and willing to show affection that will soon turn to embarrassment.

I take Elsa on my lap, kissing the top of her downy head of curls. She smells like milk and soap and something sweetly unique to tiny children. I imagine, just for a moment, what it would be like to bounce Daniel's and my child on my lap, a little boy or girl with his green eyes, my chestnut hair. The thought frightens me almost as much as it excites me. How will it be for two orphans like us to be parents, to continue the legacy of our families? Will we live in fear every day of something befalling our child...or us? For is it not every parent's second greatest fear, having to leave their children behind, unable to guide and soothe and love, unable to witness who they become? I hug Elsa to my chest, but she is having none of my maudlin affection, wriggling until I loosen my hold, then twisting to make a grab for my necklace. Before I can stop her, she has popped the pendant into her mouth like a candy attached to a chain. After a moment, she spits it back out, clearly disappointed by its lack of sweetness.

"You silly girl," I say, tickling her chin. She gurgles and leans against me, her small body pleasantly solid in my arms. We chat and play a while longer with the children, before I say goodbye to return to Grosvenor Square and ready myself for the evening ahead.

I am greeted by Wilkins, who looks remarkably better than he has in weeks. I am relieved once again that Hugh took heart and confessed. Wilkins made mistakes, but he was desperate and is repentant. Were I in his shoes, perhaps I would have done the same, and then hoped for the forgiveness of those I consider my friends. Hugh and Wilkins are more alike than they realize, and both are loyal to Daniel. One might assume this would create a bond of friendship between them, but for the moment, I am content with civility. It is Wilkins' sister, Maisie, who helps me dress, when I am getting ready for dinner. The maids are lovely, but I especially like Maisie's company, even if, as our housekeeper, her job is not to button me up. She doesn't seem to mind, and it gives me a chance to talk to her in private. It must have been strange, moving from the home she shared with her husband in Whitechapel to Mayfair, where the only people she knows are Daniel, her brother and me. Yet she looks better than she did when we first met, when she was reeling from her husband's death and her brother's arrest. Her face has rounded a little and her body has acquired a healthy softness where before were angles and gaunt hollows. She is still young, too young to hide herself away as a widow forever, but I will leave the matter for another time.

"How are you, Maisie? I have been rushing about so much lately and hardly had a chance to speak with you. Are you are settling in well?"

"Very well," she replies, fastening the final button at the back of my navy silk dress. "Adam told me Mr. Lawrence admitted to following him. He is so relieved. It was making him mad." She smiles at me in the mirror.

"I am glad at least that mystery was easily solved. You mustn't hold it against

Hugh. He only did it because he cares for Daniel as he would for a brother."

"I understand. I daresay Adam does as well. He even admitted he might do the same if conditions were reversed."

"Daniel is fortunate to have such devoted friends."

"Well, two slightly mad, if devoted, friends can be a bit of a millstone, but I suppose we should all be so lucky." She holds up a string of pearls, and I shake my head.

"Something simpler, I think."

"Hm...these?" A pair of tiny sapphire earrings.

"Perfect. Thank you."

"Happy to help. It is almost like being caught in another world, living here. So different." She hurries to add, "I hope you don't mind me saying so."

"Not at all. It's the truth, I suppose, but I hope you are beginning to feel at home, too. Do you go back to visit old friends sometimes?" I ask, putting on the earrings, watching her in the mirror as she sorts a few rejected pieces back into their velvet cases.

"No, not often. Well, only twice, to be truthful. I never had many friends there. Terry saw to that. He owed everyone money." Though she would have every right to be bitter, there is no rancor in her voice as she speaks of her late husband and his many debts. It is a fact she has come to accept. She and Wilkins are still paying off the arrears, months after he was buried. Daniel offered them a loan, but neither would accept it.

"There we are, very nice," says Maisie, stepping back. I do a little twirl, making the layers of silk below my knees rustle like dry leaves dancing down the street on a gust of wind.

"What are you doing with your evening off?" I ask, smoothing out the front of the dress. Maisie shrugs.

"I will probably have dinner with Adam and the others and then settle in with a book."

"I must say, I envy you a little. It takes some determination to go out again into the cold and dark."

"I could be persuaded, if I had anywhere to go." Maisie touches her mouth after the words leave it, as though wishing to lock them up again. She and Wilkins are likely saving every bit of their wages to rid themselves of Terry's debts. Little will remain for pleasure, for small trinkets or the odd evening show. A thought comes to me, but I tuck it away for another time. Maisie does not want to speak of personal matters anymore, that much is evident from the sudden rigid set of her shoulders and jaw. I smile at her, hoping to convey my understanding without furthering her discomfort.

I find Daniel dressed in a charcoal gray suit in the bedroom, tucking a silk square into his pocket, then taking it out again.

"Very dandy!" I observe from the doorway.

"I could think of a few better adjectives for you," he says with a smile.

"Let me hear them!"

"I would not like your head to burst," he replies with a grin. "Now, what are we to expect tonight? You have met Graham Markby before?"

"Once. Adeline invited a few of the ladies from the WI to her house. Juliet was there as well, and Briony, Aunt Louise, Edith, Priscilla. Did I tell you they are organizing Juliet's funeral?"

"Generous of them, given that they hardly knew her."

"They take the idea of sisterhood seriously. After all, Edith is the one who hired Hugh and me."

"It might not be as selfless as you think. A murder among the ranks of the WI does not exactly promote the best image of the institution."

"Likely it has nothing to do with the WI."

"Scandal sticks. If they are engaging in political pursuits, asking for more women police officers and such, this murder could be twisted and used against them."

"I had not considered that," I admit.

"It only just came to me. I spoke with Harold earlier. He is keen to take advantage of the upcoming by-election and asked whether the Harper family is willing to endorse him as a candidate. I agreed, naturally, and even Dominic did not oppose the notion, which surprised me, given Harold's politics."

"Perhaps you underestimate your cousin."

"Perhaps." Daniel shrugs and sits on the edge of the bed. I join him, wishing we could stay home, have cheese on toast for dinner, then play a few mindless hands of rummy. "In any case, it made me consider how words and events are warped in the realm of politics and organizations, likely in the WI, too."

"I don't think the WI is viewed as much of a threat. Their efforts have largely been by way of letters and petitions. They are not the suffragettes of a decade past, waving banners and hurling demands."

"You sound quite wistful." Daniel observes with a smile.

"Maybe I am."

"I can imagine it, you in white with a purple sash."

"Yes, but then I am grateful I need not take up that cause, grateful others did it before me, even if much work is still to be done. Change is happening, slowly but surely. One day we will have a woman prime minister. Maybe Iona's daughter will be an MP."

"Maybe she will herself."

I smile at Daniel, glad for the thousandth time to have found someone to finish my thoughts and echo my sentiments. Soon he will be my husband, and we will be a family. Come what may, the thought fills me with excitement.

Chapter 32

A gleaming black Rover is parked in front of Adeline and Graham Markby's house when Daniel and I arrive. Light spills from the windows onto the damp pavement, and a soft fog has risen from the ground.

The house is familiar from my last visit, though quiet this time, no busy chatter, no clanking of porcelain and scraping of chairs. Adeline wears bright colors as ever, her vibrant grass green dress a vast contrast to her husband's somber gray suit.

"Don't you look lovely!" Adeline takes both my hands. She has a motherly manner which sets me at ease, although she cannot be more than seven or eight years my senior, if that. I remember Louise telling me they have no children and wonder why. Perhaps they are happy as they are, or maybe it is not possible for them.

"Adeline says you work in shipping?" Graham asks Daniel, as we follow the couple into a lounge where a fire is crackling in a massive hearth and colorful expressionist art hangs in clusters on the walls. The furniture is similarly bright, and though the riot of color seems in keeping with Adeline's favor, it is almost dizzying to behold, like being caught in a vivid dream.

"My cousin and I run the family business. And you?" Daniel asks. He is reluctant to speak of his work, especially given the current and precarious state of affairs at Harper Ltd.

"I work for the War Office. I am a barrister by training. During the war, my focus shifted. I am blind in my left eye and was disqualified from serving in the capacity of a soldier." Unlike other men I have met, who were unable – or unwilling, in the case of conscientious objectors – to serve, Graham Markby seems to feel no discomfort admitting he was spared time on the front. He has a straight posture and slightly roughhewn features, which make him not exactly handsome, but interesting to look at. When we met before, I hardly took notice of him. Our interaction was hurried, and the many others present offered too many distractions. Judging by this second impression, I rather like the man. Adeline is chatting away, smiling and offering drinks, then forgetting them again until her husband takes over the task. They met as children, Daniel and I learn, when we settle into the plush dining room for a first course of leek soup.

"I was five and Graham eight and our parents were dear friends. At the time, he thought me irritating and I thought him horribly dull," Adeline observes, reaching out to pat Graham's hand, as if this ancient slight might still sting. "We drifted apart when Graham's family moved to Cambridge. Eight years ago, we met again at a wedding and I didn't think Graham quite so dull anymore, nor, I daresay, did he find me quite so exasperating!" She chuckles. I am surprised at the ease of their company. I anticipated somber musings about Juliet to darken every moment, but neither has even mentioned the murder. Perhaps they believe it would not befit dinner conversation, and their cook would be most displeased if uneaten meals were sent back to the kitchens because the diners lost their appetite. Whatever it may be, conscious or not, I am relieved to speak of lighter matters for a while.

"When is your wedding to be?" asks Graham, when the maids clear away the empty soup bowls to replace them with the next course, pink slices of duck with roast carrots and potato puree.

"In a few weeks," I reply, catching Daniel's eye.

"Will you continue with your detecting business afterwards?" Adeline asks, surprising me. I expected someone raised by Edith Ashbourne wouldn't think twice of a woman maintaining her profession after marriage.

"I will most certainly continue," I say, trying to mask my vague irritation with a smile.

"Ah, yes, Adeline told me Edith has hired you herself," Graham observes. Do I detect a hint of a challenge in his eyes? He blinks, and I push away the thought.

"She has. I am looking into Juliet Nelson's murder." So now the conversation has, after all, turned to the subject on the forefront of my mind. "Sadly, it has been a slow process thus far. Have you learned anything about Juliet since we last spoke?" I ask Adeline.

"Nothing, I am sorry to say. Have you questioned her colleagues? I did not know much about her, except that she worked at the British Museum in some capacity."

"Yes, I spoke to a few of them. Most hardly knew her, and the woman who did could only offer some stories about her as a child. She had been close to Juliet's parents, you see."

"Are there many women working at the museum?" Graham asks. "Adeline is always complaining of the vast inequality in opportunities." His wife playfully elbows his side.

"Not many. I only met three in the department."

"A sign of progress, small though it may be," Adeline observes. "You have probably heard that Mother intends to organize Juliet's funeral." Her tone suggests disapproval, and she hastens to add, "It is wonderful that she is willing to do so, of course, but it seems strange no one has come forth claiming to be her family, wishing to take responsibility. Priscilla told us of a brother who apparently called, and now we know there was never such a person at all. It is very disconcerting. Pris is troubled that she may have actually spoken to the killer that morning."

"If the funeral is publicized, perhaps her murderer will attend. It is not uncommon."

"How utterly grim!" Graham pronounces, taking a sip of wine.

"Perhaps we should speak of other things," Daniel suggests. "Do you have much family in the city, Graham?"

"None close by, but a multitude of distant cousins. My parents moved to the country after the war. Then I married Adeline and remained here. What of you? Are you from the city?"

"I grew up in Kent. After the war I traveled and rarely return to the place where I lived as a child. My parents died long ago, and both my brothers were lost in the war."

"I am very sorry," says Graham, his expression somber. Perhaps he understands. Few in this city, maybe in this country, lived through those terrible years without the loss of someone they knew and held dear.

"It was quite a long time ago." Daniel tries to sound more at peace than he will ever be on the subject.

"One never does forget," Graham replies with a small nod.

"No, never."

By the time a light pavlova with figs and apricots is served, conversation has thankfully turned to lighter matters. The Markbys speak of plays they have seen, and Daniel mentions his cousin, Johnny, Dominic's son, who is finally treading the boards in a West End production, after a long battle with his father over his choice of profession. It is a pleasant evening in good company, and when we say goodnight, we promise to repeat the occasion at a near opportunity. No more mention of Juliet was made. I think we all preferred to pretend we were simply new friends, and I am beginning to think of the Markbys as such. Graham was easy company, personable and quick to engage both Daniel and me in conversation, more willing to listen than to speak himself, unlike his wife. Despite her penchant for almost silly amounts of color and outward frivolity, Adeline is not a flippant woman. She is quick to laugh, but her upbringing has made of her a woman capable of speaking as comfortably about politics as chatting about the latest fashions and the causes of the WI. I like them both, and Daniel echoes my sentiments on the way home.

"It went well."

"Quite. I was worried when talk of the war came up that the mood would turn melancholy. Graham was moved by your history. One could not fail to be, I suppose."

"He understood."

"What do you mean?" I ask, slightly tired from the conversation, food and wine, my mind in a pleasant fog.

"He recognized my loss. I feel certain he has gone through something similar. He gave me this look. It is difficult to describe. I have seen it before many times. It says, 'I know, because I have felt the same grief'."

"You can tell a lot from a look." I raise my brows.

"Trust me, Evie. He has lost someone very dear to him."

"I always trust you." I hold a hand to my mouth to stifle a yawn and lean against his shoulder. "Maybe he did not wish to speak of it. You don't like talking about Henry and William to strangers."

"True enough," he agrees. "He mentioned his family lives in the country, and it did not sound as if he sees them often. I suppose I see something of myself in the man. His family consists of his wife and her relations, much as it will be for me." He falls silent. I hear the echo of his heartbeat as I lean against him.

"Are you sad your family cannot be at the wedding?" I ask, knowing the answer, of course, but willing him to speak of it all the same. Even with me, he is reluctant to mention his parents. I sometimes think he is uncertain how, without sounding as though he blames them for leaving him. His mother's health deteriorated badly after Henry and William died and his father, after losing his wife, took matters into his own hands with a shotgun. Daniel struggles with the idea that he was not enough for them to stay.

"Of course, I am, and you feel the same about your parents."

"I always had Agnes and Robert and Louise," I say, hoping it does not sound like gloating.

"I am glad of it. What sort of rascal would you have become without their influence?" he whispers. I hear a smile creeping into his voice. I reach for his hand.

"I haven't asked anyone to give me away, or to lead me down the aisle. I thought it would be Uncle Robert, but…" I let my voice drift.

"It should be Agnes," Daniel notes, his voice firm.

"Maybe she wouldn't agree. It is untraditional."

"She is less rigid than you give her credit for. Ask her. I am convinced she will agree, and Robert will understand."

"Perhaps I will." I close my eyes for a moment, feeling the rumble of the car's engine as we roll through the city, and Daniel's heartbeat, his chest rising and falling. "I was playing with Elsa earlier and thought about our own children."

"Oh?"

"And…I wondered, what if something happens to us, too?" I feel him tense for a moment, before he replies.

"It could, but we cannot live like that, Evie. For so long after my parents and brothers died, I kept running from everything that tied me down, including love and friendship. It did not make me happy. You make me happy and our family, in whatever form it comes, will make me happy and that is all I allow myself to contemplate. Anything can happen to anyone at any time. That is a fact of life, but we may also live to a ripe old age, bounce grandchildren on our knees and finally retire to an island in the sun, like the one where we met. Those are my plans."

"I am quite happy with such a forecast."

"Then we are in agreement." He kisses the top of my head, and I am strangely soothed by his words and his confidence. "And ask Agnes," he whispers into my hair.

Chapter 33

The following day I drive to Bloomsbury for a meeting with the WI. Aunt Louise is standing by the door when I arrive, breaking into a smile when she sees me. We haven't spoken in a few days, since Jeffrey's arrest, and I am glad the shock of it seems to have worn away. She tucks her hand into the crook of my arm, and we go inside together.

"You have probably already heard, Edith is organizing Juliet's funeral," she says in a low voice, nodding at another – to me unfamiliar – woman writing her name in the ledger. "Are you closer to solving the case? The police have hopefully abandoned the mad notion that our Jeffrey is connected to the crime."

"I believe they have. To tell you the truth, this case is proving rather difficult to crack."

"Is it terrible that I am curious to see who comes to the funeral? It has been made public, after all. I expect someone from her past must have caught wind of it."

"I hope it will be so. Let us have lunch after the meeting, and I will tell you what we have learned."

Louise's eyes widen, and she lowers her voice to a conspiratorial whisper. "Do you suspect anyone from the Women's Institute?"

"Let me put it this way, I have no reason not to at this stage."

"Oh, dear. I have grown fond of these ladies and feel rather useful here, even if our efforts are not met with quick success. I should not like it to be tainted."

I give my aunt's arm a gentle squeeze. "I am glad you enjoy it and I must concede, I underestimated this organization. Edith has me convinced that introducing women into roles of authority is the way of the future. Don't tell Harold I said so. Though having married Agnes, I don't suppose he would need convincing."

Louise giggles and shakes her head. We have gathered in the hall and find our seats as Edith steps to the front. Priscilla at a small table to her right is taking the minutes.

"Ladies, if I may have your attention!" Edith's voice cuts through the chatter, silencing us, capturing our attention. She has a commanding presence, and I imagine her as she might have been a decade ago, righteously uncompromising, marching in white.

"As you all know," she announces, "I have decided to take on the task of organizing Juliet Nelson's funeral. She was one of us, for however short a time. Thanks to Priscilla, who has been such a help, we have arranged for the burial to take place on Tuesday morning at Kensal Green Cemetery. Please, if you can, plan to attend. We do not know whether we can expect members of Juliet's family, since we had no luck in locating anyone." She casts me a quick look, and I note a hint of displeasure in her gaze. I have failed her, she must think, yet she does not understand that the game of detection is never a speedy affair. I will be expected to give her a summary of recent events, though I am not at all inclined to tell her about finding the box and its contents just yet. I like and respect the women I have met here, as I said to Louise, yet I cannot entirely trust any one of them.

After Edith calls an end to the meeting, having shifted easily from funeral plans to the progress of the latest petition, Louise is pulled aside by a group of women, so I drift towards Priscilla. She is just closing her notebook and tucking her pen into a leather case as I approach.

"Oh, it's you," she says, mustering a smile.

"Hello, Priscilla. How are you? Have the past few days given you some respite after the shock of recent events?"

"I try my best." She gives a little shrug and gets to her feet. "My Bertie does not have the patience for an upset Mama. So I had to swallow my anxiety, which is probably for the best. In a way, helping plan the funeral has given me something useful to concentrate on. I feel I was unfair to Juliet in life, so perhaps this goes a tiny way in making up for my hasty judgement. Not that she will benefit from it, sadly. Are you making progress?" She lowers her voice, though we are unlikely to be overheard.

"Slowly, frustratingly slowly."

"And the police? They spoke to me, but I could tell them nothing more than I told you."

"I am afraid I can't say, though I am in contact with the investigating officer."

"Ah, secrets among professionals?" she observes with a smile. It softens her taut features. Then her attention shifts, and I feel her eyes moving beyond my shoulder. I turn and see a man, his back to us, speaking to Edith. He is tall and broad-shouldered, gray hair peeking from beneath his hat.

"Who -" I begin, when he shifts and recognition dawns. It is Lloyd Ashbourne, Edith's husband. "Does he often attend WI meetings?" I ask Priscilla in a whisper. Unnecessary, for he would have to be blessed with near superhuman hearing to register my words, and even if he did, what harm is in them?

"No, not at all. I can count the number of times I have met him on one hand, and I have been with the WI for years."

"My aunt is acquainted with the family from long ago, but I can't remember her ever speaking of him."

"He was a bit of a controversial figure for a while. He owned a weapon's manufactory during the war. Came under a fair bit of scrutiny until he sold up."

"Priscilla! Can you come here for a moment?" Another woman calls out from across the room, waving a hand. Priscilla sighs and shrugs.

"Forgive me, I am needed. Will I see you on Tuesday?" I nod and watch her go, turning back towards the Ashbournes. However, the space they occupied just a moment ago is empty.

Shortly thereafter, Louise and I step into the cold to find a place for our midday meal. We settle into a small café nearby, with a bright blue door and fogged windows, telling of cozy warmth inside.

Over chicken pie, I relay the recent developments to my aunt, and she listens with marked curiosity. Of all my aunts, Louise has the most adventurous spirit, and I do believe I detect a hint of envy when I tell her of Hugh and me sneaking into Juliet's flat and finding the box.

"You ought to ask Harold about the medals, he might be able to give you more information. He has quite a few of them himself, as Agnes likes to remind me." Louise winks.

"Speaking of Agnes," I hesitate.

"Yes?"

"I am thinking of asking her to give me away at the wedding. It should probably be Robert, and I would be honored for him to…It's only that -" Louise raises a hand to silence my explanations.

"That sounds perfectly reasonable. Robert will understand. Don't you waste a moment worrying about it," she says, her voice gentle but firm. "Agnes is like a mother to you, and I am so very glad you two have mended your relationship in recent years. I know she is, too."

"Does she speak of me often?" I ask, strangely hungry to know.

"Of course, she does! You hear me going on about Briony. Well, imagine the same coming out of her mouth. Evelyn is going here; Evelyn is doing that. You two cannot see what is right in front of you sometimes. Trust yourselves a little with one another. Agnes loves you above anyone and I know you love her very much as well, despite your mutual bickering. Ask her, she will be nothing short of delighted, I promise you."

More encouragement could hardly be wished for. So, after our meal comes to an end and I drive Louise home, I stop in Eton Square. The day is fine, soft cotton clouds chasing each other across a bright blue sky, a cold breeze sweeping the pavement clear of dry leaves. Two children in elegant coats and shiny shoes kick a ball back and forth in front of one of the mansions. As I climb out of the car, a red-faced woman runs outside. Her chastisement, "not in your Sunday best!" can be heard from across the street.

"Evelyn, how good to see you! Were we expecting you?" Harold asks, when Mr. Harris, Agnes' butler, leads me into the sitting room, where I find my aunt's husband reading the Sunday paper. He puts it aside, and I kiss his cheek.

"No, I am just dropping by. I hope I am not disturbing you."

"Never, my dear. Your aunt went to fetch her embroidery. She will be delighted to see you." He lowers his voice. "It made her very happy that you liked the dress she chose."

"I could say the same for myself," I reply, smiling. "Tell me, how does your campaigning go? Daniel said you now have the endorsement of Harper Ltd."

"Yes, what a boon. It is still viewed as a working man's industry, which appeals to my voters in Shoreditch. I think there is a good chance for me, Evelyn, I truly do."

"I wish you success," I say, concerned that the endorsement of Harper Ltd. may prove a burden rather than a boon, if they start sending spades of workers into unemployment by closing the shipyard in the new year. Harold must be told, but I do not feel I should be the one to share this with him. Yet how can I allow him to associate himself with a business that will do exactly what he is campaigning against? Still, there is time for the situation to improve, or so I hope.

"Evelyn, what are you doing here?" Agnes' voice interrupts my thoughts. She smiles, even though her words seem to carry a hint of accusation. I get to my feet and give her a quick embrace.

"I wanted to speak to you. Do you have a moment?"

"I believe that is my cue to make myself scarce," Harold observes, gathering up his paper in a disorganized bundle and slipping from the room. We can hear him in the hallway, before settling in, me on the sofa, Agnes straight-backed in an armchair opposite.

"Is everything all right?" she asks, caution in her voice.

"Yes, yes, everything is fine. Well, apart from the fact that Juliet's murderer is still running free, but that is not why I came today. I have something I want to ask you."

"Oh?" Agnes raises one of her perfectly arched brows in a gesture that used to rile me, but which I have come to accept as a mere punctuation to her question.

"It is about the wedding."

"There is little I can do to change things now, Evelyn."

"No, no, it isn't that. I wanted to ask, well, whether you might want to be the one to give me away?" I realize how feeble my voice has become, as if I am expecting her to reject my proposal with the wave of a hand. I push aside the thought, remembering what Louise told me and watch for her reaction. Agnes' surprise is evident, but the tension in my shoulders eases, when she smiles.

"You have thought about this?"

"Naturally."

"Robert might -"

"He will be fine. What do you say?"

"If it is truly what you want..." She hesitates, meeting my gaze. "I would be honored."

I cannot help but laugh with relief. "Thank you!"

"It is I who should thank you. You looked so worried for a moment, did you really believe I would say no?" Agnes is smiling, and I feel a fool for having doubted her. Old habits die hard, I suppose, both hers and mine.

"Only a few more weeks now. I am beginning to look forward to it."

Agnes huffs and exclaims, "I should hope so!"

"Is your newly married life everything you hoped it would be?" I ask, genuinely curious, for before her wedding to Harold, Agnes confessed her fear of change, of everything she had grown used to being turned on its head.

"It is not my first marriage, of course." Agnes sighs and leans back in her chair. "My marriage to Brendan was different. I was so young, younger than you are now, only twenty when we wed and looking back, I hardly knew what I wanted or expected. Brendan was so good to me and I am grateful for our time together, too short though it was. Yet it was fraught with difficulty as well."

"Oh?" I ask. Agnes has never been very willing to speak of her life with Brendan. She mourned him much of the past decade, after he died during the Spanish Flu outbreak. I cannot recall her ever having spoken a harsh word about him.

"He could be stubborn, like me. Two such determined heads knocking together could lead to some bitter disputes. Thankfully, we were both too fond of one another to allow bad feelings to linger long. Then there was our inability to have a child, the death of your parents, the war..." She shakes her head, and I wonder whether images of our life as it once was flash before her eyes like scenes in the moving pictures. I try to imagine her, young and in love with Brendan, the charming military man, the eldest son of a grand landowner. I remember her when I was little, her forehead creased so frequently with displeasure, her words so often sharp and cold; the way she held herself at Brendan's funeral, where I sobbed into Louise's coat and threw Agnes angry glances for shedding not a single tear, as we watched the casket being lowered into the ground. For so long, I compared her to the idealized mother I lost and hardly knew. I considered Agnes stony and indifferent, traditional and unbending. Looking back, I must acknowledge that she was always there. She did not offer me a shoulder to cry on, but she gave me a home and fought to keep me with her and Brendan when my other aunts wanted to raise me with them. In recent years, we have grown closer. She has confessed that she struggles to be affectionate; that she made mistakes, and I have done the same. Perhaps Daniel and Harold deserve some credit, for they have, in their gentle ways, pushed us together again and again. They made us realize that we are not so terribly different, and that underneath all the silly words and childish resentment rests profound love.

"With Harold," Agnes continues. "It is different. I met him more fully formed, and he has accepted me as I am. I was worried at first, I told you months ago, that marriage at my age would mean having to change, just when I am happy the way I am, but Harold expects nothing of me that I do not wish myself. Daniel strikes me as a man with a similar temperament."

"He likes to say I have inherited a few qualities from you as well," I say, unable to hide a smile.

"I take that as a compliment."

"Do. You know he is fond of you."

"I trust you will be happy together. Don't think I am unaware you two already live as married couples do." She raises her brows, and the heat of a blush creeps into my cheeks. "Not much will change except, perhaps, expectations, both from within and without. You will learn to cope with them. Daniel is right, we are both obstinate creatures and I do not worry, you will get your way in the end."

"The key to a happy marriage, a wife who is always right?"

Agnes laughs. "Quite, my dear, and I have been fortunate that both my husbands realized this very quickly!"

When I leave number 12 Eaton Square, I feel relieved and light on my feet, making my way to the car. Speaking with Agnes and her reaction to my request brightened my mood and distracted me, for a short while, from my worries about the case, about the wedding and everything in between. I will always mourn my parents and ache from their absence, sad that they will never meet Daniel or our future children, but I am luckier than most always to have had a family. So many people are not so fortunate. There are Hugh and Dulcie, Mr. Button and poor Juliet. The former two at least have dear friends they can depend upon, though. So it is that my mind circles back to the case. Driving home, I cannot help but think there must be someone who knew Juliet, someone who can give us a clue, a motive, a suspect to lead us to her killer.

Chapter 34

Ask and you shall receive...Even if it requires some patience. That evening, who should stop by the flat, just as I am planning to leave, but the reporter and our source, Hollis Napier. Hugh stopped by earlier, despite my urging him to take the day off. He wanted to see if any other case had come in. He frowns at Napier, but the newspaperman ignores him, sliding breezily into the chair opposite me, forcing Hugh to drag his own chair over to us.

"I found a cousin!"

"Juliet's?" I ask, my heart-beat quickening.

"Naturally." He rolls his eyes. "Name is Victor Stanley, a beat copper. I took the train out to Reading yesterday morning, and met an old friend – Mark - who writes for the local rag and knows everyone. Mark didn't remember Juliet's family, but he pointed me in the direction of Victor Stanley. They had crossed paths when he investigated a robbery a few weeks ago. Mark wrote about it. When I described Juliet to him, he said he did not know her, but was able to discover that this Victor chap's mother's maiden name was Nelson."

"Did you speak to him?" Hugh asks, unable to hide a glint of excitement in his eyes, reluctant though he is to credit Hollis.

"Of course, what do you take me for!" Hollis puts on an expression of deep affront.

"Apologies, do continue."

"It was easy enough to find him after I had his name and to my surprise, he was willing to talk. Seemed a bit of an odd one. He rents a room in a boarding house of sorts. Unmarried, no children...as far as I could tell, at least." Hollis gives us a wink.

"Facts, please, not gossip," I remind him, yet I can't help but smile. He has such an easy manner. One has the impression nothing in the world could weigh him down, though I suspect this is most certainly not the case. He remains human, after all.

"Oh, do let me have my fun! Is she always this impatient?" Hollis asks Hugh, a hand on his heart.

"Only when it comes to murder," Hugh replies evenly.

"Fine, fine," Hollis says with a shrug. "As I was saying, he was odd, but not in a dangerous way. Cheery fellow, spoke of his bridge club and rugby – though he is not built for it!"

"Juliet, Hollis, what did he say of Juliet!" I urge.

"He remembered her. He was her cousin on the mother's side, knew her as a child. I gather they were near the same age." Hollis pauses, takes in our expectant expressions and coughs. "Any chance of a cup of tea? I am simply parched."

Hugh lets out an exasperated sigh and gets to his feet. "I'll ask Maeve. Anything else?"

"Oh, now that you ask, a biscuit or two wouldn't go amiss." Hollis grins widely, clearly taking pleasure in riling Hugh further. He watches him slip out of the door, and I follow his gaze.

"Must you tease him?" I ask, shaking my head, arms crossed.

"It is too easy," he replies with a cheery shrug. "He is a mysterious fellow. Couldn't learn a thing about him. You, on the other hand, are an open book."

"Why are you investigating us?" I ask, irritation rising within me. "Leave Hugh out of your nosy missions. Have you ever considered that the reason people are reserved is because they wish some things to remain private?"

"Some, maybe, but everything? No, if someone is as standoffish as Mr. Lawrence, I gather he has something to hide, and I am a bloodhound, when -"

"I am warning you, Hollis. You stay away from Hugh, or our arrangement is at an end." I fix him with a stern gaze. He watches me for a moment, then smiles that typical, easy smile which says he is never quite serious about anything, and raises both hands like a cornered criminal.

"All right, all right. You will have your reasons for trusting him."

"I do. Implicitly."

"Very well. He does remind me of someone else, though, someone who tried to live as quietly as possible."

"Juliet."

"Got it in one! Silence masks secrets, Lady Evelyn."

"People are entitled to secrets. Juliet, however, was murdered. The argument for privacy is lost when it is weighed against the significance of finding her killer."

"I hope you feel the same when I publish my article at the end of this investigation," he says, eyes fixed on mine.

"Don't make an enemy of me, Hollis."

He is quiet for a moment before chuckling and shaking his head. Just at that moment, Hugh comes back. He is carrying a tray, which he unceremoniously places in front of our guest, china cup jumping in its saucer.

"Why thank you, Mr. Lawrence." Hollis takes a sip and makes a sound of satisfaction. "As I was saying, I met Victor Stanley. He remembered Juliet from their childhood, described her as a quiet girl, kind, too. I had the sense he himself was often the target of neighborhood ruffians. In any case, his education ended at sixteen while she completed her schooling. They hardly saw one another until her parents' funeral. Victor's family attended, and he told me she was distraught, wouldn't allow anyone to comfort her. They were a close little family. Juliet sold the house and went away. Victor heard she drifted around. His parents once received a card from Manchester, another from Brighton. They thought she was doing well, away from the memories. Then the war rolled around and Victor enlisted at the very beginning in 1914. This is when his story gets interesting. In '15, he was home on leave after contracting a bad case of pneumonia in Belgium. His father and brother were both away. They, too, had enlisted, and it was only him and his mother in the house. His mother had become very religious, going to church every day to pray for her sons and husband – who all survived, I am happy to say.

"There was a knock at the door, and Juliet was standing there in the April rain. She looked pale and thin, and her eyes were frightened. I had the sense it was an image Victor never quite forgot. Maybe because it was the last time he ever saw her. His mother let her in, gave her a cup of tea and a towel to dry off, but Juliet could not sit still, she paced about and kept muttering to herself. She was in a bad way and seemed beside herself. Victor's mother was disturbed and told him to get the doctor. It took a while, because the man was on a house call, but when he came back with the physician in tow, Juliet was gone. Later he asked his mother what had happened. She was reluctant to speak, but she finally confessed that Juliet had spoken of being with child, needing help. The father was a stranger who had stolen her money. She was alone. His mother was distressed and, compelled by Victor, admitted she sent Juliet away. Gave her some money and got rid of her. Too embarrassed of the shame associated by supporting an unwed mother. Victor was visibly upset by the memory, particularly knowing that it was the final time he saw his cousin alive."

"She must have either lost the child sometime after seeing her aunt, or she gave it away for adoption," Hollis observes, and for once his voice is lacking the sarcastic edge I have grown accustomed to.

"So, she came home to ask for help, was sent away and disappeared again?" Hugh scratches his chin, leaning back in his chair, a crease between his brows. "The woman Victor described seemed different from the one Evelyn knew, less controlled."

"But then I hardly knew her at all," I say.

"Victor has promised to attend the funeral and plans to ask his parents and brother, too. He did think it was unlikely they would agree to come, though."

"You have no reason to suspect he was lying?" I ask.

"I tend to have a strong sense of a person. I am very intuitive," Hollis grins meaningfully. "And no, I do not think he possesses the guile to dupe me. His reaction to learning of Juliet's violent death struck me as genuine, and what motive would he have had? He lives a quiet, bland, little life with his card games and his rugby and fortnightly visits to his parents. He struck me as the sort who is content with his lot. Why cause trouble?"

"A lot of killers are content until something happens that they perceive as a threat to their world order. They become compelled, not realizing that murder will never restore the equilibrium."

"True enough, Lady Evelyn, true enough, but if you had met Victor, I wager you would have come away from the encounter sharing my opinion."

"This story tells us more about Juliet, but does it bring us closer to her killer?" Hugh wonders aloud.

"If we strike Victor from the list – or at least move him to the bottom – it leaves the man who she claimed stole her money and left her pregnant."

"But why now? He got what he wanted at the time. Even if she recognized him all these years later, I doubt she would bother accusing him, or go to the police." Hugh shakes his head, dissatisfied. I agree, yet I cannot quite shake the feeling that Juliet's past is linked to her death. She had been living quietly in that flat for years, a phantom. The more I think of it, I believe she chose that life to keep her past at bay or to hide from it. Was she afraid? I remember the flat, so anonymous in its décor, the home where she had lived for years. It looked as though she wanted to be untraceable, as if she wished nobody to know who she was. I think of this office, my room here, the house in Grosvenor Square. Small mementoes of who I am and what I like are everywhere. As Hollis said earlier, I am an open book. Was it exhausting for Juliet to be so closed off, or was it simply who she had become?

"What are you thinking?" Hugh asks. I feel his and Hollis' eyes on me and sit up.

"I was wondering whether Juliet was afraid." I explain my theories to the two men, and they listen without interruption.

"Do you think she suspected someone wanted her dead since coming to London?" Hugh finally asks.

"I am beginning to wonder," I admit.

"Why stay, then?" Hollis asks. "If she had neither friends nor family, nor particularly fulfilling employment, why stay in a place where you are afraid for your life? She disappeared before, she could have done it again, couldn't she?"

"Maybe she was tired of running away? Or there was, after all, someone in her life in London whom she trusted and to whom she wished to be close."

"Someone," Hugh observes darkly, "who may very well have killed her. If we are right in assuming she knew her murderer and let him or her into her flat, there is clearly a person we are overlooking with whom she had some sort of a relationship and didn't see as a threat."

"Such as the women in the WI?" I say warily. The men don't object, leaving me to face the unsettling possibility I had hoped to dismiss.

Chapter 35

When I stop by the police station the next morning, a young constable unceremoniously informs me the inspector is out. Asking when he is expected to return earns me only an apathetic shrug, so I decide to leave Stanton a message to contact me. I want to tell him in person what Hollis has learned and hear what he has to say about it. I doubt he could know already. Ignoring curious glances, I make my way out of the station and back into the freezing cold. I am beginning to wonder whether a winter wedding is such a brilliant idea after all. I hope the place Daniel has planned to take me afterwards is one suffused in warmth and sunlight.

My mind is in a muddled state this morning, contemplations about the wedding, of Juliet and her past, of the funeral and tonight's séance mingle in a confused thought-soup. I cannot concentrate. It does not help that, upon arriving at the flat, I am met with a distraught young woman who has lost a diamond and ruby necklace which her husband expects her to wear this evening. She is afraid to ask her staff for help, insisting they all loathe her, for she is the second wife and the first was apparently an angel! I feel sorry for her and agree to take on this search and rescue case, which takes me to her Mayfair home and absorbs the next three hours of my day. In the end, I find that the necklace is not all that has been taken. When threatening that I will alert the police, a hard-faced housekeeper approaches me, claiming to have *found* the stash in one of her maid's rooms. I realize immediately she is lying and say as much to my client, but the young woman is too relieved and frightened by the housekeeper to act against her. There is nothing I can do, so I collect my fee and make my way back to the flat in St. James. What great fortune to have found the kind and trustworthy Maisie and the bright and reserved Maeve! Neither, I am certain, would ever betray me. When I arrive, I find that Maeve is out at the market, and Hugh is upstairs at Dulcie's helping her and a reluctant Mr. Singh set up for the evening's event. I am just writing down my notes for the morning's case, when I notice a sound. Aidan is standing in the doorway, a small blue blanket in one hand, a slightly damp looking half of a biscuit in the other.

"Well, hello," I say and give the lad a wave. He hesitates, then offers a shy smile. I walk over to him, crouching down. "Are you bored? Would you like a story?"

Aidan's big eyes widen, and he crams the remainder of the biscuit into his mouth. Before I can say any more, Kathleen appears behind her grandson, two spots of color in her cheeks.

"Oh, I do apologize. I only took my eyes away for a moment. You mustn't bother Lady Evelyn, Aidan," she reprimands gently, ruffling his copper curls.

"I don't mind one bit. The distraction is welcome, in fact."

"Working too hard?" she asks, a rare display of curiosity. Typically, our conversations consist of brief niceties, polite chit-chat about the weather or meals. I take her question as a sign that she is warming to me, and I welcome it.

"I should not complain. Hugh and I are very fortunate, yet this case is giving us trouble and then there is the séance tonight. I can't say I am looking forward to it."

"A séance?" Kathleen asks, and I realize she may not know. I explain, feeling slightly foolish all the while. Watching for her reaction, I see not judgement but curiosity.

"She wishes to contact her son?"

"Yes, well, I do not know if she truly believes it. She will try anything."

"I have never met Mrs. Hazlett, though I ran into the chap with the head scarf a while ago."

"Mr. Singh," I say, not explaining the significance of his turban. "He is her friend, though they do not agree on this evening's event."

"I can't blame him for doubting, but then I can't blame her either. When you lose a child, you never recover fully. I am fortunate to have found Maeve and Aidan to distract me. I see my boy in him every day. He looked just like Aidan at this age, maybe the hair was a bit closer to brown. They have the same eyes, though. And they have the same name, of course."

"Maeve mentioned you go to the graveyard often," I observe, realizing as soon as the words leave my mouth that she may not wish to speak of her visits to her son's final resting place with me. In her eyes, I am an employer, not a friend. Yet despite her assertion that Aidan keeps her company, she must feel lonely sometimes. She goes to church, but mostly, I think, she is with her grandson.

"I go as often as I can," she replies, her voice somber. Grief has its claws in her, and it will likely never quite let go. She looks near Aunt Agnes' age, though she must be ten years her junior, having lived a life of labor and loss. Perhaps it is this thought compelling me to ask, "Would you like to join us tonight?"

She looks taken aback by the proposal, and I hope I have not offended her Catholic sensibilities. Kathleen may well think it is some manner of sin to try to communicate with the dead, or with the spirits, while in some ways it is not so different from visiting her son's grave and praying there.

She opens her mouth as if to speak, then closes it again.

"Of course, it is entirely up to you," I hasten to add. "Perhaps it goes against your beliefs. I must confess, I am not convinced by any means, but Dulcie is my friend."

"I can't," she says, finality in her tone, though her expression remains soft. "I wish for you all to find what you look for. I speak with my Aidan every day. I go to his grave, I pray for him. That is how I connect with him."

"I understand," I say. At that moment, we hear the front door, and Aidan, who seems to sense his mother's return, runs into the hallway as quickly as his stout little legs can carry him. Kathleen and I exchange a smile, before she follows her grandson and I return to work. Nothing has changed, yet I feel a sense of calm come over me. I hear Aidan giggle in the hallway and the Irish lilt of his mother and grandmother speaking, and once more I am glad to have found them.

Hugh, previously most at ease with the notion of the séance, has grown anxious, pacing about the office. I cannot concentrate and close my notebook. Daniel should be here any moment. There is a knot in my stomach at the thought of sitting around a table in Dulcie's cozy flat, trying to summon...Who? My parents? Will I be able to bring myself to try? The thought of some strange woman putting on airs, being able to communicate with them when I cannot, strikes me as appalling. I know Daniel feels much the same, and I am all the more grateful he let me bend his will to join us. I wonder why Hugh agreed to come. He has experience with death, and lost many a comrade fighting in France. Is there one person he wishes to reach, or does he merely wonder whether it is possible, the way a tiny part of me does, too?

When Daniel arrives, we go up together, each of us silent in our unease. I grip Daniel's hand, and he gives me a knowing nod. He is pale and I feel guilty for asking him to attend, but I am suddenly frightened that this woman Dulcie found is not a charlatan. What if, by some strange magic, I can contact my parents? Or Dulcie her son? I take a deep breath before knocking. We are here now, come what may.

It takes hardly a moment for the door to open and Mr. Singh to beckon us into the dimly lit hallway. It smells of the usual spices, marsala and chai and something else, dust and candlewax. I worry that this experience will spoil the peace of Dulcie's flat forever, though hope I am simply being melodramatic.

"Dulcie is in the sitting room. The séance will be held in the dining room. Apparently, a large table is required," Mr. Singh says, his voice heavy with disapproval.

"You will not join us?" Daniel asks, while Hugh fidgets at my other side.

"My religion teaches me death is not the end. The soul is reborn until it is ready to join Waheguru." He speaks quietly but with conviction, and I wonder how life would be if I, like Mr. Singh and Kathleen, had such a powerful faith in that which I cannot see? Of course, they believe everything around us is the creation and will of God. It does Mr. Singh credit, however, that he has helped Dulcie organize this evening, for I do not doubt it is largely due to his efforts and devotion to his friend that we are here.

Dulcie steps into the hallway at that moment. "What are you whispering about? Come in, Madame Rose will be here soon!"

Daniel throws me a meaningful look when Dulcie turns, mouthing, "Madame Rose?" and I have to stifle a nervous giggle. "Do you think she will come in black lace like a weeping widow?" he whispers in my ear, as we join Dulcie in the sitting room.

"I shall be rather disappointed if she does not."

The sitting room – thank heavens – is as always, warm and welcoming and somewhat odd, its décor ranging from traditional English with an overstuffed green brocade armchair, to decidedly more exotic, with piles of silk cushions and the grand feather of a peacock in a vase on a gilt side table. Dulcie looks brighter than the last time I saw her, cheeks rosy as if she has been for a brisk walk. Sadly, I know it was not so. She wears a dress of fine emerald green silk with gold embroidery on the sleeves and hem and a scarf in her hair. I feel underdressed in my plain blue woolen skirt and jumper. Mr. Singh brings out a tray with a carafe and tiny copper glasses. From the scent in the air as he pours, I can tell this is to be liquid courage.

We sit a while in silence, sipping and throwing glances at the clock, when finally, ten minutes past the agreed upon time, comes a knock at the door. Mr. Singh, who has been waiting, though not drinking with us, gets to his feet. He casts Dulcie a fleeting look. She merely nods, and he leaves the room. A moment later, he returns with a woman in a dark dress and blood red scarf draped around her neck. Another younger woman stands behind her, in a plain gray dress, eyes to the ground.

"Madame Rose," he says, as though the woman requires any introduction. She is of indeterminate age, yet if I were forced to guess, I might put her close to fifty. Her hair is dark with a strand of white at the front and tied into a loose knot at the nape of her neck. She wears no jewelry, her only adornment a swipe of bright red lipstick across her mouth. She has something exotic about her, although it could simply be the circumstance in which we find ourselves that paints such an image. We go around and introduce ourselves.

"Good evening," she says in a low, unaccented voice. "I am Madame Rose and this," she gestures at the woman by her side without averting her gaze from us, "is my assistant, Kat. Shall we begin?"

"Oh, er...yes, yes, of course," Dulcie agrees eagerly. I have rarely seen her flustered, but this woman has unnerved us all. All except Mr. Singh, who stands calmly at the door, arms crossed over his chest.

"I must see the room first," she demands as Hugh helps Dulcie to her feet.

"I will show you," says Mr. Singh and the two women leave with him. A moment later, he returns alone. "They are inspecting the energies," he grumbles.

"Oh dear, I hope..." Dulcie begins.

"It will be all right." I pat her hand, wishing I could say, "Don't get your hopes up,"yet understanding it is the last thing she wishes to hear.

"Madame Rose is ready," Kat announces, appearing silent as a mouse in the doorway after a few minutes have passed.

"Right," Daniel says, taking a deep breath. We follow the young woman down the hall to the dining room. I have never been in this room before. It is grander than I anticipated, although Dulcie has not, to my knowledge, hosted a dinner party in a long time. The windows have been darkened with black sheets and a cloth of the same opaque fabric has been draped over the large round table at the center of the room. In the gloom, I see a few framed paintings by artists I recognize. On the side tables stand solid silver candlesticks. There are lit candles everywhere and my body goes rigid with a fear of accidentally causing one to tip over and send the tablecloth or curtains aflame! The flickering light, however, does infuse the room with a sense of mystery, the thick scent of candlewax cloying and heavy in the air.

"Sit," commands Madame Rose and we take our places. Dulcie sits beside the medium, I beside her, Daniel, then Hugh and finally the assistant, Kat. I notice that the three extra chairs have been pulled away from the table and pushed against the wall, so our circle is not interrupted. "Place your hands on the table, palms up." She demonstrates, and we follow suit. My gaze flits around our little group. Hugh sits rigid, as though he regrets having agreed to come. Daniel's expression barely conceals his suspicion. Dulcie, however, wears a tiny smile of anticipation, reminding me why we are here. I only hope she will not be too badly disappointed. At this stage, I almost hope Madame Rose and Kat are charlatans and will at least pretend to produce some connection to satisfy Dulcie's need.

My thoughts are interrupted by a low hum emanating from Madame Rose, and my eyes find Daniel's. He grimaces, and I give him a little kick under the table.

"Spirits!" Madame Rose calls out, her voice low. I wonder whether Mr. Singh can hear. "Spirits!" she calls again. "Hear me!" She closes her eyes and Kat bids us to do the same. I do not like it, but comply, the room going from dim to black. The sound of Madame Rose's hum intensifies, broken by the intermittent call for the "spirits" to hear her. Suddenly, there is a sound, a sort of knocking, just once.

"What was that?" I ask, opening my eyes to find the others have done the same. Another knock.

"Yes! I hear you! Come to me!" cries the medium, raising her hands just above the table. Then she gives a violent shudder that has us gasping aloud, and her eyes roll back in her head. She inhales deeply, audibly and closes her eyes. "I see a man," she says. "He is young."

None of us respond. Even Dulcie, requires more details before providing the name of her son. Who among us has not known a young man who died? We live less than a decade after a horrendous war!

"Green eyes, he has green eyes, and his hair…brown. I see a scar -"

"Rupert had a scar!" Dulcie cries out, unable to restrain the hope that has blossomed within her. A scar. Daniel has brown hair, green eyes and bears a scar. The description could be his own!

The medium nods. "Is that you, Rupert? Tell me." Another knock.

Dulcie cries out. "Rupert?"

"Quiet! Yes, I hear you. What is that you say?" Madame Rose nods, and I wish I could kick her, too. Fury towards the woman rages within me. Can she not see Dulcie's pain? Toying with her so, making her believe –

"Mother? Is that you?" Madame Rose's voice has changed, shifted ever so slightly, and it sends a chill down my spine.

"Rupert? Darling, I am here, I am here!" Dulcie says, eyes wide. I ache to bring an end to this charade.

"I miss you, Mother. Do you think of me often?"

"Every day, my boy, every day," she says, her voice thick with tears, though she dares not raise her hand to wipe them from her face for fear of breaking the supposed connection.

"I am all right. I am not suffering anymore," comes the medium's eerie voice. "Here I am free."

"Why did you do it, Rupert? Why did you leave me?"

Madame Rose is silent for a moment, rocking ever so slightly back and forth in her chair. "There is someone else," she says, her voice as it was before.

"Where is Rupert? Call him back, please!" Dulcie's desperation sends a dagger through my heart and I open my mouth to object, when the woman orchestrating this farce begins to speak once more.

"A woman is looking for her child," says Madame Rose, her voice entirely monotone. "A child no more now. Come closer, let me hear you. Who do you seek?"

Against my better judgement, my heart beats faster suddenly and despite my reasoning mind, dread descends upon me, heavy as a cloak.

"Is Rupert gone?" Dulcie whispers.

"Evelyn?" Madame Rose says, again her voice has adopted a different cadence, and gooseflesh rises on my skin. "My daughter's name is -"

"Enough!" Daniel's voice is loud and angry, angrier than I have ever heard him before. He pulls back his hands. Madame Rose ignores him completely as though she is not present in the room but somewhere else. She did not so much as flinch at his voice. I find myself frozen to the spot, eyes on the medium. The room feels stuffy and airless. Smoke from the candles burns my eyes.

"Come into the light," she says, coaxing. "Speak, you are among friends." Once again the knocking rings through the silence, yet this time, it sounds as though it is coming from close by. "If you can hear me, send a sign." A moment's silence, then another, louder knock. It is definitely close by, almost as if... I pull my hands back and look under the table. It is too dark to see anything.

"What are you doing? You are disrupting the spirit circle!" Madame Rose shrieks, breaking her composure. It is enough proof for me to get to my feet and fumble for the electric lamp.

"Evelyn, please!" Dulcie cries out, but the spell is broken. Bright, artificial light floods the room, and everyone blinks blearily. I am on the ground in time to see exactly what I was expecting. The source of the knocking.

"You charlatan!" I cry out, pointing at Kat. The girl is bright red and stumbles to her feet, a mistake, perhaps, for now everyone can see my discovery. The woman is wearing the plain black boots she arrived in, but ankle straps hold two wooden balls in place, to produce the knocking sound which signaled the arrival of the spirits. Dulcie gasps and presses a hand to her mouth. I am glad Daniel and Hugh are here to steady her. Anger courses through me. While I had no expectations of a genuine communication with the spirit world tonight, this barefaced and uninspired deception is startling and infuriating.

Madame Rose stands, trying to appear dignified, staring down her long, straight nose at me as I get back to my feet. "What I said is still true. People always want sound effects, but the spirits speak to me. I -"

"That is quite enough," I say firmly and walk across the room, opening the door. "Leave!"

"We are owed -"

"Nothing, except to be reported for trying to take advantage of a grieving woman. If you do not wish me to call the police, you will be gone by the time I have blown out these blasted candles!" There must be something in my manner that convinces the women their act is over, and they quickly pack up and disappear. My heart is still hammering in my chest by the time the front door has closed. Rationally, I know they were liars and that it is no secret I am an orphan, yet when Madame Rose said a woman was looking for her child, and spoke my name - a name I had given moments earlier - I hate to admit a flicker of hope came alive within me, even if it was extinguished a few seconds later.

"What happened?" Mr. Singh is standing in the doorway, concern creasing his brow. It would have been impossible for him not to hear our shouting and the two frauds hurrying from the flat.

"They were impostors," Daniel explains. He is still holding onto Dulcie's arm, for she is pale and shaken. Her hope has collapsed, and she likely feels all the lonelier and more foolish for it.

"I expected as much. Now at least we can -"

"You found them, Sunil! Did you choose blatant imposters to prove me wrong?" Dulcie's vehemence shocks me, and I can see from the expression on the others' faces, I am not the only one.

"You know that is not true, Dulcie," Mr. Singh replies in a measured tone, though I can tell from his expression, her words have stung. He is the most loyal of friends to Dulcie and to be accused in such a manner must hurt.

The fight drains from Dulcie as quickly as it appeared and she sighs, shaking her head and sending a curl of silver-gray hair tumbling into her face. "You are right. You all believed it was a farce, and maybe I did too. But when she said..." Another shake of the head. "I was a fool. Do not think less of me, please?" She addresses us all, but her eyes are on Mr. Singh.

"Never, Dulcie," I promise. Daniel and Hugh nod their agreement. Mr. Singh offers a conciliatory smile.

"Come, let us leave this room. I will sort it out later. Come to the kitchen. I am sure, if you are anything like Dulcie and myself, you will not have eaten."

We agree, for indeed, none of us could muster an appetite at the thought of conjuring up spirits of the dead, and I am suddenly famished. The dining room out of commission, we sit at the long kitchen table. Mr. Singh serves bowls of fragrant yellow rice, a sort of lentil stew he calls *dal* and a bright orange dish of chicken so spicy it makes my eyes water.

"A simple meal, but it will put some color back in your cheeks," he says, inviting us to begin. Dulcie is listless, pushing her food around her plate, but the rest of us tuck in. Hugh especially, who has never tasted Mr. Singh's cooking, is impressed. He seems immune to the burn of the chili that has me continually reaching for the jug of water Mr. Singh thoughtfully placed on the table. He was right, though. The warmth and nourishment, the bright light of the kitchen and the scent of foreign spices lingering in the air reinvigorate us. I feel the tension of the previous hour slowly ebbing away. Even Dulcie looks better, though she is quiet while the rest of us try to distract her. Daniel and I speak of the wedding, to which she and Mr. Singh have naturally been invited, even if I suspect she will not come. Hugh manages to elicit a tiny smile, recounting one obscure case after another, of lost pets and mislaid jewels. Mr. Singh is mostly silent. Once in a while, I catch his eye and he gives me a nod. This evening did not bring closure. Dulcie will not forget her grief or her son, and Mr. Singh feels helpless in the face of it. There must be something that can be done, something to distract Dulcie, to ease her mind a little and alleviate the guilt of a parent who had to bury her child.

When we leave, it is as though the séance was nothing but a strange dream. All through our meal, none of us spoke of it. I, for one, would be happy to completely forget the travesty altogether. It is late, and we persuade Hugh to stay in Grosvenor Square for the night instead of trekking out to Lambeth. Juliet's funeral is tomorrow morning, with a small gathering to be held at the WI's hall afterward. I dread the event, yet I cannot possibly miss it. Daniel is lending Hugh a dark suit for the occasion.

"You do know she was a fraud?" Daniel asks, as we lie in the darkness. He has an ability to tell whether I am sleeping or not, even when my eyes are closed. So I abandon the charade and push myself up on my elbows. I can just see the outline of Daniel's face.

"I know she was."

"And yet…"

"Maybe someone else isn't?" I sigh and drop my head back to stare at the ceiling as if the answers to my questions can be found there.

"You don't believe that. Evie, don't let false hope do to you what it did to Dulcie. I miss my family, too, but I am convinced some stranger will not reach them if I can't."

"You are right, and I agree. There is only the tiniest sliver of doubt. The world is too mysterious for me to be certain about much of anything."

"Doubt can be a burden and a boon," Daniel observes quietly. "Remember when I thought Henry was alive?"

"How could I forget?" I reply, recalling the tense weeks spent in France, after a tenuous thread of hope had sprung up that Daniel's eldest brother survived the war after all.

"I think the wedding has brought on my maudlin mood. There is so much I want to share with my parents, so much I wish they could be a part of. Agnes is here, and I have family, I know, but it isn't the same."

"I understand," Daniel says after a moment's silence. "But if you are willing to believe a stranger can connect you to the people you lost, you can also believe in God, in a life after death, in the possibility that they are somehow ever-present."

"Reason does not get us very far in this respect. I do not know what to believe, even if I know what I would like to believe."

"At least you can differentiate between the two," Daniel offers.

"What do you think Hugh believes? He was surprisingly keen on taking part tonight, even if nerves got to him in the end."

"We haven't discussed it."

"Men," I say in a huff.

"Do you make a habit of chatting about the afterlife or lack thereof with Briony?" Daniel asks, and I hear the smile in his voice while the darkness hides his features.

"That is hardly the point. I think he believes more than we do. Maybe it makes him feel less alone."

"Almost certainly." He hesitates, then asks, "Do you feel alone?"

"No," I reply quickly, truthfully. "Or no more than anyone might. I have encountered so many people recently who seem to be missing something, or rather someone in their lives. London is such a large place, and being alone here can make a person feel invisible."

"Like Juliet?"

"Maybe." We are silent for a few moments, thinking of the past and the present, and how they collide; of the yet unformed future, both frightening and exciting, and for some, entirely out of their grasp.

"Are you still awake?" Daniel asks after a little while.

"Yes." His hand tries to find mine, and I reach out to take hold of it. We do not speak any more of death and spirits and loneliness. My eyelids are heavy and at some point, though it seems a long time, sleep comes for me and I drift away into the land of dreams.

Chapter 36

"I dreamt I was underwater," Hugh tells me as we drive to Kensal Green. The day is surprisingly mild, though it is only morning and a scattering of sparrows lazily picks at something on the pavement, dispersing when the motor's engine roars into life. Clouds hang lazily in the pale blue sky, barely a breeze ruffles the barren branches.

"Perhaps it symbolizes something," I suggest, wishing I could remember my own uneasy dreams. I woke up with my hair in tangles and a sense of dread, though unable to recall where it came from.

"Fear of washing?" Hugh proposes with a wide-eyed grin.

"Oh, stop it!" I say, amused by his attempts to distract me.

"Do you think Wilkins told his sister that it was me following him?" he asks. "I spoke to her this morning, and she was friendly as ever. Maybe she doesn't know."

"She knows but wasn't angry. I think Wilkins probably just wants to forget and move on."

"She seems happy here."

"I hope so."

"Is Stanton coming to the funeral?"

"Yes, and Hollis is, too. I know you do not like him much, but you must admit, he is helpful."

"The problem is what he wants for his help. He will write about the murder, but how will he write? The thought of him turning Juliet's death into some sensational tale strikes me as deeply macabre."

"If he does not do it, someone else will. At least with Hollis, we have a tiny degree of influence, or so I hope."

"Her cousin Victor will attend. I hope we get a chance to speak to him. Hollis may have learned all there is, but I want to get a sense of the man."

"I do not rank him highly on our list of suspects."

"As yet, we do not rank *anyone* very highly on our list. That is the problem," Hugh complains, and I cannot disagree. Patience may be a virtue, but time is a slippery eel, and I am afraid soon too much of it will have passed for us to solve the case. For all we know, Juliet's killer has disappeared and is half-way to Timbuktu by now!

The drive to Kensal Green Cemetery takes the better part of an hour, and by the time we arrive, I am eager to stretch my legs and arms, which have grown stiff in the unpredictable London traffic. Several other motorcars idle outside the cemetery gates, and people in black and gray mingle in clusters. I take a deep breath. There have been too many funerals to attend in my relatively short lifetime already.

The ceremony is short and superficial. No loving anecdotes to add character to the woman in the casket. Outside, as the coffin is lowered into the earth and the vicar speaks in somber tones, I glance around. Not surprisingly, there are mostly women present. I recognize a number of familiar faces from the WI. Aunt Louise stands beside Adeline and Edith. To my surprise, even her husband, Lloyd, is in attendance, wearing a dark suit which makes him appear even broader and taller somehow in this sea of women. Frances Bell stands to the side, no Lara Bennet in sight. I give her a nod when I catch her eye and she returns it, her mouth set in a tight line. She attended the funeral of Juliet's parents, and now she must bear witness to their daughter's as well. Stanton hovers near the Ashbournes, his eyes roving around. He arrived late, missing the ceremony, and is likely trying to get a sense of the attendees, just as I am. A man with white-blond hair waits at the edge of the congregation, next to him Hollis Napier who, despite the occasion, appears to have a sly grin on his face, his natural expression. Another man lingers behind them, though I can barely make out his face, for Hollis wears a tall hat and shifts perpetually from one foot to the other, obscuring my sight. I take a step back for a better view. Hugh gives me a strange look, but follows my gaze. The man is slim with dark hair poking out from under a hat. From a distance, I judge his age to be near Juliet's. Is this the man from her photograph? I would not make such a leap were it not for the distinct lack of male attendees, particularly ones unknown to me. I cannot say I notice much of a resemblance between him and the younger man in the photograph, though. His face is longer, thinner, and his mouth wider. He has the look of someone who smiles often and easily, though I am unlikely to see it on this occasion.

"Do you recognize him?" Hugh whispers, as the vicar's monotone voice commits Juliet to the earth. I shake my head.

"I thought…"

"No, he looks different," Hugh finishes my thought. "Even if the photo is ten, fifteen years old."

"I want to speak to him after this, learn what his connection to Juliet is. Edith made the funeral's time and date public, so anyone might have found out about it." I add, "Especially if they were looking for such an announcement."

The vicar closes his bible. The final prayer is spoken, and the congregation turns away. I notice the man facing the open grave a moment longer. The women of the WI have moved on, shivering and eager to escape the chill of the graveyard. Hollis is saying something to Victor, and they approach Stanton. I seize the chance, Hugh by my side. The man notices us but, to his credit, does not make any attempt to escape. His expression is curious, eyes slightly narrowed as we approach.

"Good morning," I say, realizing too late the words are not quite suitable given the circumstances. I extend my hand. "Evelyn Carlisle, this is my colleague Hugh Lawrence." The man looks at my hand, as if uncertain what to do with it. Before the moment grows too awkward, he gives it a limp shake.

"Michael Ellroy," he says, and I detect a hint of an accent. American, perhaps?

"May I ask, how you knew Juliet?" I smile to illustrate I am aware of my nosiness.

"I met her long ago. She helped me once."

"You're American?" Hugh asks.

"From Canada, though I have lived in London these past five years. My wife is English." His expression softens a little, and I dismiss the notion he was Juliet's lover. A married man may well be unfaithful, but it strikes me as unlikely that he would come to his murdered lover's funeral and mention his wife to strangers with an affectionate smile on his lips. A friend, then. I would wish it for Juliet, even if friendship does her little good now.

"I met Juliet only shortly before she died," I admit. "Were you in contact with her?"

"I...no, and I do not think -"

"Pardon me, I should have explained. Mr. Lawrence and I are investigating Juliet's death." I decide to be honest and hand him a card. If he is going to lie, he will lie regardless of our explanation. To my surprise, his expression relaxes.

"A detective? Juliet would have liked that, I am sure. No, sadly we lost touch long ago. Someone told me she had returned to the city some years ago."

"Was it Howard Bell?" I ask, the name slipping past my lips before I can stop myself. By the shift in Ellroy's expression, I see I have hit the mark. Recognition and surprise flicker in his eyes.

"How do you know Howard?" he asks. I throw a quick glance around to see if Frances is about, yet she has faded into the distance with the other mourners, eager to escape the cold. Perhaps she recognized Ellroy? But then, it seems, there was much her husband kept from her.

"I know his wife."

"His widow," he corrects me.

"So, you heard he died," Hugh observes.

"I did. Sadly, I could not attend his funeral. Yet I thought it only right I should try to be here today. I read Juliet's obituary in the paper. Terrible. She was so young, so clever." He shakes his head, rubbing his roughly-shaven chin, glancing around at the huddles of people, the lichen covered gravestones and the fresh hole in the ground, now being filled by two men, sleeves rolled to their elbows. "I should go."

"Please, Mr. Ellroy, just a moment," I plead, but he is already moving. Hugh and I trail alongside him, keeping pace. "Juliet was murdered. We are working with the police to find her killer." I decide there is no point in trying to make the truth sound more appealing. Better to be blunt, given the circumstances. If Mr. Ellroy is the killer, he was aware coming here was a risk. Stanton must have noticed him, too.

"And you think I can help you?" he slows and looks at me. I cannot tell whether his expression is one of disbelief or admiration.

"Juliet knew her killer," I say and watch for his reaction.

"You suspect me?" he asks, stopping in his tracks, and I almost collide with him. Ellroy stares at me through narrowed eyes, but there is no anger to be found in them, only bewilderment. "I have been in Canada the past month. My father was poorly, though he has since recovered. I returned a week ago. There are arrival logs testifying to it. Besides, I never wished Juliet ill, quite the opposite. I owe her a debt. Now I can never repay it."

"A debt?" I ask, unwilling to let go.

Ellroy lets out a sigh, then chuckles. "You are a bloodhound, Miss Carlisle, and you may take that as a compliment." He looks around. Stanton and the others have disappeared. A few steps away, another funeral is taking place. I shiver, not only from the cold.

"Are you going to the memorial?" I ask. A reluctant nod. "Let us drive you, or have you taken a car?"

"I came by taxi. Oh, all right. I don't suppose I can evade you."

"Don't sound so enthusiastic," Hugh says, and we trudge in silence through the graveyard, leaving behind all that remains of Juliet Nelson, daughter and friend, as it says on her gravestone. *But who were you really?*

Chapter 37

"Nice motor," Ellroy observes when we climb into the Bentley. The leather seats are freezing, and I feel the cold through my coat, my skirt, my stockings. Hugh is driving, and I sit in the back, leaving the passenger's seat to Ellroy with his long legs.

"You mentioned Juliet did you a favor?" I ask.

"Is she always this nosy?" Ellroy says to Hugh, who grins traitorously.

"Comes with the territory," he observes.

"So, you really are trying to find Juliet's killer?"

"We have been successful in the past," I say quickly.

"Who hired you?"

"My client's identity is confidential."

"Look, I am interested in helping if I can," Ellroy says, looking over his shoulder at me. "But you have to meet me halfway."

I take a moment to consider, then explain, "Juliet was invited to join her local WI. A woman there hired me, that is all I can say. She was very troubled by Juliet's death."

"Rich, then," Ellroy observes, rubbing his chin.

"An answer for an answer," I reply. "What sort of a favor did Juliet do you that you still feel indebted to her?"

"Your question demands more than a simple answer. Not a fair exchange, but my mother taught me to be a gentleman, so I will play your game. Juliet saved my life."

"That is indeed a debt!" I marvel as Hugh slows the car, turning down the wrong lane, buying us time with Ellroy.

"It is, and you turned too early," Ellroy says. There is a wry note to his voice, telling me he is well aware of what Hugh is doing and doesn't very much mind. "My turn for a question. How did Juliet die? I don't quite trust the papers."

"She was strangled," I reply, my hand moving instinctively to my throat, the image of Juliet with her necklace of bruises flashing before my eyes. Ellroy watches me over his shoulder and his jaw tightens.

"Poor Juliet. Strangled, after everything…" He presses his lips into a tight line and shakes his head. "And you believe she knew her killer?"

"Yes. We think she must have known him or her."

"Was she still so slender a woman? It wouldn't take much to physically overpower her, even if she always had a few tricks up her sleeve."

"What do you mean?"

"Oh, I suppose I owe you another answer. Juliet was clever, as I said. Experience taught her that. Experience, serious training and even more serious circumstances."

"You are a puzzling fellow! Has anyone ever told you that?"

He laughs. "Do you want that to count as one of your questions?"

"No. Mr. Ellroy, this is not a game. Please, if you can help, do so before the trail goes cold. If you take your debt to her seriously, help us find some measure of justice for Juliet." My impassioned plea finds receptive ears. Ellroy twists in his seat to meet my gaze.

"You are right. It isn't a game, but you may not realize what you have stumbled upon. Juliet Nelson was no ordinary spinster. I knew her many years ago as Minette Laurent. She was a spy."

Chapter 38

"A spy," I repeat slowly, and pieces of the scattered puzzle fall into place. The medals, her ability to make herself practically invisible. I hardly notice when Hugh pulls into a side street and stops the car, turning in his seat.

"You really didn't know?" Ellroy asks with a hint of a smile. "Then again, Juliet was intensely private. Howard refused to give me her address. I only learned her real name after the war."

"This is all quite…shocking," I stammer. "Juliet Nelson was a spy for Britain during the war."

"Got it in one, Miss Carlisle," he says. "I met her in Valenciennes. A number of Canadians were stationed there along with some Brits."

"The name has a familiar ring."

"I recall hearing of the Battle of Valenciennes in '18," Hugh notes somberly.

"Part of the Hundred Days Offensive," Ellroy says. "I was there in '17 already, which was when I met Minette – Juliet – I mean."

"I remember now. Mrs. Bell said Juliet's mother spoke fluent French and that Juliet did, too."

"No one would have taken her as anything other than the girl from Lille she claimed to be, well, almost nobody."

"Please, tell us what happened." I lean forward. Ellroy hesitates, perhaps already regretting that he spoke at all, that he did not simply turn away at the graveyard and leave us none the wiser. Maybe a remnant of the secrecy bred into him from the war?

"I heard of the female spies," Hugh says quietly. "Or rather, I heard of one of the best, Louise de Bettignies."

I shudder at the mention of the name. Bettignies was deemed a brilliant mastermind in the realm of British Intelligence. She ran a spy ring around the area of Lille and saved countless lives by providing information gathered from the German occupants, supplying it to the British. Her end was far less glorious than her bravery would have warranted. She was arrested, imprisoned and died of mistreatment. Only after the war was she was given a worthy burial and military honors to suit the great service she did Britain and France. To think of Juliet in a similar vein is almost unimaginable. Slight and silent Juliet…

"Bettignies was a legend, even when I was over there, and she had been in captivity for years. When she died, it sent a collective shudder through the ranks. Juliet was not prominent like Louise de Bettignies, but she was a hero to me and many others." Ellroy takes a deep breath and rubs his chin. "I can only share my own story, for as grateful as I was to Juliet, I knew very little of her, just as she intended. Her secrecy was in part to protect herself and her cover as the baker's assistant, as well as to protect me. If I knew nothing, I had nothing to tell either.

"It was late 1917, ten years ago, when I met her. I was stationed in Valenciennes and because I spoke some German, decided to do a bit of spying on my own. I was young, eager to prove myself, to stand out amidst a sea of soldiers. I had ambitions and a false sense of heroism." Ellroy lets out a cheerless laugh. "It took a while for me to realize there are not many heroes in war. The long and short of it is, I was caught. I was familiar with the restaurant across from the bakery where the Germans liked to drink. It was a fine establishment, and the owner a traitor, even if he was a desperate man himself. He supplied good wine, fine sausages and stews while everyone in the town around him scrounged for bread and hadn't eaten meat in months. I donned a plain civilian coat and snuck into town alone. What a fool I was! Perhaps I deserved what I got. I had heard my lieutenant trying to convince the delivery man, who supplied the restaurant, to do a bit of spying. The man declined, but he let slip that there was a back door, and no one paid attention to it. I made my way inside. The man had been right. No one guarded the door, which struck me as fortuitous then, but like a trap in hindsight.

"I was listening at the door of the private dining room, well concealed, I thought. They spoke about the transport of ammunitions. I believed it was my big chance to prove my worth. If I could supply my superior with news of the German ammunitions transport schedule, we could stop it from arriving." Ellroy frowns and shrugs. "As you can imagine, I was unsuccessful. While listening, I suddenly felt something hard poking into my side and when I turned, I was faced with a man in a German uniform, his pistol pointed at my ribs. Unwilling to let them capture me, I was reckless. I seized the moment and slammed my head forward, cracking the fellow's nose. He was distracted, but his howl of pain roused the officers in the room beyond and the door flew open. I had seconds - mere seconds! - to run and so I did. Not quite fast enough, though. I rushed outside, darkness all around me and began to run. I heard the crack of shots being fired. They had to be shooting almost blindly, for there was no streetlamp, no light spilling from open windows. Everything was dark, blacked out. I ducked my head and was about to slip into the alley behind the bakery to make my way across the field, back to my company. It was then the bullet struck." He pauses, eyes glassy, distant, as though he is once again in that moment of darkness and terror, feeling the bullet slice into his body. I wince and see the pain of memory reflected in Hugh's eyes as well.

"What happened to you?" I ask gently, on the edge of my seat. Ellroy's eyes still have a faraway look, and I feel a stab of sympathy for this man, who must have been near my own age, alone, afraid and wounded.

"I kept moving, when I felt someone grab my arm and yank me back. Suddenly I was in a room. It was dark, too, and I was half unconscious from fear and pain. I felt a hand on my arm. In the shadows was a face I vaguely recognized, the baker's assistant. She told me to be quiet and dragged me to the next room. She opened a door in the floor, and pulled me down the stairs. My eyes swam in the gloom. I remember thinking afterwards that she must have practiced this in the dark, for she did not hesitate or stumble. When we were below stairs, she lit a torch. I could see her face more clearly. 'I will help you, but you must be quiet,' she whispered in clear English, which startled me. She asked for my name and told me hers was Minette. My mind swam as she pressed against the wound at my side, applied something that stung so badly I almost screamed had she not pressed a twisted handkerchief between my teeth. Suddenly, we heard movement from above. 'They've come for me,' I said, but she stayed calm. For a moment, I wondered whether it was a trap and she was going to deliver me to the Germans. I had heard whispers that the baker spat into the dough of the bread he made to feed the occupiers, but those were rumors. There was the sound of fists pounding on the door, the mumbled, *Oui, oui, j'arrive, j'arrive!* as the baker moved on the floor above us. I heard him pause on the trapdoor, the sound of something being dragged, then his steps moving away again. Minette pressed a finger to her lips, eyes wide, as if I would think of making a sound. We heard badly spoken French, barked commands, heavy footsteps moving around, shifting furniture, loud and angry, while the baker whimpered that he knew nothing, had seen no one. I could not believe it when they finally left, and the house was silent once more. I remained there in that basement for two days. Minette tended to me. Thankfully the shot had been clean, the bullet gone straight through muscle. Minette told me the baker supported what she did, although he wished to have no active part in it. After two days, I worried my comrades would think I was likely dead. I was desperate to return to them. Minette promised she had a plan. She did not let me down. On the third day, the baker was meant to take his rusting heap of a motorcar to deliver goods to a small village outside Valenciennes, something he did every fortnight. This time, however, Minette would make the delivery, and her cargo would contain more than loaves of baguette and brioche.

"The drive was terrifying, and I was in agony from fear and pain as the car jolted over uneven, rutted roads. Minette had made contact with a fellow member of her network who would take me back to my people. We were to meet him at a crossing, which turned from the main road to the village where she was to deliver her goods. I had the sense she cared for this man, for she blushed when she spoke of him. By then, I had learned she was English, though she still insisted her name was Minette Laurent and never to call her otherwise. The man we were meeting remained nameless. In hindsight, so much could have gone wrong. We could easily have been caught, but the only checkpoint we passed gave the bread barely a glance, his eyes focused on the pretty girl behind the wheel. Minette flirted a little and drove on. I heard her sigh with relief once we were out of range. I was sweating and miserable under my canvas cover, but endlessly grateful. Our contact was where he promised to be. He and Minette helped me out of the back of the car. I remember the pain, the ache in my muscles, and also the relief. I saw right away, they were fond of one another. He was a handsome fellow, tall, light brown hair, broad-shouldered. Minette spoke to him in French, but slowly, as though his fluency could not match her own. She touched his arm and he smiled at her, promising to contact her soon. Then she pressed a kiss on my cheek and said, 'Be safe, Michael.' That was it. The man did as he promised and I was soon in the hands of my very disapproving, if relieved, lieutenant once more. When I recovered, I tried to learn what had become of Minette, wished to send her a message of thanks somehow, but I could never return to the occupied Valenciennes."

Hugh and I are silent for a moment, allowing the weight of his story to settle. Juliet a spy…Minette…a young man, her lover? The way Ellroy described him, it could have been the man in the photograph. I wish I had it with me but will instruct Stanton to show it to him. Maybe he would recognize the man who, with Juliet alias Minette, helped save his life.

"How did you learn Minette and Juliet were one and the same?" Hugh asks, the first to find his words. Ellroy sighs and runs a hand over his face. Sharing these memories has tired him, as though he had to relive the harrowing experience.

"I never forgot what she did for me. After the war, I spent some time at home in Ottawa, then started to work for the government and was dispatched to London, where I met my wife Jane." A smile touches his lips. "The memory of the young woman, who claimed to be French, but spoke to me with an English accent, never quite left my thoughts. I began to investigate, which finally took me to Howard Bell, or rather my clumsy investigation brought him to me. I had asked around and put in a request at the War Office, which called attention to me. Bell showed up one evening at my door and introduced himself as an employee of said office. It was evident he was no mere clerk. He was an unobtrusive fellow, but in possession of an undeniable air of quiet authority. He asked me point blank why I was searching for a woman called Minette Laurent. I gave him an honest answer, which softened him towards me. We went for a drink, and I told him everything I remembered. I was desperate to find Minette, to thank her properly, to make sure she was alive and had made it through the war. She was English, I was convinced, though her French must have been strong enough to allow her to pass as a native."

"How did he react?" I ask.

"I could tell he knew more than he was willing to disclose. This took place in 1920, people were still reeling from the devastation. Memorials were still being built, medals still awarded. It wasn't over, not really. For some it never will be. Howard Bell was the sort of person who asked few questions, but just the right ones to get you talking."

"You became friends?"

"Something like that. He never met Jane, and I never met his wife. We would have a drink the last Friday of every month and talk." Ellroy closes his eyes for a moment, a look of pain on his face. This display of vulnerability surprises me, though I suppose nothing should surprise me now. It does not feel like we are strangers anymore.

"Was he able to help you?" Hugh asks.

"Yes and no. I never saw Minette – or rather Juliet again, but I was reassured she was alive. After I told Howard of my time in France, he promised to see what he could do. That was all. He got up and left, not so much as naming a place where I could reach him. Yet ten days later, true to his word, he was waiting for me at the same corner outside my office. We went back to the same pub. He paid for our pints, and we sat in a corner. 'Minette is alive. Her name is Juliet Nelson, and she has agreed to meet you.' You will understand my shock at his words. He did not elaborate much, but I trusted him. Despite knowing him hardly at all, I felt there was something broken in Howard Bell, that he felt a yearning to make amends, though for what I never knew. I told him I would meet her any time she wanted, any place. I was confused but excited and told Jane all about it that evening. The next time I heard from Howard, however, it was with far less welcome news. Juliet had changed her mind. She wanted me to know she was well, but could not face a reminder of that time. Howard seemed crestfallen when he told me, then made me swear to leave it at that. I didn't know what to do. She was so close, and yet...I wanted to respect her wishes, despite my eagerness to meet. It was the least I owed her."

"So, you never met again?"

Ellroy shakes his head, and I see a glimmer in his eyes. "Never. I hoped she would change her mind, but after Howard died, I lost my connection to her, and to be honest, she faded from my mind a little. Howard rarely spoke of Juliet, but he would let a few bits slip here and there after a couple pints. He was unhappy, I think. Once he confided that six of his agents were killed. He felt responsible, although they all understood, at least on some level, what they were getting into."

"He recruited Juliet," I observe, slowly piecing parts of the puzzle together. "She must have come to London after leaving Reading that final time and met Howard."

"He never told me how he met her, but I felt he thought of her almost as a daughter. How someone could send a person they were so fond of into Valenciennes at the height of the war is beyond me. Yet if he had not, I would not be here today."

"She must have saved many more lives," I muse.

"Howard hinted she was one of his best. She had an affinity for languages and easily picked up German in her training. I had the impression she obtained many valuable nuggets of information for British Intelligence."

"She received war medals of the highest order," I say, eliciting a smile in our new Canadian friend.

"If anyone deserved them..." he mumbles. "I wonder what became of the young man who smuggled me back to my people. Since I never knew his name, I could not ask about him. I suspect he was English as well. His French was not as good as Minette's, though he spoke nothing else to me. My own French was modest at best."

"We found a photograph." I explain. Ellroy promises to speak with Stanton and take a look at it.

"I remember his face. I would never forget."

"Do you have any suspicion who could have wished Juliet harm?" I ask hopefully.

"I haven't seen her in ten years! You would be better off asking those close to her, though I suppose you already have."

"She did not allow anyone to be close to her," I say.

"She had been disappointed and hurt in the past. Maybe she could not face growing attached to someone only for them to let her down," Hugh says quietly.

"Perhaps that is why she changed her mind about meeting me all those years ago. I asked Howard again a few times, but he insisted once Juliet made up her mind, there was no changing it. She must have led a lonely life." Ellroy frowns. "The war did things to us all, to our minds. Some are able to move forward, while others remain anchored in a time that changed the way they viewed the world." I glance at Hugh as Ellroy speaks. How very true his words are, even if, in the case of my dear friend, he was able to escape the confines of his memories.

"You know," Ellroy continues, "I am tired. Maybe I can give the memorial a pass. Would you mind dropping me off a few streets down, so I can take the Underground home? You can give your policeman friend my details, but I can't face repeating all of this again today."

"We will drive you home, of course," Hugh decides, and Ellroy is too weary to argue. The plunge into his history has exhausted him, and he is silent as Hugh starts the engine and we roll back into traffic. Engrossed by Ellroy's story, I hardly noticed how frigid the inside of the Bentley has become and shiver even in my many layers. Perhaps it is not only the cold giving me chills, though. We have learned so much about Juliet, and yet I cannot distinguish a clear path to guide us to her killer. Was it, as we suspected even before we knew so much more, a person from her past, who caught up to her as Michael Ellroy finally had? Driving towards Hammersmith, I imagine what Stanton will say when I share our discovery with him.

Chapter 39

We arrive at the memorial event so late, many people have already left. Plates with smears of jam, half-eaten sandwiches and teacups with crimson half-moons of lipstick on the rim are left abandoned on the tables. Edith and Adeline stand together talking. Lloyd Ashbourne is nowhere to be seen. About a half dozen other ladies, among whom I notice Priscilla Lewis and my aunt, mingle quietly. Louise waves us over, and we oblige.

"Where on earth have you been? Everyone has gone already. That policeman kept asking after you, and then he left in a bit of a huff fifteen minutes ago."

"It couldn't be helped," is all I offer. "Is Hollis still here with Juliet's cousin?"

"Hollis?"

"The reporter. Thin, pale, permanent grin-"

"Oh, that chap. Yes, he's still about." She glances around. "Look, over there," she gestures towards a corner, where the two men sit on hard-backed chairs, plates daintily perched on their laps. Hollis catches my eye and raises his brows, glancing meaningfully at the clock on the adjacent wall. I mouth an apology and raise a finger to indicate I will be with them in a moment. Louise is frowning at us, her expression one of bewilderment. I owe her an explanation, but not right now. Instead I reach for her hand.

"Please do not be angry, Aunt Louise. I will explain everything, but I must speak to Victor."

"About the murder?" She whispers the word and leans a little closer. I nod. "Oh, all right, go on then. But I will hold you to your word. For what it is worth, I had a little chat with Victor, and he seems a kind fellow, a policeman. His family did not come with him, though."

"There was a rift between them and Juliet. To them I fear she was dead long ago." Louise tuts disapprovingly and lets us go. Victor Stanley must be near Hugh's age, although he looks younger. He is slight of build, similar to his cousin, with light hair and near translucent blue eyes. There is an innocence about him, which I fear today's event may have tainted. Hollis makes the introductions and Victor stands to offer me his chair, but Hugh has already found two for us and carries them over.

"I am sorry we must meet under these circumstances," I say. "Hollis told us about your last encounter with Juliet. It must be very hard to be here today, but I am grateful you made the journey."

Victor shrugs and colors slightly. "I couldn't let her down again, even if it is too late, really. And if I can help discover who...who killed her, I want to do so. I am a policeman. Still on the beat as yet, but I hope to be a sergeant one day. I spoke to Inspector Stanton, told him what I told Mr. Napier. He said it was useful. I don't know if that's true." He shrugs.

"I am convinced it is." I glance around, noticing no one within hearing range. "You are sure you don't have a clue what happened to the child Juliet was carrying?"

Victor sighs, his shoulders sagging. "No, not with any certainty. If she had no money, how could she have supported herself, let alone a child? The sum mother gave her could not have stretched far. We were comfortable enough, but by no means well off. I thought...No -" He shakes his head, as if to dislodge an unpleasant notion.

"What is it?" Hollis probes.

"This sounds mad, given that the reason my mother offered for sending Juliet away was religious fervor, but I wondered whether she gave the money to Juliet so she might rid herself of the child. I never asked, but it seemed plausible. Inspector Stanton said he will speak to Mother. She won't be happy, but Juliet is dead." Victor sits up a little straighter. "In any case, Juliet never contacted us again, at least not to my knowledge. She was the type who, once slighted, would not quickly forgive or forget."

Hugh and I exchange a glance. Michael Ellroy said Howard Bell echoed a similar sentiment about Juliet. Perhaps such a steely nature was useful in the game of spying.

"Would anyone else in your family agree to speak with us? We would be very discreet."

Victor bites his bottom lip before answering. "They might, but I would not depend upon it. With the police, they can hardly say no. As for private detectives...Please do not take this the wrong way," he adds hastily.

"Not at all," I reassure him. "Nonetheless, it may be helpful to hear what they have to say."

"My brother might be willing, but he was not even home when Juliet came for help. He hardly knew her. The only person worth questioning is my mother. As I said, though, she will likely have little to add to my account."

"And your father?"

"He was away then, too. Beyond that, he had no quarrel with Juliet. It was through his side of the family that we were related.

Juliet's father was my father's cousin. He never spent time with us as children. I doubt he spared much thought to Juliet in the past decade. Mother may not even have told him of her final visit."

"Too many unanswered questions," I observe later, when Hugh and I are on our way to St. James. Hollis took Victor back to the station. We managed to extricate ourselves from the memorial after offering apologies – if not justifications – to Edith and Adeline for our delay, and appreciation for their generous efforts. The two women seemed somber and quite willing to let us go without prolonged conversation. I will have to drop by Aunt Louise's later today or tomorrow morning. She is owed an explanation. Briony, too, may wish to learn more, for she was with me when we discovered Juliet's body.

"I want to at least try to question the mother," Hugh says.

"I wonder whether Stanton could be persuaded to allow us to join him. We have quite the bartering tool with everything Michael Ellroy told us. I am still shocked by the revelation!"

"It opens up a whole new world of possibilities. Maybe she had old enemies, even if she was careful about maintaining her false identity during the war."

"It explains the medals, yet not the reason they were so damaged."

"That much seems clear to me," Hugh notes. "Juliet did not want them. She did not believe she merited them."

"That is a leap, don't you think?"

"She scratched away her name. To me that is a sign she did not believe she deserved such decorations of valor."

"Maybe." I remain unconvinced.

"I wish Howard Bell was alive to be questioned."

"We must speak with Frances again. There has to be something she knows, some clue to guide us closer to the truth. I feel ever more certain Juliet's killer is bound to her past. In her present, she was hardly acquainted with anyone, and no one knows much about her. If she made an enemy, if she caused trouble for someone, it could be a motive, even many years after the event."

"Do you think her killer was at the funeral today? It was mostly women, I noticed."

"We have not excluded the possibility that a woman is the murderer," I remind Hugh. "Let us not rule out the chance that the killer did attend. In my experience, they often return. Perhaps to confirm that their work is truly complete."

"Stanton will be speechless when we share our new information with him." Hugh chuckles.

"I will telephone his office straight away. With any luck, we will reach him there." We climb out of the car. A thin mist has settled in the square, hovering like a spectral sea above the pavement. I shiver, glancing around at the silent street. Did Juliet move through London always peering over her shoulder, always afraid? But why then remain here? Why stay, when she was frightened to be anything other than unseen and unheard? But then, maybe that was all she knew to be. Perhaps she never fully laid the shroud of a spy to rest?

Chapter 40

Stanton finally appears in the evening, just after I persuaded Hugh to go home and get some rest. The flat is silent, the sky beyond the window dark as pitch, save the silvery orb of the moon high above. Earlier I knocked on Dulcie's door, but no one answered. I hope yesterday's ordeal was not too much for either of my friends in the flat above. When Stanton walks into the office, he glances around with a wary expression, before accepting my offer of a seat and a glass of cognac to warm his bones.

"I have quite the news," I say, eagerly perched on the edge of my chair as Stanton takes a sip, eyeing me cautiously across the table as one might a serpent.

"You spoke to that man at the funeral? I gather it is related. Victor Nelson, though eager, was not able to offer me more than he had told Hollis. The pregnancy is a surprise, yet not as shocking as one might think. Poor girl, orphaned and desperate, turned away by her family. I am trying to find out whether there are any recorded births registered to her name. It is a tedious task. Nelson is not an uncommon moniker."

"If you thought news of the pregnancy was shocking, prepare yourself, Lucas."

"Why am I worried now? Tell me you haven't gotten yourself in trouble?"

"Oh, stop being so cynical. I can take care of myself, thank you very much."

"History suggests otherw-"

"Do you want to hear what I have to say, or not?" I interrupt.

"Go on." And so I do, happy to note the way his jaw seems to sag a little when I share the revelation that Juliet Nelson was a spy. His glass is empty by the time I fall silent. "What do you think? It could very well be someone from her past, who took this long to find her, don't you agree?"

"Yes," he replies slowly, as if my words are taking their time to reach him. "A spy. It explains the medals. I haven't been able to trace them, and it's not necessary now. I have to speak with Mr. Ellroy."

"He gave me his details. I take it you haven't made much more progress?" I ask, trying not to let my disappointment show.

"I have been so busy, but it's no excuse."

"There are only so many hours in the day. Thankfully you have a private detective at your service." I grin and he grimaces. "How do you like working in the city after Oxford?"

Stanton sighs. I top up his glass. "When I left Oxford, I was ready for it. If I hadn't thought it for the best, I would never have taken Thom out of his familiar surroundings."

"I sense a however."

"However, the workload is much greater, too. I never appreciated how little crime there was in Oxford. At the same time, I am more useful here, even if it means long nights and seeing too little of Thom."

"Is he all right? Iona mentions him sometimes."

"He is well enough. Children often adapt much better than adults. He does not notice the darker side of this city, thank goodness. Just three days ago we pulled a fourteen-year-old out of the river, his throat slashed. The mother was out of her mind with sorrow, the father couldn't speak. I witness these horrible things and feel powerless to stop them," he continues, alcohol loosening his tongue. "But if I step away, find some other profession, I would still know such villainy exists and that I am not even trying to stop it."

"No one ever claimed it was pretty work," I say gently.

"Thom insists he wants to be a policeman, but I am hoping some of Iona's scholarly ambition rubs off on him. I would rest easier, if he were on a different path."

"No one is entirely safe, no matter their profession. Or have you forgotten, we met when my professor in sleepy Oxford was murdered?"

"How could I forget? My life became more complicated after that day," he says with a laugh. It has a bitter ring to it, and for a moment I worry for my friend. Shadows sharpen his cheekbones, and his skin is pale. His weary demeanor could be the effect of winter or work, still I fear there is more to it. Perhaps he was never suited to city life, and perhaps I have been unfair in seeking out his friendship. Stanton notices my silence and forces a smile. "Oh, do not look so glum, Evelyn," he says softly. "Leave the frowning to the rest of us. You are getting married soon."

"Lucas -" I begin, but he pushes back his chair and gets to his feet.

"I ought to go. Thom will be waiting at the neighbor's, and I don't want to keep him." I consider protesting, but understand it is best for him to leave before words that cannot be unspoken are uttered. I do not walk him to the door and hear it close a moment later. The flat suddenly feels hollow and too silent. I am relieved when Maeve pops her head in to ask if I need anything or whether she can go to bed.

"Of course, sleep well." I smile at her and sense she wants to say more. Then she thinks better of it and nods, disappearing into the hallway. Sitting for a moment longer, I stare at the window and the darkness beyond. I feel sorry for Stanton, even if that is surely the last thing he desires. And yet...What he wants, I cannot give, at least I think it is so. Briony, Hugh and even Daniel himself have warned me, but I would not hear them. Seeing Stanton, hearing that bitter laugh, I realize they are right. I care for Stanton, took to him almost from the start, but it is not the same as the love I share with Daniel. I was intrigued by him and his profession, glad to have an ally in Oxford, someone who respected me and my abilities, yet in my mind, that was as far as it ever went. I felt a certain ease from the first time I met Daniel, a sense of having found something vital that was missing. When I think of losing Daniel, I think of a hole opening up that could never be filled. In a few weeks I will marry him. Yet does our union mean the end of a friendship between Stanton and me? The question troubles me as I put on my hat and coat, as I drive the short distance from St. James to Grosvenor Square. Perhaps it is the way of life, beginnings and endings. The realization, however, does not make accepting it any easier.

Daniel is awake when I arrive. It is not as late as the darkness outside suggests. I sag onto the sofa opposite him and tell him of the day's events. He listens without interruption, even if his expression is one of surprise as I illuminate Juliet's remarkable past. I have told her story twice now, trying to be as faithful to Michael Ellroy's account as possible. I have even written it down, and yet no obvious clue leaps out at me to be grasped and dissected. It has been a long day. Perhaps a night's sleep will expose something that was hidden before.

"If the man in the photograph is one who helped rescue Ellroy, it may prove significant," Daniel mutters, more to himself than to me, for I have obviously reached the same conclusion. "Have you told the police?"

"I spoke to Stanton. He was surprised, but agrees with us."

"He was at the funeral?" I nod, eager to turn the conversation away from the policeman. "Mostly women from the WI attended. Apart from Ellroy and Victor, there was no one I didn't at least vaguely recognize."

"It makes you wonder. If she was such a hero, why would no one from her past have come to honor her? Surely, someone must have known her true identity, former associates or so. You are certain Ellroy is innocent?"

"He was on a ship on the Atlantic Ocean, so unless he had an accomplice, he cannot have anything to do with the murder. Besides, if what he said was true, he has no motive whatsoever, quite the opposite."

"The question of her child, or at least her pregnancy, remains."

"Too many questions!" I huff and slump against the cushions. "Tell me something diverting, won't you? Something far removed from murder and lies."

"A fairy-tale?"

"I said no murder. Fairy-tales are full of burning witches and slain dragons."

"But they are the villains," Daniel says. "The hero must conquer the villain to arrive at the happy ending, does he not?"

"Or she," I correct him. "Perhaps. But can an ending ever be truly happy if violence was involved to achieve it? Wars are won, but the soldiers returning home are not truly victors. Look at Hugh! What did winning the war do to him for so many years?"

"Maybe a fairy-tale is best saved for another day, then," Daniel soothes. "Shall I read you a business report? It will put you to sleep faster than a mug of warm milk." I laugh.

"Sounds wonderful!"

Chapter 41

It is snowing when I wake the next morning, the sky beyond the window brilliant white. Delicate snowflakes sail through the air only to melt away on the damp pavement below, while bare tree branches have held on to a white scattering, as if sprinkled with fairy dust.

The enlightening dream I had hoped for did not come. I fell asleep as soon as my head touched the pillow and woke a solid seven hours later to the smell of tea and toast coming from downstairs. I get dressed in soft gray trousers and a warm green jumper. Daniel is already halfway through the paper when I arrive.

"Any good news today?" I ask, helping myself to the toasted bread and dollop it with ruby red marmalade.

"Hm…let me see," Daniel rustles the pages. "A great tunnel has opened in America, right under the Hudson river."

"Is that the best you can do, a tunnel?" I raise my brows.

"A trove of Norman coins was discovered in Cricklade," he offers weakly.

"Oh, I do despair," I reply. "Coins and a tunnel? I was hoping for something more like the rescue of orphans or the liberation of a besieged nation."

"I am afraid none of that is on offer today. If you like, I can make something up?"

"I might hold you to that, if today proves as challenging as yesterday." I take a bite of toast and thank the maid when she pours my tea. "What are you doing today? Any developments at work?"

"Nothing to speak of. I am having lunch with Harold. He asked me to help him with his campaign, though he hardly needs any help I could give. People gravitate towards him, and they will vote for him, too. I am confident of that. You will soon have an uncle in Parliament, mark my word."

"Your trust does you credit. I only hope Harold will not be disappointed when he recognizes his objectives may not be so easily realized."

"He lacks your cynicism," Daniel teases. "Ideology is a valuable asset for a politician. And Harold is worth more than words."

"I wish him every success. It is good you two get along so well. I feel our whole family is coming together after being fractured for so long." I say the words without much thought, but as they come out of my mouth, I realize how true they really are. Agnes has found Harold and, more than that, she and I have found a way back to one another. Briony has her family, and hopefully matters will mend with Jeffrey, too. And I have Daniel, who gains a whole family through mine, after being adrift for many years when he lost his brothers and parents.

"Any guesses where I am taking you after we are married?" Daniel asks with a playful smile.

"Hopefully somewhere warmer than here!" I say, nodding at the window, where snow flurries dance through the air. "Spain? Italy?"

"I couldn't possibly say."

"You mustn't tease me!"

"I must tease you often, and you me. I intend for us to have faces creased with laughter lines in our old age."

"Our grandchildren will never believe us when we say we were once young, too."

"No, they will sit on our laps and we will tell them stories, even fairy-tales," he says with a wink.

"I suppose it will do them good to know there are ogres and wolves in the world."

"And that they can be defeated."

"That, too. All the same, let us hope no one we care for ever has to be a hero."

"Heavens, no!" Daniel says with emphasis. "Let them have peace, even tedium. There have been adventures and villainy enough in our lifetime." He adds, unable to hide a grin, "But with a grandmother like you, who attracts trouble like a magnet, we may be in for a rather dramatic future. Laughter lines, yes, but prematurely gray hair, too."

"Oh, you'll enjoy it," I tease.

"I enjoy seeing you excited. I only wish it were about tranquil pursuits like knitting or croquet."

"You haven't played croquet with me yet. It is anything but tranquil, I warn you, future husband."

"I will be certain, then, to keep out of range of your mallet, my love."

We chat a while longer, following an unspoken agreement to avoid unpleasantness, straying far from the subject of the murder or the demise of the shipyard. It is good to savor these moments of normalcy within an eddy of uncertainty. After we finish eating and notice the time, Daniel hurries off and I wrap up in a coat and scarf to drive to Briony's house. I arranged to meet Louise there, so I am not forced to repeat Ellroy's story two more times.

The streets are slick, and I drive slowly as the snow continues to fall. It seems too early in the year for flurries, but then the weather gods have always had minds of their own. Nonetheless, it takes me a while to complete the journey to Belgravia, and when I arrive, my fingers feel stiff from gripping the wheel with such concentration.

I am ushered inside by a maid I vaguely recognize as being new. When she has taken my snow dusted coat and hat, I am led into the sitting room, where my aunt and cousin sit near the crackling fire. The children, apart from Elsa, are in school. The house is too quiet, merry voices conspicuously absent.

"Evie, finally! We have been waiting on pins and needles!" Louise exclaims, accepting a kiss on the cheek.

"Mother told me about the funeral. I am sorry I could not come, but then, I hardly knew her."

"You will know her a lot better once I have told you everything I learned yesterday," I promise and proceed to explain. The women are suitably stunned, yet neither can think of any clue emerging from this newfound knowledge that Hugh, Stanton, Daniel or I have not considered already. "Did anything happen after the funeral, something I missed when I was speaking with Ellroy?" I ask my aunt. "Did you notice anything out of the ordinary?"

"Well, it was all out of the ordinary. I did speak with a few of the women. Most could not have identified Juliet if she had been in the same room. They attended the funeral mostly as a favor to Edith. I was surprised to see Lloyd, but he left shortly after we got to Bloomsbury. I barely exchanged a few words with him. He invited Robert and me to dinner next week, though."

"That is all?" I ask, unable to hide my disappointment. A dinner invitation is not what I am after.

"Well, let me try to remember." Louise taps her chin with her forefinger and Briony and I exchange a glance. "Priscilla was flitting about as usual. Adeline was her usual chatty self. She hardly knew Juliet, after all. One cannot be expected to truly grieve a person with whom one hardly exchanged so much as a greeting. Thankfully, on this occasion, she did forgo one of her blinding wardrobe choices in favor of gray."

"Did you speak to Frances Bell? She was at the gravesite. I meant to seek her out, but then we met Ellroy."

"Oh, yes!" Louise raises a triumphant finger into the air. "I did speak to her. She was one of the few people present who looked genuinely distressed. In other circumstances, she may be rather formidable, tall and imposing as she is, but she seemed sunk into herself. Maybe it was the black. It isn't really anyone's color, is it?"

"What did she say, Mother?" Briony asks, a hint of exasperation in her voice.

"Right, right. Well, she didn't say anything incriminating, if that is what you are after. When I asked her whether she had been close to Juliet, she appeared on the verge of tears. She said, 'If only I had been'. Before I had a chance to ask more, Lloyd came over. When I turned back to her, she had disappeared. I think she left just then. I felt sorry for her. You said she is alone, her husband gone. No one should be lonely when they are grieving. I asked Edith whether she is a member of the WI as well, but she said she had not met the woman before."

"I want to talk to her again in any case. I will drop by the museum around the lunch hour and ask if she can spare a few moments."

"Do that, my dear. If her husband recruited Juliet and Mrs. Bell genuinely did not know about it, discovering his secret life is probably deeply distressing. I suspect she will learn the truth soon, one way or the other. Better to give her fair warning. Unless you believe it is all a farce, and she is playing the game even better than her husband did."

"You mean they were both spies, or something of the sort?" I ask, marveling that the thought hasn't crossed my mind until now.

"It sounds like a story taken from a sensational novel," Briony says with raised brows.

"Mrs. Bell seemed genuinely shocked when I told her of Juliet's death, and of the secret flat which belonged to her husband. I may be wrong, but I do not believe she is so talented an actress. Besides, she drew attention to herself by following me and asking me to verify that Lara Bennet's claim was true, and Juliet truly was dead. Why would she do so, unless she has nothing to hide?"

"Some criminals have a macabre desire to be in the middle of the action," Louise observes like an expert on the matter.

"Perhaps. I certainly can't wholly discount the notion."

"Since she lives alone, she probably doesn't have a useful alibi for the hours of the murder," Briony muses.

"No, she does not. Yet if she is the killer, would she not have made certain she did have a convincing alibi?"

"If a murder takes place at night or in the early hours of the morning, few people will have convincing alibis. Even I might have snuck out of the house without anyone taking notice. It seems more dubious if someone under suspicion claims to have been among company at a time when they should naturally be in bed."

"True enough," I agree. "All of this speculation doesn't lead us very far. I hope speaking with Frances again might offer greater clarity."

"Will you tell her everything Ellroy shared with you?" Briony asks.

"I do not think it wise just yet, though I feel sorry if she is blind-sided by a revelation she could not have imagined about her husband. Especially now that he is no longer here to explain himself. I will have to take it by ear."

"Come over for dinner tonight, won't you?" Briony asks me at the door.

"I would like that very much."

When I leave my aunt and cousin, my head is spinning with the possibility, vague as it is, that Frances was a part of Howard's scheme during the war. Then again, this was at the time when she attained her position at the museum. Perhaps she could have followed both paths, but it strikes me as unlikely. She seems dedicated to her work. Even if she was part of the spying ring, it is possible Howard kept Juliet's recruitment from her. Maybe he thought she would oppose it? I must learn more about the enterprise. Whom to turn to? Who can tell me more about espionage during the war?

I skip over a puddle of gray sleet and climb into the Bentley. It has stopped snowing, yet now a sharp wind whistles through the square. I close my eyes for a moment, picturing the faces of all those involved in the case. There is Graham Markby, who works for the War Office. Would he be able to offer insight into the network of spies Britain employed in France during the war? Would he be willing to get involved? I could ask Adeline but am reluctant to do so. If I ask her for this favor, I must explain why, and it will be easy enough for her and Graham to draw a connection to the case. For the moment, I want to keep Juliet's past between those I trust completely. Then another name comes to me: Harold. He has friends in all areas of the military and surely that includes members of government working in the War Office ten years ago. Harold, who is always eager to help. I glance at my watch. He is meeting Daniel for lunch, but it is only ten. Can I catch him at home? The engine comes to life, and I push down on the accelerator.

Chapter 42

"Evelyn, what a pleasure! I am afraid Agnes is out at the moment," Harold greets me with his customary warmth.

"Actually, I have come to see you."

"What brings me the honor?"

"It is rather a delicate matter. You have heard of the case Hugh and I are investigating?"

"The murder of a woman you met at the WI," Harold replies with a somber nod.

"Precisely. Well, long story short, she was a spy during the war. It is a matter of discretion, you understand."

"Completely, my dear." Harold taps his nose and gives me a wink. "How may I be of service? I never joined the ranks of spies myself."

"Do you know anything about espionage during the war? So little is public knowledge, which is, of course, the intent."

"There was quite an effective network of spies acting for Britain in France. You have heard of the famous Mata Hari, Louise de Bettignies?"

"I know the names and a part of their stories. However, I gather there were few well known female spies."

"Few famous male spies as well, yet both existed all the same. Women were often underestimated, and perhaps were and are still more adaptable and able to go undetected."

"How were they recruited? Who decided on the requirements?"

"Steady on!" Harold says, holding up a hand to stop my flow of questions. "I can tell you only what I have heard from friends of friends, you understand?" I nod. "Recruitment is a bit of a mystery. One way or the other, the person catches the eye of someone in the War Office. In the case of male spies, they may have displayed bravery in battle, with women it has to be another skill."

"An affinity for languages?" I offer.

Harold raises a finger into the air. "There you have it. Particularly during the last war. French and German fluency was terribly valuable, particularly the former, if the spy was stationed in France or Belgium. If they understood German, too, they must have been truly prized. They could work undetected, as long as they kept a straight face when they heard it spoken around them and did not let on they understood.

That is, apparently, how Bettignies and her agents operated. Can you imagine? Mingling with the enemy while they discussed war strategies, hardly noticing you, thinking you deaf to their words?" Harold sighs and shakes his head. "Remarkable, and very dangerous, as was proven."

"Did many get caught?"

"Since I have no idea how many existed, I cannot say. One would hear of executions sometimes. I am sure there were far more that did not make the front pages during that turbulent time. But back to recruitment, for a moment. As far as I understand, a select few were approached by someone from the War Office or Secret Service Bureau, who then trained them – teaching linguistic skills as well as more practical ones in wartimes, such as shooting and the creation and deciphering of code. They had to learn how to blend in, and how to turn situations to their advantage. Spy craft at its finest reportedly saved thousands of lives and provided an element of surprise, sometimes preventing an attack or weapons delivery in its entirety. It is impossible ever to fully appreciate what an impact these men and women made. Perhaps they turned the tide of the war."

"Astonishing," I marvel.

"Utterly. Courage comes in many forms. Women who picked up their husband's factory jobs on the home front while raising their family alone were undeniably brave as well."

"What about the time after the war? Did they come home like soldiers and try to assimilate themselves back into society? Was it known that they had been spies?"

"A thorny question," he replies, crossing his arms and leaning back. "Since the war was over, they could have broken their cover, especially back at home, but one hardly hears that anyone did. Such few names are public knowledge, which leads me to believe the cautious manner in which they lived during the war was difficult to shake."

"That fits with what I have learned in the course of this investigation. The spy in question, Juliet Nelson, lived as quietly as she could until she was killed. I also learned she used a different name as an operative in France. Have you ever heard of Minette Laurent?"

Harold scratches his chin. "Minette Laurent?" He shakes his head. "Sadly, no, I have never heard the name before. I take it Juliet spoke fluent French to have been able to pass as a native?"

"Learned it from her mother. She also picked up some German in training, so she could spy on the enemy. Juliet must have had a talent for languages. She was in Valenciennes and appeared as the baker's assistant. He was in favor of the cause."

"Goodness, what a tale! I heard of locals trying to rebel against the occupants in any way they could. It would have posed a grave danger to the baker, though. He must have considered the risk worthwhile, and she must have been good at what she did and discreet, too." Harold raises his brows in admiration.

"I rather think she was, and I would have liked to have heard her story from Juliet herself. What a sad waste," I sigh.

"Now you think someone from that time in her life has come back to take revenge?"

"I see no other motive," I admit. "She lived unobtrusively. Whoever hated her to the point of wishing her dead must have known her when she was almost literally a different person. Or do you disagree?"

"It sounds rational, and experience," he smiles as he speaks, "has taught me to trust reason. It often led me a roundabout way, yet never entirely astray. Do you have any suspects from her past?"

"No one I can pin down firmly, and the one person who might have offered more clarity died eight months ago. He was the one who recruited her. His wife professes to have known nothing of what he did. I wonder whether this can be true. Could he have led such a separate, secret life away from the woman with whom he shared a happy marriage?"

"Maybe it was not so happy? People often turn a blind eye, when they think it will protect them or preserve the status quo. Sometimes, it is easier to pretend everything is well, even if there are plenty of clues in plain sight that speak of the opposite being true."

"I think you may be right."

"A phrase I hear very infrequently since giving up my bachelorhood!" Harold says, laughing.

"Oh, you are but at the beginning, my friend! Try living with her for twenty years, then we shall compare stories," I reply, laughing, too.

"I should be so lucky. If I can have another twenty years as your aunt's husband, I will die a happy man."

"She would wince hearing this sweet sentiment," I observe.

"My Agnes? You underestimate her."

"I did, but I hope to rectify that."

"She made her share of mistakes, she will readily admit that," Harold says gently. "Yet it is better to realize late than never. Time is not our friend, after all."

"I wish you wouldn't speak like that, Harold."

"I am a realist, Evelyn, but never fear. I am quite determined to make the most of whatever time remains, starting with joining the government."

"It is not long now until the by-election. Are you prepared?"

"As much as anyone can be. When I lived in India, I tried to be active, to mix with everyone and help where I could. I have missed feeling involved in something worthwhile since returning to London. Dinner parties and watching cricket are well and good, but I cannot spend the rest of my days busy with such pursuits."

"And you won't," I reply with confidence. At the door, Harold promises to contact some of his old friends and see if they can add anything to his knowledge of espionage during the war. Invigorated by our chat, I make my way to the British Museum, hoping a conversation with Frances will serve to be similarly rewarding.

Chapter 43

"Frances is in a conference through lunch today," Lara Bennet tells me in a bored voice, when I ask to see the archivist.

"Oh, I had been hoping to see her."

"Try tomorrow."

"Could I leave a message with you?" I ask. Upon her shrug of assent, I scribble down the number and address where I can be reached. "Can you make certain she gets this? It's urgent."

"Something to do with Juliet?" Lara asks, sitting up a little straighter, curious cat eyes meeting mine. "The police have been round a few times already. Making slow work of it, I must say. But then, I gather they have little to go on. Juliet kept herself to herself and then some. I never heard her say a thing about her life outside of work. We like a bit of a chin-wag here, but she never joined in. It wasn't our fault we never got close to her." Lara falls silent. Juliet may have seemed rather aloof to the young secretary, and thus offended her.

"Juliet was simply a very private person. I am sure she meant no offense."

"Maybe," Lara sighs. "I'll give this to Frances when she gets back." She holds up the folded note, and I must be satisfied with that.

Disappointed, I leave the museum and return to the office. Hugh is out, but left a message that he is chasing up Hollis, to hear if there is a story in the paper's archives about war heroes. I am proud of his cleverness, though this means he must reveal at least a measure of the truth to Hollis. How much discipline does the reporter have to hold off on publishing such a titillating story before we have solved the case? Hopefully, my faith in him is not misplaced.

I write down what Harold told me. It is a struggle to imagine Juliet, who appeared so fragile and reserved, to be utterly capable and determined in situations that tested her bravery beyond comprehension. I wish, not for the first or even second time, that I could have known her better, that one day she might even have shared all of this with me herself. There is a knock at the door. "Yes?" I call out. It opens a crack to reveal Kathleen.

"Am I disturbing you? Maeve took Aidan out for a walk, and I've made some lunch and wanted to see if you're hungry. It is only a cottage pie."

"Cottage pie sounds lovely. Thank you, Kathleen."

"Shall I bring it in here?"

"I'll eat in the kitchen, actually." Kathleen seems a little confused by my response. The kitchen smells delicious and the warmth radiating from the oven feels like a comforting embrace, when I enter the room. Kathleen serves me a generous helping, thick gravy oozing out underneath the creamy potato puree. "Won't you join me?" I ask, suddenly awkward, sitting in her domain while she stands beside the counter.

"Oh…all right," she replies, and ladles herself a portion. After a moment's hesitation, she sits down across from me.

"This is delicious, Kathleen!"

"Do you like it? It was my mother's recipe."

"Wonderful. I am afraid the most even patient Maeve has been able to teach me is how to make fried eggs."

"The girl is a good cook," Kathleen acknowledges.

"And a good mother, I daresay," I add, carefully blowing on my fork.

"Yes, she'll keep her boy safe." Kathleen looks down. Unspoken words hang in the air. *I was not able to do the same for mine.*

I hesitate. Then, hoping to distract her, I tell her about the séance. "You were right, it was a farce."

"I take no pleasure in it. That poor woman still has no comfort."

"I fear she never truly will."

"No, maybe not."

We are silent for a while, the only sound the scrape of cutlery on china, the ticking of the kitchen clock. I am surprised when Kathleen is first to find her voice.

"Do you think I could speak to her? Perhaps I can take her to church with me. If she is able to believe in a medium, maybe the power of the Lord can reach her, too."

"That is a kind thought, however, she does not leave the house. It is as if her grief has crippled her, and the outside world is sandpaper against her wounds."

Kathleen nods thoughtfully, her fork forgotten in her hand. "I understand, but I would still like to visit her, if she is willing."

"I am going to see her in a bit and shall broach the matter. Please do not be offended if she rejects the notion. Dulcie is in a bad way at the moment, and she is proud, too, and very private. Although the latter may be a side-effect of her self-imposed exile. I believe she was once rather a social creature. She grew up in India, did you know? She misses it."

"So, she is homesick and grieving, poor woman."

"Do you miss Ireland?" I ask, feeling emboldened to delve a bit deeper with the woman who, though living in my flat for months, has seemed a little distant most of the time.

"Not often. I miss the sea, my parents, but my home is here now with my grandson. I could never go back, could never leave my son in the ground far away from me, even if I know his spirit is in heaven."

"When spring comes, you must take Maeve and little Aidan to the seaside. I remember when I was very young, before my parents died, they took me to Cornwall. We ate fish and chips and watched the seagulls as they tried to snatch our food. I remember it, the smell of the sea, the sound of the waves as they crashed against the rocks. I am afraid of losing such memories all the time, but this one I cling to." I smile, heat creeping into my cheeks, suddenly abashed by my candor. Kathleen reaches out a hand and touches mine, just for a moment; just to show me without words that she understands. She must recognize the fear of forgetting as I do, but she knew her son twenty years and I my parents only four. She had the chance to amass two decades worth of memories, and I have a mere fraction. Loss cannot be measured, yet I wish for the thousandth - ten-thousandth - time that I could have had longer with them. Those first few years when a child hardly understands which way is up do not count for much. I remember their smiles, though. Sometimes I think I even remember how they smelled or the sound of their laughter, before convincing myself it is only a dream. I have built up their memories, built them up and fleshed them out without certainty of what is real and what imagined, or whether it even matters.

"My Aidan and I used to go the shore together since the time he could walk. He liked to collect stones, smooth round ones he held in his hands like little treasures. He ran down to the water and then up to the shore as the waves chased him. Often, when we returned home and he went to bed, I found his pockets weighed down by the round pebbles from the beach. Sometimes on those occasions we got scotch eggs and ate them sitting on a bench looking out at the sea. I haven't eaten one since he died." Kathleen's eyes have attained a faraway look, as if she can see through time and space a scene with a younger version of herself, playing with a little boy who looks something like her grandson. Then the moment passes, and she blinks, back in the here and now, a single tear glistening in the corner of her eye.

"I do not think you need to worry about forgetting," I say gently.

"Maybe. My mind these days is filled with my grandson, with new memories being made. I sometimes worry they will crowd out the old."

"Perhaps your son would not mind so much. He would like to see you happy with his little boy, not weighed down by perpetual grief the way Dulcie is."

"Yes, I think you are right. My Aidan was a kind boy, he would have hated seeing me suffer."

"I will speak with Dulcie, ask whether she is amenable to meeting," I promise, though I worry the two grieving, childless mothers put together may only stoke each other's unhappiness. Yet there may be a measure of comfort in reminiscing about their shared loss. I finish my pie and thank Kathleen. She is relieved when I go, already regretting her openness after holding me at arm's length for months.

My knock at Dulcie's door is answered quickly this time. Mr. Singh opens it with one hand, while restraining Dulcie's dog, Rudy, with the other.

"Hello, I hope I am not disturbing you?" I ask, patting the pup's head.

"No, no, Rudy and I just got back from our walk. It was a short one today. Despite all my years in this country, the cold still creeps too easily into my bones. I yearn for the mild winters of my younger days."

"Do you miss home?" I ask, as he beckons me into the hallway and closes the door.

"Sometimes, yes, sometimes not at all. I can be at home in many places if I have a friend. Here I have found several," he says with a smile. I am glad to find him livelier than the past few times we met. His skin is still a little sallow, yet his eyes are not bloodshot, and he does not lean quite so heavily upon his cane. "Are you looking forward to your wedding, my dear? Only a few more weeks now."

"I am, though nerves may set in at any moment. Can I expect to see you there?" I ask, having sent him and Dulcie invitations weeks ago in the hope she might be coaxed out of doors.

"I would not miss it. I have always loved weddings. One day, I must tell you of traditional Indian weddings. They are very different, and once in a while, even an elephant will make an appearance."

"Oh my! I fear I can offer no such spectacular entertainment. You will have to make do with flowers, food and family antics." Mr. Singh chuckles.

"I look forward to it."

"How is Dulcie?" I ask, lowering my voice. "Has she recovered a little from the shock of the séance?"

"At first, I worried it would set her back even more, but she has returned to the way she was before. Quiet, tired and desolate. I cannot think what to do, though I have been able to rid us of that pesky so-called physician. I simply turned him away at the door. His help is not the kind Dulcie requires."

"A wise move," I say with a nod of approval. "Perhaps I have an idea." I tell him of Kathleen and her proposal to visit Dulcie.

"I think she is a little lonely, too, despite having her grandson and Maeve in her life. It may do them both good. But I do not want the encounter to appear contrived. Maybe I can bring her along one day and slip out, leaving them alone once I see that they get on."

"It is worth a try," Mr. Singh agrees, scratching his bearded chin. "I met Kathleen a while ago. She was coming into the building with her grandson when I was leaving with Rudy. Seems a friendly lady, even if my beard and turban may have given her cause to stare." He laughs to show no offense was taken.

"Can I talk to her, or is she sleeping?"

"She is reading in the lounge, go on through. She will be happy to see you. Shall I bring you a cup of chai?"

"That would be perfect, just the thing on a day like today."

I find Dulcie in her usual position, propped up by two brightly colored silk cushions in her lounge. She puts down a book when I enter, a smile on her face. Despite her welcome and the kiss she presses on my cheek, I note that she is not well. She is considerably thinner than a few months ago. Her cheekbones, once hidden under soft flesh, have pushed forth like blades, making the hollows in her cheeks more pronounced, and darkening the shadows beneath her eyes.

"How have you been?" I ask. She waves away my question with a frown and insists I tell her all about my new case and about the wedding plans. Unable to deny her, I speak freely, and she listens with an expression of relief upon her face, as if this distraction offers her a momentary reprieve from her perpetual heartache.

Mr. Singh joins us after a while, bearing a tray of steaming chai and small squares of a white sweet called burfi, which melts on my tongue with flavors of cardamom, almond and rosewater. After a while, Dulcie begins to nod off and in silent agreement with Mr. Singh, we slip out of the room to let her have her rest.

"I did not mean to weary her," I whisper, taking in Mr. Singh's creased brow.

"Oh, it is quite all right. She can use some more sleep," he says absently and brushes his bearded chin as he frowns.

"Is everything all right? Have I upset you?" I ask, sensing something amiss in his altered demeanor.

"No, not exactly," he says slowly, meeting my gaze. "What you said about Miss Nelson…" He bites his bottom lip and shakes his head.

"Yes?" I prompt, anxious in the face of his agitation. Mr. Singh is usually the very picture of composure.

"Perhaps you have considered this already, but you mentioned the coroner found a network of scars upon her back and arms, and in light of your most recent discovery, I venture to guess, well, that she was tortured."

I gasp, though it seems as though this conclusion should have come to me immediately. Somehow, I did not quite slot those pieces of the puzzle together. Tortured. A spy caught and tortured. It makes a perverse sort of sense. Did her torturer catch up with her and complete the job by taking her life?

"Are you all right?" asks Mr. Singh, a look of gentle concern softening his features.

"Yes, fine. I simply cannot believe I hadn't made the connection myself, though I realized she had been abused, of course."

"Your mind does not hurry to such dark places."

"You think she must have been caught?"

"I cannot be certain, of course, but yes, I do. Your Great War was not the first and will not be the last to be fought in this world. I have seen fighting, and I have seen the cruelty and viciousness that can blossom in a man's heart when tribal loyalty comes into play. It is no different whether the conflict is great or small. I have been called a cynic, but I am merely a realist. People are capable of great good and great evil. Sometimes we find both in the same person."

"She was rewarded for her service with military medals of the highest honor."

"And so she should have been, regardless of capture or not."

"I wonder, if we had become friends, she might have told me something of her past?"

"In all likelihood, she was trying to forget. If, as you say, she hid the medals, the money and photograph, it may have been to keep them out of her sight as much as to keep them secret."

"True enough. There was a ring, too, in her wardrobe. I have to believe that it was given to her by the man in the photograph, though who he is, we still do not know. Stanton will show it to Ellroy, and hopefully he will tell us whether it was the man who helped rescue him in France. Even so, we are left without a name or other clue pointing to his identity."

"Not quite. If Juliet Nelson and this man were British spies, there must be a record of it. The recruiters must have kept logs – coded possibly – of the people they drew into their secret organization."

"Harold will contact some friends who work at the War Office, though this information may be so deeply classified that only a handful of people knew. I wish Howard Bell was still alive. I feel he is the key to solving this mystery, yet he is entirely useless to us now."

"Don't be so certain. Everyone leaves a trace. Sometimes the greatest challenge is simply to locate the trail of breadcrumbs. Following it is easy."

"Do you remember where those breadcrumbs can lead?" I ask.

"To a house made of biscuits?"

"To a hungry witch."

"I have always believed the real villains in the story were the woodcutter and his wife who abandoned the children in the first place. The witch is only acting in accordance to her nature. You would not expect a lion to spare a zebra or a hawk a mouse. But parents are expected to love and protect their children."

As I leave the flat and descend the stairs, Mr. Singh's words do not leave my mind. There is something in them that bothers me, something out of my grasp. I close my eyes to concentrate as I pause at the door. Nothing comes to me, so I give up and go inside.

Chapter 44

My mind is spinning with all the questions that still need to be answered. Who is the man in the photograph? Was Juliet hiding the money in case she had to disappear? Was she captured in the war, tortured even? Did Howard Bell leave any significant clue to lead us onto the right path? Something stands in our way. Some hidden door remains unopened.

"Hello," I hear Hugh's voice.

"I hadn't noticed you," I say, straightening in my seat.

"You seemed absorbed. Anything new?" He is not quite as startled by Mr. Singh's observation as I was.

"Did you have any success in the archives? You had to tell Hollis the truth, I assume."

"Afraid so, but I think he is so eager for one big story in the end, he will keep his word and hold off publishing until we are ready. I did learn a few interesting tidbits." Hugh slumps into the seat in front of me. His cheeks are pink from the cold. "I wanted to read about war heroes, and it wasn't difficult. In fact, there was almost too much information on the matter. Britain was keen to stoke the morale of the nation and printed stories of valor on a regular basis."

"I remember it well. I read the papers and often felt a sense of relief, trusting it was going well, even as my uncle had the true measure of the situation and raged against the propaganda."

"Since I was in France, I did not pick up an English paper until I returned to England last year." Hugh shrugs.

"It must have been difficult to go through the archives and read about that time."

"Words on paper in some dusty vault can never hurt me the way my memories do, and they are forever trapped within my mind. All the same, reading about these men and their bravery, I kept thinking of William and Henry and all the others who disappeared, remembered only by those who loved them. Who decides which deed is heroic during war? Henry was my friend. If anyone was a hero to me, it was him and yet he received no mention, nor medal of honor. He simply ceased to exist, another replaceable ant in the teeming anthill of the army."

"But he is not forgotten," I remind him. "As you said, what do words on dusty pages matter. You knew him and Daniel knew him, and you love and honor him thus."

"It isn't enough. Reading those pages upon pages, seeing those names, I realized that memory is short. How long until we have forgotten not only the names, but the battles, the wounds, the war itself?"

"You mustn't think like that," I say, though I cannot deny the same thoughts have crossed my mind. How quickly have we forgotten the bravery and sacrifice of our men and women? We let them line up at the workhouses and Salvation Army for scraps and discarded clothes instead of lifting them up in repayment for all they have done. Will the next generation overlook them completely? Will they be nothing but shadows and hazy memories of which the young had no part? I fear for such a time, yet sense it is inevitable. How rarely do I myself think of conflicts that took place before my lifetime? They are words in history books, and time has proven most cruelly that recounted truth in dry tomes is not enough to truly make us learn. More wars will come, more fighting, more death, more faces to be forgotten. Yet ruminating on the reality of this terrible premonition will not bring me any closer to my current aim of finding Juliet Nelson's killer. I must focus on the here and now, that is all I can do.

"Only around six-hundred Victoria Cross medals were awarded, many posthumously. The papers wrote about them fairly frequently, though Juliet's name never came up. In fact, hardly any women were mentioned, save a few suffragettes and a few instances of women taking on men's work or praise of the land girls."

"Quite tragic," I observe, thinking of all the women left behind to hold up their roofs, feed their children and work backbreaking jobs.

"Edith Cavell was a name I came across a few times. She was a British nurse in Belgium, who helped many soldiers escape from occupied territory. She was executed for her trouble."

"I have heard of her." I shake my head.

"It made me think of Juliet. A nurse, a baker, no one would be likely to suspect them, don't you think? They could do their work without arousing suspicion, at least for a time. It would only take one instance of bad luck, of course, for all that to be over."

"I wonder what went wrong." My thoughts drift to that fateful day, Juliet on the floor, pale and lifeless. Hugh takes out his notebook and flips through the pages.

"I wrote down some interesting points. Here, have a look, maybe you will notice something I did not. Whatever I found does create a stronger image of the world at war time, but I cannot see anything in particular to help with Juliet's case." He pauses, allowing me to scan his notes. It is useful information on the war, though little comes as a great surprise since I lived in England at the time.

Added to that, everything printed in the papers must be taken with a pinch of salt. They intended to strengthen morale, and fact and fiction could thus be blurred. I remember the terrifying posters everywhere, blatant propaganda, effective all the same. They depicted images of the German soldiers in their pointed helmets, tall and grim as Huns, as apes even; they showed images of collapsed homes with weeping children. There was truth in them, of course, and yet the posters displayed in Germany surely depicted the British and French in much the same light. At the end of the war, after the Armistice was signed, the placards read "Never Again", advocating remembrance. It ended only nine years ago. In that time, there have been wars in Russia, Greece and Turkey, revolts in France and uprisings in Ireland, to name a few.

"Anything?" Hugh asks, drawing me from my dismal musings.

"This is interesting." I hold up the notebook. "The mention of Cecil Aylmer Cameron who worked in the War Office and acted as a staff officer, recruiting and running spies during the war."

"It reminded me of Howard Bell."

"You wrote Cameron's British spies were trained in Folkestone, here in England, with other stations in Rotterdam and Montreuil."

"Did you see what the codename of the operation was?" Hugh asks with a smile.

"Evelyn!" I reply. "How uncanny. It says he was later made Chief Intelligence Officer during the Russian Civil War in Siberia, and even Commander of the Order of the British Empire. Goodness!"

"And shot to death in an army barracks three years ago. The verdict was suicide on account of insanity."

"What a horrible ending."

"If several of his spies were sent to their deaths and he had a conscience, it is unlikely he ever forgave himself. Louise de Bettignies was one of his, you know. I could not find much more about him, nor the success of his missions. The paper only wrote a short paragraph after he died. I suspect his family wished for privacy. There were some murky issues in his past, when he spent time in prison for fraud. It isn't clear to me what exactly happened. In any case, he redeemed himself admirably with his dedication to the crown."

"Even if it destroyed him in the end. If Howard Bell played a similar role, how could Frances not have known?" I set down the notebook and lean back in my chair, my fingertips drumming against the tabletop. "I must try to catch her after work. This cannot wait any longer."

"Shall I come with you?"

"No, I think she will be put off if we both approach her. I will be careful. There are so many people around the museum."

"All right." Hugh hesitates. "I was wondering whether we could persuade Stanton to take me along when he interviews Victor's mother, Juliet's aunt. I could pretend to be a constable and wouldn't have to say a word. Do you think he might agree?"

"It cannot hurt to ask. Frankly, I think you would be better off making the request yourself. He does not seem particularly fond of me at the moment."

"Do I want the details?" Hugh asks with a grimace.

"Better not, I hardly know myself. In other news, Dulcie is a tiny bit better, and Kathleen wants to meet her."

"Might be a good idea. Remember when we were in Scotland when I met all those veterans who had suffered as I had? It helped me to be among those who understood without us having to explain that our wounds are not always visible. Maybe Dulcie and Kathleen can do one another some good."

"It cannot hurt to try, at least." I glance at the clock above the mantel. "Best set off soon. I do not want to risk missing Frances. Briony invited me to dinner tonight, so maybe I can ask Jeffery a few more questions as well."

Wrapped up in my coat and shawl, I set off. The sky is already purpling, and the sun has bid another farewell, while the pale shadow of the waning moon gleams above the rooftops. It isn't late, yet the onset of darkness rests like a heavy blanket upon my shoulders, and I wish I were at home with a good book and a cup of tea.

Traffic is dense, and people crowd into buses and step onto the street without a care, in their eagerness to get home. Halfway, the bus in front of me breaks down and blocks the road with its red bulk. I peer nervously at my watch, seeing the minutes tick by, while I stand idle. Frustrated, I thump the wheel. At a quarter to six, I give up, dip into a side alley and turn around. I will have missed her by the time I arrive, no point in making the rest of the journey. Disappointed, I turn towards Belgravia where I am to meet Daniel at Briony's house for dinner. I am of two minds, both wishing for distraction and eager to continue on my path, desperate to get closer to the truth.

Daniel is already at the Farnham house when I arrive. Timon has coaxed him onto the floor to show him his new train set, while Areta launches herself at me as soon as I walk through the door, eager for attention.

"At least Elsa is asleep," Briony whispers. "Sometimes I think I live in a zoo. Children, your dinner is waiting in the kitchen!" she announces, clapping her hands like a schoolmistress. Iona rolls her eyes at being categorized as one of the children, but closes her book and gets to her feet. It often seems she is the only one who can make her younger siblings listen. Reluctantly, they trudge off for sausages and mash, while we wait for Jeffrey and a more sophisticated, if perhaps slightly less satisfying evening meal. Daniel gets to his feet, kissing my cheek. Ensconced on one of the sofas around the crackling fire, I tell them what I have learned. Both share my reaction when I explain the likely origin of Juliet's scars.

"Horrifying!" Briony exclaims.

"I wanted to speak with Frances Bell after work, but got stuck in traffic and had to give up. Maybe that's why Jeffrey is late?"

"He promised he would leave early tonight." Briony shrugs. "I expect, as ever, time ran away from him." She does not sound terribly aggravated, however, so I take it matters have not deteriorated again so soon after their tête-à-tête. We sip our Vermouth, hearing the children's chatter ringing out from the kitchen, while Daniel talks about his lunch with Harold. At some point, Iona steals into the room to explain that the younger ones want Briony to kiss them goodnight. It is eight. Where is Jeffrey? I exchange a look with Daniel and note a trace of anxiety in his eyes.

"I don't understand what is keeping him." Briony paces the room when she returns from saying goodnight to the little ones.

"I will try calling the museum, find out if he simply forgot the time," I reassure her. When no one answers the call, however, I quickly realize the museum is closed, its only inhabitants are relics and mummies now. Where is Jeffrey?

"Should we telephone the police?" Daniel whispers to me, meeting me in the hallway out of earshot of my cousin.

"It may be premature, but I have a bad feeling, Daniel. He may be late sometimes, but it's been hours since he should have arrived and he knew to come home early tonight."

"Maybe I should drive over there? Ask if the night guard can tell us anything?"

"Let us wait another twenty minutes or so, then we can decide." I try to put on a reassuring front when we re-enter the sitting room. Briony waits by the window, peering out at the street beyond. It is dark, save for small pools of light cast by the streetlamps. She turns to face us, her features tense, mouth pressed into a thin line.

"We should not worry too much. Maybe he simply forgot and had a drink with a colleague," Daniel says in an effort to sound optimistic, yet failing.

"Do you think something has happened to him? Be honest. Or has he…has he left us?"

"Briony, don't be silly, he would not leave you! I thought you had established that much," I exclaim.

"No, yes, I mean, you are right. But where is he, Evie?" Just as she turns back to the window, there is a noise from outside, the rumble of a motor. Daniel and I rush to join her, breathing a collective sigh of relief when it stops in front of the house. This sentiment expands considerably when we watch Jeffrey emerging from the taxi and paying the driver. Briony hurries from the room and pulls open the front door just as Jeffrey climbs the steps. She throws herself into his embrace and, with a slightly bewildered expression, Jeffrey holds her tight for a moment.

"Where have you been?" she says, her voice laden with anxious accusation when they part. Before he can answer, I notice a stain on his white collar. Red.

"What is that? What happened to you?" I ask, stepping forward, pointing at the spot which is, undeniably a drop of blood. His face appears uninjured and he stands upright, as if unscathed.

"Let me get a drink, all right? Then I'll explain everything." What can we do but grant his request and follow him into the lounge where, with shaking hands, he pours himself a generous measure of whisky, grimacing as he takes a sip, then another. In the warm light of the room, I see how pale he is and am eager to hurry him along, to learn what transpired tonight. Briony is more patient now that she has him home, safe and sound. She helps him out of his coat, and he slumps into an armchair.

"Firstly, it isn't my blood. I am fine," Jeffrey begins in a weary tone. "That being said, I have spent the past two hours at the hospital. I am sorry I didn't call. The line to use the telephone was endless, and I didn't expect to be there so long."

"Why were you there at all?" I almost shout with exasperation.

"There was an accident. Or, at least, I think it was an accident. It's Frances, Frances Bell, the archivist."

I gasp, and Daniel takes my hand. "What happened?"

"I was leaving the museum at just past five. I really wanted to be early as I promised, Briony." He attempts a smile, and she nods. "I saw Frances ahead of me. It was drizzling and everyone was hurrying, unfurling their umbrellas. I called out to her, intending to offer a ride home, though I suppose, after Juliet, I should have learned my lesson. She did not hear me. She was crossing Great Russell Street, when I heard the roar of an accelerating motor and -" Jeffery shakes his head, rubbing his eyes. "It drove straight at her." He winces as if feeling the impact. "The sound of it...God, it was awful, just awful! The motorcar just drove on, turned onto Bury Place and was gone. It took me a moment to realize, then I ran to her. A man and a woman were already kneeling on the road. When I got there, the woman hurried off to call an ambulance. I felt for Frances' pulse, and it was there, but weak. Her head was bleeding and her left leg...It was crooked, bent the wrong way. It was horrifying. I went with her to the hospital. We don't know one another very well, but she is a widow and alone."

"Was she responsive in the ambulance, speaking at all? Could you see who was driving the car?" I rattle off my questions. "Did you call the police?"

"Give the man a chance to breathe, Evie," Daniel says gently.

"She made some sounds, but I couldn't understand anything she said. In the hospital, they took her away. The police must have been called. As I was about to leave, they arrived and wanted to question me. Did I notice anything, know the victim, think it was an accident? It went on and on. But no, I did not see the driver. However, by the way the engine revved the moment Frances stepped onto the street, I have to believe it was intentional. Added to that, the driver fled the scene. If it had been accidental, they are still guilty of criminal behavior for driving off and leaving her there."

"What sort of a motorcar was it?" I ask, frustrated and worried for Frances.

"Dark, ordinary." Jeffrey shrugs. "Had I known it would matter, I would have paid closer attention, but it happened so quickly. It was raining and I wanted to get going, as I suspect most people did. The police seemed irritated to have so little to go on. I suspect they will never discover who drove that car."

"What of Frances?" Briony asks, hands fidgeting in her lap.

"She was alive when I left. They would not allow me to see her. I fear she is in a bad way. The car struck her, and she hit the ground with such force." He sucks in a breath and shakes his head, bringing the glass to his lips and draining it. "Whoever was driving had the intention of killing her, I am sure of it."

Chapter 45

"I was on my way to speak to Frances," I tell Daniel on the drive home. "I turned back because of traffic, but maybe the traffic was so bad because Great Russell Street ahead was still blocked from the accident?"

"Do you think this attack is related to Juliet's murder? It feels too coincidental that two women working in the same place, acquaintances from long ago, would come to harm in such a close timespan without some thread of connection." Daniel glances at me, maneuvering the car onto Park Lane. We did not stay for dinner. Jeffrey was shattered and he and Briony needed space to think, to be alone after his shock. For my part, I am happy to be in Daniel's company. I could not have made light conversation over roast chicken with thoughts of Frances, broken and alone, in the hospital crowding my mind.

"It cannot be a coincidence. Frances must know something she did not share with me before, something related to Juliet or to Howard and the past."

"Or at the very least, someone believes she knows more. Maybe her presence at the funeral drew attention to Frances. It could have given the killer reason to believe she attended due to a deeper connection with Juliet than she truly had. Do you remember everyone who was at the funeral? It must have been one of them, surely."

"There are Victor Nelson and Michael Ellroy. They were both there and probably saw Frances."

"Ellroy has an alibi for Juliet's murder," Daniel reminds me.

"That does not mean he is innocent when it comes to Frances' attack. That being so, I had the impression he genuinely cared about Howard. Would he have tried to kill his widow after confessing quite as much as he did?"

"I agree, it sounds unlikely. And Victor?"

"Possibly, but as far as I know, he is back in Reading. It is a workday. He could not easily nip over to London, stalk Frances outside her place of work and acquire a motorcar to run her over. Then there were the women of the WI, Edith Ashbourne and her husband and Adeline, Priscilla…" I slump in the seat and throw my hands up. "Anyone could have lingered near one of the other graves and gone unnoticed. It is maddening. I wonder whether Stanton has heard about what happened to Frances?"

"Probably not."

"And I can only tell Hugh tomorrow," I grumble in frustration. Hugh lives in a rented room in Lambeth and the proprietor refuses to acquire a telephone. Daniel and I have tried to convince Hugh to find lodgings closer to the center of town, but he is being stubborn, even if money is not as tight as it once was.

"The news will keep," Daniel soothes. My fear is that it will not. What if Frances does not survive? Has the same killer struck twice? Another thought forces its way into my mind just as Daniel pulls to a stop in Grosvenor Square, an idea twisting my stomach into a painful knot.

"What if our investigation called attention to Frances? What if something we did put her in danger?" I ask as Daniel opens his car door. He pauses, turning to face me.

"Do not take on such guilt, Evie. The person who drove the car is solely responsible. This story started long before you even met Juliet. The past holds the answers, and whoever tried to kill Frances feared her memory. You wanted to ask her whether there was something she remembered, something she had neglected to share with you. Well, her attacker may have reached the same conclusion, but instead of words, he chose violence. It is reckless and tells of desperation. The driver could have been seen. It could have gone very wrong for them. To be so rash means they believed they had less to lose being caught running her down than letting Frances continue to live in possession of some critical information." His words take some of the weight from my shoulders, though I remain unconvinced that I may not carry a portion of the blame.

"If they had been caught, they could always have pretended it was unintentional. No one could prove premeditation, even if Jeffrey had made his claim that it appeared to be willfully done," I say, climbing the stairs to the house. I shiver, whether from the sudden cold or the thoughts swirling about in my mind, I cannot tell. Wilkins is at the ready, taking our coats and hats. I try a smile, too weary to make polite conversation. I trudge ahead into the sitting room, hearing Daniel ask Wilkins if he could arrange for some sandwiches to be made. When Daniel finds me, I am sitting in the armchair near the fire, my knees tucked under me, staring into the flickering blue-tipped flames which lick like tongues of hungry beasts at the blackening logs.

"Wilkins is bringing something to eat," he says.

"I do not have much of an appetite. I keep thinking of Frances, wondering whether she is awake, whether she is still alone. They will not allow me to visit her at this time of night, but I feel so useless just sitting here." Daniel rests his hands on my shoulders.

"There is nothing you can do now. Evie, you have to remember, this person - if it is one person - is dangerous. If they had no qualms about killing one woman and attempting the same with another, they will not hesitate to use violence against anyone who gets in their way." I lean back, looking up at him.

"You know I always do my best to be careful."

"Your best efforts to keep safe, I hate to say, have not been terribly successful in recent years, my love. I will never try to hamper your ambitions, but you must grant me the right to worry." I cannot but smile at his diplomacy, resting my head against him and reaching for one of his hands still on my shoulders.

"You know what you are getting into. Are you certain you want to marry me?"

"Unquestionably," he answers without hesitation.

"You have been warned," I tease.

"As long as you still love me with creases of worry etched into my forehead, I will have to cope."

"Hopefully, they will be vastly outnumbered by laughter lines," I reply, more earnest now. Daniel smiles, though upside down as I see it, it looks more like a frown.

"Can you imagine us in forty years? I wonder what will have changed by then, what our lives will be like."

"Would you look into the future, if you could?"

"Unlike that quack of a medium, you mean?"

"Would you?" I persist.

"No. Better not. I already know there will be good and there will be bad, that is the lottery of living. What would I gain in knowing the specifics? To think always with dread of unpleasantness to come and never be able to revel in happy times? Would you?"

"I think not. Perhaps some disasters could be averted, but others would spring up in their place. The world will spin, and we can only do our best to keep up and be as good as we can, hoping the mistakes we make are not irreparable."

"Very reasonable," Daniel agrees.

I twist my body around and look up at him. "Though I would like to know whether we will solve this crime. Peering into the looking glass of the future might deliver the killer's identity."

"Would that not be cheating? You are a detective, after all."

"Ah, yes," I sigh. "I am a detective, am I not?" The word, despite everything that has happened, still tastes sweet on my tongue. I am filled with a new vigor that Hugh and I will solve this case and be worthy of calling ourselves such.

Chapter 46

Hugh is suitably disturbed when I tell him what happened to Frances the next morning. I am glad he came in early, for I am eager to get to the hospital. Hugh agrees to contact Victor to verify his alibi. The police will likely, at some stage, do the same, but there is no harm in being a step ahead of them. Later, I want to talk to Ellroy once more, to hear where he was last night and whether Stanton has shown him the photograph. I feel an even greater urgency than before to solve this case, to find the person willing to kill not once but possibly twice. There is something so ruthless, so cold about the way they acted. Strangulation, staring the victim in the eye as their life ebbs away, then ramming a body with a beast of a car, feeling the impact as bones shatter and simply driving on.

The hospital is crowded, people with various degrees of injury sit in the waiting area, some holding red-stained handkerchiefs to their head or wrapped around a hand; a few women wait with crying children. The odor of antiseptic hangs in the air, making my eyes sting. A harried nurse directs me to the ward where Frances can be found. She lived through the night, which I hope is a promising mark of her recovery. When I arrive at the ward, another nurse meets me at the door. She is small, but built to be intimidating with broad shoulders and a scowl etched into her face. She eyes me warily, and I pull myself up to my full height. I can be formidable, too. Agnes might have rubbed off on me in certain ways.

"Mrs. Bell has not awoken," she grudgingly says.

"But she will, I mean, she will recover?" My anxiety seems to soften the matron, whose name "Beth" is embroidered above her left breast. She leads me to a row of chairs against one wall and we sit.

"Are you a relative?" Her expression tells me what my answer ought to be.

"A niece." The lie trips easily from my tongue.

"Right." She pauses and takes a deep breath, clearly gauging whether to go along with my deception, then deciding in my favor. "She has a broken leg, arm, shattered bones in her left hand, injured her shoulder, has a head wound which indicates a possible crack in her skull, and she sustained severe bruising to her left hip. We have found no significant signs of inner bleeding or ruptures, but she is very badly hurt. The head wound is most worrisome. She was delirious when she was brought in and hasn't spoken since or regained consciousness. The doctors are hopeful, but the longer she remains unconscious..." Beth sighs and lets the thought trail away, for me to fill the silence with the worst possible outcome.

"Have the police been here?" I ask.

"Came last night. It was no mere accident, it seems," Beth says, raising her brows, her frown deepening.

"No, it was not. Someone tried to kill Frances. They may try again, now that she is unable to defend herself. There should be a guard stationed by her room. Did the police mention whether they will send someone?"

"Do you see a guard?" Beth asks, shaking her head. "A widow without family is not a priority, not when gangs and robberies call."

"I will make it their priority, you can be sure of that. Frances will be protected. If I have to hire a guard myself!" I announce, frustrated by this oversight. With the amount of people entering and leaving these premises, anyone could slip in undetected and press a pillow over helpless Frances' face!

Beth nods, approval shining in her eyes. "Good to hear someone is taking control. I say, if women had the run of the world, matters would look quite different."

"I heard someone else make much the same observation not long ago," I note with a smile. When I leave, I extract a promise from Beth to look in on Frances often. In return, I will try to arrange for a guard within the next few hours.

As soon as I find a telephone kiosk, I call Stanton. Fortunately, he picks up and is forced to listen to my rant about Frances being in danger and police incompetence. By the time I fall silent, my anger spent, he promises to send a constable to the ward immediately. As it happens, he only learned of the attack an hour ago and was going to leave for the hospital just as I rang.

"You have saved me the journey, if she remains unresponsive." His sigh sounds through the line. I imagine an expression of frustration tugging at his features.

"Have you interviewed Victor's mother?"

"Tomorrow. I spoke with Ellroy yesterday, only on the telephone. He promised to stop by during his lunch hour to look at the photograph. His alibi was confirmed, though obviously this was before Mrs. Bell was attacked. The fact that he was so forthcoming makes me want to eliminate him as a suspect, but if he is devious enough, he could be concocting the whole story in order to fool us."

"I think it unlikely, still I want to speak to him again as well."

"Take Hugh along, would you?"

"Yes, yes. Speaking of Hugh," I begin, hoping to have found Stanton in an amenable state, "Would you perhaps take him along when you interview Victor's mother? He could pretend to be your constable and remain silent. We did deliver you Ellroy and, for that matter, Victor himself."

"Is that your way of telling me I owe you?"

"When you put it that way…"

"Fine. Hugh knows how to handle himself. I'll take him along. This better never reach the ears of my superior."

"Why would it?" I ask, ignoring his implication that, unlike Hugh, I cannot *handle myself.*

"Tell him to come to the station tomorrow at eight. I want to be back by midday."

"Still working several cases?"

"Unfortunately. In this city, as soon as one is unscrambled, another two take its place. It is endless. I am proud to be a copper, but sometimes solving a case merely seems like a drop of water on a hot stone." He stops himself, yet I can tell it would do him good to grumble a bit, vent his frustrations. Maybe another time.

"If you help one family to find a measure of justice, that makes it worthwhile, surely?"

"It would feel all the more so if I could give everyone some peace."

"If we lived in a society with everyone at peace there would be no need for your profession, or mine, for that matter."

Stanton chuckles. "We both know that is a bargain we would both gladly make."

I have to wait until the evening for Hugh to return and visit Michael Ellroy with me. When I called him earlier, he said he was working until five, but we could meet him at his house after that. He sounded eager to help, likely curious to know what happened. Hugh has brought news of Victor. After some investigation, he learned that not only was Victor out on a beat with another copper from morning to evening yesterday, he does not own a motorcar, perhaps does not even know how to drive. I am relieved to strike him from our list of suspects, at least as far as Frances is concerned. It seems too far-fetched for him to have learned who she is and her husband's connection to Juliet. He came across as a friendly fellow, and I would hate for my intuition to be so terribly mistaken. Besides, the thought of the only person in Juliet's family who attended her funeral being responsible for putting her into the ground is too tragic. There is little about this case to which that word does not apply, though.

"Stanton agreed to take you along to interview Victor's mother tomorrow," I tell Hugh as we finally set off to Hammersmith, where Michael Ellroy lives with his wife. I wonder whether she is aware of his past. Then again, he was a soldier, not a spy, so there is little need for secrecy in that regard. If it is a secret, he could easily have asked to meet us elsewhere.

"I doubt Victor's mother will be very forthcoming. Nonetheless, I am curious to hear what she has to say."

"She may be defensive. Perhaps I would be, too. She sent away a young, pregnant girl and the next time she hears about Juliet, she's been murdered," I say in a wry tone, glancing at Hugh in the passenger seat.

"Which is not her fault, as far as we know," he reminds me.

"True enough. I suppose I am eager to find someone to blame. Maybe she will at least be able to say something about the pregnancy. It is possible Juliet contacted her again. It could be useful to have a chat with her husband and Victor's younger brother, too, while you are there, even if they were away at the time. See if it can be done."

"Aye, aye," Hugh says with a mock salute. "From what Victor says, however, I have the impression his mother rules the roost. Perhaps she never even told her husband about Juliet's visit all those years ago."

"It's possible. No doubt she felt some degree of shame, else she would not have instructed Victor to keep quiet."

"It would have been difficult for everyone involved, but even in a small community, people do eventually get over the shame of a child out of wedlock. I think, if Mrs. Stanley had supported Juliet, let her stay with the child, people would have grown to accept it."

"It is unlike you to be so optimistic," I observe with a smile.

"It is, isn't it? Maybe we are all changing." Hugh laughs.

"How am I changing?" I ask, curious and slightly affronted. Was I not quite perfect to begin with?

"You are becoming more cynical, while I am becoming the optimist," Hugh explains with a chuckle, and I poke him with my elbow.

"I am not!"

"Maybe cynical is not the right word. Maybe realistic is better. You see the world for what it is."

"I did not before?"

"Do not be offended, Evelyn," Hugh says, warmth in his tone. "You lived in a castle much of your life. When you left London and went to Greece, and then started out on your own here and in Oxford, you became aware of some aspects of the world once entirely hidden to you. Before you began detecting, you had never encountered the poverty of the East End, the vast disparity between the people who live in this city. I do not judge you for it. If I could have been shielded from so much of the darkness in this world, I would have chosen that path without question. But once you see the truth, it cannot be unseen. It has changed you. For the better, I believe." He falls silent. Hugh is never much of a talker, so this has come as a surprise. It makes me wonder how he saw me when we first met. Did he think I was a rich, ignorant madam, interfering in his life? He is not wrong to observe my view of the world has changed. It is true that while I knew of the poor in our city, volunteered with other ladies once in a while, I had never stepped foot in the East End, had never seen the hungry-eyed children, men with their shoes worn through to the sole, women with little ones on both hips, unable to feed them. I had not come across murder, the villainy of some, the desperation of others. I had known grief and sadness, but it was internal. Hugh is right, I have changed and while he claims it is for the better, a tiny part of me yearns for the ignorance of my past, even if that life was not always as blissful as it may have appeared. Detecting is fascinating work and quite satisfying at times, but every murder I have helped resolve has shown me a side of humanity I wished I never knew. It has made me contemplate the value of justice, whether it is possible when something as irreversible as murder has occurred. It makes me contemplate justification, too. I am ashamed to have, on a rare occasion, sympathized with a killer, learning their motive and finding myself wondering whether, in their shoes, I might have done the same. I shake the memory away and try to focus on the present moment.

We are nearing Hammersmith and night has crept up on us, even though it is only a quarter to six. The area was named for once housing the many blacksmiths of the city, when the clanging of their hammers was heard at all hours. Now it is a lively area, with industry and factories along the riverfront. Ellroy gave us his address, and we stop in front of a neat little house with a bright blue door and a holly wreath in one of the windows. A light shines in the lower level, illuminating a patch of the pavement outside. The house has an altogether welcoming appearance, I only hope Ellroy will feel the same towards us once we have questioned him.

"Come in, come in!" He opens the door, a smile on his face. "My wife is visiting her sister in Leeds. We can speak openly. That said, I did tell her of our conversation after the funeral. I am no disciple of secrecy."

"Have you seen the photograph?" I ask, when we have settled into his cozy sitting room and been offered tea.

"I stopped by on my lunch hour and saw it," Ellroy confirms, crossing his legs as he leans back in the chair, which seems too small for his lanky frame. Hugh and I sit squeezed onto the sofa opposite. Everything in the room seems a size too small. Perhaps Mrs. Ellroy is a dainty creature.

"Did you recognize the man?" Hugh asks, leaning forward in his seat.

"I believe so. I am fairly sure it was the man who helped rescue me that night. I only saw his face by torchlight, but it is imprinted upon my memory. The photograph is grainy and creased, so there is a chance I am wrong, but the face looked familiar, even after all these years. Of course, I never knew his name. Even if he had provided one, I do not doubt it would have been false, just as I later learned Minette Laurent was not Juliet Nelson's true identity. Does knowing that the man was connected to her during the war bring you any closer to Juliet's killer? I do not believe he wished to hurt her, rather the opposite. To me, they seemed quite clearly enamored, even in the brief exchange I witnessed."

"Love and hate are sometimes not far removed from each other," Hugh observes.

"Though I would prefer to think, had they been in love, he would not ten years later choose to murder her. We must discover his identity. I wonder..." I hesitate.

"What is it?" Ellroy asks, eyes focused on mine.

"I wonder whether it might be wise to run the photograph in a paper and ask for anyone who knows the identity of the man to come forward."

"It could produce a lot of false leads," Ellroy notes, adding, "All the same, it could be worth a try."

"We will speak with Hollis," Hugh says to me, without explaining further. I decide to move the conversation down another path.

"We have come with other news related to the case."

"Any progress?" Ellroy asks. I suspect he is beginning to feel a part of the detection process, which suits me well enough, if he is innocent. If not he could be playing a wild game with us. He does have an alibi for Juliet's murder. Yet is it too tidy?

"Another woman, Frances Bell, has been attacked. A driver hit her and left her to die on the street." I watch Ellroy carefully, but detect only horror in the way his features shift, his jaw slackening and his brows knitting close together.

"That is...goodness!" He rubs his chin. "Just terrible, terrible. Is she...did she die?"

"She is in a very bad way. The doctors cannot predict whether she will wake up again. Police guards are watching her round the clock," I add, to emphasize that any repeat attack is futile. My implied warning seems unnecessary, for Ellroy appears nearly as disturbed as Hugh and I were when we learned what had happened.

"The poor woman. She was Howard's wife, Frances Bell, was she not?"

"Yes, I am afraid so."

"I didn't know her myself. Howard kept his private world very separate from the public one. When I learned of his death, I first suspected his secrecy had caught up with him; that some old enemy had taken revenge. Then I heard it had been an ordinary heart attack. In a way it was a relief, and in another, a great irony that so clever and brave a man was felled by the treachery of his own body like so many others. In my mind, there was an aura of immortality about him. I thought he always was and always would be, but it is foolish to think so. All the more foolish of a man who has been to war, who knows as well as anyone that immortality is a myth. Men, capable and courageous, can drop to their graves with the pull of a trigger, the impact of a small piece of metal embedded in their hearts." He lets out a sad sigh. "And now his wife unwittingly takes on the story that by rights should have been Howard's, to die at another's hands."

"She is alive yet," I say with more vehemence than I intended. Ellroy straightens in his seat.

"Of course, of course. My apologies. I grow morbid when the day is long and memories return. I only meant, it is a sad irony that a man with so many secrets, who played an instrumental role in the war, died of natural causes and his wife was brought down by someone eager to keep her out of the way. It makes you wonder what she knows."

"If, indeed, she knows anything of significance. The driver may have been mistaken, believing her to be better informed than she is. You are sure Howard kept his work a secret?" Hugh asks.

"Yes, quite. In fact, he told me that he sometimes regretted being so secretive. In the beginning, it was to protect her and himself. After the war, he had lost some operatives and did not wish to speak of that time, the memories too painful, the guilt too tangible. As years went by, it became impossible to confess it all to his wife. He had kept such a significant part of his life from her, he couldn't find a way back. I remember this conversation well. It was the last time I saw him. He had been drinking too much, and the words burst from him without his usual restraint. Perhaps he sensed something was wrong. Do you believe in such things, in premonitions?" Ellroy seems genuinely interested on our reply.

"I believe in intuition," I say. "Omens and the like, I find, are slightly beyond my comprehension."

"I feel the same," Hugh agrees. "Howard may have felt unwell already, added to that the drink and the growing need to unburden himself could have made for the right combination to get him talking. Maybe even to his wife, once he returned home that night."

"Possibly. But since she claims not to have known, Howard probably went to his grave with the secrets he held close for more than a decade of his life, his wife none the wiser." We let Ellroy's words fill the space between us. Not a person alive exists without regret, but to hold such a secret and to keep it from the person one should trust the most must have been a tremendous burden to bear. Once again, I wish I could have met and spoken to Frances' enigmatic husband, not least because I think he could have helped us learn who might have hated Juliet enough to wish her harm. After all, he was the one who helped her find her footing after the war and protected her privacy. Howard Bell was shielding Juliet, but from whom? He knew of her past and likely feared it could spill into her present, but in what way? Did he anticipate someone's hunger for revenge and therefore installed her in the flat he himself owned, then convinced his wife to pave the way for her to work quietly at the museum, far from the offices of government where her name might be recognized? What happened that might have required such a shroud of mystery to be draped around Juliet Nelson?

All of this I discuss with Hugh on the drive home. Though Ellroy was willing to chat for some time longer, it quickly became clear he was mostly curious and had no particular insight to add. His alibi for yesterday evening is reasonably solid. He was at work, seen by his colleagues, which is easy enough to confirm. To his credit, he did not balk when I asked where he was at the time of Frances' collision with the car. He even offered to show us his own motorcar to prove it is undamaged. We agreed to look at it, and indeed, it is pristine, not a mark on it. Michael Ellroy, unless he has a vicious accomplice and is himself a talented actor, appears entirely innocent.

"At least we now know that the man in the photograph was someone she met during the war, and that he was likely English. Does this not beg the question whether Bell recruited him, too?"

"It is fairly likely, which leads me to wonder whether he survived the war. Ellroy told us Bell was troubled by the deaths of a few of his spies. Maybe the man was one of them."

"Possibly. Yet even if there had been some flirtation between the two during the war it doesn't have to mean anything. Everyone lived differently then. People were afraid for their lives, and what initially may have seemed a passionate connection could feel far less exciting after the war. Maybe they realized they were not compatible and parted ways."

"There is the ring, though, the wedding band in her wardrobe," I remind Hugh.

"Not necessarily hers. Both her parents died, she could have held on to her mother's. It was small, likely a woman's size."

"All right," I concede. "I may be allowing a fantasy to take hold, but you must admit, there is a chance that they were in love, that they married. She could have kept the ring and photograph as a memento. Evidently, if they were a couple, they were no longer one at the time of her death. There is no record of Juliet having married, and she kept her maiden name."

"It could have taken place in France. During the war, the task of keeping records often fell by the wayside. I doubt there is much use chasing after this lead without even knowing the man's name. How many people passed through Valenciennes in those years?"

"Our next task should be to place the photograph in the paper and hope somebody responds to it. What do we have to lose? Whoever killed Juliet and tried to kill Frances was likely searching her flat for the medals or the money – if the ransacking was not a false trail – and not for the photograph. No one could have known she had it. It was clearly a privately treasured possession."

"Hollis will be happy to have something he can publish, even if it is merely a photograph with a call to memory. He is restless, but too hungry for the full story to go to press before the case is solved."

"Hopefully," I say. "What will you ask Mrs. Stanley tomorrow?"

"I thought I was meant to sit quiet as a church mouse and do nothing but listen?" Hugh asks, grinning.

"What would be the use in that? You are better informed than Stanton! To be fair, you ought to tell him what we have learned on the drive to Reading."

"And if I can think of nothing else to say, we can always talk about you?" he teases in a rare show of humor.

"Don't you dare! You are my friend, remember?"

"How can I forget?" he counters. His affection and loyalty to Daniel includes me, and I consider myself quite fortunate for it. Whatever mistakes Hugh made in the past, his tendency to fixate – as he did again by trailing Wilkins – aside, he is as steadfast as they come. If he were to talk to Stanton about me, I do not fear he would be anything but complimentary.

"You must try to establish whether Victor's mother truly never heard from her niece again after sending her away all those years ago. Most importantly, she must be set at ease. She will feel defensive, confronted by two male policemen – since you are impersonating one. You must make it clear you do not blame her. Sympathize, be on her side. Perhaps she regrets what she did. Reminding her of her harsh behavior will not earn you any favors. A woman who sent away her desperate and pregnant niece must have a steely core." I try to picture the scene, young and frightened Juliet asking for help, turned away by a hard-faced woman, too worried about what the neighbors would think to consider the well-being of not one, but two people she should have held dear. I am glad it is Hugh going to question her. I fear I would let my emotions betray me, and she would see how harshly I judge her actions.

"I will do my best. You know I have a talent for putting on a front," Hugh says with a smile.

Chapter 47

All good plans, we learn the following morning, can go awry. Hugh arrives at the office with the pallor of one risen from the crypt, perhaps slightly greener. He is so uneasy on his feet, I wonder how he made the journey from Lambeth to St. James in one piece. Maeve rushes to fetch him a hot tea and a cool cloth for his burning brow, while I force him to rest on the sofa. We quickly determine it is entirely impossible for him to join Stanton on his excursion to Reading.

"I must have caught a bug," he moans apologetically.

"You rest up and don't move! Maeve will keep an eye on you. But I will not allow Stanton to use your illness as an excuse to go on his own. There are female Police Constables, even if I have learned at the WI, there are remarkably few. I can pretend. At this point though, I wonder whether it matters if we simply tell the truth and say I am a detective in my own right?" I pace about the office, wrapping a scarf around my neck, grabbing my coat and hat.

"Maybe it would be easier that way, fewer deceptions to remember," Hugh manages in a raspy voice.

"Right, I am off. If I do not find you resting here when I return, I shall be very cross indeed!"

"I do not have the strength for a cross Evelyn. Your wish is my command."

"That is what I like to hear!" With newfound energy, I hurry out of the door. Stanton might make a bit of a fuss, as he is prone to do when he thinks I am meddling, but I will be at that interview. If he will not take me, I will follow him. After all, Hugh and I were the ones who found Victor – well, Hollis, admittedly – and it was our team, too, who discovered Michael Ellroy.

Stanton, as predicted, is less than thrilled that I am to be his companion on today's outing, though almost disappointingly, he does not put up an argument. Why bother, when he knows he cannot win it, I suppose. Besides, I promise him a few nuggets of new information to sweeten the drive. It should not take much longer than an hour, but westbound traffic is dense this time of day. By the time we reach the outskirts of the city, driving through Richmond towards Hounslow, I have told Stanton of our meeting with Ellroy the previous evening and shared what we learned.

"I knew he recognized the man in the photograph, of course," he says, and I roll my eyes.

"Yes, yes, but were you able to eliminate him from your enquiries?"

"No, I was not. Very well done," he replies not without sarcasm. "He did not bring his motor to the station when he looked at the picture, so I could not examine it."

"Do you have any other suspects? I trust Jeffrey is now firmly crossed off the list, and Victor has been rejected as well?"

"He still has a mother, brother and father, who might have done it, though I do not see why they would. I have also not ruled out several members of the WI. Their alibis are flimsy, but those of innocent people usually are. The guilty make certain theirs are iron clad."

"Who has an iron clad alibi, then?"

"Ellroy, to begin with. Victor's is quite solid. Edith Ashbourne was with her family at home, which is not dependable, but as she hired you, I am inclined to trust her, unless she has some masochistic desire to be caught? What do you make of her?"

"I respect her. Are you familiar with her history?"

"Her involvement in the suffragette movement? Yes, she was quite the figure, right-hand of Emmeline Pankhurst."

"Indeed, and still very commanding."

"Do you like her?" he asks. Do I?

"I do not know her well enough, really. I do not dislike her," I reply thoughtfully. "She is a bit…intimidating, perhaps."

"I thought the same when I met her," Stanton confesses.

"Would you make such an observation about her husband? Lloyd Ashbourne carries himself in a similar manner as his wife, yet in a man it is viewed as natural, impressive even. Edith Ashbourne's commanding air should, by that token, be viewed in the same light, should it not?" I do not wait for his reply, barging on, "And really, women are constantly judged by very outmoded ideals. I cannot tell you how many strange looks I have received from people when they hear I am a detective. I can almost see it written on their forehead, 'But that is men's work'!" I cross my arms. "I should like to see men doing what women do all the time!"

"Such as raising children?" he says, humor in his tone, a twitch at the corner of his mouth.

"Precisely!" I announce, before realizing that, in fact, he knows quite well, far better than I do, what it takes to raise a child alone. "Well, maybe not all men are ill informed," I amend, feeling the fight drain from me as quickly as it flared up.

"I do not disagree that the standards by which women are judged are old-fashioned, but it is difficult to shake ideals which were held true for so long by a large segment of society."

"There is the inherent difficulty in effecting change, and then often times a complete unwillingness to even try. It is no wonder women only received the vote nine years ago, and I for that matter, still do not have it! Until men – for it is men making the rules, we cannot forget – accept women as full and capable human beings, able to carry the responsibility of voting and working as we choose, there can never be equality."

"Maybe that is how some prefer it to remain. Some women, too, prefer the current order of things and opposed the suffragettes and all they stood for. There will never be equality in any case. If women and men have equal rights, there are still the obstacles of poverty and class to overcome. I cannot see us living in a utopia of socialist ideals, where all are equal and where jealousy and greed do not eventually topple the equilibrium. Humans are not meant for realized idealism, they would not know what to do with their natural instincts."

"Hugh claims I am growing cynical, but to hear you, one could think the end of civilization is nigh!"

"When you spend your days tracking down the dregs of this so-called enlightened society - murderers, robbers and rapists - you would question whether we were ever civilized at all."

"True enough. I feel myself growing less willing to trust already," I concede, thinking of the way I suspect even the ladies of the WI. The only exception being my dear aunt. When one has faced true wickedness, it is difficult not to see the potential for it all around. Yet I am not so far gone that I cannot find the counterbalance of each evil deed in the vast numbers of good ones. They may not undo the bad, but at least offer a contrast, light to crowd out the dark. For all those who seek to harm, to destroy, there are many more who will soothe and create and rebuild in their wake. As long as such balance remains, there is hope, and one ought not forget it.

"You are right, still it does not allow me to forget what I have witnessed. Yet for Thom I must try to remain optimistic, to believe in a bright future. What sort of a father would I be, if I could not conjure up a happy world for my son?"

"Thom is a bright boy, and very lucky to have you," I say, relieved to hear a note of lightness return to my friend's voice. I was beginning to worry he is growing too gloomy for this work. We are silent for a while, driving along near empty streets, towns giving way to patches of open countryside, before we reach the outskirts of Slough.

My gaze shifts to the landscape outside the window. I haven't left the city in some time, and the sight beyond makes me yearn to once again be astride a horse, unencumbered by traffic and buses and the clang and clamor of London. The sun is bright and high in the blue sky, shining onto the pale, hoar-frosted fields. Farther on, I see the dark outline of a woodland. The trees are barren, but dense still, one can only imagine the lush hedge of green when spring arrives. I yearn for the warmer months, the smell of blossom in the air, vivid flashes of bright magnolia all across the city, patches of crocus and daffodils and the twittering of the birds. Winter is a heavy coat in this country, and we wear it for months, until it bends our backs and we ache to stretch our stiff muscles in the invigorating sunshine of spring. The warm breeze is a balm to weary souls, enveloping us in its welcome embrace.

Yet I cannot wholly deny this season brings its own charms. Christmas is around the bend, the scents of cinnamon and clove hang in the air in every house I visit. Spirited carols are sung on street corners. There is the beauty of dancing snowflakes observed from a window from the cozy indoors, or a cup of cocoa warming one's hands. There are the trees, shimmering with tinsel and flickering candles, the food, the roasts and the gingerbread. Even as I am eager for warmer climates, I think with fondness of what is yet to come in the next weeks and months. How strange it was at times, living in Greece, to observe only the smallest changes in the weather, such mild shifts in the seasons. Though Greece is the land of Homer and Aeschylus, neither would have been able to write an ode to vastly different seasons as they appear in my native land. I missed them when I lived on Crete, even if now I often yearn for the persistent sunshine. At the time, I thought of the respite of a rainy day, the riot of color as the leaves turned from lush green to orange and fiery red, the chill of first snow and witnessing the glee upon the faces of children at play who would launch themselves into the white expanse. There is so much in the world to make it worth living. I may be more cynical than I was some years ago, but I am not beyond accepting this as a fact.

Soon the scenery changes again, as Slough appears ahead and fields yield to rows of houses, an occasional factory, a tall chimney spitting soot into the air. The town was a center for repair during the war, and damaged motors and vehicles were sent to the depot. So many places I visit, or even pass through, played a role in that tumultuous time, a role often entirely forgotten, overlooked by history, but vital, nonetheless. This country may not be the largest, but it tells countless tales. Every city, every town and every village has a history to shape the character of its residents, fill them with pride or with regret.

After Slough comes Maidenhead along the River Thames, a lively market town with a well-known clock tower, built in honor of our late Queen Victoria's diamond jubilee.

"Not long now." Stanton's voice reaches through my silent musings. I pull my eyes from the view and back to him.

"How shall we proceed? Will you come straight out and ask her whether everything Victor told us was true, and whether there is more?"

"She already knows what we heard from Victor, since I had to arrange the meeting and needed to tell her something. So it's best to be straightforward. I think – and in light of our previous conversation, do not hold this against me – I should be the one to speak more brusquely and you more gently. That way we can gauge her reaction, unnerve her a little, so she cannot lie too easily. You can be the kindly one to coax answers from her. Do you agree? Before you reject my plan, it is either that or you remaining quietly in the background."

"I was not going to reject your plan. I do not oppose being the softer one in this exchange. Gentleness can be as much of a strength as force can be."

Stanton sighs. He is quite evidently on the verge of saying something he might come to regret. "Fine, we are in agreement, then," he finally mumbles.

"Exactly. Aren't you glad I came along?" I ask, which makes him smile.

"Ask me that after we are done. Right now, I think Hugh would make for rather more peaceful company."

"Then you do not know Hugh as well as I do."

Reading is not terribly far from Oxford, and yet during my time there, I never visited. From what I see as we drive into the town, past rows of cozy semi-detached houses, past medieval churches and over a bridge spanning the River Kennet, I think it might have been a mistake. Reading possesses a certain charm unique to English towns, and I wish we were not here on such a fraught errand.

Stanton slows while I consult a map and direct him onwards. It is no simple task to locate the house, which is tucked away in a side street at the edge of town. It is a small house, two-up-two-down, well-kept as far as I can judge from outside. The windowpanes look freshly painted and a wreath of holly hangs on the door. The lane is quiet, not another soul in sight. It is a working day, which likely means Mrs. Stanley's husband and her sons will be out of the house. A shame for us, though it might serve to loosen her tongue, knowing they are not around to judge her behavior.

Our knock is answered quickly, as though Mrs. Stanley has been waiting by the door. She is taller than I envisioned her to be, with a soft figure and a head of brown curls, streaked with strands of silvery gray. Her eyes, blue like her son's, are her most striking feature, bright despite the guarded expression she wears when greeting us. Introductions are made and she, hesitating just a moment, guides us into a small sitting room. It is cozy, if spare. A few watercolors hang on the walls, a photograph of two young boys with pale hair on a side table.

"Tea?" she asks, eyeing us carefully, as though we might pounce at any moment. We nod our thanks and she disappears into the kitchen.

"She seems nervous," Stanton whispers.

"Only natural when the police come calling. It does not mean she has anything to hide. Though of course, I am hoping she does." Stanton sits on the faded, pale green sofa, and I take a quick stroll about the room. The furnishings are old, but well cared for. The room itself is tidy to the point that not a speck of dust clings to my finger, as I trail it across a shelf. I imagine Mrs. Stanley scrubbing the place, anxious about our visit, shooing her sons and husband out from under her feet. The books are the typical volumes one might expect. A number of religious texts, two bibles, yet also *Tess of the d'Urbervilles* and *Bleak House*. There is a small, framed photograph of a couple on their wedding day on the top shelf. It has gone slightly yellow with time, but from her stature, it is easy to recognize Mrs. Stanley. Mr. Stanley is a bit shorter than his wife and broadly built. I remember Victor mentioning he is a joiner and the other Stanley son is likewise occupied. I pick up the framed photograph of the two boys just as Mrs. Stanley enters the room, a tray in her arms.

"That's Vic and Pat. Vic was six and Pat four. Look like butter wouldn't melt, don't they? But they were rascals, the two of them." Her tone is chatty, but it does not camouflage her evident discomfort. The china clatters when she sets down the tray, and a drop of tea spills from the pot as her nerves spill into the room.

Sympathy takes hold of me, despite my readiness to dislike this woman who pushed out her desperate niece. Perhaps she has lived all this time with regret and now realizes she can never atone for what she did. Some wrongs can never be righted. I replace the picture frame and sit down, trying to put her at ease as she pours and talks without meeting our eyes, asking whether we take milk, sugar, a biscuit, perhaps? Only when nothing remains to be done and she is forced to sit in the remaining armchair, does she look up and let out a weary sigh.

"So, you have come about the murder," Mrs. Stanley says, closing her eyes for a moment, as if in pain.

"Sadly, we have," Stanton says. "Juliet Nelson was your niece?" The question is pointless, since we already know it to be so, but it is easy enough for her to answer and thus a good way to begin.

"My niece, yes. She was my sister's daughter. Margot and I were not very close after childhood. She changed."

"Adulthood demands it of us," I observe, adopting a light tone.

"She had ideas after she was married, plans of living in France, of becoming...Oh, I don't know, *somebody*," she says with a dismissive wave of her hand. "It wasn't good enough to be a mother, a wife. She always thought she was a bit above everyone. I spoke French, too, but she loved being viewed as exotic. I should not speak ill of the dead. Maybe I was simply envious." She shrugs and takes a sip of tea, lowering her gaze. Her reflection surprises me, perhaps she will be more forthcoming than we expected.

"What of Juliet?" Stanton asks. Broad questions allow for broad answers. We still know too little of our victim, after all.

"Juliet," Mrs. Stanley repeats the name, as if it is new to her, as if she has not considered it or the woman behind it for many years, and the letters strung together taste foreign on her tongue. "I have not seen her in over ten years." She swallows. "And I suppose now I never will see her again." Her voice is even, and her expression gives away nothing of what is felt beneath the surface. Does she have regrets? Or did she find closure with the subject of her niece long ago?

"She came to you pregnant," Stanton says, not a question this time.

Mrs. Stanley nods, licks her bottom lip, nods once more. "She did."

"You sent her away," he continues. I try for a sympathetic smile, to soften his blunt approach, but she does not seem to see me. She stares ahead at a distant scene, invisible to everyone else.

"I did not want to do it, but she was in no state to stay, and in no state to be a mother. I understood how difficult it could be, and I had a husband at that. She had no one and nothing, except a wildness in her eyes. It frightened me."

"You thought it was for the best?" I ask, playing the game Stanton concocted, even as more pressing questions – judgements? – crowd my mind.

"Maybe." She shrugs. "Maybe I was selfish, too. I had an ordered life, and there she was, strange and difficult, a hand on her flat belly, asking me to take her in, to take on her troubles. Juliet had some romantic notions, even though she did not share the father's name, nor cared to discuss him. But it takes more than love to raise a child. Juliet was almost a child herself."

"You told her to get rid of it," Stanton continues, choosing words that will sting.

"It was for the best!" she exclaims, finally abandoning the pretense of calm, raising her gaze to meet first Stanton's, then mine, searching for sympathy or understanding. "It was for the best," she repeats, more quietly now, setting down her cup and resting both hands on her knees as if they might steady her. She has suffered, even if she has done her best to forget, to convince herself her words are true.

"Can you tell us what happened that day?" I ask, my voice as gentle as I can make it.

Mrs. Stanley hesitates, presses her lips together before speaking once more. "I had not seen her since Margot and John's funeral. She sent the odd letter or card, that was all. To be truthful, I had enough to worry about with my own family. The war was on, my husband and Pat were gone. Every week, neighbors and friends received those dreaded telegrams, which told them of the deaths of their sons, or husbands or brothers. I was wrung out, expecting one to come for me every day. When Juliet arrived, at first, I was happy to see her, happy for a distraction, but the feeling faded quickly. She seemed almost mad. Her hair was tangled and her eyes wild, her voice too loud. I was overwhelmed. She was a tiny thing, but she seemed to take up all the space in the house. I couldn't bear it. I felt choked by her presence, by the words she spilled into the room, their implications. Vic probably told you I sent her away, because I am some sort of religious zealot. It isn't true. He is a good lad, but he broke with the church when he was sixteen and condemns everything connected to it. Maybe I was afraid of what the neighbors would say. Fine, I admit it." She shrugs. "That wasn't all, though. I watched her that day, and I thought this girl cannot be a mother. She could barely get dressed, it seemed. How would she care for a child? I certainly could not do it for her. I gave her what money I could spare, and for my sins I thought it was for the best."

"You wanted her to find someone to end the pregnancy," Stanton observes. His voice, too, has softened.

"It is a terrible thing, I know!" she cries suddenly, making me jump. "I knew it an hour after I sent her away, but it did not change the fact that Juliet could not have cared for that child. She couldn't. You did not see her! You did not know her!" Mrs. Stanley's voice rises and in her manner, in her reaction, I can see this unburdening is long overdue. Even if she hates us for having asked it of her, saying the words, making her confession, will do her good in the end. I suspect the version she told Victor was the simplest one she could muster.

"Did you ever tell your husband or Pat?"

"Why would I?" Mrs. Stanley shakes her head. "It was over by the time they came back. They had enough to think about, known enough tragedy."

"So, you heard from Juliet again? Did she tell you whether she took your advice?" I try to sound diplomatic, keeping my expression even.

"She got in touch two weeks later. My nerves were shattered at the time. Victor had just returned to the front."

"What did she say?"

"She wrote it was done and I need not worry, I would never hear from her again." She falls silent, her hands folded tightly in her lap, her jaw trembling. Did Juliet obey her aunt's wishes? There was no child in her life when I met her, so either she found a way to end the pregnancy or gave it away. One thing is certain, she never forgave her aunt for pushing her away when she was desperate. Even if Mrs. Stanley was right in assuming Juliet was unable to care for the child, she could have tried to help her, could have made it clear that she was not alone, whatever decision was made. I sympathize with Mrs. Stanley, who was clearly overwrought with fear for her sons and husband at the time, yet my greater feeling goes to Juliet. Whatever state she was in, she was alone and afraid. We must retrace her steps and learn what happened next.

"Did you try to find out where she was, what had become of her?" Stanton asks, his expression impossible to read.

"No. I respected her decision." Mrs. Stanley straightens in her seat. The truth is not that she respected Juliet's wishes, but that she was too cowardly, too afraid to be rejected herself, to ask her niece's forgiveness.

"You did not hear anything more until you heard of her death?"

"Not a word. We were strangers to each other. Occasionally, I thought of her and hoped she was well, that she had straightened herself out, married, become a mother in the right way."

"She had not. She died alone," Stanton says. I notice a crack in his façade, a sliver of his disdain for Mrs. Stanley shining through. She senses it, too, and shifts uncomfortably in her seat.

"I am sorry for that, yet I cannot take responsibility for Juliet's life. I told her what she should do. It was her decision to do it or not to. I am sorry she is dead. She was so young, and it is awful she has been murdered. But Juliet was a stranger to me, and though I am sad for her, I cannot truly grieve someone I barely knew. You cannot ask it of me."

"I ask nothing of you, Mrs. Stanley, but the truth. I trust you have given it?"

"I told you what I know. Is that all?" She gets to her feet, forcing us to stand as well, calling an end to the interview. "I would appreciate you leaving my husband and Pat out of this. It is bad enough Vic got involved, the other two have not seen or heard Juliet's name since the funeral of her parents. They have nothing to add. I wish you well in your investigation," she says curtly, showing us to the door. Is Juliet's murder of the same interest to her as anyone's death she might read of in the papers? A moment of vulnerability exposed her regret, but she shut that door quickly and I believe it will not be reopened. She is finished with the subject and I come away from the meeting uncertain what to think of her. All I know is that she offered little more than what Victor told us. At least we now know Juliet contacted her once more. Whether or not it matters, I cannot yet judge. Did she listen to her aunt and end the pregnancy? Did she go through with it? Maybe she lost the child naturally? And even if I had answers to these questions, does it bring us closer to solving the crime, or closer to understanding a person who is the very definition of an enigma?

"Was she was being honest, do you think?" Stanton asks, as we trudge back to the car. I am dissatisfied with our visit, and it seems he is as well.

"I think so. She more or less repeated Victor's story, with a few more details. I did not like her much but felt she had been waiting to unburden herself for many years. You noticed how agitated she became. I do not believe it was an act."

"Neither do I. The timeline of events intrigues me. First came her parent's funeral, the last time Juliet supposedly saw Patrick and Mr. Stanley. She went away, distraught, but sent the odd letter to confirm she was well enough. At some point she must have met a man. She was young and vulnerable, I do not doubt the story that he used her and then stole her money. She returned to Reading at the beginning of the war, and less than two years later, she was in France. Four or five years after the end of the war, she was back in London. There are large pockets of time we cannot fill."

Nodding, I glance around, spotting a small tea shop at the end of the street. "Let us get something hot to drink before we drive back," I suggest.

We soon find ourselves ensconced in the tiny shop, two large cups of steaming, milky tea in front of us, the clatter and chatter of other patrons loud enough to make it unlikely our conversation will be overheard. I suppose no one here would care enough to bother anyway.

"Let us go with this theory for a moment," I begin, setting down my tea. "What if, alone and afraid, Juliet turns to the one person who knew her before, and who knew her parents as well."

"Frances Bell? She claimed not to have heard from her in years, and only helped Juliet find employment at the museum recently."

"She might have lied, if Juliet swore her to silence."

"To lie, even after Juliet was murdered, suggests more than respect for the other woman's privacy. It is obstructing the investigation," Stanton says with a frown.

"Yes, yes," I say, waving away his affront. "Let us assume for a moment she went to Frances and begged her for help."

"All right, I am assuming. Go on."

"Frances finds someone who can end the pregnancy for Juliet. Naturally, the women would not speak about this to anyone. It is illegal after all. Maybe Frances felt unable to turn the young woman away? In any case, she may have introduced Juliet to Howard. Then he, realizing she needed a purpose and had an affinity for languages, sensed an opportunity. He made the offer to Juliet, asking her to keep the matter between themselves to protect Frances. Juliet, at this point, would have felt she owed them a debt, and she also needed a task, so agreed to Howard's plan. She went off to Folkestone where she received her training and was sent to France." I shrug. "Frances was likely unaware of any deal having been made, but I think she might know more than she let on."

"Clearly, whoever tried to kill her felt the same." Stanton grimaces and wraps his hands around the teacup.

"You agree, that is how it might have gone?"

"Entirely possible," he concedes. "Little would surprise me at this point. The revelation that Juliet was a spy and Frances Bell's husband some sort of master of espionage are startling enough. Next we will see pigs flying and the sky turning green."

"It is a whole world I never truly considered before this case. There must have been so many men and women working on these secret assignments in other countries, without ever being celebrated for their bravery."

"Juliet received those medals."

"True enough. However, she kept them hidden, seemed unhappy to have them in her possession, ashamed even. I have to believe it was Juliet who tried to scratch away her name."

"Maybe she wanted to forget. She would not be the first to come out of the war a changed person, who could not bear the reminders of that dreadful time."

"Perhaps. I read up about espionage during the war, and Harold filled in some of the gaps. Like Juliet, many spies took on new identities, learned languages, cracked code and created their own. They ferried messages and stowed away people under threat, at risk of their own lives. Many were caught and executed. Can you imagine keeping all of that, a whole separate life, secret from your family, your friends?"

"No, I cannot. They must have had a talent for acting as well as being clandestine. Juliet had no family and no friends, apparently, so keeping her double life a secret would not, perhaps, have been quite so difficult."

"When she returned, she continued to live like a hermit, quiet, unobtrusive. Maybe she never allowed herself a circle of friends, a family of her own, because she was afraid of telling them what had happened?"

"The war is over. She could have been honest," Stanton says.

"For some people it is never over. You know how it is even now. We see men who came home nine years ago, and so many cannot shake the terrors they witnessed and live as society demands. It is difficult to strike a balance between remembering the past and pretending it never happened."

"Maybe Juliet did not want a new family, because she was mourning her old one, or one with the man in the photograph, which never had a chance to blossom?" Stanton leans back, crosses his arms over his chest. "Somehow, the more we learn about her, the more questions arise."

"That may have been exactly why she was so closed off. The questions everyone might have had, if they learned of her history, would have demanded answers she was unwilling to give. Easier to exist as a phantom, than to be flesh and bone with vulnerabilities and a painful past."

"But she was flesh and bone. Even if coming through the war gave her a sense of invulnerability; even if she hoped to live a peaceful, long life by remaining inconspicuous. Someone did notice her, and that was the end."

"But who and why?" I throw my hands in the air. "Discounting Michael Ellroy, Victor and his family, we are left with the ladies of the WI, Mr. Button – who can hardly climb the stairs! – and the mystery man in the photograph."

"No one said this was easy work, Detective Carlisle," Stanton teases.

"No," I sigh, "not easy, yet I feel I am running into a wall again and again and not learning from my bruises."

"That is modern police work for you. Fool's errand after fool's errand and then, when you least expect it, the door to the truth appears."

"What a pretty picture. And what if the door is locked?"

"You find the key."

"What if the key is lost?"

A smile twitches at the corners of Stanton's mouth. "You find the weak spot and break it down."

Chapter 48

Stanton and I do not return straight to my flat in St. James, rather, we take a detour and visit Frances in the hospital. A guard sits on a chair outside her room, busy picking something from a fingernail when we approach. To his credit, he snaps to his feet when Stanton's shadow looms above him and he states his credentials.

"Has anyone apart from a nurse or physician tried to enter the room?" he asks the young man. The stern note in his voice almost makes me pity the fellow.

"No, sir. Nobody but one nurse…Beth, and a doctor earlier in the day. It's been quiet," he stammers, eager to convey that he was not negligent in his duty.

"All right, well done," Stanton says with a nod. The other man's shoulders slump. What must it be like to carry such authority? I have the weight of my wealth and title, but I am still a woman and, in this world, considered the weaker sex. It is damnably frustrating!

"What are you thinking? You've gone puce," Stanton mumbles, as we walk along the corridor to the nurses' station to be apprised of the patient's state.

"I have not!" Stanton only raises his brows.

"No change," a harried looking nurse tells us when we inquire after Frances. "The doc's been in to see her, but she's not yet responsive."

"Is that a very dire sign or normal with such an injury?" The nurse sighs, sets down her tray and regards me with a look that mingles pity with irritation.

"It's not a good sign, love. The longer she's unconscious, the worse it is for her recovery." Noting my dismay, she adds, "Still, it's early days, and she was very badly hurt. Every night she lives is a good sign." She gives my arm a pat before sweeping past us, intent on her tasks.

"I cannot help but wonder whether we should have expected something like this?" I muse as we leave the hospital. We looked in on Frances, but apart from whispering our well wishes to her unresponsive ears, there was nothing we could do.

"Frances assured us she knew nothing. We had no more reason to assume she was at risk than to consider her the killer."

"I still feel guilty."

"Evelyn." He turns to face me once we are outside the hospital. "There was nothing you could have done to prevent this. No one but the driver of the car is to blame, and we must find him -"

"Or her," I interject.

"Or her." Stanton shakes his head. "That does not exactly narrow our search, does it? A man or a woman, who may somehow have been connected to Juliet, which we cannot know, because Juliet was as secretive as they come." He rolls his eyes skyward.

"Not an ideal scenario. At least we have eliminated some of the suspects. I will double down again on the women from the WI. I have neglected them since Victor and Michael Ellroy appeared on the scene. Edith will be keen to hear a summary of our progress, too."

"Be careful what you tell her. Even if she was the one to hire you, it could have been a diversion," Stanton warns when we reach the car.

"I don't want to believe it, but I will be cautious."

"Good. Send Hugh my wishes for a speedy recovery," he adds with a wink. I nod and wave him off then hail a taxi to go back to the flat. In the back of the cab, I lean into the seat and contemplate the events of the day. I wonder whether it is possible to learn if Juliet Nelson gave a child away for adoption. There must be records, even during the war years, when everything was less organized. Would Juliet have disclosed her real name? What would it tell us to know she had given away the child? The timeline suggests she could just about have delivered the baby and had enough time for her Folkestone training before she was recorded as having been in France. The child would now be near Iona's age, if he or she was ever born.

I close my eyes to order my thoughts, feeling the rumble of the taxi rolling down the street. The question of the child is, in all likelihood, less critical than that of the man in the photograph. Juliet was working and living unobtrusively when she joined the WI, the singular novel element in her life, as far as we know. A short while later, she was killed. Is one of the women from the institute responsible? The question has, of course, crossed my mind before, yet with so few suspects, I must turn back to it, reluctant though I am to do so. The killer knew Juliet well enough to call the WI and excuse her absence, likely assuming it would provide a substantial window of time before anyone discovered the body. Who is capable of such calculated underhandedness? We can all, I feel certain, be devious creatures when circumstances push us into a corner, yet there is a difference between acting in desperation and scheming to commit murder. Could Juliet's death have been an accident somehow? Perhaps the killer arrived to talk to her; they argued, fought and Juliet did not emerge the victor in this battle. The murderer panicked and ransacked the flat as a means of distraction. By the time they made the call, they must have calmed down enough to think more clearly.

"Miss? Miss, we're here," the cabbie announces, and I wonder whether he had to repeat himself a number of times already. I was so lost in my thoughts, I had not noticed we came to a stop in front of my building. The fine blue sky of the morning has been shrouded by a swathe of gray clouds, and raindrops spatter the pavement. I hurry inside and greet Mr. Flynn, the caretaker of the building, who hands me a parcel.

"This was delivered for you earlier. I was about to go up and bring it to you."

"Thank you." I take the parcel, a brown paper wrapped package no larger than a small stack of books, but much lighter. There is no return address. "Who delivered this?" I ask, turning back. Mr. Flynn narrows his eyes, his bushy gray brows knitting together.

"A lad came in, one of the urchins hanging about on the off chance someone will spare them a coin. Happens often enough. I did not take note of it."

"Do not worry yourself. I was only curious. I wasn't expecting anything."

"An early Christmas present, perhaps?"

"Perhaps."

In the flat, I find Hugh not quite where I commanded him to stay, but in the kitchen, bent over a large bowl of soup, looking decidedly haler than hours ago.

"Evelyn! How did it go? What did you learn?" he asks, eyes bright as he sets down his spoon.

"Not as illuminating as I had hoped," I reply, sinking onto the chair opposite him before I share all that transpired in Reading. "In summary, you did not miss much."

"Hm..." Hugh considers my words, a tendon in his neck twitching. "It is convenient how some people can pretend the past never happened, while others are consumed by it."

"Mrs. Stanley did not forget. The woman struck me as aloof, but I believe the past troubled her considerably."

"She sounds like a coward to me."

"Maybe."

"So that leaves us with the possibility that Juliet may have followed her aunt's directions," Hugh observes, leaning back in his chair and giving me a meaningful look.

"I have been thinking, we need to examine the WI more closely. It was the only new element in her life, as far as we are aware."

Hugh nods. "Hollis telephoned earlier. He trawled some record office – by some miracle that man has friends everywhere! – yet he could not find any record of Juliet having been married. There were a few Juliet Nelson's, but their dates of birth made it clear they are not ours."

"I do not trust the records entirely. We know what a mess we faced after the war and during it. People wed so quickly, sometimes it may not have been registered. Then again, the wedding band we found could have belonged to her mother. If we find out who the man in the photograph is, we may be much closer to discovering the identity of the killer."

"You don't think he did it, do you?"

"Not truly, no. But the fact that he knew her during the war, that Michael Ellroy said they seemed very fond of one another, and that she kept his picture for quite a long time, tells me he is not to be overlooked."

"Hollis agreed that running the photograph in the paper is a good plan. He is going to ask Stanton for it later."

"At least that sets things in motion," I say. The thought, however, does not fill me with optimism. What are the chances someone will recognize the man from a grainy newspaper print and be willing to come forward? Nonetheless, there is the smallest of possibilities that just this will come to pass.

"Have you brought me a present?" Hugh asks, nodding at the parcel I set on the table and forgot about almost instantly, my mind whirring with questions.

"Oh, that, no. It just arrived." I get up and take a knife from the drawer, slicing open the brown paper. Inside is a box about the size of a brick. Glancing at Hugh, I open it, and immediately step back.

"What is it?" Hugh, alarmed, turns the parcel around and grimaces. Inside the box is something red and congealing. Revulsion makes my vision swim. Hugh is already pulling a note from the mess, and reads aloud. "Stay away!" He raises his brows and meets my gaze. "If ever there was a warning..."

"What..." I swallow. "What is it?"

Hugh leans down and frowns. "It's a heart. Pig, I would guess by the size."

"Good God!"

"I think it is safe to assume the murderer sent us this little gift. Who delivered it?"

In a shaky voice, I repeat what Mr. Flynn told me. Hugh closes the box and pushes it aside, placing the card on the lid. It is typewritten. No signature, of course.

"This disturbs me, Evelyn. Whoever killed Juliet tried to do the same to Frances and nearly succeeded."

"What do we do?" I ask, beginning to pace about the kitchen. "Where are Maeve and the others? Should we warn them? They live here and the killer sent the parcel to this address."

"We must tell them, yes, but I think this warning does not apply to them. The person who sent it would not get past Mr. Flynn unnoticed the way they got past Mr. Button. But we must be very careful. Maybe we should inform Stanton. He can send a bobby to patrol the square, take note of anyone suspicious hanging about."

"Yes," I nod, more to myself than to Hugh, troubled by this gruesome gift. I realize it was purchased at a butcher's shop, but there is something so dreadful about sending me the heart of a slaughtered animal. Particularly as the person who sent it is likely guilty of murder themselves. It is easy enough, even without the words printed on the accompanying card, to appreciate the meaning of this parcel.

"It does suggest the killer believes we are onto him or her."

"Since the funeral, there has been the attack on Frances and now this threat," I observe, still pacing.

"And since then, we have interacted with Victor Stanley and Michael Ellroy," Hugh completes my thought.

"Even though we have pushed them to the bottom of our list of suspects, they strike me as impossible to strike off completely."

"If either is guilty, how can we explain away their alibis? Ellroy was in the middle of the ocean, after all!"

"It doesn't make sense, but something shifted after the funeral to make the killer grow desperate."

"I am calling the police to report this," Hugh gestures at the closed box on the table. "And to ask for a bobby to patrol the square."

"And I must speak with Maeve and Kathleen. They have to be made aware that a killer knows this is my flat, which could pose a danger. I will suggest they come to Grosvenor Square for a time, until the case is solved."

"You intend to go ahead with the investigation, then?" Hugh asks, hovering in the doorway, expectation in his eyes.

"More than ever," I reply with as much conviction as I can muster. "A pig's heart in a box is a pig's heart in a box."

"Next time it could be something worse."

"Only if we are not careful and clever. We must act as if we are losing interest in the case, be more cautious, take on a few more mundane ones like missing jewelry or lost pups to make anyone watching believe we have taken their warning to heart."

"The photograph will still run in the paper."

"It is in police possession, nothing to do with us, right? Besides, the photograph does not necessarily mean anything to the killer."

"Though we are hoping it does," Hugh reminds me.

"We will proceed as planned, do you agree?" I ask, giving him an opportunity to back out, which I know he will never take. He grins and nods. A moment later, I hear his muffled voice on the telephone in the other room. I let out a nervous sigh, a measure of the prior moment's bravado leaking out of me. It would be foolish not to be afraid, but I refuse to submit to the threat of an anonymous shadow. I might be frightened of the murderer, yet I cannot ignore that the murderer is frightened of us as well. This is not a game, yet if it were, would Hugh and I be the cat or the mouse?

Chapter 49

Maeve and Kathleen take my news with remarkable stoicism. Kathleen makes the sign of the cross, while Maeve merely crosses her arms.

"A pig's heart is to frighten us out of the flat?" Maeve asks, affront heavy in her tone.

"If Maeve and Aiden are staying, I am staying," Kathleen insists. "I have lived through quite a different kind of horror. A piece of meat won't frighten me."

"Besides, we wouldn't leave you behind, miss." Maeve gives me an encouraging nod.

"Do not worry about me. You are most welcome to come to Grosvenor Square. Think on it. I do not believe you are in danger, but you deserve the truth."

"And we thank you for giving it to us," Kathleen replies, her Irish accent stronger than usual, convincing me she is not to be dissuaded.

Nodding, I cannot but feel a rush of pride. I had worried making friends of my housekeeper would prove impossible, after Maeve's initial formality when she arrived here. Now I sense a bond has formed between the three of us, and I hope they feel it, too. Perhaps we are not quite friends, but we are allies and that is something.

The women return to their tasks, and Hugh leaves to meet the bobby in the square and explain what has happened. I go back to the study and write my notes about the morning's visit to Reading. I struggle to concentrate, my thoughts repeatedly turning to that slimy heart in the box. Never would I have expected someone to send me such a cruel warning and I consider vegetarianism just thinking about it.

A knock sounds at the front door, and I wonder whether Hugh forgot his key. I vaguely hear Maeve moving in the hallway to answer it, then her voice. I cannot make out the words, but her tone is too formal for Hugh. Curious, I get up to investigate, surprised to find Adeline and Edith in the hallway.

"Good afternoon," I greet the pair. Ushering them into the office, I wonder what they want.

"I hope we are not disturbing you. We were in the area and Mother wanted to know if there had been any progress," Adeline says, her eyes roving about the study, curious, I suppose, what the workspace of a detective looks like. I suspect the fairly tidy desks, our file cabinet, the plain furnishings and simple charcoal sketches framed on the wall, disappoint, for her expression drops a little and she sinks into the chair beside her mother. Maybe she was expecting chalkboards of scattered notes and crumpled pages with discarded ideas scattered about the floor?

"It is moving slowly, but every day we are learning more," I explain, not willing to disclose too many details. In light of recent events, I am taking particular care to heed Stanton's orders to remain discreet, even if Edith is our client. That being said, and judging by her unimpressed expression, I cannot remain entirely restrained. "We have determined that the murderer's motive must be connected to Juliet's past."

"In what way?" Edith asks, narrowing her eyes.

I have to think quickly to measure my words and what they may reveal. "Juliet chose a very private existence in London," I begin, "and we have yet to find anyone who knew her well during the past five years, leading us to believe whoever killed her was holding on to an old grudge." My explanation is not particularly insightful, for without sharing that Juliet was a spy, rejected by her family and possibly left heartbroken by a wartime romance, there is little to ground my hypotheses in fact.

"Do you have any suspects?" Edith asks, her expression difficult to read as she watches me, sharp eyes on mine.

"There are some names. I cannot say anything with certainty yet. I am afraid it takes time. The police inspector on the case is working closely with us."

"That sounds reassuring, though if I trusted members of the police to be in possession of the necessary competence to solve this case, I need not have hired you," Edith replies and finally a tiny smile touches the corners of her mouth. "I understand you wish to keep your theories close to your chest. Far be it for me to meddle. However, I expect to be told the truth once you know it. It has come to my attention that you are acquainted with that reporter, Mr. Napier. He was at the funeral, after all. I would not wish the whole city to know what happened before I do. I meant it when I said Juliet was one of us."

"You have my word," I reassure her, hoping I can keep my promise.

"The funeral was such a sad affair," Adeline observes. "I hardly noticed anyone I did not recognize, no family apart from that cousin, and the tall man I saw you with." There is clearly a question in her observation, and I cannot fault her for it.

"He was an old acquaintance who had come across the funeral announcement and wished to pay his respects. He did not know her very well, though."

"At least someone from her past cared to come. What a hermetic life Juliet lived!" Adeline marvels. "I assumed living in a city of this size, one could not but form relationships. There are too many people to avoid it!"

"My dear, not everyone is endowed with your temperament. There are many lonely people in London, and I imagine they feel all the lonelier for its size."

"Well, Juliet would have found herself quite overwhelmed with friends had she remained at the WI," Adeline observes with a smile.

"I hoped it would be so. We have our causes, but in the end, we are a community above all else," her mother replies.

At the door, Edith turns to me and says, "Louise and I are organizing a fundraiser to be held at my house next week. I understand you have been too busy to attend our regular WI meetings, but we would be delighted if you joined us."

"Of course," I reply, happy to wave them off. The day has been tiring and yielded both too little and too much. The trip to Reading confirmed only what we already knew, apart from the fact that Juliet did contact her aunt again. The parcel sent to me demonstrates that Juliet's enemy has now become our own.

Chapter 50

"Look, they've printed the photograph!" I hold up a copy of the paper for Daniel to see over breakfast. He reaches for it, squinting at the page.

"It's a bit grainy."

"The photograph was creased, so the print is not perfect. Still, I hope someone might recognize him. It is worth a chance, is it not?"

"It can't hurt, especially since the inquiry does not mention you as a contact. The threat you received yesterday cannot be taken lightly." Daniel lowers the paper and gives me a meaningful look.

"I will hardly run headfirst into danger, if I can avoid it," I reply a little huffily.

"Please see that you don't." Daniel smiles and shakes his head. His concerns are not groundless, I admit, if only to myself. On more than one occasion in the past, I found myself in the hands – sometimes quite literally – of a killer. It could have ended badly, yes, but the point is it did not. That being so, they were rather frightening experiences I am not eager to repeat. I will proceed with caution, that much I can promise with absolute sincerity.

"Are you visiting Frances today?"

"Yes, I want to see if she has woken. The nurse suggested every day she remains unconscious could be very bad for her recovery."

"And she is alone?"

"Yes. It surprises me, since she has lived here for so long. I suppose she will have the odd visitor, but no one is waiting by her bedside. Edith noted yesterday that loneliness in large cities is even worse than in villages and towns."

"Probably true. People often come here to start afresh, thinking adventure awaits. They do not realize that a city like London can afford new experiences, but it can also make you feel small, like an ant in an anthill, and swallow you whole. What would happen to Hugh, if he did not have friends here? I can see him reverting back to an anxious, hermetic state. If you are alone and do not wish to be, London may be a terrible city to call home. If you are like Juliet, though, eager to blend into the background, there is no better place."

"That sounds rather glum," I observe.

"Perhaps, but the truth is glum sometimes. I, for one, am quite happy to be here now. Yet had I come back after the war, wretched and alone, with too much money in my pockets for my own good, I do not know what would have become of me."

"You had some friends," I say, taking a sip of tea and burning my tongue.

"The way Frances does?"

"Hm..."

Daniel nods. "At least in the army, we had camaraderie. Even if many of those men did not survive the war. Afterwards, I cut myself off from them entirely, unable to cope with the reminder, as if it were ever possible to forget. Maybe Juliet had a similar intention."

"Adeline said she was confident they would have become friends had Juliet become a part of the WI community," I say, wondering whether it could be true. Would Juliet ever have allowed us more than a glimpse into her life? And if not, can one truly be a friend to a person one does not know? The more I learn about Juliet, the less I am able to gauge her character. Was she fragile and afraid, abandoned by her family? Or was she shrewd and clever? Or both? Did Howard Bell notice some spark in her that prompted the recruitment? We are all a vast amalgam of opposites, yet certain traits reign supreme and mold our personalities. With Juliet Nelson, I cannot pin down who she truly was. Each time I think I am closer to understanding, I learn something that dashes my theories and sends me down a new path. Undeniably Juliet was a victim, not only of her murderer, but of circumstance. Yet something about her riled someone to the point of wishing her dead. What was it? Is the motive fueled by love? By hatred? By a combination of the two?

"Evelyn?" I only now register Daniel must have said my name more than once, and I look up to meet his gaze.

"Away with the fairies." I smile.

"Rather away with the murder suspects, no?" Daniel tilts his head and raises an eyebrow. "I was asking whether you have already questioned Frances' colleagues? Maybe she was upset? Maybe something happened before she was hit by the car?"

"You have a point. Goodness, so much seems to be happening all at once, and I cannot order my thoughts. I could drop by the museum after breakfast. Perhaps I will run into Jeffrey while I'm there. It would be good to see how he is. He was so shaken after the police questioned him and then witnessing Frances' accident...I have been a negligent friend. What are you doing today? Any progress in finding a solution for the ailing shipyard?"

"Dom and I are searching for a potential buyer. It isn't ideal, but better than closing it down. We have a responsibility to our workers. Harold reminded me of that again a few days ago. He was quite upset to hear of our troubles, not least because he had just received our endorsement. I wanted to warn him that it could become somewhat fraught."

"Harold is a loyal fellow. He may even come up with a plan to help you. I do so hope he wins his seat!"

"He is charismatic, and people are often drawn more to that quality than experience – which can, of course, lead to disaster. In Harold's case, however, I am convinced he will grow in the face of his challenges."

I remember this description of Harold as I drive to the museum. Perhaps it applied to Juliet as well. I knew her as a silent, almost frail woman, but she was not dealt an easy hand in life. Her appearance and outward manner may have disguised a steely core, which hardened as her situation worsened.

The museum has only just opened when I arrive. Few people mingle in the galleries, taking in the icons of another age, another place in reverent silence. I pass through the exhibit of mummies and elaborate obelisks, then one dedicated to marble statues of ancient Greece. How much drama, treachery and wickedness have revealed themselves in the time between then and now? How anonymous the countless victims? In five-hundred years from this day, no one will remember most of the people crowding this city, and yet in the here and now, they hold that very future in their hands. Children born today are the heroes and villains of tomorrow. Battles of today will contour the outlines of the world in the years to come. Yet memory is a strange thing, slippery as an eel, which once out of our grasp delves back into black waters, soon to escape our minds entirely. How many decades will pass until no one remembers the Great War, just as we have forgotten many that came before our time? Passing the sculptures of orators and emperors, I cannot but think their world seems one of myth much more than reality. Will future generations look at the paintings and photographs the past decades produced and think the same, that history is a story, not a lesson? Perhaps I underestimate humanity? Perhaps, I wonder with a smile, Hugh is right in calling me a cynic.

"It is quite dreadful, isn't it?" Lara Bennet says with wide eyes when I ask whether she has heard about Frances. "The members of this department are dropping like flies. Can't say I feel particularly comfortable at the moment. Maybe there is someone out to get women working at the museum, some sort of male vigilante." Her tone, however, is more excited than afraid, so I do not feel the need to conjure soothing words.

"Were you here on the day Frances was hurt?"

"Naturally, I don't get weekdays off. More's the pity. I was already on my way home when it happened. How ghastly for poor Mr. Farnham to stumble upon her like that!"

"Quite. Do you know Frances well?"

Instead of questioning by what right I am making these inquiries, Lara seems happy to chat, leaning forward on her elbows, small button nose as pink as her rouged cheeks. "Frances has been here for ages! She is quite old. I wonder why she doesn't retire. She has the money. I've seen her house, a good set-up, and she wears expensive clothes, if rather dull. I suspect she's a bit lonely," Lara observes, her voice softening by a fraction. "Her husband died very suddenly of a bad heart not a year ago. I had just started here then, and she was away for several weeks. Frankly, I was surprised she came back, but as I say, I do not think she has much other family."

"Is she well liked at work?"

"Oh, sure," Lara makes a dismissive gesture with her hand. "Frances spends most of her day hovering over some dusty book, but most people here prefer ancient things." Her nose crinkles with distaste, and I almost laugh, though I refrain from asking why on earth she works at the museum and not in any ordinary office if she dislikes old things.

"What is your impression of her, if I may ask?"

"Hm…" Lara frowns and taps her forefinger against her chin. "Frances gets along with everyone, but she doesn't seem to be friends with anyone, not here at least, not as far as I can tell. She chatted with Juliet more than the others when she passed through the department. Never told me much about herself, never asked me much either." Lara shrugs, as though this hardly matters. It strikes me, however, that the young woman herself is not the type to show much interest in others, yet takes affront when others do not appear very interested in her. Perhaps we are all a little like her in this respect, but I sense it is a stone in her shoe when it comes to Frances. I dig a little deeper.

"Does she act above herself?" I ask carefully, lowering my voice as I might when speaking to a friend.

"Maybe, though I like her better than I did Juliet, God rest her." Lara lazily makes a sign of the cross. "Frances is a lonely old lady. Juliet…Juliet thought she was something better than the rest of us."

"What gave you that impression?"

"Oh, you know, she never laughed with us, never joined in when we had a catch-up over a cuppa; never even offered to make us one when she was brewing a kettle!" This, it seems, is the height of offense in Lara's eyes.

"She was reserved?"

"More than that, I'd say. But then, I can't actually say much about her, since she kept herself to herself as if she was writing the book on it," Lara's voice is heavy with disdain.

"And Frances?"

"Well, she is reserved, too, as you say, but more because she's a bit odd, a bookworm. Maybe she thinks she's too old to chat with Joan and me. I hope she gets better. I haven't anything bad to say about her. For that matter," Lara quickly adds, sitting a little straighter, "I certainly never wished any ill on Juliet either."

"Of course not!" I say with as much reassurance as I can muster. The police have interviewed Lara. She has a sound alibi for both events. Besides, she would not likely admit her antipathy for Juliet and her apathy towards Frances, if she is the killer.

"I should be getting back to work," Lara announces, eyeing me warily, as though I hoodwinked her into an unwilling confession instead of her volunteering these opinions quite willingly.

"I understand. Just one more question, please. Was Frances behaving any differently than usual the day of the accident?"

"Differently? Let me think." Lara frowns, and she narrows her eyes. "Maybe she was a little distracted? I don't know if this means anything, but when I asked her what she was doing the coming weekend, just to be friendly, she said something like, 'I have to go to the bank'. The bank is closed on the weekend. But then she is old, maybe she was confused." A little shrug.

I refrain from reminding her that Frances is but sixty, not a wizened old crone, and that, should Lara be fortunate, she herself will learn what old age truly is one day.

"Are you certain that is what she said? Was her behavior unusual?" I ask instead, wondering whether Frances heard anything distressing, that might have led her onto the path of the killer – quite literally.

"She said it. I have very good ears," Lara congratulates herself. "I did not see her much the rest of the day. I was busy. There were some letters to be typed up and sent out as usual." She shrugs.

"Would you prefer to work elsewhere?"

"Naturally." She leans forward again. "I am only doing this until I find myself a husband. It's all very well and good to speak of the modern woman entering the workforce and all that. But when you do the same dull job day in and day out for a pittance and no appreciation, it does not feel like a purpose, nor like power."

I am struck by her sudden insight. She is right, I suppose. Yet what she hates about her job, Juliet enjoyed. Going unnoticed and even the low pay did not seem to concern her.

"Do you have a fellow in your sights?" I tease.

"None of yet, sadly." She sighs, fluttering her eyelids. "But I am a choosy creature, and there are many frogs in the pond."

"As you should be," I say with a smile. "Keep your eye out for a prince."

"I intend to. If one crosses your path, you might send him my way."

"I will remember you, Miss Bennet," I say before leaving the department.

Frances' apparent confusion tells me little. Did she remember anything pertaining to the murder, or was her mind simply occupied with work? The latter seems the more likely, even if we have considered the possibility that she is keeping something from us. I decide to make my next port of call the hospital.

There I find the same young copper sitting on his chair in front of Frances' room. He rises to greet me, glancing around as though I might be hiding Stanton somewhere. When he realizes I am alone, he visibly relaxes.

Frances remains prone on the only occupied bed near the window. The sun filters in, bathing the sterile room in a pleasant light. A small bouquet of flowers sits on her bedside table and another on the windowsill. So she has had a few visitors. The thought pleases me, and I pull up a chair and sit beside her bed. She is almost as pale as the sheet that covers her up to the collarbone; even her lips are drained of color. Frances Bell is a tall woman, imposing even, but here and now she looks small and fragile as a bird.

"Frances?" I whisper, awkwardly speaking into the silence. "It is me, Evelyn Carlisle." I hesitate, uncertain how to continue, what to tell someone who cannot reply, someone who may not even hear me. "Frances, if you are listening, try to open your eyes. You mustn't give up." My words are platitudes, but I can think of nothing better to say. I cannot evoke cherished memories or loved ones, because I am not her friend or confidante. In truth, I hardly know her. Nonetheless, I feel a strange bond with this woman and a need for her to recover, not to be another victim of this faceless killer.

"Frances? Think of Howard. He would wish you to continue on, to do the work you love, to live. Soon will be Christmas and then a new year, new opportunities, new friendships. You must wake up, Frances. You-" I fall silent. Her hand has twitched! "Frances? Can you hear me?" I ask, more loudly. Her mouth moves just a hint. Unable to decide whether to run for the nurse, I wait, watching for a further sign. It comes in the form of a sound, then a fluttering beneath her eyelids. Her eyes open the tiniest fraction. I sense she has seen me, noted my presence. I reach for her hand to confirm she is not dreaming; she is not alone.

"I am here, you will be all right," I mutter, knowing, of course, I cannot offer such assurances. "Wake up, Frances."

"Car...Carlisle..." she stammers, and I feel my heartbeat quicken.

"Yes, yes, it's me, Evelyn Carlisle. Shall I get the doctor? I will-"

"What…?" Frances rasps, her throat dry. I pour a glass of water from the jug on the bedside table and hold it to her lips. A few droplets dribble down the side of her mouth.

"There, rest and I will get the doctor for you." As I get to my feet, however, Frances takes hold of my hand. Her grip is weak, but her eyes have opened wider and in them I read a plea for me to wait.

"What is it? Is there something I can do for you?" I ask, bending down, so she does not have to strain her voice.

"It hurts. I went to Queen Victoria Street…" She catches her breath and swallows. "Howard-" A rattling cough shakes her.

"Frances, do not exert yourself. There will be time to speak later." I try to reassure her. She does not release me.

"Sixty, twelve, ninety-eight, twenty-two," she mumbles. At first, I think I have not heard correctly. "Key is in…office drawer. Howard left -" Another round of coughs, this time shaking her body so violently, I pull my hand free and run into the hallway, shouting for a nurse. Beth comes running, followed by a doctor.

"She is awake!" I cry, and they hurry past me into the room. I am not allowed entry again. I pace about the hallway for some twenty minutes only to be told they have given her something to ease the pain and she is resting again, but that her waking up is a promising sign and I should return tomorrow. I feel a mixture of frustration and immense relief. Frances is awake! Hopefully this bodes well for her recovery. Yet I cannot get the words she uttered out of my mind. *Queen Victoria Street* and the string of numbers. I took care to write them down as soon as Frances was seen to. *Sixty, twelve, ninety-eight, twenty-two.* What did she mean about a key in her office? She mentioned Howard, but was it merely a yearning for her lost husband, or something else? I decide to call the flat and see if Hugh is there. A nurse directs me to a telephone kiosk.

"Hugh? Are you well again?" I ask, relieved he is there.

"Yes, fine. Is everything all right?"

"Frances woke up!" I say, and explain what happened and what she said.

"The numbers sound like an account or something like that, don't you agree?" he suggests.

"Yes, that could very well be it." Another thought comes to my mind. "And the National Safe Deposit Company is on Queen Victoria Street, if I am not mistaken. I have passed the building countless times."

"Frances mentioned a key, didn't she?" I hear the excitement building in Hugh's voice.

"I think she was instructing me to go to Queen Victoria Street and open her box. Why else would she have told me the numbers and where to find the key?" I glance around and lower my voice. "Hugh, Frances must have remembered something important."

"You are sure she wasn't just rambling? Did she understand it was you she was speaking to?"

"Yes, definitely. Meet me at the museum. We have to find the key!"

"Maybe Jeffrey can be of some assistance?" Hugh suggests. "I will try to be there in half an hour. Remember to be careful, Evelyn!"

"You, too!" I replace the receiver and hurry to the doors, my mind buzzing with the prospect of a new clue just within our reach. Of course, we could be wrong, but I feel we are onto something. Sense does battle with temper, as I want to speed towards the museum as fast as the Bentley can carry me.

Hugh arrives moments after I do, and his eyes are as bright and eager as I imagine mine are. Together we climb the steps of the grand entryway and slip into the museum I left only a few hours earlier.

"You should go in first and distract the secretaries. Lara is on the hunt for a husband. Make yourself amenable. Then I will slip in and go to Jeffrey's office. If he can't be found, I will look for Frances' desk on my own."

"You have the better task!"

"Well, she will hardly wish to flirt with me. Besides, we already had a lengthy conversation earlier."

"Fine." He rolls his eyes.

I know where Jeffrey's office is, and while Hugh distracts Lara and Joan is nowhere in sight, I easily slip into the office and tap Jeffrey's door. A moment later, it opens, revealing a scattered looking Jeffrey, his hair standing at odd angles where he ran his hands through it, and his spectacle lenses are smudged.

"Evie? What-" I push him back and into his office before Lara notices. I do not want to draw her attention.

"I must look around Frances' room. She woke up and said some curious things. I have to look into her desk," I whisper.

"She woke up? Oh, thank goodness!" Jeffery sighs and runs his hand through his hair again.

"Yes, though she was asleep again when I left the hospital. I hope it is a good sign. But, Jeffrey, she mentioned something about a key and a number and an address. I think she was pointing me in the direction of a safe deposit box."

"Is that legal?" Jeffrey grimaces in doubt.

"We are dealing with a criminal, Jeffrey. I admit, I am forced to go about this investigation in rather dubious ways, but the ends surely justify the means."

"I am not sure I follow your logic, but all right. I am simply grateful she is awake. What do you need from me?"

"Can you show me to her office? Will it be locked?"

"Probably," he shrugs, walking around his desk and opening a drawer. "The locks all use the same master-key. It's quite silly, really. I can open any of the department's offices with my own key."

"That seems quite haphazard! Who has a copy?"

"Only a few people. Besides, the treasures are not in the offices but in the galleries."

"Right, well, can you show me?"

Jeffrey hesitates, giving me a look of unconcealed reservation, yet he must sense I am a terrier on a scent and finally relents. "Come with me."

Hugh is still chatting up a storm when we slip out of Jeffrey's office and proceed down the hall to another door, slightly out of view of the entryway and Lara's desk. Jeffery unlocks the door to reveal a small, dark space with a desk and chair crammed in one corner and an overflowing bookcase along one wall. A tiny window allows some light to filter in, but all in all, it is a sorry space. I notice a framed photograph of an older man, handsome yet with a somber expression, on one side of the desk.

"Howard Bell," Jeffrey whispers, quietly closing the door as I begin to examine the desk drawers. It is easier said than done, for they are chockfull of all manner of debris – pencil stubs, folded pages, tiny notebooks, larger notebooks, envelopes, stamps, creased maps and a half-eaten packet of ginger biscuits.

"Did you know him?" I ask.

"Bell?" Jeffrey shrugs. "Vaguely. I saw him once or twice. Remember, we haven't been back in London very long, and he died eight months ago. Seemed a quiet fellow, genial enough, though. Didn't look unwell, but he did appear a bit tense, couldn't stand still. I remember thinking he had probably been in the war and acquired some sort of nervous twitch that I have observed in others."

"He wasn't a soldier himself, but I'll explain later. Don't just stand there like a tree, help me!"

With obvious reluctance, Jeffrey pokes about the desk, lifting papers here and there, while I sift through the untidy drawers. If Frances kept the key here, instead of at home, she must have recently gone to open the box. Why would anyone leave a key to their valuables in an office that can't be properly locked? Did someone discover a secret she should have tried harder to hide? What provoked the killer to go after her?

I prod about the bottom drawer when my fingers, seeking blindly, touch a metal object. I tug on it to find a small key attached to a piece of twine.

"Look!" I say slightly too loudly in my eagerness, holding up the object for Jeffrey to see.

"Very good, now can we go?" He is the embodiment of discomfort and I, too, prefer not to linger longer than is necessary. We slip out of the room, Jeffrey locking the door behind us. He gladly waves me off when I make a gesture to leave. I note with relief that Lara has abandoned her desk and is nowhere to be seen. I hope she has not ravished poor, innocent Hugh while I went about my work!

Happily, I find him leaning against a pillar outside the museum, a cigarette dangling from his lips. He takes a final draw and stamps it out beneath his heel.

"Since when do you smoke?" I ask, wrinkling my nose to make my opinion of this habit known.

"Only when I must steady my mind. That woman can talk for England. My head was spinning!"

"My sincerest apologies, but your sacrifice was worthwhile." I give his arm a pat while holding up the key. Hugh's eyes widen.

"Off to Queen Victoria Street!"

Chapter 51

Gaining entry to the vaults proves easier than we anticipated since we can present both our key and the number Frances provided. An attendant with a matching key leads us down a flight of stairs, then to a lift and deeper into the bowels of the building. The corridors are long and narrow with sconces mounted on the walls, throwing out pools of light and lengthening our shadows. Our footsteps sound unnaturally loud as we make our way. The man leads us to a small room and draws a box from a tall cabinet, containing countless other boxes of the same appearance yet with different numbers imprinted upon small metal plates on their sides. I hope once more we are acting as Frances intended us to. The man waits for us to turn the key in the tiny lock and hear it click, instructing us to ring the bell at the door when we have finished. Then he leaves us alone.

"Ready?" I hold on to hope that this is not an exercise in futility. Hugh nods. It is a small box, just big enough to contain a stack of slim notebooks, the pages slightly yellowed, a few brown drops – tea, I presume – spattering one of the covers. I pull out the first, open it to its front page and read the date in the upper left corner. "1916. The next line reads: Howard Bell." I look up at Hugh. "His notebooks, Hugh! We have his notebooks!"

"There are six of them. We cannot read them all in here," Hugh says, his implication echoing my own thoughts. Our eyes travel to my bag, discarded on one of the chairs. Hugh nods. I carefully take the notebooks out of the box and slot them into my bag, pushing away a slight feeling of unease and convincing myself, with moderate success, we are simply following Frances' wishes. I will go back to the hospital tonight or tomorrow morning at the latest and tell her what we have done. Hopefully we will have gained some useful information by then. I should pull Stanton into the fold as well, but not before Hugh and I have a chance to examine our findings.

We close the box and ring the bell for the man to return and replace it in its original space. Hugh and I keep glancing at each other as we follow the attendant out of the building.

"Let us go to Grosvenor Square," I suggest, as soon as we are in the chill outdoors once more. "Daniel has a safe. We can lock up the notebooks when we have finished."

"Good plan," Hugh agrees. We hurry down the street to find my car. It is cold and windy, but I hardly feel it, heat coursing through me in anticipation of our new discovery. I am forced to exercise great self-control driving home, for my foot itches to press down on the pedal and speed home. We hardly speak while I drive, both of us lost in thought, theorizing, no doubt, what those precious notebooks might contain.

When we finally arrive, we hardly exchange more than a quick greeting with Wilkins who meets us at the door, hurrying into the library and closing the door behind us. It is not distrust of the staff, rather a sense of reverence for what we are about to read; respect for a man now gone, who sacrificed for his country and who may never truly be appreciated for all he did.

Setting the notebooks on the large round table, I start to organize them chronologically. "They only begin in '16. Perhaps he was not very active yet at the beginning of the war."

"Or he did not keep elaborate records yet," Hugh suggests, pulling out his own notebook and opening it to a blank page.

Pushing my chair close to Hugh's so we can read together, I pick up the first of the volumes and open it. After a few pages of nothing particularly striking, we arrive at a mention of Verdun, that battle of battles, the stuff to fuel nightmares, swallowing hundreds of thousands of lives in the span of less than a year. There is something sickening about reading his recollections, finding slivers of hope in his words, while knowing what would happen, that it went on and on, bodies piling upon bodies for years to come.

"In April he writes, 'Reports are worsening. Germans have gained ground and are advancing steadily. M arrived in Souville and found work at a hotel. No word from K. Very worrying.'" I read aloud. "So, he was already sending spies to France by then."

"M could be Minette, the name Juliet used," Hugh proposes.

"Maybe, but as far as we know, she was in Valenciennes, which is hours north of the battlefront."

"It would be helpful to know if the initials stand for code names, real names or surnames."

"I imagine he felt quite close to his recruits and used given names, but we cannot be certain. We have to hope he writes something to help us identify Juliet, given what we have learned thus far."

"I didn't think there was British involvement in Verdun," Hugh muses. "I thought it was essentially a French and German battle, while the English focused on the Somme. But then I suppose the point of espionage is not to be noticed."

"We have to assume they were working closely with the local French."

I scan the following pages. Howard records the development of battles with greater British involvement. It looks like he scattered his spies in the most dangerous of places, those with a strong German presence, but I suppose that was the point. Still, it strikes me as playing dangerously close to the flame. It does not help that I know the ending of this story already.

"He has no great fondness for General Pétain," I observe, pointing to a scathing passage where he describes the celebrated Frenchman at the helm of his army in the Battle of Verdun as an "arrogant frog, leading his men to the slaughter".

"Some in command forgot where they came from, forgot that they were on the ground once, too, small and vulnerable as an ant." Hugh sighs heavily. "Others remembered and fell apart, realizing they could not save the men in their command. There were no true winners in this war. From the way Michael Ellroy described Howard's outlook later in life, he belonged to the latter category. He could not forget the part he played."

We read on and stumble upon a passage from May of 1916. I read aloud.

"Listen to this: 'Met J again today. She has recovered and is willing. Slightly risky, but she is eager to prove herself. Completely fluent and quick with languages. Sending her to the training in Folkestone. Hope my intuition is not wrong. Lost contact with K entirely. Germans are catching spies like spiderwebs catch flies. Two Frenchmen were executed last week. Met with Cec. Bad news. Op Evelyn compromised. LdB sentenced. Not likely to be rescued. Cec in a bad way.'" I look up and meet Hugh's eyes. "J has to be Juliet, doesn't it? And then there is Cec who could be Cecil Cameron, the spymaster who committed suicide in '24."

"Then LdB has to be Louise de Bettignies."

"She was sentenced to death in '16, but only died in '18."

"Read on."

"The next entry doesn't mention J. He comments on the Battle of Jutland and the losses. I can read the growing desperation in his words. One battle after another; one horrendous death count following the next. How did he hold on to hope that his work and that of his recruits was worthwhile?" I shake my head and read on. "'Fort Douaumont op a success. Explosion killed over six-hundred Germans. Terrible to consider it good news, but S and M did well. Still no word from K. J is getting better quickly. Her grasp of German much stronger than others, good aim, too. Want to send her to Lille area. Now LdB is out, need to build new network.'"

"He wanted Juliet to be a part of a new set of spies in Lille, a focus of German occupation in France. He must have thought her remarkably capable after so short a training," Hugh marvels.

"His respect for her could explain why he helped her after the war as well, why he let her live in his flat. What is Fort Douaumont?"

"It was held by the Germans, they stored munitions and weaponry there. At some point – evidently in 1916, though I had entirely forgotten about it – there was an explosion which killed many people inside the fort. I thought they had called it an accident, but Howard seems to suggest it was deliberate. I do not know whether to admire the reach of his spies or to be disturbed."

"The latter, I should think," I say. Hugh shrugs.

"War does strange things to the mind. When a battle kills a million men in the course of six months, six-hundred do not seem so great a number. Appalling but true." He shakes his head, ears reddening. I reach out and give his hand a little squeeze.

"You do not need to justify yourself to me, Hugh."

He inhales deeply, then says, "When we heard of German losses, we celebrated, realizing it meant hundreds or thousands of men, not much different from ourselves, going to their graves." He folds his hands in his lap, fingers laced tightly together. "I often wonder what my life would have been like had the war never happened, then I think at least I survived, at least I have a chance to exist at all. That chance was stolen from so many, and for what?" Hugh shrugs helplessly and meets my eye, seeking an answer I cannot give. "It was for nothing but to feed the self-importance of greedy men, and how many of those has history seen? How many more does the future hold?"

"I do not know," I mumble uselessly.

"Nobody does. But will it ever change? Or will we continue to send our people to die again and again and never learn?"

Once more, I have to admit that I do not have an answer. "We can only hope, Hugh, and do our part."

"Yes, I suppose, though it doesn't feel like enough. Reading this, hearing the details I was myself guilty of trying to forget, I realize that is precisely what we must never do. We must always remember!" I am unused to hearing him speak with such passion, and I cannot think of what to say to equal the power of his words. So, after a moment, I continue reading aloud.

"This was written a few weeks later. 'Conscription has begun. Only a matter of time, but a bad sign. End of war not in sight. J leaving for France next week, to make contact with M on arrival. He is in Lille. Souville was a mistake. J will be sent to Valenciennes.' There is another entry from the next day. His handwriting is a little shaky." I continue. "'K has been caught. Nothing can be done. Hope she is sent to camp not executed. French have not recovered bodies of both executed spies, likely never will. J is unconnected, no family to miss her, but I hope the girl pulls through. She's clever as they come.'" I scan the next few pages, but Howard mentions only a few logistical points, observations about the progress in Verdun. His anger in face of the propaganda he sees everywhere. He is growing more anxious, more frustrated as we move along. "Here, I have found the next mention of her. 'J arrived in Valenciennes. Met by M in Lille and taking cover as baker's niece. If all goes well, she will help with deliveries of bread and overhear plans. We have contact working in town as waitress in restaurant Germans frequent. M proving his worth. Derailed train delivery of munitions before it reached Saint Quentin. Will slow movement, if temporarily.'"

"Are you thinking what I am thinking?" Hugh asks.

"M is mentioned frequently," I say.

"And is a man."

"We mustn't be hasty," I warn.

"He could be *the* man. The one in the photograph."

"Let us keep going." I hold up the notebook, so we can read together, scanning pages and pages of scribbles without mention of either J or M. He does note the execution of K in a place called Mons and having to tell her parents. So not every one of his recruits was an orphan or unconnected. The more we read, the more surreal it seems. We lived through this time, yet neither of us knew the details of what occurred behind the scenes. Were it not so horrifying, it would read like a choppily written espionage novel. Again and again, I think: *How was this possible? How could it go on and on like this for years on end. The dead piling up, and the very reason the war began forgotten in the fray?*

"Look," Hugh points at a line. "'J met me in Calais today with news. She was delivering her usual order to the restaurant and overheard one of the Germans. Nobody knows she understands the language, and if anyone can blend into the background, it is J. They are expecting a visit from the Duke of Wüttemberg. He is celebrated for his triumph in the Ardennes, but under his command the bastards used gas in Ypres. He must be stopped, even if another man just like him or worse will spring up in his stead. J must learn when his train arrives. It can be done, I am sure. She was calm, no more mention of the past. What providence to have one such as her in the service of the crown. Thought about telling Fran, but it is too late.' Since Frances told us about the safe deposit box and assumed its contents would interest us, does that not suggest she is aware of them? Even if she had forgotten when you initially interviewed her after Juliet's death."

"Maybe the night she was hit by the car, she was going to tell the police? But how could the would-be killer know of her discovery?"

"Perhaps they did not know, merely assumed she was aware of her husband's activities and could make some critical connection."

We read on and learn that Howard Bell's network gathered considerable amounts of information, which occasionally managed to cripple the enemy in frustrating ways, delaying deliveries or destroying munitions. The local population of the occupied territories was often recruited as well, another advantage of the Allied Powers over the Central Powers, since they were unlikely to feel loyalty towards those who tried to steal their land and resources.

Moreover, we discover that photography was frequently used as well as tiny scrolls of paper in miniscule handwriting sewn into hems or hat brims, until they could be handed over to Howard or others in his position. The nerve of these people, and their cleverness has me once again wishing I could have known Juliet better. We read of her contributions, the one time she smuggled a whole family out of town, because the Germans were going to arrest the father; the time she and the baker hid Michael Ellroy in their cellar; the many secret tips and snatches of information she stole from careless German officers, lubricated with drink when she occasionally waitressed at the restaurant and passed the facts along as stealthily as a black cat in the night. She saved numerous lives, yet she slipped into obscurity – willingly, it seems – when the war was over. Others, too, are mentioned in Howard's notes again and again. I feel as if I know M and G and the baker, called P, by the time we reach the end of the journal. The second volume begins with his rage and frustration about the German announcement of an unlimited submarine war. It seems a world away from the towns in France and Belgium with which he is concerned, but as we discover more and more, it is impossible not to notice the deterioration of Howard Bell's conviction. His frustration shines through the pages, and worry for his recruits echoes that of a parent. One more is killed at the beginning of the year, another discovered and sentenced to hard labor in a camp. Contact between Howard and Juliet and his other agents is sporadic, and it is obvious this troubles him, for he mentions sleepless nights and the burden of lying to Frances.

"I wonder why he did not simply tell her at some point? If they were so devoted to one another, she would not have betrayed him."

"Lies can grow and grow until they are stuck in your throat, too big to escape," Hugh says.

"That is a convenient excuse," I counter.

"Maybe it is. Liars need excuses like fish need water."

"And yet Howard was a hero of sorts as well."

"One does not preclude the other. No person is all good or all bad, though there have been times in my life where I certainly thought the latter was true."

"He died nearly a decade after the war ended. I wonder what role it played in his life, even after all that time. He was still hiding the truth from his wife, and I suppose he was still working for the War Office. Then there was Juliet. I hope his diaries mention what happened to her after the war and whether they maintained contact until his death."

"To some extent, probably, since it was Frances who helped her find employment at the museum." Hugh shrugs.

"Maybe Howard did not know Juliet approached his wife?"

"Let us read on." We nearly reach the end of 1917 in Howard's notes when something catches my eye.

"'Met J in Calais. Seemed distracted and when asked about M, she blushed. Worried they are growing too close. Must consider moving him. She is too well placed to relocate, too valuable. She reported movement in the German camp, constant streams of trucks coming and going. Something big is afoot, and I did not need to tell her to chase it up. She is one of my best. I hope she works with the same care as she has thus far. It is a boost for enemy morale when they catch one of ours, and we have sacrificed enough to them already.'" I raise my gaze to meet Hugh's, who gives me a nod and I continue reading. "This one is from a week later. His handwriting looks a bit different, as though he scribbled it in haste. 'Damn!'"

"What?" Hugh frowns.

"That's what he has written. Shall I go on?"

"Yes, yes."

"'Damn! P sent message. J compromised. I was worried about this. She was caught at the restaurant and her room at the bakery raided. Not sure if anything was found. She is too clever to leave incriminating evidence in plain sight. P was arrested but released again. The blasted Boche like their bread, I suppose. What can be done? Do not know the charges, even if I did, I could send no aid. This cannot be happening again! What have I done? Trying to contact M. Must see him as soon as possible. Worried he will do something stupid.'"

I feel a tightening in my chest and see in Hugh's pallor, he must be experiencing the same. Juliet was captured. My mind flits instantly to previous mentions of executions, of the tragic end Louise de Bettignies faced. Juliet survived her ordeal, but I remember the coroner's observation about her scars and her limp and feel a queasy knot forming in my stomach.

"What was the date of that last entry?" Hugh asks quietly.

"The twelfth of October 1917."

"Still more than a year until the Armistice was signed."

We flip through the next few pages, but Howard sounds disjointed, scattering his thoughts upon the paper without much reason. It is strange how much one can tell about a person's state of mind by their writing, even long after they are gone. He was disturbed, and growing increasingly more so. I wonder how he covered his unease in front of his wife. The war was raging, the losses high, so she may have believed his bleak state was due to the bad news all around. And she must have been busy herself at the time, the role of archivist having been settled upon her during these years. Only after another two weeks does something seem to shift.

No word from J. M is in enemy hands, too. P sent word. Not certain what to do. I have failed them. J is twenty-three, M twenty-five. Has this war and my recklessness sent them to an early grave? I spoke with Cec, but he is in a bad way. LdB still doing hard labor. There is hope she will survive, but we cannot predict when the tide of the war turns, when it will finally, finally end. At the moment, I feel it will stretch into eternity. What has happened, what we have witnessed can surely never be forgotten. When the last bullet is fired, when the silence descends and we see, in the smoke and the fog and the gas, the bodies of our dead, we must surely ask, how did it come to this? I think it every day. How did it come to this? It is a perpetual echo that accompanies me like a spiteful spirit day and night. Maybe I would better serve this mad world by putting a bullet into my own head. Were it not for my poor, unknowing Frances, I would.

The despair in his words rests like a heavy shroud on my shoulders. Juliet and M in captivity.

"I know how this story ends," Hugh says in a quiet voice.

"If only it were merely a story, not history."

"Spies were not treated kindly. It is a marvel Juliet survived."

"But what sort of life did she lead afterwards?"

"It explains why Howard felt a responsibility towards her after the war; why he helped her and kept her privacy when Ellroy wanted to meet."

"But what of M?" I ask, dreading Hugh's answer, for I can guess it myself.

"I think we both know. Read on."

Howard's mind was often occupied with J and M, as the weeks went by and he struggled to learn something new. At times, he seemed relieved to hear nothing, for an execution would have been celebrated by the other side, and made widely known to bolster morale. A few more recruits were sent to France, but not to Valenciennes. E and S were set to Lille, and he mentions locals who did all they could to thwart the occupiers. By the beginning of 1918, Juliet must have been in captivity for months. Then comes the entry we have been dreading. News of M's execution. It happened on a cold sixth of February 1918. He was twenty-five. It was a week before his birthday. Howard noted it down in short sentences, a staccato of words which needed no embellishment to convey the burden of his grief. Juliet was sentenced to a life of hard labor.

"We have to assume M was the man in the photograph. Though these are not Juliet's journals, I have the sense she took her work very seriously. No one would have been likely to divert her attention except for a man with the same devotion to the cause."

"And then he was killed." Hugh sighs, running a hand over his face as if to erase the thought.

"She was sentenced to hard labor, and by the looks of her, according to the coroner, she served some of it."

"At least the lifetime sentence was reduced when hostilities ended seven months later. Though I do not doubt she suffered more than anyone should."

"Howard goes on," I say as I pick up the next notebook. "He threw himself into the task of negotiating her release. He was desperate to prove he would not desert the men and women he recruited. His style of writing has changed. Before it was quite spare and to the point. Now," I show Hugh a page, "he rambles, and his script is careless."

"He must have known so much more than the public or soldiers did at the time, been aware of the true state of the war and whether the propaganda was true, or whether it was a lie in the face of likely defeat. It was such a muddle at the time, wasn't it?"

"It was. In addition, we were coping with another threat, the Spanish Influenza." My mind conjures my uncle, Agnes' first husband, who was one of countless victims of the disease.

"Those four years stole human lives with Midas' greed."

The months go by and Howard's despair grows. In September 1918 Louise de Bettignies dies from what should have been a simple surgery, and moral takes another dip. Two months later the Armistice is signed at last. By this stage, though, Howard has grown bitter and writes.

It is only a piece of paper, only signatures of fallible, weak-minded men. It won't be a lesson. This war will have been a mere tremor in human history, forgotten as soon as the ground settles beneath our feet. I will remember, though. I see their faces every night before I try to sleep. I see them in crowds, in the streets, only to realize my mind is playing tricks and they are gone. The one crumb of good news is that J is alive. She was freed last week. I am going to France to see her. She is in a bad way. Fran suspects I am lying to her. I think she believes another woman has come between us. It is true, yet not in the way she thinks. I am frightened of seeing J again. Will she hate me? Scorn me? Will she be willing to accept whatever help is mine to offer?

"What happens next?" Hugh asks, for we have finally reached the point leading to Juliet's life after the war. Howard was not shunned when he saw her, he wrote, rather she smiled at him and took his hand. He recalls the injuries, the scars and bruises, noticing her limp when she was finally allowed to get out of her sickbed. They did not speak of what happened. They did not discuss her suffering, for its causes were obvious. He still refers to her as J. A few of his other recruits survived the war as well, but it is clear that J is the one he holds dearest, the one he feared lost but found again.

She was in the hospital for two months. Her injuries terrible, her body weak. I hardly recognized her at first, an old haggard woman, tiny in the hospital bed. Then she said my name, and I heard the familiar voice. She knew of M and would not speak of it, yet when I mentioned his name, she looked confused. She had only known him as Louis, just as he had only known her as Minette. She loved him, and so I respected her wishes and never speak of him. Last week, I brought her back to England. I thought of taking her to stay with us, but how to explain it to Fran? Though she will remember J from the past, she cannot have an inkling of our connection now, what we have been through together. I found her a hotel for a time, brought her the small suitcase of her belongings I had kept safe before she left. She unpacked slowly, asking me how I am, how Fran was, as if we were ordinary friends. A small box tumbled out of her case and I picked it up, for her hip still gives her trouble when she bends. It was a jewelry case. "Mother's wedding band," she said and showed me the plain gold ring within. There was such pain in her expression. Even if she did not lend it word, I understood what she was thinking. She and M would never have a future. She would never wear his ring. I felt shattered when I went home. That night, I wondered whether to connect her to M's family, but they were so distraught and angry when they were informed of his death, I did not know if they could bear another reminder. J does not plan to stay in the city. It is too much of everything. She startles at the slightest noise, looks panicked in crowds and tires quickly. I have a friend in Plymouth who runs a guest house and have arranged J to stay with her, maybe work there for a time. The sea air will do her good, so will getting away from the memories. All around the city, I see young men returning home, so many maimed, savaged by the gas or walking in a dream, dazed and unaware. I wish I were dreaming, too. I wish I could wake and wipe the past four years away, blink into sunlight and start afresh, be honest with my wife. I feel a stranger to her sometimes. I feel like a stranger to myself. Who have I become, a mercenary who sent young people to die? I thought I was a sort of father figure, but I see now that it was good I never had children of my own. I would have ruined them. I have done so badly by Fran, by J. How can I repair so much damage? My hair has gone entirely gray within the past two years. I am an old man, what have I to show for it? There was talk of medals being awarded and Cec is being made Commander of the Order of the British Empire. Are such misplaced honors in my future? My colleagues think I did well, clap me on the back for the part my spies played in the war, the successful missions and intercepted information we procured. I feel a fraud all the same. I considered leaving the city, too, but it is not right for Fran. I must devote myself to her now. I will leave the War Office as soon as is reasonable. I will retire. Read, go for walks and live a quiet life until I am gone and Howard Bell is but a fading memory.

"Here it ends," I say and place the final notebook on the table.

"He never did leave the War Office, did he?"

"No. Though he tried to deny it. His work must have become a fundamental part of his identity."

"Now we know Juliet's story. After Plymouth, she evidently felt a desire to return to London after all and Howard helped her. Maybe enough time had passed, and he arranged a meeting between her and Frances and that is how the latter helped Juliet find employment."

"The hidden cache of money could have been a safety net for Juliet, in case she wanted to leave again. She may have hidden the medals because, like Howard, she did not feel she was any sort of hero."

"Does her story bring us closer to finding her killer? We know of her past and Howard's, too, but they are both dead and can offer no further explanation. Maybe Juliet made an enemy when she lived in Plymouth. Maybe she truly did move around a lot as she told you, never quite settling."

"Let us sleep on it. There must be something in these notebooks that will push us in the right direction."

Hugh leans back in his chair and stretches his arms toward the ceiling, cracking his knuckles and his neck. I grimace at the sound, even if my own shoulders feel stiff from bending over the notebooks for hours. Only now do I realize how time has sped by. My stomach rumbles, reminding me we haven't eaten in ages. I persuade Hugh to stay longer and join me in a sandwich and cup of tea. We carefully pack up the notebooks, and I place them in the safe Daniel keeps hidden behind one of the shelves. At least we know Howard's precious writings are secure. I wonder whether Frances read them and thus sent us to find them, or whether the memory that Howard possessed this box only came back to her the day she was struck by the car? I do not believe she lied, that she knew much more than she claimed, but there might have been something. Howard mentioned Juliet's recovery at the very beginning of the notebooks. Maybe he helped her find someone to end the pregnancy and waited for her to get better again? Maybe she lost the child and was thereby forced to rest and recover? Maybe we will never know. One thing, however, seems clear. No baby was ever born, for there was not enough time for a full term pregnancy and no mention of such an event in Howard's journals. In a way, it makes me even more sad for Juliet. How different might her life have been? A child could have posed a challenge, yes, but I think she would have made do. Though I never knew her well enough to form such an opinion, Howard's recollections make me believe she was a most capable young woman who grew with the challenges that came her way. Who wanted such a person dead? A woman who sacrificed so much, showed such bravery? Who could have hated a distinguished war hero enough to murder her?

Chapter 52

It is late by the time Stanton drops by to pick up the notebooks. Refreshed after tea and sandwiches, Hugh and I agreed not to waste time in alerting the police. Daniel knows the bones of what Hugh and I learned and now offers Stanton a drink while I go and fetch the notebooks from the safe. I hurry, for leaving the two of them alone for too long strikes me as less than ideal, even if both always behave like gentlemen towards each other. Indeed, when I return to the sitting room, notebooks in my arms, they are sitting amiably by the fire, the amber in their crystal glasses shimmering like liquid gold in the flickering light. Shadows thrown by the fire deepen the hollows under Stanton's eyes and sharpen Daniel's cheekbones. I wonder what would happen if I left them alone. Could they not, perhaps, become friends? They are more similar than they care to admit.

"Here we are," I say, when they turn to me, noticing my presence. I set the notebooks on the table and pour myself a drink, before sinking into an armchair. "The man in the photograph was probably Juliet's lover, a fellow spy who was executed in '18. Howard refers to him as M, his code name was Louis." I give Stanton a short summary of what we learned, and he listens without interruption, only nodding, taking small sips.

"Those internment camps were terrible," Daniel says quietly. "We were there when one of them was liberated by the Allies. The prisoners of war looked like ghosts. Juliet must have suffered terribly."

"As her scars can attest," Stanton agrees with a shake of the head.

"What next?" Daniel looks at me.

"I don't know," I admit. It has been a long day, and everything is whirling around in my mind. I cannot decide how to proceed until my thoughts settle, and the air clears. "I don't suppose there have been any worthy leads when it comes to the photograph you printed in the paper? We saw it this morning. The quality is not very good."

"Unfortunately, the creases and its age made for a less than perfect printing. Hollis was not pleased," Stanton admits, wrapping his hands around the glass. "There have been a few calls, nothing promising, though. Some callers are still searching for lost ones, even after all this time. Then there are those who take pleasure in deliberately misleading the police." He glances at his watch and grimaces, lifting the glass to his lips and draining its contents. "I really must be going. I am late again. Thom chastises me as though he is the father and I the errant son."

"How is he?" I ask, when Daniel and I accompany Stanton to the door.

"Well enough. Adjusting to the city, looking forward to the holidays. He is meeting Iona this weekend. Your cousin is taking them to a circus."

"I am glad they are friends, or do you think a little romance is blossoming?" I tease.

"You would know before I do. Men don't speak of such things," Stanton replies and winks, though his tone carries a hint of sadness.

"Good night," Daniel says and Stanton nods, turns and disappears into the square. Daniel closes the door and gives me a meaningful look.

"What?" I ask, crossing my arms.

"I do not know whether to feel sorry for the man or whether to resent him."

"What would you have me do?"

"Nothing," he says. "I should not have said anything. Working with you must be frustrating for him – well, more frustrating than for others." He grins.

"Maybe we should work on finding him a match instead of Hugh," I suggest, half-seriously as we return to the sitting room.

"Speaking of Hugh, I have found someone, or have you forgotten our little wager as you waded about in the sea of wickedness that is your profession?"

"I have not forgotten and have found someone, if she is willing, naturally."

"Do I know her?"

"As well as I do."

Daniel pours us both another measure and hands me the glass before sitting down across from me. For just a moment, I let my mind conjure a scene many years from now, both of us wizened, creases around our eyes and mouths, hands speckled, sitting together in front of the fire. The thought sends a flutter of warmth through me, a strange feeling of satisfaction, as though I have finally arrived after a long journey at sea. We do not know what the future holds, but this image is one I would not be unhappy to see realized.

"Who is it?" Daniel asks, drawing me out of my musings, a faint smile on his lips. "There are few women I know as well as you do."

I twist in my seat to make certain the door is closed. "What do you think of Maisie for Hugh?" I raise my brows, awaiting his answer. The sagging jaw I am faced with is not what I was expecting. "Come, it is not a bad notion!" I begin to defend myself, but Daniel's disbelief shifts into laughter.

"Maisie is the very person *I* chose!"

"What? Are you teasing me?"

"I am as serious as the taxman. Great minds, as one says." He smiles and taps his temple. "I do believe they could be compatible. Both are, in their way, lonely, and too young to give up on changing their lives. Maisie is a widow, true, but I think she and her husband were not very close during the last years of their marriage."

"But is she ready for someone new?" I wonder aloud.

"She cannot be content living with her brother as a housekeeper for the rest of her life, not when she once desired all that a marriage entailed. She is young enough for children, if she wants them."

"You have given this some thought, I see," I observe, unable to hide a smile. Hugh is Daniel's closest friend. He is evidently quite invested in helping him find something like what we have found with each other. "How do we engineer a romantic encounter between them? Both are too reserved to act themselves, I think. Or if they did, it would take a decade."

"We should first learn whether there is any mutual interest. Maybe you can speak with Maisie and I with Hugh. If they are agreeable, we shall seat them together at the wedding banquet. Perhaps compel them to share a dance?"

"It is certainly worth a try. I would be happy to see Hugh with someone. I do not think he has much experience with romance, or have you heard him mention anyone?" A thought comes to me and I carefully add, "You do not think he prefers…"

"The company of men?" Daniel finishes my thought and shakes his head. "I am fairly certain he does not."

"Would Wilkins oppose such a match? Hugh and he are not exactly bosom pals."

"I believe they have sorted out their differences, mainly who is more loyal to me," Daniel says with a chuckle.

"Very well, then, let us play Cupid."

"Eros, my love! You and I met in Greece. It is the gods of Olympus we must invoke."

"Maybe this time next year we will have another wedding to look forward to," I whisper conspiratorially.

"Don't put the cart before the horse quite yet."

"Very romantic, but I see your point. I will have a little natter with Maisie tomorrow, and we shall see. In other news, can you believe we will be married in a month's time? I have hardly noticed the past weeks fly by. I've been so busy running about. Not planning the wedding, mind you. Agnes has that firmly in hand."

"It feels strange to have so many people missing who ought to be there, doesn't it? One never quite gets used to the idea."

"No, one does not. We will simply have to be grateful for all the people who are there on the day and hope that makes it easier to bear. It is a joyous occasion, and I think our parents and your brothers would have been happy for us."

"I am convinced of it." Despite my assertion that we must be grateful for the company of our friends and family at the wedding, I cannot shake Daniel's comment even as I try to fall asleep. I am thankful for Agnes and happy she will be the one to give me away, yet my mind wanders all the same to a scene in which my parents are with us, sitting in the front pew, smiling at me as I stand with Daniel and exchange vows. I have lived without them so much longer than with them. Perhaps we would argue all the time, had they survived. Perhaps we would not be half as close as I dream we would be. And still, even if we loathed one another – a picture I cannot truly grant any credence – they would be alive. Death is so terrifyingly final. I cannot allow myself to contemplate it often, but when I do, I wonder what frightens me more, no longer existing myself, or leaving behind people I love and who love me and being unable to comfort them. I squeeze my eyes shut tightly, making spots appear, tiny black holes in front of my eyelids. Forcing my morbid thoughts aside, I try to remember a blue sky, clear and cloudless, a gentle breeze, carrying the fragrance of springtime blossom. Slowly I drift away, carried on the imagined gust of wind into the land of slumber.

Chapter 53

"Another anonymous letter was delivered this morning," Maeve tells me when I arrive at the flat after visiting Frances at the hospital. She was sleeping, but slowly improving, the nurse told me. I whispered our discovery of the notebooks and gave her hand a little squeeze, promising to return soon.

"Just a note this time?" I ask, my mind instantly leaping to the memory of the box and its contents, now rotting away in the bin outside.

"Here, I didn't open it, of course. Mr. Flynn said a different lad delivered it this time."

Slicing open the plain white envelope, I find a card identical to the first. *Stay away. Do not force me to act again.* The ominous message is typewritten once more and reveals nothing of its sender. I show it to Maeve.

"I repeat my offer: Stay in Grosvenor Square for a time. You are quite welcome. It isn't your fault my work has attracted such unwanted attention."

"I will talk to Kathleen, but I think she'll agree that we should stay."

"It is your decision."

"Are you afraid, miss?" Maeve asks, eyes wide, even though she has been through a number of ordeals herself and always shows herself stoic in the face of trouble.

"I would be foolish not to be a little frightened, but I am angry, too, Maeve. This person is a coward and a monster who has caused unspeakable damage to two women. He or she is sending these threats because they realize time is running out."

"People do bad things when they are desperate," Maeve observes.

"And they make mistakes, too. I feel we are close to the truth, I really do, and when we discover it, this nightmare will hopefully come to an end."

"Won't bring the murdered woman back to life, though."

"No, nothing will. Yet I firmly believe it is better to have some small measure of justice in catching who killed her, than none at all." I look at my watch. There is a meeting of the WI today, and I plan to attend. Aunt Louise will pick me up, and we will drive across town together. I think she is itching to hear everything we have discovered, and I wonder what I can rightly share. She can be trusted, but she is also talkative, and Edith is her friend. Though I do not suspect my employer, I do not fully trust her either. My mind persistently returns to the fact that the WI was the one area of Juliet's life which had changed in recent weeks. She lived for years escaping everybody's notice, then died so soon after joining the organization. I cannot let go of the connection, even if there have been no clues supporting any dubious hypothesis I could conjure up. The women have been cordial and welcoming; Edith trusting in my abilities and quick to take responsibility for a lonely, murdered woman she barely knew. *What to think? What to think?* Then there are Adeline and Priscilla, both similarly welcoming, both helpful when I made inquiries at the beginning of the investigation. I cannot discount Graham Markby, Adeline's husband, for he met Juliet, too, if briefly, when we were at Adeline's house. It is impossible to take on the role of detective without growing suspicious of nearly everyone!

"Tell me, how are you getting on?" Aunt Louise asks when I climb into the backseat of her car. She never learned to drive and I have known her chauffeur, Patrick, from the time I was an adolescent. I give him a nod and he taps his hat, before closing my door and climbing back behind the wheel. A moment later, the engine roars to life.

"I think we are close," I explain in a low voice, even if Patrick is as trustworthy as they come.

"Briony mentioned you received some threat? You are being careful, aren't you? Your wedding is in a matter of weeks."

"And if it weren't, I could afford to be reckless?" I ask, teasing. Louise rolls her big blue eyes, the mirror of her daughter's, who, by the by, I swore to secrecy!

"You are lucky indeed that Daniel is such a tolerant fellow. I tell you, Robert may seem all ease and joviality, but if I were to start prancing about, mixing with murderers, he would have something to say about it."

"If Daniel were to prevent me, I would have something to say about that as well! Where is this coming from? I thought you were championing the empowerment of women! Or is it only women you do not know?"

Louise lets out a deep sigh. At first, I cannot tell whether it is from exasperation with me or weariness. Then she smiles and touches my arm. "You are quite right. I just worry. You are like a daughter to me, my dear. Although you have proven yourself capable on many occasions, I am entitled to worry for you. At least you are working with the police, I take some comfort in that."

I soften instantly in the face of her concern. "I will be careful, Aunt Louise. Yesterday Daniel and I sat by the fire, and I imagined how it would be when we are old and gray."

"Like me?" Louise chuckles.

"I would be pleased, if I became anything like you," I say. "But yesterday I thought, I could count myself lucky indeed if we sat together in forty or fifty years. Life is so unpredictable. Juliet, no doubt, hoped to grow old as well, but the chance was stolen from her. She was only a few years older than I am. She will never be a mother, a wife, never travel the world and fall in love again. I owe it to her to keep at it, and I truly believe we are close."

"Fall in love again? Was there a man, then?" Louise asks, latching on to my words.

"There was, though he, too, was not met with a happy ending. Are you certain you want to hear?"

"I already guessed it would be a sad story, so tell me." As I do, Louise's expression shifts, her mouth tipping at the corners, her eyes acquiring a glassy sheen and when I finish, she dabs at them with her hankie.

Her voice is hoarse when she says, "When will new tales of horror from that time ever cease?" She takes a deep breath, and I give her hand a gentle squeeze. We are approaching the hall, and I ask Patrick to circle around the block to give my aunt time to compose herself before facing the other women.

"At least we can better understand why Juliet was so closed off, living such an intensely private life."

"How cruel not to leave her to it! Who was she hurting, living as she was?"

"The question may be, who did she hurt before? Or rather, who believes she did them harm?"

"I cannot imagine one of her German captors finding her now to take revenge," Louise ponders, tucking the hankie back into her sleeve. "They punished her enough. Maybe other people in the resistance movement felt Juliet had betrayed them in some way?"

"Even so, would they have bothered to find her now, a woman they knew under a different name? So much time has passed. I cannot quite connect the dots to create the complete picture, but I sense we are close. We discovered too much about Juliet's life for the truth to evade us much longer, or so I hope, even if Hugh believes I am growing cynical."

"It is funny, for me it is the opposite. When I was younger, I thought much more cynically of the world than I do now. Perhaps being a parent and a grandmother has something to do with it. I want to believe in the good of people and the world my loved ones inhabit."

"I shall hope to follow that way of thinking." The car has done its circuit and we climb out, shivering as we hurry into the building. In the entry, we hear the busy hum of voices. Suddenly, I regret having come. I am in no mood to make idle chatter for the next few hours, but it is too late to turn back now. At least I have my aunt by my side.

"Louise, Evelyn, how lovely to see you!" Edith greets us, coming our way, hands outstretched to take ours. We accept her embrace. "Pris and I are discussing the fundraiser. So much remains to be done. We are meeting with Adeline at my house tomorrow evening, if you can spare the time, we would welcome any help and your company, of course."

"I am taking my eldest granddaughter to see Macbeth in the West End," Louise says with an apologetic shrug. "The girl is infatuated with the most morbid of stories! I cannot stand these tales of endless vengeance, one death begetting another, but she begged me and my willpower melts away like snow in summer when faced with those big brown eyes."

"I wish I knew the feeling. Adeline and Graham have been married for years and not a single grandchild to bounce on my knee," Edith says quietly.

"Ah, she is young. It will happen," Louise replies with a wink.

"She will be thirty-two come March," Edith laments.

"I thought you were all for women making their own decisions, bucking the trend," Louise teases.

"Oh, I am, I am, but I would like a grandchild before I am too old to chase him or her around and spoil them rotten. Lloyd isn't getting any younger either, though he is quite proud he is keeping so fit at his age."

"He should join Robert at Chesterton come spring. We have a new tennis court and Robert has no one with whom to play apart from the gardener's son, who is a third his age. I worry the young man will push my poor husband to his limit, for he can be too competitive for his own good."

"We will arrange it. Now come in, have a cup of tea. June made some excellent scones. You really must try them before we begin. There has been a slight development, I don't mind telling you already," Edith says, walking with us to the table, set up as a small buffet with cups and saucers, a large pot of tea and two platters of scones and biscuits. "We have been able to arrange a meeting with the police commissioner! I think he is sick of us sending petitions and letters to all the MPs and to him as well, so he has agreed to an 'informal chat', as he called it."

"Good news, hopefully. Evie's work shows us that women are as capable of solving crimes and enforcing the law as men, maybe even more so."

"I entirely agree. Speaking of which, has there been anything new?" Edith turns to me, her gaze direct and impossible to evade. I am saved from answering by Priscilla, who interrupts just then, asking Edith to call the meeting to a start. Edith shrugs and touches Louise's arm, promising to chat later, and gives me a nod. I am not excused just yet.

For the next hour, we listen to Edith outlining the new development, speaking encouragement and rousing the women in the room. Even when she calls the meeting to an end, excited talk amongst the ladies does not cease. Edith, I have noticed on previous occasions as well as today, has the skill of a born orator. She engages, seems to be making eye contact with everyone in the room, and has the strange ability to thrill, even when the progress of which she speaks is modest indeed. It requires no great leap of the imagination to see her as an MP or political figure herself, championing her cause like she has for more than a decade. How I hope she is who she claims to be! That she hasn't tricked me with this investigation and is, in some way, implicated. Our world needs more women like Edith Ashbourne and Juliet Nelson, not fewer.

"I can guess what you are thinking." I turn to see Priscilla standing next to me. "You understand now why I admire her so?"

"I do."

"Do you have children, Evelyn?" She asks, eyeing me with curiosity.

"No, I am to be married in a few weeks," I reply, though we both appreciate one does not preclude the other.

"Then you will not quite understand yet. I have a son, but my sister has three daughters. I want them to have a future in which they are respected, valued for who they are, rather than ignored for what they are not, namely male. Edith and the women here give me hope for the future."

"I think Juliet would have done the same." The words slip past my tongue before I can catch them. Priscilla's smile stiffens.

"I am sure she would. Have you heard anything new? Have arrests been made?"

"No arrests yet, but the police are very close, I gather." I watch for her reaction, for a flicker of fear, yet if she feels any, she does not betray herself. Instead, her expression softens to something like relief.

"Finally, I still wake up in the middle of the night, picturing Juliet's coffin being lowered into the ground. Adeline was saying much the same. Part of a generation that lived through war and the

Spanish Flu, we have all attended too many funerals already, but hers felt almost like an attack on the WI. We receive a few threats now and again. There are always men – and even some women – who think we ought to remain in our place and be grateful for it, too, but there has never been violence until now."

"For what it's worth, I have found no indication the crime was related to Juliet's attendance here. She was only a member for a few weeks. It saddens me, but I think hardly anybody took much notice of her."

"Someone did," Priscilla observes and takes a sharp breath.

"Yes, someone did," I agree.

"Evelyn!" I turn to see Adeline coming towards us, wearing a bold dress with green and purple stripes. "I am glad you came! Mother says you are getting on well. Very good! Hopefully, we can put this nasty business behind us soon. Oh, and I heard your uncle is in the race to be the new MP for Shoreditch, how intriguing! Can we hope for his support should he win?"

"I do not speak for him, but I am fairly certain the answer is yes. His wife is a rather formidable woman."

"Then you must put him in contact with the WI of his district. It may aid his effort to have women championing his cause in their homes and perhaps to vote for him themselves."

"What a marvelous idea! I shall put it to him later." I smile, genuinely touched she has thought of a way to help Harold. I sincerely believe he will do his best to prove worthy of the faith of his voters, male and female. Much as I wish to see more women in positions of power, until that time, we must make allies of the men who have everybody's interests at heart, and attempt to convert those who are capable of shedding their inflated self-worth. Leadership and responsibility are all well and good, but the mark of good governance, to me, is the willingness and ability to listen and to learn.

Chapter 54

In fact, I call my uncle as soon as I reach St. James. Hugh is meeting Hollis to discuss tips the paper received regarding the photograph. I have low expectations, but low expectations are not no expectations.

"Having the support of the WI would be wonderful," Harold enthuses on the other end of the line.

"I will put you in touch with Edith. Agnes could get involved, too."

"At the moment, her sole focus seems to be your wedding, my dear."

"I am not sure whether that should delight or disturb me."

"The former, surely, the former. How is your investigation coming along? Have you found out more about our tragic spy?"

"Too much and still too little. She came to a terrible end, indeed, but her life was not without some measure of happiness."

"There was a boy?" Harold guesses, a smile in his voice.

"A young man, rather, but yes, there was romance." I give him a summary of what we read in Howard's journals.

"Terrible, terrible. Will there ever come a day when we are not confronted with more tragedies of this war?"

"I have to believe so."

"But that may mean people have forgotten, which is worse than mourning. I spoke to a former friend of mine, who seems to know everyone, even a few chaps at the War Office. He told me that, at the time, there was little public knowledge of the network of espionage Britain was building. There were interior conflicts, apparently, within different branches of the Office, in particular the Secret Service Bureau. Communication was not at its best. Freddy, my friend, told me most agents were recruited locally, meaning in France, Belgium and so forth. Juliet had to have been quite remarkable to draw a recruiter's attention."

"By Howard's account, she was that and more."

"Her imprisonment strikes me as intriguing. Did she disclose something significant in captivity? You told me of her scars, probably a result of torture. Now this could have occurred in the camp where she was a prisoner, but more likely it happened when she was caught. Did Mr. Bell mention whether she let slip any secret that she told him about?"

"No, he was vague on the matter. Perhaps he did not know himself. It was a chaotic time. Who could ever know whether Juliet revealed something, or whether it was simply bad luck when an allied plan went awry?"

"I was a military man, and I abhorred the use of torture. That does not mean everyone in my company did. In my experience, if the captive did not speak, they did not always live. Sometimes - often times even - the point was to get them to confess, guilty or not."

"You are insinuating Juliet survived and was sent to the camp instead of being executed, because she gave the Germans something useful?"

"I hate to say so, but I would not discount it. Do not think less of her, if it was so, Evelyn. From what you have told me, she was an astonishing and brave young woman, but everyone has a threshold when it comes to suffering. The mouth betrays the mind."

"I can attest to that, even without having faced torture," I admit, and Harold lets out a laugh.

"Most of us think far too little about the words slipping past our tongue. Yet in all seriousness, from what you have told me, Juliet did not strike me as such a person. If she told her interrogators anything, it was because she was broken, not callous."

"I cannot say this chat has been very uplifting, Harold." I sigh, crouching on the edge of the desk and frowning at the wall.

"My apologies, I wish I could have offered something better."

"You made me think, which is as good as anything, even if the thoughts are disturbing." When I end the conversation, I sit in silence, unmoving for a few more moments, allowing Harold's words to settle in my mind. Juliet must have been tormented by her captors, but what did she reveal? I shake myself and pull out our notes on Howard's recollections. After an hour of poring over them, I find nothing indicating Juliet was guilty of a betrayal. Still, it is clear Howard took on the role of her protector. Maybe he preferred not to know the truth of what happened when she was a prisoner. What good would it do? The war was over by the time she returned to London, and any admission would not have achieved a thing apart from causing both of them pain.

Before I sink deeper into despair for Juliet and Howard and the rest of them, I hear the front door swing open and hurried footsteps approaching. A moment later, Hugh stands in the doorway, eyes bright.

"What is it?" I ask, sitting up.

"The paper..." Hugh takes a deep breath, before continuing. "The paper got a call from someone who recognized the man in the photograph!"

"A viable source?" I ask, a rush of excitement quickening my heartbeat.

"They said they recognized him from school."

"School? Anyone could say that."

"They said his name was Martin."

"Martin as in M," I say.

"Precisely. It could be nothing, but all the other tips sounded unlikely. This one, however, may be worth pursuing. What do you think?"

"Who was the caller?" I ask instead of answering his question. Could this Martin be Juliet's M, the man who worked under the code name Louis?

"Hollis wasn't the one to take the call. The receptionist said it was a man who sounded older. He said he saw the photograph and thought it was Martin, a lad he taught in school. I talked to the woman who received the call, and she said the man spoke very clearly and seemed sure of himself. We – or rather the police - can find him at his address in Paddington. What do you think?"

"Impossible to ignore. I suppose Hollis has informed Stanton?"

"He is duty bound, but Stanton wasn't in the office when he called." Hugh raises his brows and meets my eye, unspoken words offering a challenge. I hesitate only for a moment. It was our idea to run the photograph in the paper, why should we not be first to confirm the validity of a halfway plausible lead?

I glance at my watch. "It is only four. Shall we chance it? Might he be home now?"

"He left a telephone number. Let us give him a call to ask if he will meet us. His name is Julian Francis and he teaches at St. George's Academy."

It takes a few moments to be connected, and when we are, the line is crackly. Mr. Francis' voice sounds almost like a whisper. He agrees to receive us in an hour at his home, claiming he wants to help however he can, and that he is confident he recognizes the man in the photograph.

"I am not sure how, but I feel his true identity will lead us in the right direction. The young man cannot be irrelevant, can he? We aren't making something out of nothing?" I ask.

"We have to take the small chance that this will lead us closer to learning the killer's identity."

"Of course." We decide not to sit about, twiddling our thumbs, and instead set off right away.

By the time we reach Paddington, the sky is already dimming, though it is hours until evening. The horizon above the rooftops is gleaming orange, shifting into a soft lilac the higher my eyes travel.

Hugh squints in the dim light, consulting a map to decipher where to find Mr. Francis's house. At first, we drive through residential streets, with neat, two-up-two-down houses, the occasional parish church, barren trees, black in shadow. I wait for Hugh to point at one, but he does not and tells me to drive on. After a few minutes, we find ourselves in a quiet area with large brick houses on either side.

"Stop here," Hugh announces, peering out of the window, his brows furrowed. "It should be here...somewhere." We climb out of the car. I cross my arms and survey the area. We take a few steps, walk up to the corner and back again.

"Are you certain this is the right address?" I ask, staring up at the warehouse buildings, dark windows and the empty lane.

"It has to be," Hugh replies, though he sounds unconvinced and his brow is furrowed in a frown. "But it doesn't look very residential."

"It looks abandoned." As I speak the words a thought rushes at me with such force, I take a step back. "Hugh," I say quietly. He registers the change in me instantly, but before I can speak, there is a strange sound, a pop breaking through the silence all around us. The next thing I know, Hugh has launched himself at me and we are on the ground, shielded by the bulk of the Bentley. Another pop, and my fears are realized. Someone is shooting at us. It was a trap!

Hugh's eyes are wild. Another pop, and a chunk of brick from the opposite wall breaks off and crumbles to the ground. We have to get into the car! The shooter seems to be aiming from somewhere above us, and whether by intention or lack of skill, is not terribly accurate...so far at least.

"Hugh," I say, grabbing his arm. He is frozen in place, eyes so wide, they seem mostly white. "Hugh, we have to move. We have to get back in the car. I will try to open the door from the ground and climb into the passenger's side. Can you drive?" He does not answer, his whole body trembling. "All right, all right," I add quickly, as another shot rings through the air and Hugh winces as if hit – though the bullet once more strikes the wall. "You go in first, I will drive. Hugh?" I pinch his arm, which finally pulls him out of his trance. He swallows and nods. I reach up for the door handle, hoping that the shooter does not notice what we are doing until it is too late, and we are both in the car. From what I gather, he or she is trying to frighten us, but I cannot be certain that is all, and am wary of taking a risk. The door opens and I breathe a sigh of relief before pushing Hugh with both hands, coaxing him to move. It seems to take a while – though in reality cannot be more than a few seconds – for Hugh to understand and force himself up from his crouched position on the ground. "Stay down in the car!" Once he is in, I follow, my eyes scanning the buildings around us. There is no one to be seen. The shooting has stopped, though I do not trust the lull. What if the person aiming at us is coming down to our level? With shaking hands, I grasp the wheel, all the while ducking down in my seat. The engine lets out a roar so loud in the silence that I wince. A moment later, we are moving. Just as I turn the bend, we hear a final round of gunfire, this time the bullets connect with something solid and I grimace. My car has been hit! I push my anger aside, relieved it was not one of us. My beloved motor has seen more than its fair share of bruising in my employ already.

I drive and drive until we are miles away and in the neighborhood of Fitzrovia. I hardly know how we got here, for I paid little attention to where I was going, the only thought in my mind to escape. Pulling to a stop at the side of the road, I turn to Hugh. He has not said a word.

"Hugh," I say gently, noticing the way his hands are clenched tightly in his lap. Even in the low light, I see the white gleam of his knuckles. I reach over and carefully pry his hands apart. Red half-moons from nails digging into flesh mark both palms. "It's all right," I soothe. "You are all right. No one was hurt."

Hugh lets out a shallow breath, as though he has been holding it since we left that treacherous alley. "It was my fault. I should have guessed."

"No more than I should have. We made a mistake."

"We could have died. You...Daniel would have killed me, and I would not have put up a fight."

"Hugh, never speak like that, do you hear me?" I say, my voice firm. "We are safe now. Yes, we should have considered it could be a trap, but..." Realization dawns, and my hand flies to my brow. "Julian Francis! Oh, we have been foolish indeed! Juliet and Frances, both victims. What a game this killer is playing!"

"I did nothing. I was useless," Hugh mutters, unable to process my words. "I heard the sound and recognized it immediately."

"You did not do nothing. You pushed me to the ground, before I even knew what was happening."

My words clearly do not have the intended effect. Hugh's time as a soldier left few physical scars, but many invisible to the eye. Even though he is much better than any other time since the war, he still does not quite trust himself. The past still haunts him. I ache for Hugh, yet can think of nothing to offer to ease the burden. The sound of gunshots triggered an old panic in him, transported him back to another land, another time, crouching in the trenches, the ground trembling as shells tore apart the earth and his comrades in the bargain.

"Do you think the shooter was missing intentionally?" I ask, trying to draw him back to the present, giving his mind a task on which to focus.

"Maybe. But we were shielded, and the shooter was likely firing from the building opposite."

"Then it was another warning. If they wanted to injure us or worse, they would probably have done so. Remember, we were easy targets walking down the street, looking for the house Julian Francis claimed was his. The shooter chose not to harm us. That is not to say this person will continue to spare us. If anything, this afternoon has demonstrated they are close to the end of their tether. I wish we could have rushed the building and cornered whoever it was. They took a risk, too, which means they are getting desperate."

"Desperation breeds danger."

"Not only for us," I say. "Many people may own a pistol or a rifle, not many would think to position themselves above their quarry and would know where to shoot to miss but close enough to frighten. I think our villain may have been a soldier."

Chapter 55

We arrive back in St. James weary, the rush of energy after the ambush having worn away. Hugh decides to stay at the flat. The shooter knows where our office is located. In case something happens, he does not wish Maeve, Kathleen and Aidan to be alone. There being three of them they are not alone, but Hugh needs to prove he is not a coward and I put up no protest. Before I leave, he catches my arm.

"Evelyn..." He hesitates, looks down.

"Yes?"

"Could you...do you have to tell Daniel about my reaction?" He glances up again, worry written across his features plain as day.

"No, I do not. There is nothing to tell. You pulled me to the ground. If you had not, who knows what might have happened."

"I froze -"

"You are allowed to be human. You are allowed to be afraid when we are shot at." I smile and give his arm an encouraging squeeze. "Get something to eat and don't sleep too late. Tomorrow we hunt down that murderous coward and lure him into the light."

My little speech is mostly bravado, I realize when I climb into my car, checking no one else is in the backseat first. *We could have been killed tonight.* My hands tremble as I grasp the wheel. I take a calming breath before turning on the engine. Forcing myself to focus on the road, I cannot shake the troubling thought my mind circles on an endless loop. In the moment, I was almost more occupied with Hugh than with the shooter. In hindsight, though, the encounter has left me badly shaken. We were aware that the person who killed Juliet, who entered her home, strangled her and rooted around before calling Priscilla, is ruthless and calculating. Mowing poor Frances down serves as additional proof of that. Yet even the threats Hugh and I were sent did not quite make me question the wisdom of accepting this case, of involving us in such a serious investigation. It is too late now to back away, and I meant what I told Hugh. I am more determined than ever to find Juliet's killer and bring an end to this horror. My determination, however, does not diminish the flutter of fear in my chest when I recall the events of today.

The house on Grosvenor Square is a sight for sore eyes, warm light radiating through the curtains, spilling onto the street. Still, I cannot bring myself to abandon the pleasant silence of the car just yet.

Should I be worried about Hugh? Was it right to promise keeping his reaction between the two of us? Am I doing him a service or disservice as a friend? Then again, he did pull me to the ground. His instinct was to protect. Maybe neither of us was truly in mortal danger, but Hugh's first impulse, when he recognized the danger, was to pull me out of harm's way. I owe him loyalty in turn.

Taking a few calming breaths, I peer around at the silent square to check for shadows, for lingering figures with ill intent. I see nobody but Mr. Malcom from three doors down with his wife Elspeth. I wave, then hurriedly climb the steps to our house before I am drawn into conversation with them.

"Good evening," Maisie says, coming down the hallway at the sound of the door, her hands already outstretched to take my coat and hat, when she pauses, her eyes narrowing. "You are very pale."

"I am well enough, thank you, Maisie." I smile in the face of her kind concern. "Mr. Lawrence and I ran into a spot of trouble today, but we are both fine."

"Goodness! Can I do anything for you? Mr. Harper isn't home yet. I can have dinner served in your room, if you prefer to rest."

"No, no, I will wait. But a stiff drink would not go amiss."

"Of course," she says, accompanying me to the sitting room. My eyes move to the curtains, open just a slit, and before I can do it myself, Maisie pulls them closed completely.

"Thank you." I sink onto the sofa, suddenly bone tired, every muscle stiff and sore as though I ran all the way from Paddington.

"Here you are." She hands me a glass with a generous measure of whisky. I raise my brows, but she nods and says, "Get that down you. It'll warm you up." I am in no mood to argue and take a sip of the fiery drink. Maisie does not move.

"Won't you join me?"

"I am working."

"Please?" I watch her hesitate, then pour herself a tiny glass of sherry. "Sit, sit." Maisie crouches on the edge of an armchair.

"If Terry could see me now. Sitting with a lady in a fine parlor, sipping sherry." Maisie smiles and shakes her head at the thought of her late husband's response to her change in circumstance.

"Do you miss him, Maisie?" I ask, the whisky loosening my tongue.

"I shouldn't say so, but no, or only very rarely. He had his good sides, Terry. By the time he died, though, I had almost forgotten they existed. Born troublemaker, but a kind man, mostly."

"Have you ever thought about remarrying?"

Maisie looks down at her glass, then meets my eye. "Of course. A girl has her dreams, even at thirty-four. But quite honestly, who would have me? The only men I meet are your fiancé and my brother, occasionally the grocer, or the butcher delivering his cuts, or the florist's boy." She shrugs. "And I am not unhappy. A peaceful life is not the most romantic notion, but when you have lived through all the turbulence a person can survive, it is an attractive prospect."

"A peaceful life does not have to mean a lonely one," I say carefully.

"No, it does not." She shrugs. "All the same, I have come to realize it is foolish to foster expectations."

"It is not foolish to hope," I say quietly, watching Maisie over the rim of my glass.

"I don't suppose it is. Although it is not wise to build one's life on hope either. I am still a romantic, but with time, I have become a realist as well. I loved Terry very much. He was charming and good to me for quite a while before things went sour. I still blame the war for how he became, but what use is it? The war is over and so is Terry's life. Mine is not." She takes a small sip, offering a smile, even if there is sadness in her eyes. I have seen that look before and wonder whether two people bearing such heavy burdens are truly a suitable match. Would Hugh drag Maisie down, or the other way round? But then we all have our loads to carry. Not one of us reaches adulthood without regrets, without some measure of sadness tucked into a corner of our minds. I can see them together, Hugh and Maisie, both quiet, kind, both looking for a chance to start again. Both deserving.

"I should see how Mrs. Kincaid is coming along with dinner." Maisie gets to her feet, her drink barely touched. I do not stop her as she hurries from the room. Maybe I overstepped with my questioning, still Maisie is more than a housekeeper to us. Even if she does not permit herself to acknowledge this, she has become a friend.

I lean back and close my eyes. Listening to the crackle of the fire in the grate, the hooting of an owl somewhere beyond the window. Then, jolting me upright, I hear the sound of the front door falling loudly shut, hurried footsteps. Daniel's voice is filled with urgency as he calls my name. It takes me a moment to react. By that time, he is standing in the doorway. His face is pale as milk. His eyes run the length of me, and only when he is on the sofa at my side does he speak.

"Evie," he begins in a strained voice, and I wonder at the reason for his agitation. "Can you tell me why the back of your car is riddled with bullet holes?" *Riddled?* I think in something of a stupor. The shooter left behind more than the one reminder I was aware of, it appears. I was in too much of a state of shock to check. "Evie? Are you hurt?" He takes my hands, his eyes searching mine. I swallow, realizing I must put him out of his misery.

"I am fine. I am not hurt." Daniel sighs and his shoulders sag.

"What happened? Were you shot at? Who did that? Did you call the police?"

For some reason, I cannot help a slightly manic giggle escaping my mouth, and Daniel gives me a look of unmistakable incredulity.

"I am sorry," I manage, now actually laughing to his bewilderment. Rubbing tears from the corners of my eyes, I say, "Sorry, it isn't funny. It has just been rather a strange day."

"I am glad you see the humor in it. I am afraid you will have to explain before I can join in." He hands me a hankie, and I dab at my eyes before blowing my nose.

"Hugh and I walked into a trap. We were overeager and did not notice the warning signs," I begin, explaining in as measured a manner as I can muster, what happened today.

"Have you called the police?"

"I will, I will," I promise, waving a dismissive hand. I know he is right. Someone must look at those warehouses. They will see bullet marks in the brick, if the holes in my beloved motorcar are not enough proof.

"Do you have any suspects on your list, people who were soldiers?"

"Juliet dealt largely with her contacts in the Secret Service Bureau and locals. The only soldier I can think of is Michael Ellroy. Victor Stanley, as a copper, likely knows how to shoot and his father and brother were in the army as well." I drop my face into my hands and shake my head before looking up again. "What a mess! Half the male population can probably fire a weapon thanks to that damned war! Heavens, you, Wilkins and Hugh certainly do, and Harold and Robert. Jeffrey I am not so sure about, bless him."

"It wasn't me or Hugh, that much you can be sure of," Daniel says, finally smiling a little. I poke him gently with my elbow.

"Women know how to shoot as well. We cannot discount anyone, really. Even I know how to use a shotgun from the clay pigeon games we played growing up. Though I could not claim great accuracy."

"The shooter, thankfully, was not very accurate either."

"I suspect it was intentional, to frighten, not to add another murder to the list. While both Juliet and Frances are the killer's victims - or intended victims - this person does not strike me as a serial murderer. They had Juliet in their sights, then Frances got in the way, and now Hugh and me. Their violence is, to them, self-defense, not a sadistic desire to kill as many as possible."

"So, if you stopped investigating, they would not kill again?"

"Maybe. There has been too much calculation to make me believe they are doing this out of bloodthirsty passion, but I have been wrong before. In any case, stopping the investigation is out of the question. Even if Hugh and I told Edith we could not continue, the police will not give up so easily."

"True enough," Daniel concedes. "And I know there is no point in trying to convince you otherwise. How was Hugh?"

"He pushed me to the ground. If the shooter meant to kill us, Hugh's quick thinking could have saved my life." I fall silent. Daniel pulls me closer, and I hear the rhythmic thump of his heartbeat. "Don't you ever wish you had settled down with a sensible lady?"

"Instead of the rogue that is Evelyn Carlisle?" I can hear the smile in his voice, though leaning my head against his chest I cannot see his face. "Never."

After I have called the police, explaining today's events, I take the tentative steps to the window and pull the curtain open, just enough to look onto the street and gated green beyond. My eyes rove around the darkness, settling on patches of light cast by the streetlamps. When they reach the edge of the green, I notice a figure leaning against the gate, barely touched by the illumination of the streetlight. I want to shrink back, but force my eyes to focus. The figure lingers, and I see a glimmer, the ember end of a cigarette hanging as if suspended in the darkness. Then he drops it and turns away. Did he mean for me to notice him? Was this our assailant, or simply a passerby? It is not terribly late, but this is a quiet neighborhood. I close the curtain and cross my arms with a shiver. If my intuition is right, this person not only knows where the flat is, but also the location of my future marital home. They knew I would be here, not in St. James, which leads me to suspect I have been followed before. The thought that whoever this person is knows so much about me, and I so little about them, profoundly unsettles me. But maybe I know more about them than I think, and it is precisely this fact that frightens them. I like the notion of the killer being afraid, too.

"What did the police say?" Daniel asks, appearing in the doorway.

"They are sending a sergeant to question me tomorrow morning. I suspect they think I am a bit mad."

"They got the measure of you quickly, then?"

"Very funny."

"Are you hungry?"

"Famished, but there is something I must tell you," I say, which is met by a rather dramatic sigh.

"I cannot leave the room for five minutes without trouble finding you, can I?"

"Maybe not."

"Go on." I tell him of the figure I spotted in the square, and he rushes over to the window. "Why didn't you call out? Wilkins and I could have gone to see!"

"You are always badgering me about being cautious, and now you reprimand me for not allowing you to throw yourself into the path of a potential killer?" I raise my brows meaningfully and cross my arms like an irritable mother, chastising her children.

"Well, all right, I take your point," Daniel replies like a sullen lad.

"Besides," I continue, more gently, reaching for his arm. "He disappeared in a flash. I might have imagined him, a mere shadow, were it not for the glint of his cigarette before he put it out."

"A smoker? Maybe…" Without another word, he strides into the hallway, a moment later, I hear the front door open. I hurry after him, but by the time I am in the hallway, he is halfway across the square. I watch him anxiously, walking towards the spot where I told him the figure lingered. He looks around, then bends to retrieve something before returning to the house.

"Daniel, what did you find?"

"Look what they dropped, it was definitely not a ghost. I think, if this person was our killer, we can assume it was a man." Daniel holds out something I recognize as a discarded cigar, wrapped in a hankie. "I do not know many women who have a fondness for these, none in fact."

"I have seen the odd lady sneak a puff, even if it is not considered the done thing, but I must admit, there are few I can name. Besides, the figure looked to be in possession of a rather broad set of shoulders, though that could have been an illusion."

"Does Michael Ellroy fit the description?"

"He was tall, though fairly slim. Besides, we cannot forget his alibi for Juliet's murder and for Frances' attack as well."

"He could be working with someone," Daniel suggests, placing the cigar stub on the table.

"What would be his motive? From what we read in Howard's diaries, I gather Ellroy was telling the truth about having been saved by Juliet. Why then, unless he is mad, would he wish to harm her? Why now?"

"He is married, is he not? Maybe he met Juliet and started an affair with her, his wife found out and she killed her. Have you interviewed Mrs. Ellroy?"

"She was out when we visited him. It doesn't quite add up. This killer is calculating and brutal. It takes force to strangle a person, even one as slight as Juliet. I suppose we can't discount the wife entirely, though. I will contact Ellroy again tomorrow. Maybe I can contrive a way to meet his wife."

"Leave that to the police, won't you? If you think she is in any way a possible suspect, she could be very dangerous and Ellroy, too, in case they are plotting together." Daniel holds my gaze, and I am forced to nod my assent. He is right, and after today's events, I am surprisingly willing to behave sensibly.

"I have promised to help Edith Ashbourne organize a fundraiser tomorrow in any case," I shrug listlessly. Daniel drapes an arm over my shoulder and leads me towards the dining room.

"That sounds perfectly respectable."

"Perfectly dull, more likely," I mope.

"I do believe you have had quite enough excitement recently, don't you?"

"Oh, well, I suppose," I agree reluctantly, thinking with regret of the interview I will miss with Mrs. Ellroy. "I hope there is something good for pudding, at least."

Daniel chuckles. "I am sure Mrs. Kincaid won't disappoint on that front. I think it is a frozen chocolate mousse."

"Do you know what other dish is best served cold?" I cannot help myself asking as he pulls out my chair.

"What?"

"Revenge," I reply with what I imagine is rather a mad grin.

"You are incorrigible." Daniel sighs.

"Would you have me any other way?" I ask, and the tension from the past hours finally dissolves as his mouth breaks into a smile, giving me my answer.

Chapter 56

The policemen who come to speak to Hugh and me at the office the next morning are strangers. I wonder whether this is better or worse than Stanton being involved. If he were, he would surely be more willing to lend credence to our claims, yet he would, undoubtedly, be quick to offer chastisement for our foolishness as well. It hardly matters, for we have to tell him what happened one way or the other. Hugh gives me a worried look when I mention having seen a man lingering in the square last night to the police officers. The two men seem vaguely indifferent, but it is the first thing Hugh asks about after they leave.

"You think it was a man?"

"I am fairly confident, which is not to say I am certain this person was the killer. It felt strange to know he might have been watching the house. There was no incident here last night?"

"No, everything was quiet. I ate with Maeve and Kathleen and played a bit with Aidan, that was all. It was a surprisingly pleasant evening, in fact." He shrugs. I wonder if now is a good time to broach the subject of romancing Maisie? Before I can speak, he continues. "Kathleen said she brought a cake up to Dulcie and Mr. Singh. Dulcie was sleeping, but she had a nice chat with him." Hugh lowers his voice. "I think she might be a little taken with him. She went on and on about his manners, observing that the beard and turban were actually rather masculine and becoming."

"A romance?" I ask, unable to stop myself.

"I doubt it will go that far. Kathleen is a staunch Catholic and he a Sikh. I think those differences would pose barriers for them, but maybe a friendship. Dulcie isn't the only one who feels lonely up in that flat, I believe."

"Speaking of lonely, I have to leave you on your own this morning. I promised Edith to stop by and help with preparations for a fundraiser the WI is hosting. Will you contact Hollis and tell him the man who called the paper yesterday was a hoax, or possibly even the murderer?"

"He'll be keen to hear the news. When I get back, I will try Stanton again, though I fear he will be less excited."

"I think you are right. Before I go to Edith's, I'll drop by the hospital and inquire after Frances'. Let us plan to reconvene here in the early afternoon."

I am relieved Hugh is himself again, not shaken anymore, or at least not visibly. His eyes are ringed with dark circles, but he rarely looks very well rested, so it is not unusual. I think he is happy to have a new task and, in sight of his eagerness, I warn him to be careful.

"There were six bullet holes in my car, I noticed this morning." I grimace. "Wilkins took it to a garage, and I won't get it back for some time."

"Sorry, Evelyn. I know you love that car," Hugh says, getting dressed for the cold, hat in one hand, scarf in another.

"Not as much as I value our lives," I reply with a shrug, though it did sting to discover the holes marring the otherwise smooth blue exterior of the Bentley. Once Hugh is gone, I write some notes about yesterday's events and sip a cup of tea Maeve brought, dipping a finger of shortbread into the milky brew. I have little inclination to go to Edith's house and chit-chat with her, Adeline and Priscilla. If only Aunt Louise would come, too. I eat another biscuit and lean back in my chair, closing my eyes, hoping this exercise will endow me with the wisdom of Poirot or the cleverness of Sherlock Holmes to knit the pieces of this puzzle together. We have one murder and one attempted. We have a spy with a mysterious past and a dead lover. We have medals of valor and a hidden cache of money. There are the WI, Howard Bell and his secrets, Michael Ellroy and his alibi, Victor Stanley, his family, their treatment of Juliet. The photograph. A stranger with a trigger finger and a possible penchant for strong cigars... What are we missing? I retrace my steps on the day we found Juliet's body. The cold flat, the disarray, Mr. Button who said he saw nobody. The people I met at the WI were strangers to me as they were to Juliet. Edith and Lloyd Ashbourne, Adeline and Graham Markby, Priscilla Lewis and about a dozen other women. I feel as if I am standing in front of the solution, but there is a veil obscuring my view. Every time I reach out to pull it aside, it slips from my grasp, elusive as a wisp of smoke, though sadly more opaque.

I open my eyes and blink a few times, but all I see are bright spots momentarily blurring my vision, not the longed-for answers. With a luxuriant, self-indulgent groan, I get to my feet and slip into my coat, wrapping a scarf around my neck and setting a wool hat on my head. Such an effort simply to leave the house! Summer – or what passes as such in this country – cannot come soon enough for my liking!

In the absence of my car, I take a taxi to the hospital. It is a short journey, but my driver is a chatty fellow. By the time we arrive, I know he has troubles with the wife, two good-for-nothing sons and a mother-in-law he has considered poisoning. I do not tell him that I am in the business of crime prevention, or at least in resolving it, and quickly slip out of the car, offering a handsome tip to remain in the chap's good graces.

I make my way along the by now familiar corridor, past nurses in their starched caps and harried looking doctors, hastening along. A different guard sits on a chair by the door to Frances' room. He accepts my explanation that I am her friend without question, which slightly alarms me. Anyone may say as much, but then I realize he has been told my name and was instructed to let me pass. All the same, any woman could claim to be me. I must have a chat with Stanton about Frances' safety. I suppose there is not much he can do, and I should be happy they listened and have kept a guard here for this long.

To my surprise, Frances is awake, though her gaze is bleary, and it takes her a moment to recognize me. Her face is pale and her cheekbones sharper than before, eyes set deeper into her skull, but she is alive and conscious, which gives me hope.

"How are you, Frances?" I ask softly, sitting down on the chair beside her bed. The room feels colder than it should be for an ailing patient, but I resist the urge to pull the thin blanket up to Frances' chin.

"Water, please," she stammers hoarsely, and I reach for a glass on her bedside table and bring it carefully to her lips. She sips, some droplets trickle out from the side of her mouth and I press a hankie into her hand. I think, even in this state, she would not like me mothering her, making her feel even more helpless than she must already.

"Better?" I ask, and she nods.

"What happened?"

I swallow, uncertain how to explain, then settling on, "You were involved in an accident."

"A car. I remember. I was crossing the street, and it drove at me. I heard the engine accelerating. Why...I don't understand."

"I do not understand it myself. Hugh, my colleague, and I have been investigating. Do you remember telling us a series of numbers and mentioning Queen Victoria Street?"

"Queen Victoria Street..." Her eyes are searching for a moment, her forehead creased with concentration. How terribly frustrating it must be for a woman as clever and independent as she is to feel so uncertain, to be trapped in a broken body, her mind trying to catch up to the present.

"Did you go there, Frances? The building contains safe deposit boxes," I whisper, though there is no one to listen in on our conversation. "Forgive me if we misunderstood, but we took your words as direction. We found the notebooks. Have you read them, Howard's notebooks?"

"Oh!" She groans and I worry I have upset her, but her expression is not one of anger or displeasure, but of recollection. "Yes, yes, I read them. Howard lied to me. I only found them the day before the accident." A single tear slips from her left eye, running slowly down her cheek and soaking into the collar of her nightgown.

"I am sorry, Frances. Maybe you did not want us to read them. Did I misunderstand?"

"No. I can't remember what I said, but I would have come to you the next day to let you know about them, or gone to the police. There were too many secrets already."

"We learned a while ago that Juliet worked as a spy. J is the person we take to be her in Howard's journals."

"I made the connection," she mutters with resignation. "They could have told me. Why did they not tell me? I spoke to Howard every day, and every day he lied to my face. It was a difficult time, the war years, I acknowledge that, but he could have told me later."

It is impossible to alleviate her sense of disappointment. Howard Bell is not here to explain himself, to face her questions. All I can do is listen and sympathize. Had I learned that Daniel kept such a substantial secret from me for years on end, I cannot think how hurt I would be. Frances will be torn between grief and anger, and I hope this burden will not impede her recovery.

"I would have helped Juliet, if she had come to me. I would have helped her without using her for some terrible task that could have seen her killed. She almost was, I believe," Frances says, her voice never rising above a whisper.

"Yes, she suffered, it is true, but I think she did not blame your husband. They remained friends, and he was there for her when she returned to England."

"Do you think they were more than friends, more than colleagues?"

"No. I truly do not. The notebooks suggest he viewed her more like a daughter than anything else."

"You do not send your daughter to war," Frances observes, her voice gaining some strength.

"The times were desperate. Everyone was trying to do their bit to help. Juliet needed a purpose," I offer.

"Maybe I should have noticed," Frances says after a moment of silence passes between us. "I was so excited to take on my new role at the museum. Perhaps I missed the signs. Perhaps Howard tried to tell me, but I didn't listen."

"I think he saw his silence as a means of protecting you. He was aware of many of the evils of this war, and he wanted to spare you. He likely suspected once he told you something, you would wish to know everything."

"You have the measure of him." She smiles for the first time. "And he would have been right. I would have wanted to know it all."

"Despite everything, he was trying to do his best by you, by Juliet and by the country."

Frances sighs and closes her eyes. I almost wonder whether she has fallen asleep, exhausted by our conversation, when she opens them again.

"In a way, I am glad her parents are not alive to hear how their daughter suffered. Then again, had they lived, she might have led an entirely different sort of life. She was pregnant?" Frances looks at me for confirmation. My expression must tell her what she wishes to know, for she gives a small nod. "Howard helped arrange...helped her get rid of the child."

"I have no proof it was so."

"We couldn't have children of our own," she says, her voice hoarse but measured. I cannot guess what thoughts are swirling around in her mind. Does she wish Juliet had kept the child? Does she resent Howard? Does she regret not being a mother? She lets out a weary sigh and asks, "Has reading Howard's notes helped you? Have you told the police?"

"I am afraid I handed over the journals," I admit, hoping she will not be angry that we took them from the safe deposit box.

"Good."

"The leading detective is a friend of mine. They are in reliable hands, and by rights, they belong to you."

"It does not matter to me now. He can burn them for all I care. I was going through Howard's belongings, a task I had avoided for months, when I found the key in an envelope with a short note addressed to me. It simply said, 'Forgive me'." She swallows, and I help her drink again before she can continue. "I read them right there, in that airless room. I could not, somehow, bear bringing them into my home, all those secrets, bound in paper."

"Lara said you seemed out of sorts the day of the accident."

"I had just learned my husband was a sort of spymaster who sent young people to their deaths, including a girl I thought I knew. She lied to me as well. We saw each other nearly every day when she worked here, and still she never thought to tell me the truth. The war has been over nearly a decade, surely there would have been no harm in being honest with me now. Howard must have known he could trust me."

"Perhaps he wished for you to see him as you always had."

Frances shrugs, or tries to, propped against cushions as she is. "It is the past, but for an archivist, the past is much closer to the present than we sometimes like to acknowledge. People come to the museum to look at the art, to imagine another time. They do not realize that what they see – the people in the portraits, the sculptures excluding those of deities, perhaps - are not much different than they are. Times may change, yet human beings rarely do."

"I cannot tell whether you are cynical or poetic," I tease, trying to lighten the mood.

"Oh, I have always been a pragmatist. You cannot spend so much of your life examining the drama of humanity – for that is the study of art history, after all – without shedding notions of romance." She sighs, clasping her hands together, as though they might give each other comfort. "What happens now?"

"You concentrate on getting better. Do not worry about anything else," I say, aware that my words cannot possibly make it so. Frances is a woman of action, and resting here, incapacitated and disappointed by what she has learned will be a struggle. I promise to bring something to read soon and bestow kind wishes from Jeffrey upon her before I bid my goodbye.

Waiting for a cab, I am enveloped by the icy wind howling down the street and I burrow into the collar of my coat. Clouds scud with haste across the blue sky and dried leaves dance around my feet. Everything seems in motion, except for me, static in the middle. I take a deep breath, feeling a tightening in my chest from the cold. What am I still missing?

The cab drive is shorter than I would have wished. This time the driver is silent, pleasant company. Inwardly, I ready myself for the assault of Adeline's rapid conversation and exuberance. My mind is still rehashing everything Frances said, trying to find an answer in her words. Ordinarily, a tall, almost formidable looking woman, she seemed so small in that hospital bed, broken bones and broken heart, as she recollected everything her husband kept from her. Nonetheless, I stand by my words. I think he believed he was protecting her, but men ought to realize women are far more resilient than they take us to be. Yet maybe they do know, and out of fear, have denied us the vote, material rights and autonomy for so long? But a confident man should not fear a capable woman. Perhaps Howard was not as strong as his wife thought him to be. His later journals paint a picture of fragility, of doubt that placed a tremendous burden on his mind. Frances will come to realize that he struggled with the secrets he kept, and that he did what he felt was right until he could not go back, to alter the way the woman he loved looked at him. I feel sorry to have left Frances alone, but she was growing tired. She noted that she was glad Juliet's parents did not live to see what had happened to their daughter, but such words are cold comfort. Juliet's parents would have mourned her, but they would not regret she was born because of the grief her death caused. The parents of fallen soldiers would doubtless feel the same. My aunt Iris, whose son Hamish was never found, would never hear of such a thing. The parents of the executed spies, of the mysterious M, felt their loss keenly, I am sure, but also their love for them. When the cab comes to a stop in front of Edith's house, I hesitate, my mind trying to hold onto a thought, while the driver waits for his fare.

M's parents, I think, slowly walking up to the house. Could they...? To find them, I would have to know his identity. If only Howard's notes had provided his name!

"Evelyn, come in from the cold!" Without having noticed the door opening, I find Adeline standing in the doorway, beckoning me into the warm hall. I paste a smile on my lips and accept her embrace. She smells of something sweet and is wearing a pair of burgundy trousers and a ruffled blouse today. "You are the first to arrive. Mother is reading something in the study. Won't you have a cup of tea? I must say, in this weather, I am sorely tempted to add a drop of whisky to it, but it is a little early for a tipple," she says, leading me into the sitting room where a fire crackles behind the grate. A tray of tea accoutrements and a three-tiered stand filled with various biscuits and diagonally cut, crustless sandwiches are already on the table. The room itself is comfortably furnished, not too opulent to overwhelm the eye, rather it is tasteful with dark blue sofas, a long, low table and lively seascapes in the style of Winslow Homer lining the walls. It is a rather masculine room, as it happens. Maybe Edith prefers it so, never one to enjoy an excess of frill and pomp, unlike her daughter. Adeline hands me a cup of tea. It is too sweet, and I only take a small sip, already looking around for a plant I can discreetly water with the rest.

"How have you been, Evelyn? I hope Mother has not been hounding you about solving this case! I told her, that is what the police are for, but the notion of a woman detective does so appeal to her, not that I disagree." Adeline smiles as she sinks into an armchair, motioning for me to sit on the sofa opposite.

"No, she has been very patient, a dream of a client."

"Has she indeed? I will tell her that. Be honest, did you think it odd that she took such an interest despite hardly knowing poor Miss Nelson?"

"I admit, it struck me as unusual, but she does feel a great responsibility for the members of the WI, and women in general."

"Yes," she observes with something akin to sadness in her eyes. I wonder whether her mother's projects and passions often left her daughter by the wayside. "For as long as I can remember, Mother has had her causes, which often include individuals she feels obligated to help."

"An admirable disposition."

"It is, but it also means other problems are not important enough to warrant her attention." Adeline speaks in a light voice, yet a niggle of resentment towards her mother is evident all the same. I cannot blame her. It must have been a challenge to be raised by a woman who championed causes as monumental as women's suffrage and was successful, too. Any childish complaint, any adolescent woe must have appeared inconsequential in comparison. Nonetheless, Edith always strikes me as a caring woman, though also as a woman not to be underestimated. Adeline had little choice but to follow in her footsteps, if she wished to earn her mother's respect.

"You think I am complaining?" Adeline asks, smiling.

"No, I don't," I reply honestly. "It must have been difficult at times, having a mother who was so confident about what she wanted and willing to stride towards her goals, no matter the obstacles."

"How she would love to hear you describe her in those terms!" Adeline claps her hands. "I shall tell her when she comes down."

"You seek to embarrass me!" I laugh and absentmindedly take another sip of the sickly-sweet brew, reaching for one of the ginger biscuits to dull the flavor.

"Not at all, my dear. I hope we can think of one another as friends?"

"Of course," I reply, though my eyes drift to the clock on the mantelpiece. I do not want to idle away the hours here, when I could be closing in on the killer. At the very least, I must speak with Stanton, ask if he found something in the journals that Hugh and I may have overlooked.

"Mother should be down soon, but we can begin without her. I am surprised Priscilla hasn't arrived yet. She is usually the epitome of punctuality. I suppose you spent some time speaking with her about the case? She was very shaken, poor thing. She lost a brother in the war, and her parents went a little doolally. She had to cope with quite a lot on her own before she married. Her husband is a dear, though."

Priscilla lost a brother? Yes, I remember it now, she told me she was annoyed with Juliet for begging off on Armistice Day, because her brother had been killed in the war and it was an important event for her. My head feels fuzzy, and I lean back against the sofa cushion.

"It was something we bonded over, actually. Graham lost a cousin, but it is different for the likes of Pris and me," Adeline says, pulling me out of my thoughts. "Lost brothers. Dead brothers."

I look up and meet a challenge in Adeline's eyes.

"I am sorry. I did not know," I say slowly, watching her as she watches me.

"No, you wouldn't. Mother never speaks of him, of Marcus."
Marcus.

My mind begins to swim. M. Marcus. I swallow, but my tongue is heavy and thick. I feel I cannot breathe and shrink back in my seat.

"When he died, Mother threw herself into her work, replaced one love with another and left me behind," Adeline continues, her gaze fixed on me. "Well, not entirely. I had Papa. We were bereft. Papa sold his company, retired early, hardly left his study for weeks on end. I did not know Graham then and was alone in my sorrow. But you appreciate the endless well that is grief, don't you Evelyn? You suffered your own losses."

I do understand, I understand far more than I expected to from this visit. I understand, I may very well be sitting across from Juliet's killer.

Chapter 57

I realize I should try to run, but my body feels strangely frozen in place, heavy, immobile. Something isn't right. I feel my heartbeat quicken and realization dawns. The tea! I knew it tasted strange. She must have –

"Just a little something to keep you calm," Adeline says, nodding at the cup as if she has read my mind. "Mother is enjoying a similarly pleasant rest upstairs. When I heard your aunt could not come, I thought what better opportunity to speak to you alone."

"Priscilla?" I ask, forcing myself to concentrate. I did not drink much and have to stay awake.

"Oh, Pris?" Adeline waves a dismissive hand. "I told her we had to postpone. She is an understanding woman. I knew she would not make a fuss."

Something still does not seem right. Adeline the killer? Can it be, or is she mad? She has drugged me and her mother, lured me here. I try to order my thoughts. If Marcus is M and he was killed, how did Adeline connect him to Juliet? And why kill the person her brother loved? Was it envy? Some sort of distorted claim on his affections?

"Why?" I manage, my eyes darting to the table. Unfortunately, I notice there is not a single knife or anything I could use to defend myself. Adeline takes a slow, deliberate breath and folds her hands in her lap. She is the picture of innocence and yet…

"If you knew someone had set the fire that killed your parents, would you not wish to see them punished?"

"It was an accident," I say.

"Imagine it was arson. Imagine it was murder."

"I suppose…"

"I knew you would understand," she says with the smile of a satisfied teacher, praising her pupil. "And if the police neglected to penalize the perpetrator, what would you do, clever woman that you are, with all the resources you could wish for at your disposal?"

"Adeline -" I begin, aware of what she wants to hear, but unwilling or unable to say the words.

"Think about it, Evelyn. You would take matters into your own hands. You would, I know it. I have watched you and admire you. It was my judgment that kept you alive last night. You might have been killed."

"What?" I ask, my foggy mind working to catch up with her words.

"Oh, dear, you are addled, aren't you? And I had so been looking forward to an intelligent conversation. Nothing to be done, though." Slowly, as If I am an imbecile, she goes on. "It was me who kept you from harm yesterday. I said it was enough to frighten and not kill you. Now I am wondering whether that was the right decision. Maybe I should have listened."

"You shot at us? It was you?" I cannot quite fathom what she is saying, unable to imagine this bright, chatty woman as a cold-hearted killer, lurking in the window of an abandoned warehouse, waiting for us as if we were her prey.

"Evelyn, Evelyn, Evelyn." She shakes her head, frowning. "I am disappointed. You were close, so close it was only a matter of time, especially when you put that photo of Marcus in the paper. I expected someone to recognize him, and you would have the police on us. Clever, quite clever, I won't lie. I admired the way you conducted yourself. I hoped the little present I sent would frighten you off, but you are hardier than I credited. We could have been friends." Adeline sounds genuinely disheartened. "Do you truly think me capable of shooting at you? Despite Mother's insistence that women and men possess the same set of skills, I fear I do not hold with that notion. Heaven's, I have never shot so much as a hunting rifle. I am not inclined to violence. You see how civilized I am? Have another biscuit!" She lets out a laugh. It sounds shrill to my ears.

My mind is spinning, and I clutch the edge of the sofa to steady myself. If she is telling the truth, I can guess who took on the task of attempting to frighten off Hugh and me. There are few options, really. Even in my current state, I can see the pieces of the puzzle slotting into place.

"Your father," I say, certain I am right. Adeline claps, confirming my suspicion.

"Well done! I thought you might suspect poor Graham, but he is entirely in the dark. Nonetheless, he was a great help to us, even if he did not realize it."

"His work…" I stammer. "The War Office."

"Precisely! Now we are getting somewhere." Adeline cocks her head and smiles, as if I am a child and she is pleased with me. In a way, this analogy is not too far from the truth. I feel helpless and small, though we are not, in truth, an unequal physical match. She has taken care of that, of course. My muscles feel like jelly, and if I got to my feet, it would be no challenge for her to prevent my escape. I must keep her talking, for I do not wish to know what she has planned for me. Where is the staff? Surely, someone knows I am here, someone must come to my aid. I try to calm myself, breathing slowly. *I only drank a little, I only drank a little*, I remind myself, hoping the words can force away the effect of whatever drug Adeline used to sedate me.

"Graham didn't understand what he was doing, the poor love. When I met him and learned of his place of employment, I cannot deny it strengthened the attraction. I knew he would help me. He is terribly conscientious, my dear Graham. Yet like many other men, even my darling husband still underestimates women."

"You gained access to the files on wartime spies?"

"It took some time for me to discover Marcus was a spy! He never told us anything, would you believe it? When we heard he had been killed, we assumed it was driving an ambulance, as he had claimed to be doing. Two years later, a Frenchman who knew him at the time of his death came to see us. He was ill, dying, and he wanted us to know the truth. He had been captured, too, you see, and in the labor camp he contracted an illness that never quite released its hold on him. He died a few months later. Jacques was his name."

"What did he tell you?" I ask, curious even in my muddled state, quite certain her words will confirm my suspicions, her motive and her father's for what they did. I had guessed it before, when we first read Howard's diaries. I could not then know who took vengeance upon themselves, but I suspected the need for revenge had fueled the murderer's desire to kill Juliet.

"Jacques loved Marcus. I think he might have been in love with him." Adeline raises her brows. "He was my brother's contact when he was sent to France and they got on well, worked secretly to move information into the right hands, to smuggle people out of danger. I tell you, I could hardly believe my ears! Marcus was a wonderful man, the best older brother a girl could have wished for. Naturally, I thought him courageous, but this? No, I never expected it, never!"

"Did he speak of Juliet?"

"He called her Minette. They had false names. Marcus was Louis. He spoke decent French, had a real ear for it, while I always struggled with languages at school. He helped me, was better than the tutor Mother hired." She pauses, smiles a tiny, private smile before continuing. "Marcus and I were the best of friends. He was only a few years older, and he always treated me as an equal, never pulling my plaits or ignoring me. I thought we had no secrets from each other. He wrote so many letters when he was away during the war, all filled with lies. How could he not have trusted me with the truth?" Adeline stares at me, for the first time appearing vulnerable, seeking an answer I cannot give.

"Marcus was conscientious and sworn to secrecy. Maybe he did not wish to worry you," I say slowly. If I can keep her talking, maybe the effects of the drug will wear off. Even so, I must play along, acting weary and incapacitated lest she think me a threat.

"Maybe so. He was a good man," Adeline observes, sounding dissatisfied, the corners of her mouth dipping in displeasure.

"What else did Jacques tell you?"

"They were captured two days apart. First him, then Marcus. Minette five days before them. Jacques said Marcus was careless with worry and that got him in trouble." Her expression hardens. "Yet from what he told me next, it wasn't Marcus' carelessness that got him killed."

"It was Minette?" I suggest.

"You know?"

"I guessed. You think she betrayed him. He was caught and executed because of information she gave their captors."

"And she got sent to the camps. She bargained away my brother's life and lived!" The anguish in Adeline's voice is unmistakable.

"Did Jacques have proof?"

"He overheard his guards. They spoke of the English woman pretending to be French who snapped under pressure like a twig and told them all they wished to know. Marcus was not the only one who suffered a cruel fate because of her. She deserved her punishment, she deserved it all and more."

I consider saying that Juliet loved Marcus, that she would not have betrayed him. But I remember the scars, the signs of torture she bore and think how little I truly knew her. How can I be sure she did not break? How could I be certain I would not do the same in such circumstances? Or Adeline herself, for that matter. All of this I do not say, for I am faced with a killer, who will not hear my words for what they are meant to be, only find evidence of my enmity within them.

"Marcus was a good man, still a boy, really. When we got the telegram..." Adeline swallows, and I allow myself to feel a pinch of sympathy. "Mother cried. I had never seen her cry before. She stood right there." She points at the door. "And she wept like never before or since. Papa was more stoic at first, but he unraveled from the inside even as mother managed quickly to swallow down her grief and move on. He could not concentrate on work, could not sit still. Some nights he did not come home at all. I never knew where he went and never asked. I was alone. The visitors who came to offer sympathy could not comprehend my solitude, and I couldn't bear the pity in their eyes. They handed out their condolences, while their sons and brothers and husbands and fathers were still alive. No one noticed me. I was invisible, gone like Marcus, but alive still. Do you know how it feels to awaken every morning for months with a thread of hope for just a few seconds, only to realize the world is without the person you most loved in it? There is no pain like the pain of the survivor," she says, and tears glitter in her eyes. Could this grief-stricken woman truly have conspired with her father to commit murder? I don't want to believe it, but I know it is true. She is right in claiming Hugh and I would have guessed the truth soon enough, all the clues were leading this way. As I suspected, it was the identity of the man in the photograph who would slot all the pieces into place. My thoughts begin to settle. I wonder how much of the sedative Adeline gave to her mother to incapacitate her for so long, and where is her father? I have no time to contemplate these questions, for Adeline finds her voice again, and I dare not let my attention wander.

"Jacques said Marcus and Juliet were lovers. I believed him. Among Marcus' effects was a photograph of a light-haired young woman. That makes it even worse. She could not have truly loved him, if she betrayed him so. She understood the stakes, knew what would happen. Jacques said people were caught and executed to prove a point by the enemy, to show their strength."

"I believe that is true," I admit.

"You see?" Adeline sounds as though she has forgotten we are not on the same side. "I told Papa that same night, and it was the first time in months I saw him appear affected by anything. He paced about the room, eyes blazing. I had to beg him to keep his voice down, not to wake Mother."

"You did not confide in her?" I ask in disbelief.

"Why should I have? She moved on as if Marcus never existed. She never spoke of him. Do you see a single photograph of my brother in this room? No. And you won't find one in the rest of the house either."

"I am sure she hasn't forgotten -"

"No, but she wishes she could, which is just as bad!" Adeline's voice grows louder, and her hands are clenched tightly in her lap. She is such a strange contradiction of prim society lady and unhinged madwoman!

"Your father was different?"

"I knew he would be. We became determined to discover who this Minette was, if she survived the camps. It would not be an easy task. We only knew she was English and a spy like Marcus. How to continue from there? We did not even know her real name. It was thanks to Graham that we discovered what we did, even if I had to be rather sly in that respect."

"Graham is truly unaware what you and your father have done?"

"Innocent as a lamb, poor darling. I might have stolen his keys to the office and given them to Papa on a few occasions. It was hard work trawling through the files. He finally found Juliet's, though. Howard Bell had recruited her and Marcus to work under the codename Nike. I looked it up. She was the Greek goddess of victory, but you would know that. Quite presumptuous of him, don't you agree? Papa and I sought him out, but he refused to speak with us. We were not deterred. We knew her name and that was more than nothing. It took months to find her and when we did, it was pure coincidence! We had gone through registries, Papa bribed officials for access to records, but nothing, not a sign. I thought Howard Bell's refusal to speak about Juliet signified she was still alive. He did not even speak about Marcus, which angered Papa. Maybe it was for the best he died shortly thereafter, or Papa might have helped him along." She raises her brows, as if I could have missed the meaning of her words. "We had to be careful. At that point, all I wanted was to confront the woman who caused the death of my beloved brother. I truly had no intention of harming her. I just wanted to know more, wanted to know what had happened." As she speaks, I feel I could be placing the words into her mouth. I know the ending to this story, but she needs to tell it. Besides, the longer she talks, the longer I have to come up with a way to escape. For one matter is abundantly evident, she is not making her confession intending to let me go. Another thought crosses my mind, and not for the first time, where is Lloyd Ashbourne?

Still I ask, "What changed your mind?"

"I was in the museum one day, we had a WI outing and were given a tour, when I saw her. There she stood, the woman from the picture, hardly changed despite the passage of so many years. Her hair was white blond, she was slim as a whippet, serious, though she smiled in the old photograph. I recognized her in an instant. I had spent countless hours staring at the small likeness, I had no doubt. She was carrying a book and papers and went into an office. I found out more in that afternoon than I had in months. She worked at the museum. I waited for a few days before telling Papa, following her, watching. She left work a few times with Frances Bell, Howard's wife as I knew her to be, for I had done my research. Did she know? I wondered."

"What happened then?" I ask, at odds with myself, both wanting to hear and wishing to drown out this terrible moment of truth when her story will reach the moment of Juliet's death.

"Papa wanted to confront her immediately. He had waited so long, borne his grief with outward stoicism, but I begged him to wait. I wanted to learn more about her, examine what sort of life she lived now. Did she have a husband? Children? Had she forgotten Marcus?"

"She had done none of that," I say quietly. "She lived almost as if she was not here at all."

"Which was even more insulting! She survived, had given up my brother only to lead this nothing of an existence? I couldn't bear it! She should have been dead, not Marcus. He would have known how to live."

"So, you followed her home," I continue for her.

"I had an idea," she says. "I thought, what better way to come into contact with this woman than if she joined our institute? She was always alone, so I thought she might be receptive. I instructed Priscilla to send out invitations to several houses in the neighborhood, not to arouse suspicion. To my surprise, Juliet came. Truthfully, I felt little confidence that she would. When I asked her what brought her to us, she told me she was curious and wanted to interact more with other women. You cannot imagine how I had to grit my teeth to smile at her."

"What did you make of her when you met?"

"What did you?" Adeline surprises me with her question, with the eagerness in her eyes as she awaits my reply.

"I thought she was a little distant, shy maybe."

"Cold is what she was. I cannot comprehend how my bright, clever brother was enticed by this dull, frigid person. The light she stole from the world in betraying him was not replaced by her, that much is certain."

"When did you decide to kill her?"

"I didn't simply *decide*. I am not some ruthless monster. Do you remember when we all gathered at my house?" I nod. "Papa and Graham were there, too." I vaguely recollect exchanging a few words with Graham, though not with Lloyd Ashbourne, who remained separate from the group. "Papa saw her there up close for the first time, and that night he came to my house again. While Graham was in his study, he told me he could not bear to live in a world shared with her. He wept, Evelyn." Adeline shakes her head and tears glisten in her own eyes. "I could not stand to see him lost to such despair. I told him not to worry, we would make a plan. So we did."

"You expected her to be at the Armistice Day event, so your father disguised his voice and called Priscilla," I say.

"A small but important detail."

"Did you do it together?"

"I knew from previous observations that the building's caretaker is a sleepy old fellow. In fact, he had drifted off at his desk when we slipped past him. I knocked on Juliet's door and she opened it to let me in, not seeing Papa pressed against the wall. I left the door open just a crack. When Juliet offered me tea, Papa rushed in and grabbed her from behind. I won't lie, it was more violent than I had expected. She fought, but Papa was a soldier once, too, and never let himself grow weak or run to fat as many do. She had no chance, none at all, just like Marcus."

"You ransacked the flat to make it look like a burglary?"

"We did have a bit of a root about. I thought she might have something belonging to Marcus, a memento, but there was nothing. The faithless creature had erased him from her life, just as she had condemned him to his death." Adeline takes a deep breath. "But you found the photograph, didn't you?"

"It was hidden under a floorboard along with her medals. She scratched her name away. She was not proud of her work."

"Too late. Regret, if she felt any, came too late. We would never have forgiven her in any case."

"Did she understand why you wanted her dead?" I ask, thinking of the terror Juliet must have felt too often in her life. Maybe she did betray Marcus under great duress, but she punished herself for it in all the years since, keeping herself separate from the world, forming no friendships, finding no new lover or husband, never building a family. She suffered until the end.

"I told her. I wanted her to know." Adeline's voice has acquired a steely edge.

"And Frances?"

"She knew too much. She was a threat. When I saw her at the funeral, I felt it."

"Did you drive the car?"

"I am good for something. Papa was too shaken after Juliet. He had regrets, couldn't sleep. The guilt weighed on him. My poor father."

"Do you think this was what Marcus would have wanted?" The question slips past my tongue before I have a chance to swallow it, but I am tiring of this game. If Adeline is acting alone now, I could probably escape. I have kept her talking long enough to regain some clarity of mind, even if my muscles still feel stiff.

"Juliet cost Marcus his life!" she hisses at me, anger breaking her placid veneer. Good, anger frightens me less than the mask she has been wearing since I met her. "She got what she deserved."

"She saved lives. She was brave, just like your brother." Provocative, I know, but I want to bring this farce to an end. For a while, I have been eying the silver tray with the pot of sugar and the small jug of lukewarm milk. It is heavy with sharp edges. More importantly, it is within easy reach. My fingers feel restless with a yearning to snatch it up, to stun Adeline and make my escape, yet I am afraid of hurried movements in case she will call for her murderous father. Again, I wonder where he is, and where is the household staff? "Did your father come to watch my house last night after the shooting?"

"Your house?" Adeline grins and waggles her forefinger. "Not quite yet, is it? Naughty, naughty! I don't know if he went to Grosvenor Square. He wasn't pleased with the way it had gone earlier. He felt squeamish about Frances and let me take care of it, but he disliked you."

"Does he smoke cigars?"

"Naturally."

"The man outside the house was smoking them. He left one behind, half-smoked."

"Clumsy of him," she observes with an indifferent shrug. "You really ought to be sleeping. I drugged you as a mercy." Adeline gets to her feet, startling me, but she does not pounce, rather begins pacing in front of the fireplace. The fire spits orange embers and blue flames lick hungrily at the blackened logs. As my eyes follow Adeline's progress, they travel to the stand beside the hearth, the stand which holds a sharp-edged poker. I wince inwardly at the mere thought of using it against another person, but what choice do I have? If only I can get to it.

"Where is your father, Adeline? What are you planning to do? The police are close to the truth. Give up now. You avenged your brother. Now you must stop, don't you see?"

"I can't," she says, stopping to face me, her eyes wide, hands spread out. I could run at her, push her and she would fall back into the fire! And yet...I cannot do it. Is it the drug, my conscience or fear preventing me?

"You can," I say firmly.

"It is too late, Evelyn. It is entirely too late."

"Where is your father?" I ask again, my eyes searching hers. She is crying now, tears stream down her rosy cheeks. Has the hunger for retribution reduced this woman I knew as a bright, cheerful person to a liar and a murderess?

"He regretted it," she says, almost as if to herself, and a look of disappointment flits across her face. A terrible suspicion blossoms in my mind, and my thoughts turn back to a few moments earlier. *He had regrets. He disliked you.*

Slowly, I push myself up, steadier on my feet than I anticipated. Still, I grab the arm of the sofa for effect. My head swims a little, but I try to focus. I am taller than Adeline, though likely weaker at the moment. I suspect she gave me and her mother laudanum, masking it with too much sugar. But what of her father? Adeline has not moved. She is weeping openly now, her cheeks glistening with tears.

"The war is like a wound that never quite heals," I say quietly, taking a tentative step. "If it had not happened, everything might have been very different." My aim is to keep her calm long enough for me to reach the door. Screaming will not do me much good, I have concluded. No conscious person seems to be in the house except for Adeline and me.

"I am not happy about what I have done, Evelyn. I am not a monster, but I loved my brother and my father and even my mother, absent though she may have been. Although I failed to protect Marcus, I can protect Father." *Your notion of protection is deeply flawed, if my suspicions are confirmed*, I think yet do not dare to say. How many steps until I reach the door? Eight, nine, ten? I am not sure. Added to that, it is closed. Did she lock it?

"Of course." I nod. She looks at me, searching for understanding and I do my best to convey it, even as fear courses through me. Warring emotions threaten to betray me. I need to get away, but I must find out what she has done to her parents.

"I could have borne Marcus' death, but to know he was betrayed, to know the person who deceived him lived…No, no, it could not be tolerated." Adeline paces again, making a swiping motion with her hand, like a scythe slicing through the air, cutting down the very notion.

I take another step back, then one more. She is distracted by her own agitation. Am I far enough from her to run and reach the door? Will I be able to open it before she is upon me? Will I have the strength to ward her off? My chest is tight with dread. She is closer to that sharp poker now than I am. Maybe I should have tried to attack her, but I am not strong enough to fight her off, should it come to it.

"Now that woman is gone, but Marcus is still gone, too. I am so alone. I am all alone." Her words escape her mouth in a wail. They are directed more at herself than me. I am close to the door, my body tense, my hand behind my back, ready to feel for the knob, when there is a sound at the front door. A banging that makes me wince and draws Adeline's attention. She ceases her pacing, stands stock still, wide eyes on me. It cannot have escaped her that I am inching my way out of the room. I hesitate only a moment before turning and running to the door, wrenching it open then quickly closing it behind me. I hear her footsteps and pull the door knob with the force of my full weight, lest she try to pry it open.

"Let me out! Let me out!" she shrieks and rattles the handle.

"Help! Help!" I shout, hoping whoever was at the door won't have left. The hallway is dim, but I turn my head to see the silhouette of a person through the milky glass panels. Hands cup the glass, a face peers inside, distorted and indistinct.

"Evelyn?" A faint voice comes from outside, barely loud enough to be heard over Adeline's shrill screams and banging against the door. I do not know how much longer I can hold it, my grasp is weakening, hands slippery with perspiration. "Evelyn!" the voice calls out again. This time I recognize it with a flutter of my heart. Hugh!

"Yes, Hugh! Get help, I cannot come to the door!"

"I'm coming!" he shouts, while Adeline curses me. She sounds like a rogue beast in that room, and I hope Hugh hurries.

"Let me out!" A kick to the door and the wood shakes in its frame.

Suddenly there is a clattering, the sound of breaking glass, an iron doorstop flies through the window at the side of the door, a hand wrapped in a scarf reaches inside to find the doorknob. The front door swings open and Hugh barrels into the hallway, face red with exertion and strain.

"Adeline and Lloyd Ashbourne killed Juliet!" I cry. Hugh's eyes search around the hallway. He grabs a decorative cricket bat mounted on the wall.

"Move to the side on three," he says, holding out the bat, ready to swing. I hesitate, yet my fingers are losing their grip, my arms weak. I have no choice but to obey. As soon as I do, the door flies inward, followed by the sound of something clattering to the ground, of a body stumbling. Hugh does not waste a moment, and rushes forward, ready to pounce on Adeline's prone figure, as she fell into the room from the momentum of the opening door.

"Call the police, Evie!" Hugh shouts, pinning a wildly protesting Adeline to the ground. Rather absurdly, she is now crying out for her mother and proclaiming that she is a respectable lady and Hugh must release her. I am in a daze, but manage to find the telephone and make the call before hurrying back to Hugh with a ball of twine I found, to bind our prisoner.

"Here, tie her up until the police arrive. I have to look for Edith and Lloyd. I am afraid she has poisoned them," I say, hardly knowing how I will find the strength in my jelly legs to climb the stairs. Taking a firm hold of the bannister, I slowly make my ascent, hearing Adeline's protestations grow fainter as I reach the upper level. It is dark and I fumble to turn on the light in the hallway. "Edith!" I call out, fear in my voice. What if I am wrong and Lloyd is up here, waiting to attack? *I should have taken some sort of weapon*, I curse myself. But if he were lucid, would he not have come to his daughter's aid? "Edith? Lloyd?" I call out, opening one door after another, finding empty bedrooms, a linen closet. Two doors remain closed, and I swallow before pushing the first open. A gasp escapes my lips, for the shadow of a motionless figure is distinct even in the faint light. I rush forward, pulling open the curtains, allowing the afternoon sun to stream inside, illuminating Edith Ashbourne lying flat on her back upon a made-up bed. Shuddering, I press my lips together and step closer, reaching out a hand to touch her wrist. She is alive! Her skin is warm, her pulse slow but steady. "Thank goodness," I whisper. "Help is coming, Edith." I give her hand a gentle squeeze, then hurry back into the hall and throw open the door to the opposite room. It is dark as well, but the darkness in here is more suffocating. "Mr. Ashbourne? Lloyd?" I say, edging my way across the room, past the bed and the man in it, towards the window. Light illuminates the room, but I do not want to see what it reveals. I take a slow breath and turn. It is as I suspected. Lloyd Ashbourne rests on the bed, lying on his back just like his wife in the next room. A finger to his wrists, his neck, a search for a pulse, for his chest to rise and fall, is a futile endeavor. His body is not yet cold, but he is dead. It is over. Adeline was right, she is all alone now.

Chapter 58

I leave the room with Lloyd's corpse growing cold, closing the door behind me. Before returning to find Hugh and Adeline, I take a few deep breaths to compose myself. We were too late. A murderess killed a murderer, is there some sort of justice in that? I cannot decide. My head is spinning with everything that has happened.

"Why did you come here?" I ask Hugh in the hallway. He has trussed up Adeline and placed her on the sofa in the sitting room while we wait for the police to arrive.

"It was your aunt, actually." He goes on to explain that Louise telephoned the office in quite a state. She had seen the photograph in the paper and was convinced she recognized the man as Marcus Ashbourne, the son Edith never mentioned, who died in the war. "It was not difficult to connect the dots, but I thought Edith, not Adeline, was the killer."

"Oh, it is far more complicated than that, Hugh." I sigh and sink onto the bottom step. "Lloyd Ashbourne is dead. Edith is unconscious in the next room."

"Dead? I don't -"

"He was the one who killed Juliet. He and his daughter planned it together. Apparently, Edith knew nothing, and I am inclined to believe Adeline. She drugged Edith and me, but I did not drink all the tea. She was trying to make it easier to kill me without a struggle."

"And Frances?"

"Adeline drove the car. Lloyd had grown regretful, apparently. I think she believes it was merciful to kill him, to save him from prison. She knew we were close to learning the truth, and the police, too. The game was almost up. Perhaps she didn't even mean to kill me, I can't be sure. It is possible she merely sought a confessor before it was all over."

"What of her husband?"

"He is unaware, or so she claims. It was through his work at the War Office that she learned Minette Laurent was Juliet Nelson."

"If Louise had caught you before you left, the situation today would have been very different. We would have called the police, and they could have made the arrest."

"Louise will feel terrible, even if it is not remotely her fault."

"Two people are dead, and another badly injured in the hospital and for what?"

"Do you remember we speculated that the murder was revenge?" I ask, Hugh nods. "They thought Juliet betrayed Marcus in captivity, that she was the reason he was executed." Hugh shakes his head.

"Sometimes I think the war will never release us."

"We can never be entirely certain what really happened. Juliet is gone, so are Marcus and Howard." Before I can continue, we hear a sound and a helmeted constable pokes his head through the door. What follows is a series of interviews, tedious questioning consisting of me repeating Adeline's story again and again. A doctor is called for Edith, and Hugh insists the man examine me as well. Just as we are allowed to leave, two men carry the body of Lloyd Ashbourne down the stairs on a stretcher. He is covered by a sheet, still I shudder as they pass by.

Hugh tucks my hand into the crook of his elbow and leads me away. The murder is solved, one of the killers apprehended, the other dead, but I feel no satisfaction. The cab takes us to Grosvenor Square, where Maisie ushers us inside, and registering our strange mood, offers to make coffee and sandwiches. I feel bone weary, likely an after-effect of the drug, or the shock of Adeline's confession and discovering Lloyd's body. I slump into an armchair and close my eyes.

"I will give Daniel a ring at the office," Hugh says and leaves the room. A frantic knocking at the front door follows and I groan, expecting more police interviews. However, the voice that sounds down the hall is not that of an eager copper or Lucas Stanton, but of my aunt. Louise bursts into the room and I open my eyes, seeing her curls in disarray, eyes wild.

"Oh, thank heavens!" she exclaims, rushing to my side. "When I spoke to Hugh, he said you could be in danger and he had to hurry. You are well, aren't you, dear?" Her eyes run over me, hands reaching for mine.

"I am. But I have something to tell you, and you best sit down for it." Louise gives me an uneasy look, then sits on the edge of the sofa, hands on her knees. She lets out more than one gasp of shock and surprise when I explain what happened.

"Oh dear! Poor Edith will not be happy with the resolution of this case," she observes, shaking her head and leaning back against the cushions.

"We did not truly solve it. I only realized the truth when it was too late. I guessed it before Adeline confessed, but too late to prevent her killing again."

"You brought an end to this, which is far from inconsequential. The police plodded along, while you and Hugh investigated. Even the photograph in the paper was your idea. Had that not happened, I would not have seen it, and Hugh may not have arrived in time."

I cannot but smile in the face of my aunt's encouragement, though I do not feel I deserve it. "Edith is a widow now, and she may lose her only remaining child as well."

"Yes," Louise sighs, looking down and smoothing the front of her skirt. "I cannot imagine how she will go on, yet I know her and trust she will cope somehow."

"She will regret having hired us."

"Maybe," Louise replies with a shrug. "But Edith has a strong sense of right and wrong. I believe she would classify her husband and daughter's behavior as the latter."

"Even at the cost of losing her remaining family?"

"The coming months will not be easy for her." She hesitates, twisting a ring on her finger before asking, "Do you believe Juliet betrayed Marcus?"

"I cannot prove the claims this man, Jacques, made were false."

"If it is true..." Louise pauses, biting her bottom lip before continuing. "If Juliet betrayed him, I cannot bring myself to condemn her for it." She meets my gaze. "How do any of us know we would be stronger, better able to resist, given such dire circumstances?"

"Harold said she was probably tortured."

"The poor girl. She was trying to be brave, and what did she get for it? Captivity, her lover killed, living with such guilt, then being murdered. No, I cannot feel anything but sorrow for her."

"So do I."

"Undoubtedly, the Ashbourne's and Adeline suffered, yet is it an excuse to inflict so much more pain? Harming Juliet did not make them happier, after all."

"Vengeance follows a similar path to war. It never quite ends, and the effects are felt like tremors in the wake of an earthquake. Would Lloyd and Adeline have been satisfied if they had never been caught? She said he had misgivings about what they had done. With time, they would surely have realized that Juliet's death and the attack on Frances did nothing to alleviate the pain of their loss. Killing cannot make you feel better, can it?" I look at my aunt, not certain I can expect an answer.

"I suppose there are some cruel, mad souls who find pleasure in it, though I do not believe Lloyd and Adeline quite fit that description. I pity them, despite the madness of their actions. I cannot but wonder what I would have done in their shoes. What is anyone capable of when a piece of their heart has been cut away? Make no mistake, when you have a child, they take residence in your heart, and when they are stolen from you, a part of you dies with them. I lost a child before Briony, though I carried him or her only a few months. A part of me mourns the loss still. What sort of grief does a parent or a sibling feel for a person they knew more than two decades? It is impossible to imagine, and I do not want to try."

"Juliet was someone's child, too, even if her parents are dead."

Louis sighs and nods. "True enough. I am not excusing what Adeline and her father did, only trying to comprehend how two people I thought to be decent, caring individuals could be compelled to commit the worst acts of villainy? Love, or rather passion, is the only force I can think of strong enough to sway good people to do bad things."

"Love and hatred are sometimes not too far apart," I suggest.

"Maybe not," Louise agrees, opening her mouth to speak again when Maisie enters, bearing a tray.

"I did not mean to intrude," she says, taking in the scene.

"Nonsense," Louise says, conjuring a smile. "Thank you, dear."

"Daniel is on his way," Hugh announces returning to the room behind Maisie.

"Was he very upset?"

"Well, he was not thrilled his fiancé was attacked...again." Hugh shrugs. When Maisie turns, almost colliding with him, a light flush creeps up her neck. Hugh smiles and takes a step to the side.

"He knows what he is getting into, marrying this one," Louise teases.

"True enough," Hugh agrees, perching on the opposite chair. "I must contact Hollis. If I do it now, he will have a few hours to write up the story in time to go to press tomorrow."

"Doesn't feel right," I say, shaking my head.

"If he doesn't do it, someone else will. We promised."

"Since when are you in Hollis Napier's corner?" I ask, reaching for the cup of steaming coffee and blowing ripples on the dark surface.

"I am not, really, but we promised, and he held up his end of the bargain."

"You are right, of course," I say with an exaggerated roll of the eyes.

"Why don't I hear that more often?" Hugh chuckles, takes a sip, winces and gets to his feet. "I will call now, before you change your mind."

When he is out of the room, Louise lowers her voice to a whisper, "Did you notice? I think your friend and your housekeeper are making eyes at one another!"

"Aunt Louise!" I cannot help but laugh, loosening the remaining tension in my chest. What a mad day it has been! From murder and mystery, I have gone to parlor gossip in the span of a few hours. "Do you think so? Daniel and I are planning to play matchmakers."

"I would say it isn't necessary, and I have a nose for such matters." She taps said appendage conspiratorially.

"Perhaps we ought to take you on at the agency? Bloodhound instincts come in handy when investigating crimes."

"Oh no, I prefer to spend my days chasing after my grandchildren. Besides, I will try to help Edith more at the WI. She will need the support of community and friends now more than ever."

"She will think she has awakened to a living nightmare. The poor woman." I wrap my hands around the warm cup and lean back against the cushions. This morning I thought I was close to the truth, desperate to know it. Now I do and am no happier for it, not yet at least.

Hours later, when Hugh and Louise have gone home, when I have told Daniel everything that happened in minute detail, I find myself sitting in the bath, suds floating atop the bergamot scented water. Tomorrow I will have to explain to my friends, to my family, repeat the story again and again. We will receive calls from other papers once Hollis publishes his story and the attention will create a flurry of activity for days or even weeks. Once it dies down, though, or in the evenings when it is quiet and I am alone, I will think of Juliet, Marcus, the Ashbourne's and Adeline, Frances and her secretive late husband. I wonder how policemen feel after they solve a case. Is it pure satisfaction? Or is the relief of closing a file tinged with regret that the sad story it contains was not prevented in the first place? As a detective, much of one's work is tracing backwards, searching for motives, catalysts leading to the decisive moment. One becomes a historian, an archaeologist of sorts, digging about in the debris of other people's lives. What draws me to this work, more even than solving a crime, righting a wrong, or finding some measure of justice, is learning about people in the process. Often times the victims or those connected to the case are complete strangers to me, and yet when it ends, I feel I know them in ways their closest family may not. It is intrusive, compelling work, which is why the bargain we made with Hollis does not sit quite right. I am nervous to read his interpretation of events, desperate for him to be respectful, not salacious.

Leaning my head against the rim of the bathtub, I close my eyes, taking in the calming scent of the bath oil, feeling the softening of my muscles in the hot water. I have not given much thought to what Adeline planned for me today. She drugged me, yes, but the more I think of it, the more I believe she knew it was over. She wanted a confession before her world came to an end, needed someone to hear her story, her justifications before the body of her father was found upstairs. I want to hate her for everything she did, and yet a tiny part of me feels sorrow in light of her fate. Grief and love drove her mad, I believe. She and Lloyd were not evil but willing to step into the darkness, believing their cause to be justified, as wrong as it may have been. How would I have felt in their position, knowing someone was responsible for the death of one I held so dear? Marcus understood the risks of war, that safety and survival were not ensured, and danger lurked at every turn. I cannot convince myself he would have agreed with the actions of his sister and father. I think of the photograph Juliet kept all these years of a boy she loved. Did she preserve it to punish herself, to be reminded of a past she could not forget even if she tried? I imagine her, alone in her sterile flat, lifting the floorboard, opening the box and looking at the picture. I knew her as a reserved, almost stoic woman, but she had a heart just like any one of us. I wonder whether all those years ago, it simply shattered and the pieces never came together again. Perhaps she believed she did not deserve happiness after what she had done. Howard recognized something in her, found it in himself, the mark of memory and of loss, even of failure etched into their very being. Howard kept his secrets concealed, possibly out of fear, or possibly to punish himself, to deny himself Frances' compassion the way Juliet denied herself friendships, relationships, love once she returned to London.

So much even the best detective could never know, for some secrets remain locked inside ourselves and we take them to the grave. It would have been difficult, perhaps nearly impossible for Juliet and Howard to acknowledge the part of their past for which they felt only shame and regret. Yet if they had, could their lives have turned out much happier? Another question I cannot answer. I open my eyes and stare at the ceiling, at the elegantly curved crown molding, the glitter of the crystal chandelier that makes the surface of the water sparkle like liquid gold. My fingertips are wrinkled like prunes, yet I cannot find the motivation to climb out. The world is silence and peace from where I lay. For a few more moments, I want to exist in nothing else. I sink beneath the surface, where sound bends and light distorts. As I linger, floating, the pressure in my ears builds, then my chest, my lungs and I finally burst to the surface with a gasp, sucking in a lungful of air, of life.

Chapter 59

Nerves flutter like butterflies in my chest as I approach the house where yesterday I found a dead body and confronted a murderess. This time, though, I am not alone. Louise is with me and Daniel and Hugh are waiting for us in the car outside. Daniel insisted on coming along, disturbed by yesterday's events. However, I convinced him to stay outside. So many strangers would overwhelm Edith.

To my surprise, Priscilla opens the door. She hesitates, a frown marring her features before spying a gaggle of reporters on the pavement and allowing us entry. The hallway is cool and dim, and Priscilla leads us into the sitting room, where the fire crackles in the hearth, just as it did yesterday. I shudder inwardly being back here, but the scene today is quite different. No tea or tray of treats sits ready for us, and Priscilla is far less bright and chirpy than the woman who drugged me here the previous day.

"I came as soon as I heard. Edith asked a policeman to call me." Priscilla shakes her head and sinks into a chair. We sit down on the sofa, and Louise gives my hand a little pat.

"She is resting?"

"Yes, the doctor said she could stay at home. He has given her another sedative. Edith is a strong-minded woman, still it was a terrible shock. Her own husband and daughter plotting and murdering, it doesn't bear thinking about."

"Yet it is probably all she can think of," I observe. "Are you alone? Where is the staff? Even yesterday there was no one about."

"Apparently, Lloyd had given them the day off. I still do not quite understand. Adeline killed him, and he killed Juliet?"

"I think she wanted to spare him prison. She probably thought it was merciful." I offer a helpless shrug. "She insisted she was showing me mercy, too, drugging me. I do not want to dwell on what else she had planned. I waver between hoping all she wanted was a chance to confess, and fearing she wished me harm, though she was likely aware the game was nearly at an end."

"I knew Edith lost a son, but I only met her after the war. She never spoke of him," Priscilla says, her expression somber.

"How did Edith take the news?" Louise asks.

"She has not been able to take it in properly. She spoke to me very briefly, then fell asleep. She is alone now. I don't dare consider

331

what will happen to Adeline. She won't hang, will she?" Priscilla grimaces.

"More likely she will go to Holloway for the rest of her life. She may be declared insane to avoid the noose." Edith is not likely to find much comfort in this possibility. What is worse, Adeline wasting what should have been a long, happy life in prison, or dying quickly at the executioner's hand? "What of her husband, Graham? Have you seen him?"

Priscilla shakes her head. "The doctor said he came by earlier, but left again to meet with a solicitor. He wants to help Adeline, even after everything."

"She used and betrayed him, how can he stand by her?" Louise marvels.

"Robert would do the same," I say.

"I suppose you might be right. Goodness!" my aunt declares.

"I cannot envision my husband displaying such loyalty," Priscilla mutters, blushing instantly, regretting her words. I quickly fill the silence.

"Whatever happens, it will be a long process. Added to that are the arrangements for Lloyd's funeral. Edith will need all the friends and help she can get."

"The WI stands behind her," Priscilla announces firmly, and I believe her. Anyone can see that Edith Ashbourne is loved and admired by the women of the WI. She fought for them and marched with many. I hope they prove themselves true friends when she needs them.

We do not stay long, exacting a promise from Priscilla to contact us if she requires help, or hears of any development. I did not take to the woman initially, but she has proven my first impression to have been faulty indeed, and I am glad of it.

We drop Louise off in Belgravia. She itches to be with her grandchildren, to hold them close in light of the terrible revelation of yesterday.

"Shall I come up with you?" Daniel asks, when we come to a stop outside my building in St. James.

"No, it's all right. You go on." I know he is needed at the office, but sense his reluctance to let me out of his sight.

"I'll go on ahead," Hugh says, climbing out of the car to leave us alone for a few moments.

"Poor Edith," I say. "And poor Graham. He is standing by Adeline, you know. What would you do?"

"Would I support you if you had conspired to murder one person, run over another, then killed one more?" Daniel raises his brows. I give his arm a playful punch.

"Don't think too long!" I warn him. "Must I remind you of our impending vows? For better or for worse."

"Right," he says slowly, smiling. "I suppose I am bound then."

"I suppose you are."

"See to it that you don't follow Adeline's lead, if you can, my love," Daniel says with a pained expression, placing a hand on his heart.

"What a terrible mess it is, Daniel. When I retrace the roots of this case, it begins before the war, with the death of Juliet's parents. That loss unbalanced her world and got her into trouble, brought her to London and to Howard's attention and on and on it spiraled. The war made enemies of people who did not even know one another, and turned Juliet and Marcus into pawns to be sacrificed. All actions have consequences, big or small, wonderful or devastating and everything in between."

"The way it has always been," Daniel observes soberly. "And the way it will always be. Do you find you are learning too much about human frailty in your line of work? You look tired, not elated, as you should be. The case is solved, after all. You were quicker and craftier than the police."

"I do feel a certain satisfaction, yes, but at the moment, it is overshadowed by pity for everyone involved. It need never have gone this far. Such a waste of life, when we have witnessed too much of that already."

"We will see even more of it before our lives are over. Or is that too heartless an observation??"

"Not heartless, but terrible all the same. It is terrible, because it is true. Yet what can be done? I pursue these cases, try to restore some order to a small pocket of the world, then before I know it, another villain rears his ugly head. It is as if I were trying to save a ship from sinking by using only a thimble to toss the water overboard."

"Futile?"

"Is it?"

Daniel takes a slow breath and shakes his head. "You and I know it is not. It would please me to no end, to have you pursuing something with less inherent danger involved. However, we both understand the value in your work, and you would not find the same fulfillment in much else. You cannot cure the world, but you can help improve it. You can make some lives better. That is all we can hope for, I think. To be good and to try. Even when you complain about searching for lost dogs, you are helping someone find their companion, silly as it may seem. You helped solve a murder more often now than I can count on one hand. It is quite disturbing, I have to admit, but I am also rather proud. All the same, I will probably go gray from the worry you cause me," he chuckles, and I squeeze his hand.

"Gray will suit you very well, but I will try not to be the cause of it."

Chapter 60

When I reach the flat, I find Hollis already waiting for us. He sits neat as a cat, legs crossed, hat balanced on one knee. Hugh is in his usual seat, wearing a bemused expression.

"Look who I found here."

"To what do we owe this pleasure?" I ask. "I noticed you did not print the story about the murder today. Did you not finish writing it in time?"

Hollis shifts in his seat appearing – can it be? – slightly ill at ease. Hugh gives me a curious look, and I shrug.

"I decided not to publish as a measure of good will," Hollis explains, uncrossing, then recrossing his legs.

"A measure of good will? Who are you?" Hugh asks with raised brows.

"Ha! Very amusing, but I am not without a heart, as it happens," Hollis retorts, chin tilted up.

"All right," I say slowly. "Thank you."

"Come on, Hollis, you did not do this for nothing," Hugh prods, arms crossed over his chest, tipping his chair precariously backward.

"Well," Hollis licks his lips.

"Go on."

"I want out of the newspaper business."

"No shame in that," Hugh observes.

"Has something happened?" I ask carefully.

"Let's just say, my employer learned of a situation involving my private life and decided I should no longer write front page stories. It doesn't matter. I have grown tired of the work anyway, thankless as it is. People love a good story and disdain the person who writes it."

"What sort of a *personal situation*?" Hugh asks, ignoring Hollis' commentary on journalism.

Hollis sighs and rubs his eyes with thumb and forefinger. "I suppose, considering what I am about to ask of you, I should be forthright. My employer learned that I prefer the company of men to that of women, if you understand my meaning."

Hugh immediately blushes.

"Of course," I say in an even voice. "You are aware from our last case. Your private life is of no concern to us."

Hollis' expression relaxes, if only slightly. "Which brings me to my reason for coming here, for forgetting the story."

"We are all ears." Hugh has recovered himself.

"I want to join your agency." Hollis holds up a hand, as I open my mouth. "Wait just a moment, so I can explain. I will be an asset to you. We work well together, and I am good at getting information from people. I have contacts all over the city. Besides, I need a change." He falls silent, eyes shifting between Hugh and me. I almost feel sorry for him. Hollis Napier is not a man to be easily unnerved.

"I see," I say, my mind already circling his proposition. "Would you let Hugh and me have a chat? Maeve will make you a cup of tea in the kitchen while you wait." Hollis hesitates, then nods, unfolds himself from the chair and disappears through the door, closing it behind him.

"When the case was solved, I thought we were done with surprises for a while," Hugh observes, turning in his seat to give me a bemused look.

"So did I, though this one is not wholly unwelcome. What do you think?"

"In all seriousness?" Hugh frowns and strokes his chin. "I was skeptical of the fellow before, but I must admit, he has proven his worth. Can't blame him for wanting to leave a place of employment where he is not welcome. In case you had any doubt, I have no judgment against him on that score."

"I know, Hugh. Are we ready to add to our little agency, though?"

"We will have many more cases rolling in. You are going to be away for a while after your wedding. I say, we let him stay for a trial of three months. By that time, you will be back, and we will have a better sense of whether he is any good at this job."

"You two will get along in my absence? Naturally, you are the one in control and Hollis your junior. I cannot see that as an equation for harmony."

"We will cope. I don't know, Evelyn, I feel sorry for him," Hugh lowers his voice. "This country has been through so much these past ten years alone, and yet we still condemn people for falling in love with someone society dictates they ought not to? Hollis is not my favorite person, but we can get along."

"All right," I say, relieved, for his thoughts echo my own. "Let us make him an offer." Hugh gets up to fetch Hollis, and I feel a rush of pride in him. He may have his struggles – as do we all - but he has a generous spirit and is a good man to the bone. Maisie will be a lucky woman, if Louise's instinct is to be trusted. I must perform a little subtle interrogation to get my answer.

Hollis is visibly relieved, though he tries not to show it. When he leaves, I can tell it is with a spring in his step, and I am curious how this addition to our little unit will alter it. With him joining the agency, I feel it is necessary to find more suitable accommodations. Maeve, Aidan and Kathleen live here, too, after all, and though Hollis is hardly a threat to the women's honor, it is not right to have so many people waltzing in and out of their home, including potential clients. I will have to start a search soon, or maybe that particular detection can be Hollis' first task.

"Maeve told me the telephone has been ringing all morning. A number of papers want our comment on the story, and Stanton came by when we were gone," Hugh says, when we finish our final notes and close the file dedicated to the Juliet Nelson case.

"What a shame we missed him. I would have liked to have spoken to him, since it was a different policeman who came to the Ashbourne house."

"Do you think Stanton is in trouble for failing to solve the case before Lloyd Ashbourne was killed?"

"If he is, we should be, too," I note, the guilt I pushed aside since waking sneaks up on me again.

"I struggle to decide whether he got what he deserved, or whether he should have been saved. Murder is terrible, but murdering a murderer is more challenging to judge. Wrong, yes, but somehow less so than killing Juliet or attempting to kill Frances."

"Maybe," I say, uncertain how to feel. Would Lloyd Ashbourne have faced a penalty of death in either case? Does that make it right for his daughter to have given him a peaceful way out instead of the hangman's noose? I fail to see the mercy in it, even if my mind can follow her disturbing logic.

"We ought to tell Frances, unless the police already have. I bet they removed the guard as quickly as they could, waste of police resources and all that," Hugh grumbles.

"She will be alone just like Edith, both disappointed in different ways by those they trusted most."

"I don't suppose that will forge a friendship between them. It was, after all, Edith's daughter who put Frances in her current predicament," Hugh notes with arched brows.

"Their situations are quite different. Still, stranger things have happened, though I won't hold my breath for it. I agree, we must visit Frances, but there is someone else I want to see as well."

It is nearing evening by the time I arrive at Juliet's former building. The flat is empty now and belongs to Frances. I wonder what she will do with it. It is growing dark, the sky a velvet blue edged with fiery orange above the rooftops. Somewhere in the small garden beyond the square, an owl hoots and a dog starts barking in strange symphony. I came alone by taxi, for my car is still in the garage. In my hands is a parcel wrapped in dark green paper. I hold it carefully as I navigate the slippery pavement, slick from an afternoon downpour.

Mr. Button sits at his table, stooped, face half in shadow, half in light from the small lamp above. He looks up when he hears the door, a smile touching his lips. Moving gingerly, he gets up to greet me. By the end of this case, I have met so many new people, some whom I liked, others...not so much. Yet once the mystery is solved, I cannot simply forget all the lives I came into contact with during the investigation, which is why I am here.

"Thought I'd see you again. I wanted to come to the funeral, but my back is very bad in this damp weather. Any news?"

"We caught the killer," I announce, earning a small gasp and a nod of approval.

"My, my, well done!"

"I wanted to tell you in person."

"Good thing you came by. I'll be gone in a week." He shrugs yet cannot hide the shadow of melancholy falling across his face.

"Gone?" I ask.

"Been let go," he explains with a deep sigh. "Come, will you. Let me make you a cuppa? Standing here's no good for my knees and it won't matter much, me leaving the desk unattended now."

In his tiny flat, seated at the kitchen table, I learn the building's owner dismissed him. The revelation that he was asleep when the murderous pair entered was viewed as inexcusable. I understand this reasoning yet feel for the man who has lived and worked here for so long. It is his home, people who live here know his face, his story, if they took the time to listen. He tries to push my sympathy aside, explaining he plans to go north, where his cousin lives, find lodgings with his savings.

"I won't lie to you, I will miss the city. Never lived anywhere else. People always dream of living in the country someday, not me. Still, change is good, isn't that right?"

"So they say. You don't want to try to stay here?"

"London has changed. I wouldn't be able to stay in Bloomsbury, not with my savings. I am too old to find a new profession, not suited for much of anything, really." He smiles. "Don't you worry about me, my dear. I'll be right as rain."

I can tell he is struggling to put up a hopeful front, but I nod anyway. Even if there was something I could do, Mr. Button is not a man quick to accept something he would deem charity. Besides, perhaps it is better for him to be near family. He may love the city, but from what I gather, he lives a lonely existence here. Change may truly be for the best, even if it is not always the easiest option.

Leaving him with the small parcel, an early Christmas present for a man who probably receives very few of them, I go on my way. We do not promise to stay in touch, for what are we, if not vague acquaintances? All the same, I will not soon forget Mr. Button, as I will not soon forget anyone involved in this case.

Chapter 61

"I hope you do not mind me coming round this late," Stanton says, when I open the door to him just after dinner. A breath of cold night air enters the house, and I usher him into the hall, closing the door. Daniel and I have given Wilkins and Maisie the evening off, for us to be on our own. He has been distracting me with talk of his plans for the business, having found a buyer for the shipyard, who agreed to keep on a number of the current workers. It is something, at least, even if it pains Daniel to dismantle a part of his family's legacy. Nonetheless, it is a pleasant evening after the tumult of recent weeks. That being so, I am not upset about the interruption. Stanton has questions, and I am eager to answer them, hopefully for the final time. No doubt his colleagues who made the arrest informed him of much that transpired already.

"Evening," Daniel says, when we enter the room. He acts unruffled, but he peeked through the curtain, then sighed before letting me answer the door on my own.

"Sorry to disturb. I wanted to clear up a few final questions, so we can lay this case to rest."

"Of course." Daniel nods. Obviously hesitant, he nonetheless gets to his feet. "I will leave the professionals to discuss the matter." It is a sign that he trusts me, and I value it.

"Can I offer you something to drink?" I ask, gesturing for Stanton to sit. He nods, folding his lanky frame into an armchair, making it seem too small.

"I wouldn't mind a drop of whatever you are having. It's been a long, cold day and I am, strictly speaking, off the clock." I pour us both a measure of brandy and hand him his glass before sitting down on the opposite sofa.

"I take it you heard what happened?"

Stanton takes a sip before answering. "I have. No point in telling you off, I suppose. The case is solved, and you are alive."

"Lloyd Ashbourne is not."

"No, he is not," Stanton concedes quietly, his expression somber, a dusting of stubble throwing his jaw into shadow, dark half-moons beneath his eyes. "In a way, Adeline saved the government the execution costs, at least that is how my superior put it. Still, I feel it is a failure on my part."

340

"On mine, too."

"You solve cases, yet I am sworn to protect. There is a difference, even if you are reluctant to acknowledge it."

"What will happen to Adeline? Priscilla mentioned Graham is standing by her, hiring legal representation."

"He is, for all the good it will do. She will never walk free again."

I nod and take a sip. "What a waste all around."

"I'll drink to that," he says and raises his glass in a mock toast.

"Don't be macabre!"

"Apologies," he says with a glint in his eyes.

"Your recent doubts and ennui with your profession have not waned?"

"It isn't doubt so much as frustration, but it will pass. Every copper goes through such a phase. You see too much and the days get shorter and shorter. Come spring, I will have changed my tune again, just you wait."

"Are you going to Oxford for Christmas, to visit your parents?"

"Three days of bliss." His sarcasm is impossible to miss.

"They miss you, I am sure. Thom used to spend every day at their house, after all."

"You are right, of course. And you? Off on an adventure after the wedding?"

"Yes, though I have not been told where it will take place, the adventure, not the wedding. You received your invitation?"

"I have." He looks down at the glass in his hand. "You won't hold it against me if I do not come, will you? Thom is going with Iona, so he will give you my best wishes."

"Lucas -"

"I should go," he interrupts and gets to his feet, setting his half-empty glass on the table.

"Thank you for dropping by," I say, for it is all I can offer.

"Take care, Evelyn."

When the door falls shut behind him, I have the sad feeling that this was goodbye. I contemplate going after him, yet what can I say? My hand rests on the doorknob, but I do not turn it. My future is here, not beyond the door, and I hope that with time, Stanton will be able to find contentment in our friendship. I can be patient.

Chapter 62

"I read about you in the paper," Mr. Singh says, when he opens the door. "Well done, my dear. And soon you will have even more cause to celebrate. The wedding is not far away, is it?"

"Just a few more weeks," I reply, almost unable to believe it myself. "I am sorry I have not been around earlier. How are you? How is Dulcie?"

Mr. Singh waves my apology away and leads me into the flat. It is warm, the scent of spices, at once familiar and foreign, permeating the air. "I am well, and Dulcie..." He shrugs. "I think she is on her way."

"She made no more mention of trying to reach *the other side*?"

"Thankfully not. She is in the sitting room reading. Why don't you go through? I will bring you something to drink, and you must taste some of my *halwa*. I tried a recipe with ginger to suit the season. I made a large batch, and you are the only neighbor willing to try." I laugh and nod my agreement, never having been disappointed by Mr. Singh's cooking in the past.

Dulcie is resting on the magenta velvet settee, a fur-edged blanket draped over her knees, a copy of *The Inimitable Jeeves* in her lap. Her choice of reading material leads me to believe Mr. Singh is right, and she is starting to feel a little brighter. This sentiment is supported by the warm smile she bestows upon me.

"Evelyn, what a lovely surprise! Come, sit near the fire. It really is winter now, isn't it?" Obeying, I sit down on the striped brocade armchair across from her, the fireplace radiating heat. I wonder, when was the last winter Dulcie actually felt the cool breeze on her skin, or a snowflake landing on her nose? This brings me to the actual reason for my visit.

After some pleasantries are exchanged, and I give a brief summary of recent events, I ask, "Dulcie, won't you come to our wedding?" I try to hold her gaze, but she looks down at her lap, then at the window, which frames the bright blue sky most advantageously.

"You will have your family there, your friends, you will not notice my absence," she finally says.

I am conflicted how to react. Not wishing to make her feel guilty or more anxious, I do not want to lie either. "I will notice, of course, but I do understand."

"Sunil will come, he will represent us both," she goes on quickly, her eyes seeking understanding in mine. "He will tell me all about it, and when you are married, you and Daniel must come and have a little celebration here. What do you say?"

"We would be delighted," I reply, pushing away my twinge of disappointment. It is not so much for me as for her. On the wedding day, I will likely be a bundle of nerves, hardly able to concentrate on the guests until the reception, but attending it would have been an important step for Dulcie, one I badly wish I could help her take. She has resigned herself to a half existence, as if Rupert, her son, would have demanded that a part of her die with him. I think of her and then of Edith and her husband, of my aunt Iris in Scotland, who will also not make the journey. They all have lost a child, and yet they cope with their grief so differently. Edith threw herself into her work, Iris lives in denial, Lloyd became a killer, and Dulcie a ghost of herself. Perhaps she will change her mind. Maybe Mr. Singh will have better luck convincing her. In my heart of hearts, though, I know my eyes will not find her in the church a few weeks from now, smiling at me as I take Daniel's hand. Both Daniel and I had moments in our lives of believing we could never outrun the pain of our past, and while we carry the loss of those we loved with us always, we have found new meaning and happiness. I wish the same for Dulcie, for Iris, and for Edith Ashbourne, too. Time will tell. Life can be consoling and merciless in equal measure. It gives, and it takes, and we never know whether time is our friend or our enemy. Hours become weeks and weeks become years and years become a lifetime, and then we are a memory and then we are dust. Mr. Singh comes in right at this moment, bearing a tray of steaming chai and a bowl of his special *halwa*. I push aside my musings on the transience of life and time and relish the moment I am in, the friendly company, the sweet and spicy sensation of the Indian sweet on my tongue and the pleasant crackle of the fire.

Chapter 63

It has been two weeks since Adeline's arrest, and the initial hubbub around the office has waned, if only a little. Hollis has a desk in our office now, and though I set him to the task of finding us a more suitable workspace, he has been unable to do so, for all the cases we have received have kept us busy. Nothing as consuming as the murder, though, for which I am grateful. After all, I am to be married in five days' time. The nerves everyone mentions have not yet set in. Why should I be worried when I am to be wed to my dearest friend, when we live together already – even if it is a badly kept secret. Agnes took me to another fitting for the dress, and we met Briony and Louise afterwards like a pair of mothers and daughters. While my mind often drifts to what-ifs, conjuring images of my parents here on my wedding day, of them in the church, pressing kisses to my cheek as they give me away, I am grateful for what I have. Agnes is not my mother, but our relationship has changed and improved so drastically in the past year. She and I may even be on the path to friendship, something I would have considered almost unimaginable not long ago. In this capacity, and despite her grumbling that she has too much to do with the wedding and Harold's by-election, she deigns to accompany Louise, Briony and me to the meeting of the Bloomsbury Women's Institute this morning. It is to be the first Edith Ashbourne will attend since the arrest of her daughter, and I can tell, as soon as we enter the hall, everyone is in a state of anxious excitement for her return.

The weeks between now and then have seen the city transformed. Tall Christmas trees have been erected, shop windows boast elaborate gingerbread houses and festive displays, and carolers stand at street corners, singing merrily. Holiday cheer has reached the WI as well, I note. Sprigs of holly stand in vases on the long table, which holds a tray of gingerbread and mincemeat pies. The scent of mulled wine hangs in the air, and I have a strong sense that today is meant to be a celebration, a sort of homecoming for Edith.

"I spoke to her yesterday," Louise whispers, while we find our seats. "She is putting up a strong front. No surprises there, but it will be difficult to maintain."

"The poor woman has lost everything," Agnes says with raised brows. "Who could blame her if she simply collapsed into herself?"

"She won't, though." I am confident this much is true. Edith Ashbourne will do what she did when her son was killed, throw herself into a cause once more. Her grief will be the fuel for future change, and in this way, I believe she thinks something good can come out of this inescapable nightmare in which she now exists.

We do not have to wait long. A sudden hush falls when Edith Ashbourne, straight as a rod, in a dark blue suit, enters the hall. She is pale and looks thinner than when we last spoke some ten days ago, but she is holding up, which is remarkable in itself. She gives the women seated at the front a tight smile and accepts embraces as she makes her way to the small podium erected at the front of the hall. Priscilla approaches her, takes both her hands and utters a few inaudible words. Edith nods, and we watch as she takes her place.

"Thank you for coming today, and thank you for your support. It has been a trying time, one I would never wish upon any one of you, but I am here now, and I know my friends are, too." A smattering of applause erupts. She holds up her hand, and the hall falls silent once more. "I have not come to discuss my private life, you all know what happened anyway." She swallows. "We have much to do, and my recent absence only makes our efforts and diligence more urgent. Last week, the police commissioner agreed to consider our petition. This morning, I received news that in the new year, one hundred women with arresting powers will be recruited to the Metropolitan Police. It is a small step, but a significant one all the same. I do not doubt our persistence is linked to this development. We have reason to be proud." The applause grows louder, and a few cheers and whistles ring through the air. "Next on the agenda is the push for equal pay. These women have the opportunity to rise in the ranks of law enforcement, but will they receive the wage of their male counterparts?"

"No!" a woman cries out in front of us.

"The shame!" cries another. I hear Briony giggle at my side.

"That is right, they will not, just like women all across this city and this country are still being treated as inferior workers, even performing the same tasks as men do, all the while running their home and caring for their children. Times are changing and we will continue to make our mark. Now," Edith musters a smile and claps her hands once, "let us get to work!"

That evening, Frances is released from the hospital. Hugh and I go to collect her, despite her protestations that she is very capable of getting home on her own. Her arm remains in a cast, and her ankle is broken, so I ignore her arguments. We have borrowed Daniel's motor - my beloved Bentley is still being repaired – and gently bundle Frances into the back, which I have cushioned with a blanket. She is much thinner than before, and her height makes her appear even more so. Her coat swallows her up, face pale, cheeks hollow. The recent strain and shocking discoveries are almost as much to blame for her transformation as her physical injury, I believe.

"This really is not necessary," she insists, though I can tell she is relieved not to be alone. Some friends visited her during her stay in the hospital, but Frances, it seems, has always led a fairly solitary life, excepting her marriage to Howard. I cannot stand the thought of her being alone at home with only a maid for company after the blow she has been dealt, not to mention her physical distress. A nurse will stop by tomorrow to see how she is settling in, which is something. Jeffrey and Briony plan to visit her soon as well, so she will know she is cared for.

"Are you happy to be home again?" Hugh asks, when we arrive at her neat terraced house. A young maid with a wrinkled apron and an anxious expression opens the door, unused to so much life back in the house.

"It is a relief." Frances lowers herself carefully onto the sofa in the small but elegant sitting room. Framed sketches of the Acropolis and sculptures of Zeus and Athena hang on the wall above her head. A stack of books is piled on the floor beside her, one open in the middle, as though she never left. Now that I glance around, I note that books are, in fact, everywhere. On the small desk by the window, on the shelf along one wall, even on a stool precariously close to the fireplace.

"'A home without books is a body without soul'," I quote. Frances smiles.

"Cicero."

"Will you be all right on your own?"

"I have been on my own for a long time. Even during our marriage, Howard was frequently away. Now I wonder where he actually went." She lets out a sigh.

"He hated lying to you," Hugh says gently.

"Yet he did so for years and years. I am not sure what to think, how to remember him." She laughs mirthlessly, shaking her head. "As a historian, I should be used to unanswered questions. Yet that is the part of this tale which infuriates me most, that I cannot ask him, and I cannot ask Juliet."

"Do you believe Juliet betrayed Marcus?" I ask. It hardly matters what really happened, but I want to hear her thoughts.

"Possibly. But Howard must have known and still chose to help and protect her. He must have realized that the time and circumstance in which she found herself forced her to act as she would never have otherwise. None of us can understand, no matter how much we read or talk about that terrible time, not unless we lived it ourselves. Maybe you know better than us, Mr. Lawrence." She looks at Hugh.

"You would not recognize yourself looking back," Hugh says quietly. "When you are told men you never met before are your mortal enemy, when you are terrified every hour of every day…People do what they must to survive. That does not mean life gets easier afterwards. Juliet suffered profoundly for whatever she did."

"I think you are right," Frances agrees somberly, leaning back, crossing her arms.

"You do not blame Juliet?" I ask.

"No, I do not. I am a scholar of the past, but I will try my best to let it rest in this instance."

"Have the police returned Howard's diaries?"

"They have, which brings me to a small favor I wanted to ask, if you do not mind. I am immobile at the moment, or I would do it myself."

"You want us to return them to the safe deposit box?" Hugh asks, his mind attuned to Frances' thoughts. She nods. Hugh and I agree to do so the very next day. I cannot quite understand Frances' reasoning, a thought I share with Hugh on our drive back to the flat.

"She wants to move on." Hugh looks ahead as he navigates the streets, narrowly avoiding a man in black stepping from the pavement.

"Frances understands the past is not gone simply because she banishes it to a box in a vault," I argue, struggling to imagine letting go of my beloved late husband's writings. Howard did lie, and what he wrote in those journals altered Frances' view of him and their relationship, but his secrecy does not erase happy memories, does not undo the bond they shared. Does she now question his honesty in every aspect of their marriage? I hope not. I hope, with time, she will be able to accept the explanation he gave in his diaries, and think of him fondly once more. She was right when she said impossible circumstances can force impossible decisions to be made, and if Juliet can be forgiven, so should Howard. I recall his regret, his concern for his recruits, his care for Juliet, and I believe he must have been a good man, whatever mistakes he made.

"Are you hungry?" Hugh asks, breaking through my thoughts.

"Famished! Everywhere we go we are offered tea. What I really want is a hearty shepherd's pie."

Hugh laughs and turns a corner. "I know just the place. Let us go fetch Daniel and finally celebrate the end of this case."

"We could ask Maisie and Wilkins along," I suggest, eyeing him in profile for tell-tale signs to suggest Louise's theory is true.

Indeed, at the mention of her name, the corner of his mouth twitches slightly. It could be a mere coincidence, but someone once said, there is no such thing. I repress a smile. This case may be over, but endings are the parents of new beginnings and I sense a happy one in my partner's future. In a year's time, perhaps, we will be celebrating another wedding!

Epilogue

In the morning, the sky was gray as a soiled rag. Yet now, climbing out of the gleaming Rolls Royce's, Briony carefully lifting the hem of my dress, the wind has chased the gloomy clouds away and replaced them with a canopy of peerless blue. Perhaps it is the chill in the air, but I am overcome with a flutter of nerves. I have approached the wedding with a sense almost of apathy, so this sudden thrill comes as a surprise.

We chose the small and charming Grosvenor Chapel not far from our marital home for the wedding. Upon entering, we are ushered into a small side room. I hear the din of chatter floating through the air. They are all here for us. The thought warms me, even as it sets my nerves on edge. All those eyes on the two of us.

"Evie? Everything all right?" Briony asks, drawing me out of my thoughts, while Agnes fusses about, straightening the back of my dress. It is as beautiful as I remembered, light and elegant, with long sleeves of the finest lace and a slim, flowing skirt trailing behind me. The veil is gossamer light, I hardly feel it as I move. When Agnes helped me put on the necklace Brandon gave her all those years ago, everything finally felt right, as though a part of our family's history was with us on this day. Briony's eyes are wide as she steps back to look at me. They already shimmer with tears, and I hope Jeffrey will have a few hankies at the ready. She wears a soft blue gown which matches the color of her eyes, while the girls wear white dresses with ribbons in their hair and lace gloves. Areta has already emptied much of her flower basket, and Iona generously gives her some from her own. Timon will act the ring bearer, and is being strictly monitored by his father, who fears the golden bands will not make it down the aisle, should his son be left unsupervised. Elsa is asleep, tucked up in a frilly dress, blond curls peeking out from under a white cap.

"Everything is perfect," I say, taking Briony's hands and giving them a squeeze. "Go on. They are starting the music." The sonorous melody of the organ hushes everyone beyond the small antechamber. I take a deep breath, watching Briony send her daughters ahead, casting a look over her shoulder, smiling before she, too, begins her walk down the aisle, my matron of honor.

"Ready? You look a picture. I will not have you crying yet, but your parents and Brendan would have been so very happy for you, my dear girl." Agnes smiles, giving my arm a gentle squeeze.

Despite her instruction, I feel the prick of tears in my eyes and try to blink them away. It is a happy day, after all. Agnes tucks my hand into the crook of her arm.

"Thank you for doing this, Agnes, for organizing it all. I could not -"

"Hush, dear, I would not have had it any other way." Her smile is filled only with warmth, no past resentment, no bitterness stands between us at this moment. The music outside reaches a crescendo, our sign to go. I think I should say something to her, something momentous. Then I realize today does not mark an ending, but a beginning. There will be time for us to speak, to reminisce, to laugh, even to argue, as we undoubtedly will, but now is the time to walk. I see Daniel standing alongside Hugh at the altar, both dapper in charcoal suits, white roses pinned onto their lapels. White roses have been tied into bundles with mistletoe and holly at the end of every pew. Warm light filters through the large windows, and the organ music seems to swell from the stone floor up to the vaulted ceiling. In the benches on either side sit the people we love most, our friends and family. There is Aunt Louise holding a dozing Elsa in her lap, Uncle Robert offering me a wide smile. There sit Maisie and Wilkins, Maeve and Kathleen and even Mr. Singh. No Dulcie. Not today. Friends from my days in Oxford, from childhood, too. Though I wish my parents were here today, I take in the faces of everyone who is, everyone who came and cares, and is happy for us, and I cannot be anything but grateful. Daniel smiles nervously as he accepts Agnes' kiss and takes my hands in his.

"You look beautiful, Evie," he whispers. "Are you happy?"

I cannot manage more than a nod, but it is enough. A long time has lead up to this moment and now that it has arrived, I hardly know why I hesitated. The service is over before I know it, and we laugh as we parade down the aisle, hand in hand, husband and wife, Areta and Iona pelting us with flower petals. Stepping into the winter sun, I am surprised to find the Bentley waiting for us, decorated with flowers and silver tinsel.

"I had to get it back in time for today." Daniel grins. "Good as new I am told."

"You have earned yourself a kiss," I say. "And I shall even let you drive, though I warn you, do not take it as a sign of the framework of our marriage," I tease.

"Oh, no." He smiles, giving me a wink and holding open the door. I wave to our friends and family. "I know whose hands are on the wheel, proverbial and otherwise."

The reception held at Agnes and Harold's large Belgravia home is in full swing. The children are wild from all the cake they have eaten and bounce about the dance floor between Briony and Jeffrey, Louise and Robert and, yes, even Hugh and Maisie. Agnes outdid herself. I cannot imagine how much time and work she put into the event. From the flowers to the food and everything in between, I could not have done it nearly as well had I tried. Since I was eighteen, she has been pushing me to find a husband. Now I know why, to demonstrate her excellent abilities in planning a wedding! All the same, I think she is almost as glad as I am that I waited for Daniel, whom she took to instantly. These past months, I realized I was wrong about so many things regarding my aunt, and she was wrong about me, but we have learned and have never been as close to one another as we are now. Time does not heal all wounds, yet it can, in some cases, make them less tender, less raw to the touch. Or, at the very least, it can teach those we love and who love us to be gentle. Daniel and I will dash off on our honeymoon right after Christmas, and in the new year, when we are away, Agnes may well find herself the wife of an MP. I am happy she has found Harold as I have found Daniel, and we both are the better for our companions.

Escaping the dancing and cheerful chatter for a moment, Daniel and I step onto the terrace, the moon a gleaming pearl in the black velvet cushion of the sky, our breaths white in the winter air. We hear the sound of laughter, voices and music from within the house, and I smile, knowing all those dearest to us are near. I think of the first time Daniel and I met, years ago in Greece, when I believed him to be a reserved, melancholy man. Even then, though, I thought him intriguing and remarkably handsome, I recall with a smile.

"What is going through your mind, Mrs. Harper?" asks Daniel, a sparkle in his eye as he takes my hand. I lean against him, resting my head against his shoulder.

"I was remembering the day we met. What did you think when I arrived at the villa?"

"Here comes trouble!" he says, and I can hear the smile in his voice and give him a gentle jab with my elbow.

"Very amusing!"

"Naturally, I thought you were clever, beautiful, maybe a little unhappy. I felt I recognized something of myself in you, or I wanted to, at least. You brought a different energy to our group, and you made me smile."

"Do go on. Did you know immediately that I was the only one for you?" My tone is teasing, but I want an answer all the same.

"Maybe. You were the first one who made me wonder what the future could look like." He kisses the top of my head. "Speaking of the future, any guesses where I am taking you on our honeymoon?"

"I haven't the slightest!"

"Does my little detective require a clue?" he asks, turning to face me.

"Less of the little and more of the clues, Mr. Harper," I say in mock reprimand. "Give me a morsel."

"A morsel? Like a crumb of naan bread?"

"I suppose," I say, thinking of the flat but fluffy bread Mr. Singh has made on occasion.

"No, that is the clue," Daniel insists with a smile.

"India!" I squeal. "We are going to India?"

"Am I doing well as your husband?"

"Very!" I say, rewarding him with a kiss. "Goodness, India. I wonder what adventures await us there? The Taj Mahal, Bombay or Delhi…I will hardly be able to wait for Christmas to be over, Daniel!" Visions of elephants, vibrant colors, feats of architecture, remnants of history around every bend fill my mind.

"Please, let us be spared adventure. All I want is a peaceful journey with my lovely wife," Daniel groans, though it is followed by a laugh, as he draws me close.

I think of all that is before us, of the utter unpredictability of life, the trials, joys and adventures yet ahead. For years I feared binding myself to another person, frightened of commitment, but also of the love that could be snatched away as it had been before. Yet standing here, shivering slightly under the starry sky, I feel a strange sort of peace descending upon me. It is true that we do not know what lies ahead, but I have come to realize whatever risk to my heart the future holds, choosing to love, whether a friend or a husband, a father, aunt or a mother, the rewards are greater still.

Acknowledgements

I write these words in the autumn of 2021, at a time when so much is uncertain and the world seems turned on its head in many ways. Yet this time has also made very clear just how important connection and community are. I have received much wonderful support and encouragement from friends, family, fellow authors and members of the literary community in the effort of writing and publishing the Lady Evelyn Mysteries. Such was the case once again with A Deadly Legacy, and many thanks are in order. First of all, to my mother, who is the earliest reader of any of Lady Evelyn's new adventures. Her red pen and trustworthy insight play a significant role in the book you hold in your hands. I cannot imagine this process without her invaluable input. Thanks also go to my dad and sisters, for their constant support and encouragement, to Liam for always making me smile, and to Liz Konneker for her help in the editing of this book. Much appreciation also goes to the people at Bookbaby, who have carefully guided me through the process of publishing for several years now. Last, but by no means least, dear reader, I remain grateful and humbled by your kindness and support. I hope you have found some hours of escapism within these pages and will return for Lady Evelyn's future adventures.

I love hearing from you, and if you would like to get in touch, you can contact me through my website or via social media.
